NEW ADVENTURES OF

SHERLOCK HOLMES

DONALD THOMAS

JAICO PUBLISHING HOUSE

Ahmedabad Bangalore Chennai
Delhi Hyderabad Kolkata Mumbai

Published by Jaico Publishing House
A-2 Jash Chambers, 7-A Sir Phirozshah Mehta Road
Fort, Mumbai - 400 001
jaicopub@jaicobooks.com
www.jaicobooks.com

Published in arrangement with
Pegasus Books LLC
80 Broad Street, 5th Floor
New York, NY 10004

NEW ADVENTURES OF SHERLOCK HOLMES
ISBN 978-81-8495-435-7

First Jaico Impression: 2013
Fourth Jaico Impression: 2015

Printed by
Repro India Limited, Mumbai

CONTENTS

ALSO BY DONALD THOMAS

POETRY

Points of Contact

Welcome to the Grand Hotel

FICTION

Prince Charlie's Bluff

The Flight of the Eagle

The Raising of Lizzie Meek

The Blindfold Game

Belladonna: A Lewis Carroll Nightmare

The Ripper's Apprentice

Jekyll, Alias Hyde

The Arrest of Scotland Yard

The Day the Sun Rose Twice

Dancing in the Dark

Red Flowers for Lady Blue

The Secret Cases of Sherlock Holmes

Sherlock Holmes and the Running Noose

The Execution of Sherlock Holmes

Sherlock Holmes and the King's Evil

BIOGRAPHY

Cardigan of Balaclava

Cochrane: Britannia's Sea-Wolf

Swinburne: The Poet in his World

Robert Browning: A Life Within Life

Henry Fielding: A Life

The Marquis de Sade

Lewis Carroll: A Portrait with Background

CRIME AND DOCUMENTARY

A Long Time Burning: The History of Literary Censorship in England

Freedom's Frontier: Censorship in Modern Britain

Dead Giveaway: Murder Avenged from the Grave

The Victorian Underworld

An Underworld at War: Spies, Deserters, Racketeers and Civilians in the Second World War

Villains' Paradise: Britain's Post-War Underworld

I

The Case of a Boy's Honour

1

Those of my readers who have followed Holmes and me through our investigations of "The Case of the Greek Key" and "The Case of the Zimmermann Telegram" will know of our friendship with Admiral of the Fleet Sir John Fisher. At a glance, he and Holmes were quite unlike. Holmes was a private man with a fame he would gladly have avoided. Fisher was a public figure. He was in the limelight as the creator of a modern Royal Navy in the years preceding the war of 1914–1918. Before that, he had supported the building of HMS *Dreadnaught* and her sister battleships when Germany had not laid a single keel of such a titan. His foresight ensured Britain's supremacy at sea during the dangerous decade to come.

Not everyone admired Sir John Fisher. A man cannot uproot and reform the Committee for Imperial Defence without making enemies. Government officials do not like abrupt demands for "a modern navy in a modern world." Few are comfortable with a naval policy of "Hit first, hit hard, and keep on hitting." To Mr

"The Case of the Greek Key" in *The Execution of Sherlock Holmes*, Pegasus Books, New York, 2007; "The Case of the Zimmermann Telegram" in *Sherlock Holmes and the King's Evil*, Pegasus Books, New York, 2009.

Asquith's cabinet this was very close to Fisher's advice to King Edward, that the Royal Navy should sink the Kaiser's High Seas Fleet at its moorings in Kiel Harbour without a declaration of war—and offer generous terms among the ruins.

Holmes and Fisher certainly shared the character of a trouble-maker. Each was unconventional and unpredictable. Fisher vexed and irritated the politicians and Admiralty officials as surely as Holmes got under the skin of Scotland Yard. The two men recognised this quality in one another and built a comradeship upon it.

On a May morning in 1913 my friend opened an envelope at breakfast and informed me that his elder brother Mycroft was bringing Jackie Fisher to tea that afternoon at three o'clock.

"I daresay, Watson, it is a friendly call at short notice. It is not necessary that you should stay in if you have already made other arrangements. Needless to say, you would confer a favour upon me by being here."

When Fisher and Mycroft Holmes came to Baker Street together at short notice, you could be sure that it was something more than a friendly call.

"I should not miss it for the world," I said cheerfully.

He seemed relieved.

"There must be buttered muffins," he said presently, dangling a pipe spill absent-mindedly, "I shall go and inform Mrs Hudson. Brother Mycroft is partial to muffins, especially when served with strawberry jam."

As he went out, I returned to the county cricket in *The Times*. The May weather in England had been atrocious. On several days the wind had screamed and the rain had beaten on our windows from breakfast until supper. "Rain stopped play" appeared against almost two-thirds of the batting scores. I had no idea as I scanned the list of abandoned matches how important this recent weather would be to us during the next few days.

Happily, since the previous evening, an improvement had set in. A strong morning sun now warmed the pedestrians and shopkeepers in the street below us. Surely we might hope for something better at last.

A few minutes after three o'clock that afternoon the hollow hoof-beats of a carriage, from the direction of the Regent's Park, slowed and stopped.

"Every eighth hoof-beat cries for a new shoe," said Holmes, sitting with his eyelids closed and the tips of his fingers touching lightly together. "Therefore it is a carriage and pair. Mycroft does not care to be seen driving in a single-horse cab. No other visitor to these premises would go to the expense of a pair. I deduce that our guests have arrived."

I got up, pulled aside the lace curtain and glanced down into the street. The black polish of the coachwork was immaculate. The two greys had been brushed and combed as if for the Trooping of the Colour on Horseguards Parade. Presently there was a pull at the bell and then laughter on the stairs as Fisher exchanged some pleasantry or other with Mrs Hudson.

Sir John had come to tea in mufti, a black swallow-tail coat, cravat and striped trousers. The humorous line of the mouth in that sallow complexion, plus a quiet resolve behind pale grey eyes, summed up his character. In his left hand he was carrying a slim black attaché case. It was hardly the mark of a man who has just dropped in for a cup of tea. Behind him, Mycroft Holmes seemed like a shambling bear in a grey flannel suit. Yet, as Sherlock Holmes never tired of assuring me, Brother Mycroft was not only the British government's Senior Advisor on Inter-Departmental Affairs—at certain times of crisis he became the British government.

We took four armchairs within range of the fireplace, where the kettle sang on the hob. Mycroft and Sir John were on one side, Sherlock Holmes and I on the other. Between us stretched a low tea-table laid with a white cloth of Irish lace. The polished dome of a muffin-dish reposed among Georgian silverware and Minton china. Of course, we served ourselves. No parlour-maid was permitted to enter on these occasions and, perhaps, overhear part of our conversation. While we looked on, Sherlock Holmes performed the ritual of pouring hot water from the fireside kettle into the tea-pot, his brows drawn down, intent upon this task as though it were an intricate forensic experiment. His voice remained at our disposal as the cups were filled.

"You have no doubt come to tell us, Sir John, that Admiral von Tirpitz's intelligence officers have broken the Admiralty war-code again. Or perhaps that the plans of the battle-cruiser *Queen Mary* with full details of her armour plating and gunnery ranges are missing from Woolwich Arsenal. At this very moment, I daresay they are being scrutinised by Tirpitz and his staff officers on the map-tables of the Wilhelmstrasse."

Fisher smiled rather faintly, accepted his cup of tea and pulled a face.

"What I have to tell you, Mr Holmes, will sound far more trivial. To me, however, it is more important than codes and gunnery ranges. We may lose a telegraphic code and replace it soon enough. We may lose a battle-cruiser and yet win a war without her. We would still have the most powerful navy in the world—and the capacity of defending ourselves—so long as we produce officers and seamen of the calibre and the morale to man the fleet."

Holmes straightened up, looking puzzled, and handed a cup to Mycroft.

"I fear you have the advantage of me, Sir John. Surely we already have such men."

Mycroft took his cup and said, "Sir John's concern, dear brother, is with future officers who must be trained to lead by example."

"Well," said Sherlock Holmes wonderingly, "I should have thought that I was the last person to come to for advice on naval training!"

He swept his coat-tails round him and sat down. Sir John Fisher gave a sigh.

"Then you have not heard of Patrick Riley, have you, Mr Holmes?"

"I do not think so."

"I suppose that is something to be thankful for. Just at present, the fewer people who know of him the better! The press are lying quiet at the moment, but that will not last. Riley is a cadet, fourteen years old, at St Vincent's Naval Academy, not far from Ventnor on the Isle of Wight."

"Then I have certainly not heard of him. Why should this youth be of such importance?"

Fisher put down his cup and saucer.

"St Vincent's is a private academy, but it is licensed by the Admiralty and therefore of consequence to us. Until a few years ago, in the Royal Navy, we used to take cadets for our own naval colleges at twelve years old. That was eventually thought to be too young. The minimum age was raised to fourteen. Unfortunately, this opened the way for private academies like St Vincent's to take younger boys as cadets, during those previous two years. Frankly, these private institutions are a thorn in my side and I would happily make a bonfire of them all. However, they exist, and their sole purpose is to prepare younger boys for entrance to the senior Royal Naval Academies of Osborne and Dartmouth, between the ages of fourteen and sixteen."

"I confess," said Holmes, "that such places are a closed book to me. Tell me, how are these younger boys trained? Could they not go to school in the normal way before entering Osborne or Dartmouth?"

Fisher shrugged.

"Of course they could, but their parents do not think so. They want them trained as miniature Royal Navy lieutenants. Far the greater number, even at twelve years old, are classed as Executive Officers or 'Deck Officers' of the future. Heroes of Captain Marryat's adventure stories, famous names of the fleet who steer the ships to battle and fire the guns. A preparation for a career of death or glory."

"And what of the smaller number?"

"Precisely," said Fisher with emphasis. "In the past ten years, that smaller number has been educated rather reluctantly by these same schools as Engineer Cadets. They are less glamorous. They do a good deal of algebra, trigonometry and physics. They come from less wealthy homes—often by virtue of scholarships. I have beaten my brains out to make some of my colleagues accept that the romantic days of masts and sails have gone for ever. Turbine, coal and oil are here to stay. Without the best engine-room officers, the Royal Navy may as well spend the next war at anchor in Scapa Flow. You understand me?"

"Entirely," said Holmes placidly, "You are, as always, correct. What has this to do with Patrick Riley? Is he an Engineer? And what is St Vincent's? Who, for example, is its guiding light?"

Sir John raised a forefinger.

"One moment. St Vincent's and its competitors claim to give pupils a head start when they take examinations for cadetships at the senior institutions. At that point their pupils enter the Royal Navy proper as midshipman cadets and pass out as lieutenants at eighteen. The junior schools give them a taste of it. They employ retired petty officers to impart lessons in drill and to keep a form of naval discipline. Such schools are always on the coast so that seamanship may be taught through sailing and rowing—'pulling,' as we call it. For the greater part, though, the teachers are what you would find at a fee-paying school for boys of that age."

"And the guiding light, if I may inquire again?"

"The headmaster? No one of importance, except in the scandal that is now brewing. Reginald Winter is a Master of Arts from Oxford. He has always been a schoolmaster, rather advanced in years by now. He has never served in the navy and nor have most of his colleagues. Previously he was assistant master at St Anselm's College, Canterbury. I am assured that his heart is in the right place. In other words, he talks like a man who has been present at every naval engagement since Trafalgar. But, as the song says, when the breezes blow he generally goes below. A martyr to acute seasickness."

"So, I believe, was Lord Nelson."

"Nelson got somewhat further than the Isle of Wight!"

Holmes inclined his head in acknowledgement and then glanced at his brother.

"Very well, Sir John, I understand your concern and the reason for your visit. I am not at all clear how it involves Mycroft or what his interest may be."

Mycroft Holmes turned his large head slowly upon his sibling, the firm heavy features and the deep-set grey eyes rather suggesting a battleship's gun-platform bringing a target into its trajectory.

"It is not I, Brother Sherlock, who hold an interest. What is it to me? It is the Prime Minister who is concerned."

"About Patrick Riley? Quite absurd."

"Not Patrick Riley! Mr Asquith sees clearly that it was a grave error for the Admiralty ever to become associated with a cramming-factory like St Vincent's. Such institutions carry the reputation of the Royal Navy, yet they are ill-regulated and a likely cause of scandal and demoralisation. Will that do for you?"

"Amply," said Sherlock Holmes with an ill-judged insouciance. "What would the good Mr Asquith have me do?"

I knew privately that Holmes abominated the current Prime

Minister, and his tone was, to say the least, ill-judged. Mycroft looked at him coldly and said, "To carry out an inquiry of your own. What else?"

"And where shall I find Master Patrick Riley in this mare's nest?"

Sir John Fisher dropped his voice, as if he still feared an ear at the keyhole.

"Riley has been at St Vincent's for almost two years as an Engineer Cadet. At first he seemed exceptionally gifted in that direction, but I cannot think he has been happy there. Ten days ago there was a most distasteful incident. It is charged that this boy stole a postal order from the locker of a fellow pupil in the so-called reading room on Saturday week. Cadet John Learmount Porson was the other boy. He was also an Engineering Cadet in the same class as Riley."

"A friend?" Holmes asked.

"Riley says so. Porson had received the postal order for ten shillings and sixpence from his parents by first post on the Wednesday, I believe. He had mentioned this to others in his mess because he was going to use the money to buy a model engine. The order was clearly visible upon his desk that evening, while he wrote a letter to his parents thanking them for it. They have old-fashioned double desks and Riley shared with Porson."

"Was the order cashed?"

"It was, but not at the school, of course. With permission, the boys are allowed into the village of Bradstone St Lawrence on Saturday afternoons, usually to visit the post office or the local shop. My information is that it is alleged Riley stole the postal order from the unlocked locker and forged Porson's signature to it. He is further alleged to have cashed the order at the village post office for a ten-shilling note and a sixpence piece at about two-thirty. Porson had intended to cash it himself later that day. At four o'clock he discovered it was missing."

Holmes relaxed, almost as if he found such a commonplace crime soothing. He looked Fisher in the eye.

"Since you have bothered to tell me about this, I assume that Riley denies the theft?"

"At first. Now he refuses to discuss it. He had a permit but claims he was in school bounds until three o'clock. I fear there is more to come."

"His silence is taken as an admission of guilt?"

Fisher lifted a hand.

"One moment. What has followed is far more important than any stolen postal order, but let us deal with that first. The headmaster confronted him with the accusation. Riley denied it. The matter then rested with Reginald Winter as head. He quite properly began by dealing with it himself. The only witness of importance was the assistant postmistress, Miss Henslowe, who cashed the order at the village post office."

"She identified Riley?"

"Not quite. On Saturday evening Mr Winter sent Petty Officer Carter down to question her. She first told him that all the cadets in their uniforms looked the same to her but that she had certainly cashed the order at about half-past two. She had given the boy who presented it a ten-shilling note and a sixpenny coin. He had counter-signed the receipt on the order while in the post office. She was standing at the counter but was busy with telegrams to be sent out and did not pay particular attention to him. The telegraph boy was also present but he was in the back office and apparently saw nothing."

"Did she offer no identification of the suspect?"

"Not much. She persisted in saying that the cadets in their uniforms looked much the same to everyone in the village. They are all roughly the same age, much the same size and in the same uniform. However, she recalled that this boy had a blue-grey braid or edging to the lapels and hem of his navy blue jacket. She did not know the significance of this. In fact it meant that he was one of the Engineer Cadets, who make up about thirty-five of the two hundred boys at St Vincent's."

"We may take it that the jacket was his own?"

"Who knows? In any case that was not quite the end of the matter. Miss Henslowe also recalled that this boy wore glasses, at least when signing the counterfoil for payment of the order."

"And that was all?"

"She agreed to visit the school with Petty Officer Carter and attend what I suppose must be called an identification parade. There are about eight Engineer Cadets and forty or more Executive Cadets, future Deck Officers, in the same term as Riley. For many classes, they are together. Otherwise, Riley and his group join the other engineering terms for instruction in the workshops or for lessons in algebra and trigonometry."

"And the result of the parade?"

"One moment," said Fisher fastidiously. "While the parade was being arranged, Reginald Winter questioned Patrick Riley, in the presence of the Cadet Gunner, as that petty officer is known. When Riley continued to deny that he had been to the post office on Saturday, Mr Winter gave him pen and paper and told him to write Porson's name. Riley wrote it as Porson usually signed it, 'J. L. Porson.' He was then told to write the name in full, as it had been written on the postal order. He wrote 'John L. Porson.' The headmaster remarked that this looked similar to Porson's own signature. Riley was told to go and sit across the corridor in what is known as the Parents' Waiting Room."

Holmes stared into the fireplace and said quietly, "It seems a capital error to leave a fourteen-year-old boy alone against the forensic powers of the adult world."

Fisher put his tea-cup down.

"Perhaps. Riley was then summoned back. He was again

given pen and paper and told to write half-a-dozen times, 'Parson Jones adored the unselfishness of his son Luke.'"

"In which sentence," said Holmes delightedly, "there lie concealed all the letter combinations of 'John L. Porson.' Mr Winter's knowledge of calligraphy and interrogation is not the most subtle but I daresay effective in its way. Clever enough to outwit a confused and anxious fourteen-year-old."

"More effective and more clever than you may suppose, Mr Holmes. The calligraphy, as you call it, was at once passed by the Admiralty to Mr Thomas Gurrin at the Home Office. Within two days, he gave his opinion that the signature upon the postal order and the specimen writing done in the headmaster's study were by the same hand. That is to say, two different scripts by one hand. Mr Gurrin is an expert."

"Whose evidence ensured that Adolf Beck went to penal servitude for seven years in 1896 for a crime we now know he could not have committed."

Mycroft Holmes had been uncharacteristically silent during all this. He reached for another muffin and said, "Unfortunately, dear brother, the fact that Tom Gurrin was wrong in that case alone does not mean that he cannot be right in any other. I fear your defence will be built upon sand. And what of the identification parade, Sir John?"

"A dozen boys or so from Riley's mess were paraded in the waiting room. They included all the Engineers and several Executive Cadets. Riley was allowed to remove his glasses. Miss Henslowe again complained that the cadets looked alike to her. She could not be sure. She looked into each face and studied each physique. In the end, she said that if it was any of them, it was the boy we now know to be Riley. Indeed, with glasses on it would probably be him. It was certainly none of the others."

"And what was the outcome?" I asked.

Sir John shook his head.

"In the first place, doctor, Mr Winter quite properly communicated his findings to the seven school governors, two of whom are retired naval officers. Under the agreement by which St Vincent's is licenced by the Admiralty, he also forwarded those findings to us. Having examined the boy face-to-face, he considered Riley was guilty of the theft. He had previously noted what he called certain defects of character in this cadet."

"That last remark is a grotesque distortion of the evidential process!" Holmes snapped.

Fisher held up his hand.

"Mr Winter assured us that he mentioned it only to confirm that he had made allowance for this so that there should be no prejudice on that account during questioning."

Holmes emitted a gasping guffaw of exasperation.

"The oldest trick in a barrister's brief! The name of it in Cicero's time was *'mitto,'* I believe. You list every moral failing under the sun—fixing them well in the minds of your hearers—and then promise not to prejudice the accused by introducing them into evidence against him. His chances are nil."

Sir John looked grim for the first time that afternoon.

"You fail to appreciate that a headmaster's study is not a court of law!"

"And yet he seems to have behaved as though it were!"

Fisher relented at this and said unhappily, "In the circumstances, for the sake of the boy as well as the school, Mr Winter recommended that the mother should be asked to remove him. A few days later, Mr Gurrin's opinion on the handwriting seemed to vindicate his decision."

"Why the boy's mother?" I asked before Holmes could get in again.

"It is an unfortunate case, doctor. That is why I am here. There is no father. Mrs Riley is a widow and lives in Dublin. I know little more than that. My impression is of a bright boy with very little money behind him. He has not been in trouble before. I should guess that his family has scraped everything together to pay his way through St Vincent's in the hope of an Admiral's Nomination for Dartmouth or Osborne. He seems to have the mental ability."

"Meaning what?" Holmes asked suspiciously.

Sir John took a long breath.

"When they take their exams at fourteen or sixteen for the senior Royal Naval Academies, there is usually one Nomination for each school. It is rather the same as a scholarship to a college at Oxford or Cambridge. It pays the fees, of course, but there is also a good deal of prestige and it will carry a young man a fair way in his career. Of course, the admirals do not know all the boys personally and the headmaster's advice carries great weight. Even if the present accusation proves no more than suspicion, Riley is no longer a likely candidate for such preferment. Unfortunately, he will always be known as the boy who stole the postal order, unless the contrary can be proved. I have come to you, Mr Holmes, because you are the one man I know who may be able to prove him innocent rather than not guilty."

At last the two friends were on common ground, to my very great relief.

"And where is he now?" Holmes demanded.

"He was suspended as soon as the charge was brought, and kept apart from the other boys in the school sanatorium. Once his punishment is confirmed, arrangements will be made to return him home."

"We must lose no time."

"You had better hear the rest, Mr Holmes." Fisher looked as if he did not quite know how to continue. However, he resumed. "Riley has been quarantined in the sanatorium, but, of course, he could hardly be kept a prisoner there. Last Sunday he slipped out on his own. The boys are permitted to walk in the surrounding countryside on Sunday afternoons between lunch and tea. No one seems to have thought of forbidding him to do so."

Our friend looked more uncomfortable than I had ever known him. Even Mycroft Holmes was studying his own toe-caps. I felt that some catastrophe was about to be announced.

"Last Sunday afternoon," Sir John continued, "it seems that Patrick Riley tried to kill himself by running towards the railway line beyond the school field and throwing himself in the path of a train that was just coming out of Bradstone St Lawrence tunnel. I think that says everything."

Sherlock Holmes's attitude and manner changed at once. His dark eyes glittered as he said quietly, "I think you had better give us the details, Sir John."

"Very well. As I understand it, Riley ran across a field adjoining the school grounds. It is sometimes called the School Field and is commonly used by the boys on their Sunday walks. There were still several of them around, walking back to the main building for tea. At the far side, where the railway line runs on an embankment, there is hardly a fence at all, merely a strand or two of wire between a row of posts. Anyone of moderate agility could scramble up to the track and the linesman's hut in a few seconds. A train had just emerged from Bradstone St Lawrence tunnel, when the boy stepped out from behind the hut and stood directly in the path of the locomotive. He showed no intention of moving."

"How far distant is the hut from the tunnel?"

"Two or three hundreds yards, I believe. That would not have saved him. However, by the grace of God, the young fireman in the engine cab had seen him running just before he reached dead ground below the line and was lost to view for a moment. Perhaps sensing something was wrong, the fireman shouted a warning to the driver. In a split second more, Riley appeared from behind the hut. The driver threw the brakes on even as the boy came into view. Riley stood there, staring at the train which was slowing to a crawl. But for the fireman, he would have been hit. As it was, he saw the train losing speed and knew that he would more probably be injured or maimed than killed. Thereupon he ran down the far side. Afterwards he turned back and was identified by several witnesses, crossing the field towards the school."

There was a pause while Holmes gave the matter some thought. Fisher added, unnecessarily as it seemed to me, "Had this attempt succeeded, a sordid schoolboy misdemeanour would have become a newspaper scandal. I understand that the field, which lies beyond the school's sports pitches, has been put strictly out of bounds to all boys since the incident."

Holmes murmured approvingly and then asked, "No doubt this so-called suicide attempt was taken at St Vincent's as confirmation of his guilt as a thief?"

"In the eyes of the world it will be taken as such," said Fisher coldly, "How can it not be?"

"And has he some right of appeal against Mr Winter's decision over the curious business of the postal order?"

Sir John put down his cup again.

"My dear Holmes! Nothing has so far been decided, given the boy's obvious distress of mind and the probable need for legal advice on his mother's side. He remains in the school sanatorium, but now he is there as a patient rather than a detainee. He will not, of course, be permitted to wander off again."

Holmes stood up, removed the silver cover and handed round the plate of muffins.

"Sir John, let me be clear. Have you come to persuade me that I should act on the boy's behalf—presumably not on the headmaster's behalf—or as a servant of their lordships of the Admiralty?"

"From what I have told you, Mr Holmes, I would have you investigate and see if you can find the truth. Whatever help I can give you, I will. Now of all times, we cannot afford a public scandal involving the Admiralty. Thanks to St Vincent's, that is what we are threatened with. To use a lawyer's phrase, I suppose I am empowered to retain you."

In my friend's eye, there was the glint of the war-horse sighting or scenting battle. He replaced the muffin-dish and sat down.

"Very well, Sir John. Then perhaps this is the moment when I should have sight of the postal order with its contentious signature. I have no doubt you are carrying it in that black attaché case of yours.

Admiral Fisher said nothing, but he sprang the two locks of the case and drew out a folder containing a single sheet of paper with a form pinned to it. He handed this to Holmes, who glanced over it with his pocket lens.

While Mycroft Holmes and Fisher looked on, my friend held the postal order at one angle and then another, allowing light and shade to play upon it. Finally, he drew out his silver propelling-pencil and made two or three cryptic notes on the white starched cuff of his shirt.

"You will, of course, wish to retain it for a thorough examination," said Fisher encouragingly.

Holmes looked up as he handed it back.

"You are too kind. However, I believe I have seen all that is necessary to bring the case to a successful conclusion.

Mycroft Holmes scowled at his sibling.

"You are quite certain, dear brother?"

"When I am certain, Mycroft, I am always *quite* certain. Now then, if you will allow me full discretion in the matter, I think I shall begin with the so-called attempted suicide."

"Rather than the theft with which the boy is charged?" Fisher asked uneasily.

"I believe so."

"But as yet you know nothing of the boy and little of the incident on the railway line."

"Indeed not. That is precisely my point. I must know. I shall remedy my ignorance at the earliest possible moment. I do not know the boy, of course, but I know a little about self destruction. I have yet to hear any argument from you that would convince me of an attempt at suicide. However, I cannot help reflecting that Patrick Riley's disappearance from this earth would have the convenient effect at St Vincent's of confirming the charge against him with no likelihood that anyone else could prove otherwise." He sat back with his cup of tea in one hand, a muffin in the other, and smiled.

Sir John blinked and said, "Mr Holmes, you are to investigate the evidence of theft, if you please, not theories of suicide. This is not one of your murder mysteries."

"You would be surprised to know, Sir John, how many inquiries of a quite different kind have turned into one of my murder mysteries, as you are kind enough to call them. As for Patrick Riley, it is of the greatest importance that he should remain where he is until Watson and I have had a chance to examine him. Indeed, you may tell the school that my colleague has been retained by their lordships or the boy's family as a medical consultant. However it is done, I beg that you will use your best efforts to keep him where he is until we can get there."

"And of the utmost importance that we should have the opportunity to examine St Vincent's itself," I said quickly.

"Well done, Watson! You see, gentlemen? Watson is ahead of you there!"

"And when do you suggest your examinations will begin?" Mycroft Holmes inquired sceptically.

Sherlock Holmes got up from his chair and walked across to the door of the room. Beside it, on the wall, hung a handsome wheel-barometer of polished walnut. It was inherited from his parents and made by an English craftsman a hundred years ago. He tapped the glass and watched the delicate metal hand move slowly round the dial in a clockwise direction. Its prediction settled midway between "fair" and "set fair."

"I had almost thought we should have to leave this afternoon," he said, "At present, however, the glass is rising and I think tomorrow promises to be excellent 'detective weather.' It is of some importance that it should not rain before we have a chance to go over the ground. We shall entrust ourselves to an early train from Waterloo station to Portsmouth Harbour. The steamer crossings to the Isle of Wight are frequent. If we reach Ryde Pier by noon we shall take the local train to—Ventnor, I suppose?"

Sir John Fisher inclined his head. "Ventnor indeed."

"If my geography of the island is correct, a cab will then take us westwards to Bradstone St Lawrence and St Vincent's. I suppose we should arrive by two-thirty or three o'clock. I take it the bird will not have flown by then and that the venerable Mr Winter will be available?"

"I may guarantee it," said Sir John enthusiastically. His good-natured features began to work into a smile of grateful acceptance. "I shall authorise the commissary office to book rooms for you both at the King Charles Hotel in Bradstone St Lawrence."

Sherlock Holmes stooped over the tea-table, and lifted the cover of the muffin-dish. He inspected the contents and then held it out to our Admiral of the Fleet.

"Pray take another, Sir John, before my brother Mycroft has the chance to eat them all."

2

Shortly before noon on the following day we stepped out of a green South-Coast Railway carriage on to the platform of Portsmouth Harbour station. A stiff channel breeze was blowing and a red-funnelled paddle-steamer was waiting at the jetty. An hour later we were in an island railway carriage for the coastal journey to Ventnor. I had never seen the south-east coast of the Isle of Wight and was much taken by the little resort with its coastguard station and sheltered cove. Holmes, who seldom forgot anything that he read, assured me that Dr Thomas Arnold compared it for beauty to a resort on the Bay of Genoa. Mediterranean, Alpine and herbal flowers occupied the crevices of the rocks.

Behind the line of the shore rose a green hill that becomes St Boniface Down. Gentility was everywhere in the villas, rising in crescents, row upon row, like the boxes at a theatre with the sea as their stage. The elegant terraces of Clifton or Cheltenham might have been snatched up and set down again in this quiet resort. Thanks to Fisher's efficiency, a cab was waiting for us at the station. We followed the shore westwards, until the road levelled out among gabled houses, set back in their own gardens.

Beyond the town, we passed at length through the small village of Bradstone St Lawrence. Ahead of us through a screen of trees rose the outlines of several buildings in red-brick gothic. One of them boasted a short spire and a stained-glass chapel window.

Such was St Vincent's Naval Academy, named in honour of John Jervis, victor of the battle of Cape St Vincent against the Spanish fleet in 1797. I recalled from my school lessons that his ferocity in the face of the enemy was equalled only by the grim acts of retribution by which he kept order among his men.

Our cab set us down in a gravelled yard, from which an archway led to a portico, double doors and porter's lodge. We followed the route to the "Headmaster's Corridor" on which Mr Winter's study was located. A single Persian runner lay the length of it with black varnish either side. Beyond a tall bookcase, several beechwood chairs with horsehair seats accommodated those summoned to his presence. The walls were hung on either side with long photographs of past intakes and shorter ones of Cricket XI or Rugby XV teams, and regatta crews. In a final alcove rose a hall-stand with a central mirror, hooks on either side for hats and coats, a drawer for gloves, a well on each side for umbrellas or walking-sticks and a rack at floor-level for boots and shoes. Holmes paused to remove his deer-stalker and hang it on a convenient hook.

Winter was a somewhat younger man than Sir John Fisher had led me to expect but still closer to fifty than forty. A curiosity was that his expression, even under strong emotion, appeared to alter very little. His head, almost entirely bald, shone for all the world as if he polished it.

Reginald Winter shook us strongly by the hand, indicated two chairs, but himself remained standing before his fireplace. How much does a room tell one of its tenant? Pride of place at the centre of the mantelpiece was held by the most exquisite model of HMS *Warrior*, Britain's first ironclad battleship, easily recognised by her black hull and stumpy yellow funnels. To one side stood an old-fashioned pipe-rack with a row of half-a-dozen briar-root pipes, a tobacco jar and a soft leather pouch. A new briar remained in its unopened box, bearing the familiar advertising scroll "Thinking Men Smoke Petersen Pipes." Mr Winter plainly saw himself as a "thinking man."

At the other end of the shelf, I noticed a business card advertising "William Fortescue, Army, Navy, And General Outfitter, Royal Opera Arcade, Pall Mall. Price Lists and Instructions for Self-Measurement Sent on Application." The effect of Mr Winter was to make me wonder how much commission our host received for each garment bought by the parents from Mr Fortescue.

Everywhere, the study certified the manliness of its occupant. Walking-sticks, golf-clubs, even a fencing-mask and a pair of foils, competed with a tiger-skin rug before the fender and the stuffed head of a stag above the mantelpiece.

The headmaster seated himself a little above us by perching on the padded leather top of the iron fender surrounding his hearth. He smiled without humour, as if to assure us that he was the master of the place and we should know it.

Before he could begin, Holmes said, "Let us come to the matter of Patrick Riley." His voice was cool and detached with all the amiability of a crocodile. I was unhappily aware of the instinctive mutual dislike of these two men.

Reginald Winter looked him straight in the eye.

"I have agreed to discuss this matter with you on the advice of Admiral Fisher. However, gentlemen, with the evidence of the witnesses before me I cannot reasonably doubt that an act of theft has taken place and Riley himself has ceased to deny his part in it."

"Or admit it," said Holmes casually.

"Quite so. Against this, I grieve that the shame of that act and its discovery drove the poor boy to an attempt against his own life."

"Indeed?"

"Indeed, Mr Holmes. I am a firm man, as my duty here requires. At the same time, believe me, I am neither vindictive nor callous. Between ourselves, Riley comes from what I am bound to call a starveling background. The temptation to theft must have been tragically potent. To keep him as a pupil, with all his schoolfellows knowing what he had done, would be impossible. It would be crueller to him than to them."

"Though not as cruel as to destroy the future hope of an innocent boy?"

Winter spread out his hands in a gesture of sincerity and boundless generosity.

"At the worst, I suppose, the poor fellow has been criminal. I prefer to think that, on both occasions, he was merely weak. The second occasion appears to confirm the first, does it not?"

A familiar look in Holmes's eye assured me that Winter had just stepped neatly into a trap.

"Without it we should lack that confirmation, should we?"

But the headmaster was not so easily caught.

"Mr Holmes, I have known this boy for almost two years. He is not evil. I wish him well. I hope he may thrive elsewhere. But I have taken the only course open to me."

"Elsewhere?" Sherlock Holmes put more into the two syllables than I would have thought possible. Winter became ingratiating.

"This will seem a strange world to you, sir. I have the advantage of living in it for some years and understanding the best interests of individual boys."

"Capital," said Holmes expressionlessly, and for a moment the headmaster seemed to believe that he was safe. But Sherlock Holmes never took his eyes off him.

"Patrick Riley is a sensitive boy," Winter explained, as if with a little difficulty, "whatever his faults or virtues. I believe his reaction to being caught demonstrates that—his refusal to take his medicine. I fear, gentlemen, the Royal Navy is not the best place for a boy of the sensitive poetic spirit, the young philosopher, the scholar whose whole heart is in his books."

"And is Patrick Riley such a boy?" Holmes inquired politely.

Reginald Winter smiled again and made another gesture of infinite good nature.

"The worst I could say before this incident was that during two years he had not been a good mixer. Riley prefers to keep himself to himself. Normal boys do not like that sort of thing. It makes a fellow seem as if he thinks himself better than they. A little more sociability or geniality would have made him popular enough."

"And was he unpopular?" I asked, "Do I take it that he has been bully-ragged?

"No!" Mr Winter looked startled, "No boy is bullied at St Vincent's, sir. In case you think so, perhaps it is best that you should form your own conclusions of his character when you meet him—for meet him you shall, I promise you that. He is fortunate to have such counsel for his defence!"

Having failed once, he tried a second time to smile us into friendship. Not a muscle in Holmes's face moved.

"I am not here as anyone's counsel, Mr Winter. You have found the boy guilty of theft. The boy denies it and, whatever the pressure put upon him, has not changed his plea. Sir John Fisher has asked me to establish the truth. That is all. Though, of course, there is also the allegation against him of an attempt to kill himself. Attempted suicide is a crime as surely as theft."

The headmaster shook his head sympathetically. He mistakenly believed he was out of the wood now.

"Even without the matter of theft, it would be difficult to

keep him after the second incident. We are not equipped to care for a boy who may attempt anything of that kind. Meanwhile, the others believe that it confirms his guilt. Would an innocent boy behave in such a manner? They naturally think not. Suicide is bound to be regarded as a sign of cowardice in the face of adversity."

The opinion which Reginald Winter attributed to his boys was surely his own.

"Yes," said Holmes, languidly arrogant, "the cowardice of the late Captain Lawrence Oates, who deliberately walked out into a South Pole blizzard in order that his companions might have a better chance of survival on their doomed trek homewards."

Reginald Winter tried to smile, but temper was getting the better of him.

"That was not what I meant, Mr Holmes. It rests on my conscience that a boy in my school should condemn himself twice, as a thief and a coward, by attempting such a dreadful thing. But there is a world of difference . . ." Then, as he sat on the padded top of his fire-surround, he stopped and smiled down at us, as if he realised that a joke had been practised on him.

"Are you playing games with me, Mr Holmes? They say it is your habit."

"Do they, Mr Winter? Do they say that indeed? Then let me tell you something for your comfort."

"Comfort, sir?" There was a mocking curiosity in this query, but I knew from the cold, sardonic tone in my friend's voice that the sparring was over. Holmes had got him and was about to land a decisive blow.

"In order that your conscience may lie quite easily . . ."

I winced at the savage double meaning of this statement.

". . . you may put it from your mind that Patrick Riley tried to commit suicide. He did not."

The headmaster's smile went out like a light.

"You were not there, Mr Holmes. Several witnesses were. They saw him run at the train. In law, a man must be assumed to intend the natural and probable consequences of his acts. What would those consequences have been if the fireman had not seen him as the train emerged from the tunnel and the driver had not pulled on the brake at once?"

Holmes relaxed, drew a sheet of notepaper from his breast pocket and handed it to Winter. I recalled that he had been compiling this from his shelves the evening before. It had not occurred to me to ask him what it was.

"Mr Winter," he continued languidly, "you may examine the tables of coroners' courts, not to mention the statistics of alienation. There you will find suicides of every description. Suicide by poison or firearms, by noose or by falling from a height, by drowning or by burning. It is very difficult to stab oneself, of course, which is why defeated generals of the ancient world ordered their servants to hold out a sword that they might run upon it."

"I have heard of that," Winter snapped impatiently.

"And to be sure, there are poor souls who have thrown themselves under the wheels of trains."

"Then you admit it?"

Holmes ignored this.

"You will find from the evidence that they often lingered at the last moment or even waited patiently for a train to appear. Some fell in front of trains, some jumped, some stood or lay upon the rails. But you will search long and hard, Mr Winter—dare I say until hell freezes over?—before you find one who ran to die in front of a train, as if he feared being late for an appointment. Hesitation or uncertainty, procrastination or postponement, not precipitation, is the governing impulse."

Mr Winter had ignored the sheet of paper and stared hard at

Sherlock Holmes during this recital. Now he blinked at the paper in his hand and then looked up again.

"And so . . ." he began.

"And so, Mr Winter, every statistic and every scrap of medical experience is against you on this. It is even less likely that Patrick Riley tried to commit suicide, which I do not hear that he has admitted, than that he stole the postal order. You have—to use a common expression—not a leg to stand on."

The headmaster swallowed gently and continued to stare. Holmes continued.

"Now, sir, I fear we must put suicide out of the question. What remains is the testimony of Miss Henslowe, who attended the identification parade, and the opinion of Mr Thomas Gurrin on the handwriting. None of this evidence has been subject to challenge or examination. My task is therefore to let a little light into dark corners. Unless we are to be governed by the jurisprudence of the late Tomas de Torquemada, Patrick Riley's protest of innocence stands firm unless—and until—proved otherwise. Why should anyone want to undermine it?"

"Not I, Mr Holmes." Like so many of our opponents who started out in bluff self-confidence, Reginald Winter was beginning to lose his nerve in the face of my friend's meticulous rationality. The headmaster's smooth face creased carefully to suggest a sincere alarm at being misunderstood. "I should be only too happy to find him innocent, if the evidence were not all the other way! Believe me, it does a school no good if an offence of this sort becomes public gossip. For Riley's own sake the best course is to note the facts, not all of which are known to you yet, and to leave us quietly to do what must be done."

"The facts? Yes, Mr Winter. I hoped we should come to the facts. Pray let us hear them."

"You are a man who judges by evidence, are you not, Mr Holmes? I believe you are well known for it. Very good. Listen to this. First of all, unknown to my colleagues and me, Riley and other boys sometimes played games in their leisure time which involved practising one another's signatures. They admit it. Riley and Porson were in the same class. They sat next to one another. As I am told, they became proficient at writing each other's names. Riley was one of our Engineer Cadets and had the hand of a draughtsman."

"And so, Mr Winter, when Porson's postal order was cashed on that Saturday week with a forged signature, Riley the Engineer was suspected as the copyist simply because he was a draughtsman? From what document did he copy when he was in the post office? He could hardly carry in his head a perfect image of John Learmount Porson's signature, for that is what draughtsmanship would suggest."

"Very far from it, sir. Were you not told that the *exeat* permit for that afternoon, with Porson's signature and that of the duty master, was in the locker with the postal order? Both of them were stolen, Mr Sherlock Holmes."

I confess this was a blow. Why had we—or Fisher—not been told of the additional theft of this permit? The headmaster had unexpectedly scored a point and was at ease again. Winter went over to his desk and came back with a small pad of yellow paper, whose pages might be torn off in succession. Printed at the top of each was the school name, followed by a space for the name of the boy and another for the signature of the master on duty. He handed it to Holmes, who riffled through the flimsy yellow leaves and handed it back. Reginald Winter resumed his fire-guard perch and smiled down at us once more.

"Each boy is given a small pad of forms at the start of term. Should he wish to leave the school grounds to visit the village on Saturday afternoon, he fills in his name, signature and the date. He then tears off this *exeat* permit and at one-thirty he goes to the master-on-duty that day, who signs in the space at the bottom—or sometimes simply puts his initials on it."

"How do the boys draw money?" I asked.

Winter looked pleased to have been asked.

"As to cashing postal orders, doctor, we are careful to prevent boys having too much money in their hands. It leads to borrowing and lending or buying items which are not permitted in the school. Each boy is allowed to draw two shillings a week from a sum deposited with his house master at the beginning of term. If there is a special reason, he may draw more on a single occasion. Within the same rules, he may cash a postal order, provided it is sent from his parents. To go to the post office he must have an *exeat* permit and also use this to identify himself at the post office."

"And Riley had such an *exeat* permit signed for him on Saturday week, did he?"

"No, Mr Holmes he did not. That is the whole point. He denies leaving the school grounds."

Holmes looked at him as Winter was about to continue.

"Where was Patrick Riley at two-thirty?"

The headmaster summoned up an indulgent smile.

"Of course he insists that he did not leave the grounds, let alone with a permit in Porson's name. How could he do otherwise? He claims that he spent an hour alone in the art room, between two and three o'clock. It is an alibi which a thief might choose because no one other than a type like Riley would skulk off there, for whatever purpose. He could be sure of being alone. His story would not be disproved."

"Why not, Mr Winter?"

"Strictly speaking, the art room is out of bounds outside teaching hours. In practice we would take a lenient view of a boy found there, but Riley was not so found. What normal healthy boy would shut himself in there on a Saturday afternoon, when he might be pulling at the boats or roller-skating with his class-mates? As for witnesses, a few boys might pass the art room, but none would be likely to look in. They would certainly not be surprised to find it locked. Possibly Riley bolted the door on the inside, stepped out of the casement window, closed it after him and walked off to the village. No one could then be positive that he was not there during twenty minutes or so. It falls far short of a positive alibi, Mr Holmes."

"Indeed," said Holmes coldly. "So far short that a true thief would not consider it."

"How many ways were there to the post office?" I asked.

"As many as you like, Dr Watson. A boy might walk along the road from the main entrance. He might follow that same route inside the field-hedge. He might even go through the trees at any angle he chose. It would not be difficult to remain concealed until he was within twenty yards of the post office."

"And then Riley and Porson were friends," I added. "Why should Riley rob his class-mate?"

"We may be sure that Porson did not falsely complain of theft. He gained nothing—he had only to go and get his money from the post office at four o'clock. Yet you are quite right, though, that the thief's motive and identity remained a puzzle. Very well. For that reason I invited Miss Henslowe, the assistant postmistress, in an attempt to identify the boy whom she served at the office."

"And so?" I persisted.

"The good lady came here, looked at them, and picked out Riley as the only possible suspect. Now then, what would you have me do, gentlemen? I informed the chairman of the governors, Commander Portman, and with his knowledge sought the advice of the Admiralty. The Judge Advocate to the Fleet requested the opinion of the principal Home Office forensic advisor on handwriting, Mr Thomas Gurrin. Mr Gurrin had no doubt that the signature on the counterfoil of the postal order and the samples written by Patrick Riley were from the same hand."

He turned to my friend.

"Whatever your allegiances, Mr Holmes, you cannot say we have not behaved properly."

"My allegiance is to the truth, sir, and to justice. I have no other clients. I am here at the request of Admiral Sir John Fisher."

Mr Winter did not like this last reminder, but he said, "So I understand," and battled on.

"I then recommended to the chairman of the governors that Mrs Riley should be asked to remove her son from the school. How could the boy go back and mingle with his comrades after such a finding against him?"

"I should like to interview Master Patrick Riley," said Holmes casually, "and, indeed, his friend Porson."

There was a breathless geniality about Winter which suggested an ace up his sleeve.

"You shall certainly talk to Riley, Mr Holmes." The geniality vanished as the ace appeared. "I cannot, however, order other boys to submit to interrogation by an outsider, even one who comes at the request of an Admiral of the Fleet. We are licenced by the Admiralty, Mr Holmes, we are not owned nor governed by it."

I could see that this was as far as we should get with him. He had put on a show of easy courtesy, but I should not have cared to be a pupil at St Vincent's. A crook-handled cane stood in a corner of the room. I noticed that Holmes's mouth had tightened a little as he caught sight of it. I recalled a comment of his on those who demonstrated their manhood by beating children.

In a voice like thin ice breaking, Sherlock Holmes said, "We have occupied too much of your time, Mr Winter, and our own. Perhaps before we talk to Patrick Riley, Dr Watson and I may take a walk across the field towards the railway line."

Innocent surprise, pumped up as from a well, brightened

Reginald Winter's face. He was pleased to allow us something after forbidding an interview with Porson, though not quite as pleased as by having seen the last of Sherlock Holmes for a while. Left to himself, he would no doubt repair his defences.

"By all means walk across to the line, Mr Holmes, though I cannot see how it will help you. If you go out through the back of the building, the playing field lies before you. Your route is straight ahead. The railway is clearly visible on its embankment. It should not take you half an hour. On your return, we shall have tea before your talk with Riley."

The expression on my friend's face indicated that, though nothing would prevent him from talking to Patrick Riley, wild horses would not drag him to take tea with the headmaster.

Reginald Winter watched us walk away down the corridor and stood there until we had passed the glass door which separated his quarters from the rest of the main school. As he disappeared into his study, Holmes held up his finger, a quiet gesture of self-reproach.

"My hat," he said absent-mindedly.

He went back to the hall-stand, with its mirrors, hooks and racks. Taking down his travelling-cap, he adjusted it in the glass. His eyes made a careful survey of boots and umbrellas, which were presumably the headmaster's outdoor wear, almost as if he had thought of borrowing some of it.

I was uneasy in case Winter should reappear from the study and catch us examining his effects. But Holmes had not quite done. As I have mentioned, the walls of the corridor were hung with group photographs of the pupils. They were all at their lessons just now. I had noticed the photographs were "Drake Term," "Anson Term," or "Nelson Term," each intake of boys christened after a hero of the fleet. To my relief, Holmes presently turned away from this display and walked towards me.

"And now, Watson," he said briskly, "let us make the best of the time that our reluctant host has unwisely allowed us.

3

"Hardly the companion I should choose for a walking tour or a reading party," I said, as we crossed the playing field towards a gate in the hedge and moved out of earshot of the buildings.

Holmes gave a quiet snort.

"A shabby fellow. An exceptionally nasty piece of work. The last person whom I would put in charge of children. Fortunately for our client, as I think Patrick Riley must now be called, Winter has made a strategic error. He would dearly love to massage the tale of attempted suicide into a confession of guilt. That would end the matter. He is too stupid or perverse to see that it is his weakest spot. It is where I believe we shall find the loose thread that unravels this entire conspiracy."

"Conspiracy?"

"What else? There is far more to this than Winter's obvious defects of character."

The so-called School Field, which was not strictly part of the grounds, was rough going, with chalk under a few inches of soil. It looked useless for crops or pasture, or indeed for anything else. The grass grew in brief, uneven tufts, and the broad path was something like a disused cart-track.

To judge from the present state of the earth, the rain that had spoilt so many cricket matches in the northern and eastern counties last week had probably cleared the Isle of Wight a day or two earlier. Patterns of footsteps left on the muddy surface the previous Sunday had accordingly been dried and hardened by a steady south-westerly breeze from the English Channel. Among these prints must surely be those of Patrick Riley and, indeed, whatever so-called witnesses there may have been. If Reginald Winter's order putting the field out of bounds had been obeyed, as I felt sure it would have been, the latest prints must necessarily have been preserved for a few days.

We walked almost half-way across the field, following the track, before Holmes stopped and surveyed the path ahead. It is necessarily true that more people will cross the first half of a field than the whole of it. Where we were standing, there were three prominent sets of prints which were continuous and a number of others which appeared from time to time on the track, as though someone had been walking at first on the grass but occasionally on the path. My companion stood there for a moment, staring down at these foot patterns. He looked up.

"I believe, Watson, that we have found our man, if Patrick Riley is he. Boys, being boys, will amble about all over the place, mostly on the grass of the field. But imagine that you were running to reach a particular destination on the far side of the field as quickly as you could, and that the surface was still damp from rain. You would, I think, prefer to follow the firmer ground and straighter line of the path. Would you not?"

"As you say."

"It is so obviously the best way that while you were running you would hardly think about it. It is what you would do by instinct. In any case, if you were in such a hurry that it was necessary to run, then wet grass on either side would slow you down. Now then, you will see there are footsteps here which I have been following from a little way back."

He paused, turned round the way we had come and then swung round again.

"See here. The length of the stride suggests the height. The depth of the impression in damp earth indicates the weight or build. What I have found is evidence of a lightly-built boy, about five feet six inches in height. At first, just for a little, the soles and heels of his shoes were equally printed, therefore he was walking. I have noticed several similar tracks, but his is consistent and therefore presumably the one we want. You see it here?"

I looked at the print of a business-like sole and heel, the plain uniform shoe of so many schools and colleges. At this point, however, the print of the heel was hardly visible and all the weight seemed to be on the toes. To me the stride appeared longer than that of a boy who was five feet six inches in height. In company with Sherlock Holmes, the explanation was obvious.

"By the time he got here, he had started running!"

"Indeed he had. Of course, there is nothing remarkable in that. Boys of his age, when they have leisure, are normally lazy. But they will run a few steps or a few yards in a game. However, ask yourself how many would run alone the width of a large field, almost start to finish, in a Sunday suit for no good reason. Everything here invites a stroll, not a run. According to the evidence, only Patrick Riley was seen to run towards the railway embankment last Sunday afternoon. See for yourself. There are no continuous running prints but these."

He stopped again and glanced up at the light cloud veiling the pale Solent sky. I took the chance to intervene.

"That hardly tells us more than we knew already."

"You think not? I believe it tells us a good deal more. Let us enumerate the details. So far, we were merely informed that he ran across the field. The foolish and improbable suggestion was an intent to throw himself under a train. It was not suggested, for example, that he was running away from pursuers or that he wished to avoid surveillance. If that was the case, his fear would not be that he might be late for the train which was going to kill him but that he wanted to avoid being seen or captured."

Having demolished the theory of suicide for Winter's benefit, Holmes now sought to replace it.

"I don't entirely follow you," I said.

"Just here, old fellow, there are two prints made by the boy who was running—whom we shall assume was Riley. They are the only ones so far that do not point forwards. The right foot is at a right angle from the path. The left foot also points right at a lesser angle. Now see here. Stand with your feet exactly where the prints are. It will not matter if you disturb the earth. You see? As you stand now, the slightest movement of your head or torso gives you a full view of the field behind you on your right. And a few yards further on our fugitive does it again—this time to the left."

"But why?"

"Perhaps, like Coleridge's Ancient Mariner, 'he knows a frightful fiend doth close behind him tread.' Or simply because he was looking out for someone who might be behind him—or ahead of him."

As we walked on, the same "turning prints" occurred more frequently to right and left, as if our fugitive indeed watched for pursuers gaining upon him or sought for friends.

The path on the far side of the field reached the so-called fence, a few strands of wire stretching along waist-high posts. It would have stopped no one. On the other side the slope went up roughly trodden steps to the top of the railway embankment. We stood by the linesman's hut and gazed towards the black mouth of the tunnel. Looking back, it was also clear that without realising it we had been climbing a slope as we crossed the field.

"Most interesting," said Sherlock Holmes quietly. "Most, most interesting."

He knelt and made careful measurements of the final imprints of the shoes, as well as mapping the characteristic pattern and blemishes of the sole and heel. Then I supposed we were about to walk back to St Vincent's, but he had not quite finished.

"There is something more, Watson. I cannot quite put my finger on it—call it intuition. I daresay it comes from not liking Mr Reginald Winter. Even on so short an acquaintance."

"You would hardly need an instinct to persuade you of that!"

"He is further involved in this than we believed. Why is it so important to him that Riley should have been thought to attempt suicide? You would suppose he might be pleased to discover it was not so. No matter for the moment. Do you notice a pond in line of sight from here?"

"I cannot see water anywhere. Why?"

"Ponds are generally surrounded by trees, which they naturally nourish. The trees are very often ash and elder or species that grow quite densely. As a result, quiet corners are provided for concealment, a useful shelter for observation. I have once or twice made use of them myself."

We skirted the field. In its furthest corner from which the ground sloped a little, we found what Holmes had looked for. It was no surprise in such a place. This pond, looking back along the track, was not more than eight or ten feet across, the result of a small spring, its surrounding foliage hardly more than an extension of the hedge which ran up to the railway bank on that side. The marshy ground would accommodate no more than two or three people. Bushes and saplings were packed thick enough to conceal whoever might be there, except from a deliberate search. Even this was unlikely to happen without warning, given the view of the approaches, visible between twigs and leaves. Because it was the remotest corner of the field, it was in any case the least likely to attract attention. The immediate view in that direction was along the railway line. It occurred to me that so long as a train was passing—or standing still at this point—the view of the linesman's hut would be briefly obscured.

We pulled aside two branches and soon stood in this overgrown space. It would have made an admirable hide for wildfowlers. The flowering elder provided excellent cover. My friend interested himself in the soil around us. Presently, his agile back curved as he swooped upon his prey.

"Rather as I supposed," he said with a contented sigh.

Taking his magnifying lens from his waistcoat pocket, he unfolded it and stooped again to examine two or three square feet of bare earth, still tacky in the warmer weather. Even without a glass I could see clearly that half-a-dozen matchsticks had been trodden into the ground. But Holmes was examining something I should have missed. In two places close together was the dottle from the bowl of a pipe, which someone had knocked out in order to refill it. Whoever it was had also spat several times on the soil.

"It seems that he stayed long enough to finish one pipe, light and smoke another, then knock that out as well before he left," I said enthusiastically.

Holmes straightened up.

"The number of matches may be more significant. If you look about you, this is far the best cover for a man to strike matches on a windy day. There is nowhere else. Even lower down in the lee of the railway embankment you could not do it with a south-westerly blowing half a gale."

"Not Reginald Winter," I said, "He has a study to smoke in. More likely it was one or two of the boys taking shelter here for an illegal smoke."

He shook his head.

"Dear old Watson, you have such an eye for the obvious! I am quite sure that the boys of St Vincent's stunt their growth by furtive smoking as surely as in any other school. However, I suggest that they are a little young for pipes. In any case, a packet of cigarettes is so much easier to conceal than a pipe with its cleaner, pouch of tobacco and all the rest of the paraphernalia."

I looked at the ground again.

"Why should Winter come here?"

Holmes chuckled.

"The answer to that question will illuminate a good deal—when we find it. What we have here is a man alone. He takes shelter, knocks out his pipe and refills it. He smokes it through and knocks it out again. He must have passed some time here—half an hour I daresay. I suggest he can only have been here as a spy."

"When did he do it?" I asked, "That may tell us whether he was a spy or not!"

Holmes looked about him.

"Even concealed by these bushes, it takes him several attempts on that windy day to strike a match and light his pipe. See for yourself. Of the six matches lying there, four have burnt only at the tip because they were blown out at once. Only one has burnt far enough down its length to be effective in lighting a pipe. During the time he was here, the casual movements of his feet trod four of the matches into damp earth. I also observe that our smoker spat several times. It is a frequent accompaniment to the lighting of a pipe filled with strong tobacco. On Mr Winter's mantelpiece you may have noticed an unopened packet of strong Old Glory Navy Cut. Many smokers use shag, but they are veterans rather than schoolboys."

"All of which does not put Reginald Winter here on Sunday afternoon."

"Quite true. It is John Fisher who does that, without knowing it. Before he left us yesterday I asked him to supply me with a copy of Admiralty weather station reports for the past week from coastal stations between Plymouth and Dover. They arrived by first post this morning. Dame Fortune has placed a coastal station at Osborne Royal Naval College. It is about a dozen miles north of here as the crow flies. The weather last week produced light but constant rain. A force five wind from the Western Approaches picked up at noon on Sunday and blew until the small hours of Monday morning. Since then the reports record dry and mild weather with a light south-west wind."

"In other words, the usual climate for May."

"I daresay. But if that evidence is to be trusted, it restricts our smoker's occupation of this place to Sunday afternoon or evening. The boys are permitted to walk across the field on Sunday afternoon but you may be sure they and their headmaster are at chapel on Sunday evening. If Winter was here, I have no doubt he was spying on them. Perhaps to catch them meeting or talking to those whom they should not meet or talk to. I have scanned the regulations that Fisher was also good enough to supply. Any word spoken to a female of whatever age or station during these strolls is a grievous offence. So is breaking bounds beyond the limits set for a walk. I imagine it gladdens Winter's heart to catch a handful of culprits for his delectation."

Having met the man, I had no difficulty in accepting this analysis of his character.

"Yet if he was here when Riley made his famous run," I said, "why has he never mentioned it?"

"Precisely. Unless my instincts deceive me, he was not spying on his boys—just one boy. It was Patrick Riley, who had ventured out of the sanatorium for some reason of his own. I am entirely satisfied that the lad was not contemplating suicide. Far more likely he was attempting to meet someone. Winter would give a good deal to know who—and for what purpose. And so would I."

I thought about this for scarcely a moment before saying,

"It can't see it, Holmes. Whether Riley was hoping to meet someone—or even commit suicide—how could Reginald Winter know in advance? As I understand it, the boy was incommunicado and he would hardly tell Winter himself. Unless he was there by pure fluke, Winter would not know what time to take up watch or even where."

"Winter does not strike me as a man who does anything by a fluke."

"Well, there you are. Even if he knew Riley had slipped away from the sanatorium and was running across the field, it would be far too late and much too obvious to start running after him. Winter could only spy on him at the railway bank by being in place here before him. And he could not do that unless he knew which way he was going to run and when he was going to do it. There is a hopeless inconsistency."

"No, my dear fellow, what lies at the heart of this is a mystery. It is an article of faith in our detective agency that all mysteries have a solution."

He was looking back towards the stretch of line running on its embankment. If anyone was going to spy, I thought, this was certainly the place from which to do it.

"We had best be getting back," I said.

But he was still looking about him in this little enclosure. I had no idea what else he expected to find, nor, I think, did he. Presently he chuckled, relaxed and took out his pocket-knife. He was staring at an elder branch, or rather what remained of it. Someone had cut through it at a point where it was the thickness of a large thumb. The cut was recent, to judge by the light colour of the exposed wood. It suggested to me that a walker had improvised a stick for himself, perhaps in the muddy weather. The absence of wood shavings indicated that the stick had been cut to size from the bush without any immediate need for trimming or shaping.

"Goodness knows how many boys cut sticks and whittle them," I said sceptically.

He opened his pocket-knife and cut a further length of the sapling, no more than three inches, for what good that would do. He slipped the cutting into his pocket, closed his knife and we began to walk back. Perhaps evidence of a kind against Winter had begun to accumulate in that cold rational brain. But evidence of what?

I thought we were going to walk back the way we had come, but Holmes set off on a path behind the hedge. This was parallel to the School Field though concealed from it. At the far end, a small iron gate opened into a domestic "chicken field" where St Vincent's grew its vegetables. A further gate let us into an enclosed lawn whose door was evidently the headmaster's direct entrance to his own quarters. A hand-bell had rung and it seemed that the "cadets" were now released from their classes. They were curiously dressed, like child sailors in their blue uniforms. A few wore a grey, braided edging to the lapels and the hems of their "Engineer" jackets.

In the corridor on which Winter's study was located Holmes stopped again, as if to check his appearance in the hall-stand mirror, a vanity he seldom indulged. No one who saw him would have thought twice about what he was doing. Unobtrusively, he slipped his left hand into his pocket and withdrew the three-inch cutting of the elder branch. His right hand moved cautiously over the umbrella stand. Presently he relaxed and drew out a freshly-cut stick.

"I must confess that I noticed this when we came out, Watson. I have been looking for its partner ever since."

He turned it over and joined to its end the three-inch cutting he had taken from his pocket.

It was, of course, a perfect fit.

4

Something of a change had come over Reginald Winter in the past half-hour. It was so abrupt that I wonder to this day whether he had not received a peremptory telegram or even a telephone call from Sir John Fisher. No more obstacles were put in our path. He went so far as to hint that if an interview with Cadet Porson should be necessary, he would bend the rules to allow it. Far more important, for the time being, was our first meeting with young Patrick Riley.

The sanatorium lay at the top of a winding stone staircase just above the study. It was little more than a well-lit, high-ceilinged room with a wash-room to one side. There were four beds, three of them unoccupied, and a central table with upright chairs. It appeared to be the domain of a grey-haired nurse, Sister Elliston. She seemed admirably untroubled by having as her patient one who was a condemned thief and an attempted suicide.

As we entered, Patrick Riley was sitting on his bed turning the pages of a picture magazine. His situation was not to be envied. For ten days he had been almost entirely isolated and with no idea of what was going on or what might happen to him. He was forbidden to speak to or associate with any other boy. Frankly, if he were not an attempted suicide an environment like this might go far to make him one. He got to his feet and stood at attention in his blue uniform with its tell-tale grey braiding of the Engineer Cadets.

He was indeed the lightly-built but nimble fourteen-year-old of Holmes's description. His appearance was hardly memorable, the soft features yet to be defined by manhood. An unruly flop of fair hair was perhaps the most prominent characteristic, through not while wearing his cap. His expression was downcast, as it well might be, but he appeared and sounded apathetic rather than distressed. No doubt he believed that the worst had happened and that no one would trust his explanations. He had little emotional energy left for histrionics.

"Patrick Riley?" Holmes spoke quietly as he stepped forward and held out his hand, "I am Sherlock Holmes. It is possible you may have heard of me."

Riley nodded and said, "Yes, sir," only because he felt he must say something rather than nothing

"May we sit round the table and talk?" Holmes continued courteously. "I am here at Admiral Fisher's request to ensure that justice is done, and I fear it may not have been so far. That is all. You have nothing to fear so long as you speak the truth."

"Yes, sir," the boy repeated, still as if he did not care much either way. "They said you were coming."

"I propose to see if truth is not on your side," Holmes said more firmly, obliging Patrick Riley to recognise his presence.

"I don't see how you can ensure anything, when all their minds are made up. How can you?"

"Because, my boy, I am Sherlock Holmes and there is very little I cannot do once I put my mind to it—and once those for whom I fight supply me with a little ammunition."

He smiled, lifted his arm and laid it on the boy's shoulder, shepherding him towards the table. He was not at his best with the very young, but so far he had not made an irretrievable mistake with Patrick Riley. The miniature cadet stared at him and then, to my very great relief, returned the smile, albeit half-heartedly.

So the ice was broken. I guessed there had been few smiles in the boy's life recently. But Riley was now encouraged to see himself as the hero of his own adventure story with Sherlock Holmes at his side.

"Sit here," said Holmes politely, drawing out a chair.

So the interview began. Riley now looked up at us with a helpless appeal.

"It was just a joke, Mr Holmes! A bit of fun!"

To my dismay, I thought Riley was about to blurt out a confession to the theft and plead that it had been a prank. So—I am sure—did my friend, from the expression on his face. "A joke" must be one of the oldest and certainly least successful defences to a charge of fraud.

"What was a joke, Patrick?" Holmes asked quietly, and I held my breath. The use of the boy's Christian name made the question somewhat more sinister because it closed his retreat into a shell of apathy.

"Writing names was a joke, Mr Holmes. I don't remember when we first did it. I sat next to Porson in class. We sat together in the evening too, when we did whatever prep the masters set. If we finished our prep before the bell went we used to mess around, writing, playing battleships on paper, all sorts of things. Porson sometimes wrote my name in my writing and I wrote his. Lots of fellows did things like that. It was a game. It wasn't forgery or theft any more than it's murder when you point your finger and say 'Bang, you're dead.' It was just fooling about."

"Very good," said Holmes approvingly. "And how successful were these imitation signatures?"

"I don't know, sir. How can you tell? They looked a bit the same."

"Believe me, I can tell. How many other people knew that you were doing this?"

"Anyone could watch us, if they wanted to. They must have seen but they wouldn't think anything. Lots of fellows played games like that."

"Did they? And how many other fellows' signatures did you copy?"

The young face clouded with uncertainty.

"I don't remember that I did. Perhaps I did. But no one else that I can remember. I played this game with Porson because we sat next to one another. I could see his name written on his prep book and he could see mine."

"And Porson has always been in the same class with you? He is an Engineer Cadet like you?"

"We're all engineers in our class. That's why we sit together in school prep. Lower Middle Engineers. We're above the junior engineers but below the Upper Middle and the seniors."

"Have you got a copy of your imitation of Porson's signature that you can show me?"

He shook his head.

"We never kept them, sir. They were thrown away. It was just a game."

"Could you do one now?"

"Not without one to copy from. Nobody could."

"It is said that you wrote a signature at the post office as you had copied Porson's for a game. Did you?"

"No! I couldn't do it! I was never at the post office on that afternoon!"

It was a wail of protest and despair, uttered so often in the past ten days. No hawk-nosed cross-examiner in wig and gown could resemble a bird of prey more suggestively than Holmes just then. But Riley had returned the answer of an innocent defendant.

"Very well. Now then, you must help me. Could you, for example, copy your own signature?"

The boy sat back and shook his head slowly, not in refusal but exasperation.

"Any fellow could copy his own!"

"I think you misunderstand me. I do not want you to repeat your signature but to copy it exactly. As a criminal expert it is my business to know about such things. I may tell you that even in the most innocent way, no signature is precisely the same on two successive occasions. And besides, you will please write the first one with your eyes closed. I am offering you a chance to prove your innocence, but you must do this much for me. Write it as you would normally write your signature and do not worry what it will look like."

The boy nodded. Holmes produced a fountain-pen and a sheet of paper from his pocket, handing them to him.

"You had better put your glasses on," he said casually. "You will certainly need them for the copying."

The boy looked as if he was about to ask Holmes how he knew about the glasses, but my friend anticipated him.

"There is a slight mark either side of your nose, evident to a student of physiognomy. That is unusual in one of your age. It is plain that you spend a commendable amount of time in reading and study. You do not wear glasses otherwise, but I believe you should. There is a sluggishness of movement on one side which suggests that you suffer from what is called a lazy eye."

Riley was visibly disconcerted by this impromptu oculist's diagnosis.

"Have no fear," said Holmes cheerily. "It is my business to notice such things. I believe, however, it may be of importance in your case."

The lad's inability to copy a signature without his glasses might be of importance to our inquiry, but for the life of me I could not see how.

Riley laid the paper on the table and closed his eyes. He took the pen and wrote a little uncertainly but quite fluently. It was not a bad effort, though the inconsistencies were clear. Let me just say that his name written with his eyes closed looked to me something like "Put riccc Rileg."

"Excellent," said Holmes encouragingly. "Now, imitate that, if you please, as closely as you can. Do not correct it to your normal signature. Imitate it as if it was another person's signature on a postal order."

The boy began. He drew quite accurately the down stroke of the "P" and the loop. Lifting the pen he then began the "u." He paused and lifted it again where it dropped down to join the "t." At the end of his first name, he paused to check his progress, though without lifting the pen. The copy of his surname appeared in a more rounded script than the original and only the last three letters were joined.

Holmes unfolded his magnifying glass and there was silence for a long two minutes, an eternity as it must have seemed to the poor boy, before my friend looked up.

"Capital!" he said enthusiastically, "If it will bring you any consolation, Patrick Riley, you would make a very poor forger."

The relief on the poor young fellow's face was almost inexpressible.

"Unfortunately," Holmes added, "whoever signed the postal order—which I have seen, of course—was probably also a poor copyist. But we have made a good beginning. Very well. Whoever endorsed that order produced a so-called feathering effect of the pen, as most of us do when we write something familiar like our names. That is to say, the pen is moving almost before it touches the paper. I observe that you started with the nib already on the paper, as a copyist might."

He held up the page at a slant to the light from the window.

"Twice at least in the copy you have lifted the nib clear of the paper, though you did not do so in the original. Through my glass, though not with the naked eye, it is also possible to see three places at which you have rested the nib on your work while checking your progress. This lack of flow appears only in the crudest freehand forgeries. The signature on the counterfoil of the postal order was skilled enough to avoid anything of that kind. It was not crude copying. This is copied. That was traced—or possibly written on an indentation."

"But can you prove it, Mr Holmes?" The earnestness in the young face was painful to behold. "Can you show them I never did it?"

"My dear young fellow, a negative is hard to prove. I cannot demonstrate to the world that you never traced it. But I do say that on the basis of this experiment there is no evidence that you could have produced the forgery on that postal order—which is a good long way towards the same thing."

During this exchange, I had got up and walked slowly across to the window. It looked out over the downland towards the channel. A late afternoon sun cast a burnish upon the lavender blue of the Western Approaches.

"Now," said Holmes, "please tell me exactly how you first heard about the theft."

Riley's answer was commendably simple.

"Porson came up to me about half-past five on that Saturday afternoon. He said, 'I say, isn't it rotten? Someone's stolen my money from my locker.' It wasn't real money, of course, just the order. They don't let us keep money in our lockers."

"And you replied to John Porson?"

"I said he should have another look to make sure it had gone.

If it had, he should tell the housemaster or one of the two petty officers on duty. Petty Officer Carter was on that day. I said not to waste time, the sooner he reported it, the better his chances of getting it back."

"Admirable," said Holmes, "Then you spoke as a good sensible friend, not as a frightened thief."

"I hope I did, sir. I knew nothing about it until Porson told me then, in the locker room."

As I listened, I was standing by a table on which his toiletries and other articles were set out in regulation order. Among them was a rather expensive clothes-brush, with black bristles and a polished walnut back, evidently brought from home. On this varnished back someone at home had very precisely cut the name "Riley" and his school number, "178." Next to this there were several words lightly scratched, as if to deface the varnish. They in turn had been scraped over, as neatly as possible, to obliterate them. Even under these neater scratches it was just possible to see that an unknown hand had cut four words next to Riley's name. The effect was to make the whole lettering read "Riley Is an Oily Hog."

There was also a cheap hair-brush which had been similarly treated. Once again, whatever had defaced it was scratched over in its turn but I could still make out an ominous jingle.

Tell-tale tit.
Your tongue shall be split,
And all the little dicky-birds
Shall have a little bit.

The old-fashioned clothes-brush might have been an heirloom of some kind. The hair-brush seemed a cheap replacement, perhaps for one that had already been defaced in this way.

Several more pieces of the puzzle fell into place. I picked up the clothes-brush and turned round.

"Who carved your name and number so neatly on the back of this?"

Riley glanced up.

"It was my uncle, sir, before I came for my first term. I was in Collingwood Term."

"And who scratched these other words?"

He bit his lip and shook his head.

"Don't know, sir."

I would have bet a hundred pounds that he did.

"Very well, then tell me at least who scratched them out—did you do it?"

He shook his head again. "My mother did it, when I went home for the first holidays. There were so many things to be bought for school that we couldn't throw away the brush. And it belonged to my father."

Holmes gave a murmur of approval.

"And what are Oily Hogs? I regret having to ask that. Please tell me."

The boy stared at the table-top and hesitated. To my astonishment, with his deliverance now a possibility, he was close to tears. Then he pulled himself together and said, "We are. The Engineers. The Executive Cadets—the Deck Officers—are the Ocean Swells. There are far more of them. One or two of us at a time have to go to be bully-ragged. The rest of us keep quiet because we're glad it's someone else. They gang round and rag us for half an hour or so, thirty or forty of them sometimes. There's no reason—they get excited and it just happens. Everything is quiet one minute and then they're singing "Oily Hogs, Oily Togs, Dirty Dogs and Frenchie Frogs," throwing things, punching, spitting. Once or twice they pushed the same chap's head into the wash-room latrine and flushed it. He ran away from school in the end. He got home on the railway somehow and never came back. Most get caught before they get very far. Then they cop it from old Winter for being out of bounds."

"Do they never complain?"

"We're not allowed to sneak or split. That only makes it worse."

"And what of the Ocean Swells?" Holmes inquired.

"They say they'll own the decks one day and we'll be the hogs down in the grease pit."

Again I thought he might weep, but I underestimated him.

"Deck officers—children of twelve or fourteen!" I said angrily, "Look, my boy, remember this. So far as names go, sticks and stones may break my bones but names will never hurt me."

"It was my mother's name," he said sadly, and then indeed, he began to weep. "Sovran-Phillips is one of the Ocean Swells. He found out that her name was Clemency. They thought it was a funny name. Phillips and the others went ganging round the school after me, shouting it, shouting that my father never died because I never had a father. My mother never had a husband. They ganged round me shouting lies about her. The more I begged them to stop, the more they did it. Now it doesn't matter, because I shan't ever go back or see them again."

I stood there. For the first time in my life the word "dumbfounded" meant something to me. When our case began I had never imagined such juvenile evil would be unearthed. Forging a postal order was nothing compared with this! But now that Patrick Riley had begun it was hard to stop him going on. What had he to lose? His eyes were dry again, reddened but angry.

"The worst of it is that I thought some of them were my friends. When it happened, even the ones I thought were friends . . . I could see them standing on the edge of the gang smiling and laughing at me. I'll never forget who they were."

Sherlock Holmes had listened very quietly to all this.

"And Mr Winter?" he inquired, "What does he have to say?"

Patrick Riley looked up miserably and blew his nose.

"He won't have sneaking or splitting. If a boy won't stand up for himself but goes sneaking on the others, Mr Winter sends him away or beats him for it. That's what I was warned."

The eyes of Sherlock Holmes were dark, glittering ice. His fury, on the few occasions when it overtook him, was terrifyingly quiet and cold. I was more angry than I had been for a very long time. If half of this was true, then the sooner Sir John Fisher had all such places as this closed down the better. Patrick Riley ended his pause.

"John Porson is my friend, on the same side in the same class. We share the same desk. Still we daren't fight Sovran-Phillips and his gang. But Porson is the last person I would steal from."

Listening to him, I thought that was the most persuasive argument we had heard in our young client's favour.

Holmes nodded and said, "You mention Sovran-Phillips. Tell me about him."

"He's Captain of Boats and prefect of the Deck Swells in the Upper Middle. The new boys act as servants to the captains and they get beaten if they don't. He knows how to fight, that's half the trouble. His step-brother's a lot older, a cruiser captain. Phillips never lets us forget it. His real brother was here a few years ago and at Dartmouth now. He says his grandfather was an admiral, but I don't know if that's true. I don't care now anyway. He says all the maids in the kitchen are spoony on him and he goes with them. Winter's maid mostly. That's a lie, I should say."

Holmes let it rest there for a moment. I tried to imagine the shame and humiliation of Patrick Riley, defeated at every resistance to the smug and superior Phillips. I might have doubted the truth of it all but for the sincerity and grief in our young informant's manner.

"Very well," said Holmes at length. "If I have my way, you will find on your side an Admiral of the Fleet, who will outrank a cruiser captain two or three times over. In the next holidays, Dr Watson and I will find a room for you with Mrs Hudson. I am not inexpert in boxing and single-stick combat. After a fortnight's instruction, I think I may promise that you shall return to St Vincent's and give young Phillips the thrashing of his life. It is not a matter of size—for I suspect you are smaller than he is—but of skill."

"I don't care if I never go back, sir. I don't mind not going back, but I won't be called a thief. Could you teach me to fight, Mr Holmes?"

"I have complete confidence in my own abilities—and yours. Now, if you please, we will set aside the matter of the postal order, for I see the way we must go. Let us turn to your attempted suicide. Was it anything of the kind?"

The poor young fellow shook his head yet again.

"They say it proved I could not bear to face my mother, knowing I was a thief. But what I could not bear, Mr Holmes, would be to leave her for ever. She knows I am no thief."

"Unfortunately what she knows you to be is not evidence, although to me it is proof. Why did you go to the field on Sunday afternoon?"

"I was in this sanatorium room for eight days. Alone, except for Sister Elliston and Mr Winter when he came to question me with two other masters. First of all I heard I was going to be expelled. Then they said there might be some sort of tribunal where I could appeal. There was even talk of a lawyer coming to see me, but I heard no more of that."

"And your mother and your uncle?"

"I don't know what they've been told or what they think. But last Sunday I had just had enough. No one would believe a word I spoke. There was no one here to stop me, and, surely, so long as I'm at St Vincent's, I may walk over the field on Sunday afternoons as the others do. I have friends, sir. I'm forbidden to talk to them, but I thought if I could get to them, tell them the truth, they might be able to help me."

"But you did not go out with the intention of killing yourself? That is what I need to know."

He looked at us strangely, as I thought.

"I'd gone as far as I could go. I might have done anything. But murder, rather than suicide, if I could choose."

I thought he was about to weep again. Instead he slumped dry-eyed in his chair and would say no more.

"You have done enough, Patrick Riley," said Holmes after a pause, "and by this time tomorrow justice shall be done to you."

"How can you say?" It was no more than a low murmur to himself.

"You must remember who I am," said my friend quietly.

5

Sherlock Holmes was seldom an early riser. Even though the next morning revealed a sun sparkling like cut glass on an emerald sea, he would have been more likely to stir himself for a dismal winter landscape where felony oozed from every leaf and twig. However, I woke to a sharp knock on my door at the King Charles Hotel. It was surely an early morning cup of tea or a steaming jug of shaving water.

At quarter to seven it was Holmes, fully dressed.

"We must look lively, Watson. I reviewed the evidence before falling asleep last night and I fully intend to close our case today. Therefore, I am most anxious to be in good time for Morning Prayers at St Vincent's. If the notice pinned on the headmaster's board in his corridor is correct, early prep is at six forty-five. With their appetites sharpened by intensive study, the boys are then fed at seven-thirty. Morning Prayers follow at eight-thirty and the first period of instruction is at nine. We should arrive no earlier than eight-thirty and certainly no more than five minutes later."

"Morning Prayers?"

As I rubbed the sleep from my eyes, I tried to imagine how Morning Prayers could have any bearing on our case.

"That is when Reginald Winter, in his scarlet M.A. hood and his Oxford gown, will be officiating in chapel. We shall have the main building to ourselves."

"It may be," I said, pulling myself upright, "but there is still a good deal to be resolved before we close this matter."

"Yes, yes," he said impatiently. "I shall tell them downstairs to have our breakfast ready in quarter of an hour."

"Quarter of an hour? The place is only twenty minutes' walk from here!"

"There is a call to make on the way."

"Where?"

But he had closed the door and gone.

It was almost eight o'clock when we left the King Charles Hotel for St Vincent's. We walked leisurely up the picturesque village street of Bradstone St Lawrence with its thatched and tiled dwellings. Ahead of us I noticed a bright scarlet post-box with Her Majesty's insignia embossed upon it. The post office itself was a picture-book cottage which really did have a rambling rose round its door, as well as Sweet William and jessamine in a narrow border. A notice in the glass panel of the door informed us that the office was open from 8 a.m. until 6 p.m. on every day from Monday to Saturday.

A bell jangled as Holmes pushed open the door, and we stepped into what might have been the large front room of a cottage or village house, with a smaller room behind it. The lath-and-plaster wall had been taken down, so that the near side of the wooden counter was open to the public and the far side reserved for official business. A middle-aged woman stood at the counter, sorting through pages of postage stamps. Her companion, to judge from her appearance, was surely a younger sister. She sat on a high stool in the back room, entering figures in a business ledger. To one side of her, a telegraph boy in a peaked cap and short jacket was perched on a bench with a copy of a penny-dreadful, "Varney the Vampire; or, The Feast of Blood," open on his knee.

Holmes introduced us, and Mrs Franklin at the counter summoned Miss Henslowe, who was indeed her younger sister. Miss Henslowe was a maiden lady of forty or so with a fine-boned beauty, what the weekly magazines describe as features of "a teacup delicacy." The telegraph boy stopped reading and gaped at us.

"I shall not interrupt you for more than a moment," said Holmes politely. "I have been asked to review the case of Patrick Riley on behalf of the Admiralty. I merely need to confirm with you what you have said and done already."

"There was little enough," said Miss Henslowe, responding to him with a half-smile. With such a charming smile, I wondered why she was still a maiden lady.

"Just so," said Holmes courteously. "Tell me, were you alone in the post office on the Saturday afternoon in question?"

"Alone at the counter," she said readily. "My sister and her husband had gone into town. Freddie who takes the telegrams was sitting on his stool."

Freddie, whose mouth had been gaping at the sight of us, closed it at the mention of his name and pretended to read his comic.

Holmes continued to question his witness.

"A boy came in, signed his postal order form at the counter and then handed it in? You saw that?"

"I was busy with telegram forms, Mr Holmes, so I did not watch his every movement. But he certainly did as you say."

"Very well. You took the order, then counted out the money for him—a ten-shilling note and a sixpence, I imagine. You handed it to him and he left. Was that all?"

"Not quite, Mr Holmes. I noticed that he had signed the order as 'John Porson,' when it was made out to 'J. L. Porson.' I asked him to insert the 'L.,' which he did."

"And that was all?"

"He showed me his *exeat* permit. St Vincent's won't allow the boys to have more than a certain amount in their pockets. The rest must be banked with their housemasters when they come back from holidays. To stop them getting more through the post, they have to show their permits for being out of the school grounds when they bring the orders here. We check the name and the amount. That's a school rule, nothing to do with the Royal Mail."

"Most interesting," said Holmes thoughtfully. "And you were subsequently asked to go to the school and see if you could identify the boy who cashed the postal order?"

"Petty Officer Carter came down and asked me. I went up on the Monday, two days later. Very upset he was, Mr Carter."

"In what way?"

"For the honour of the service, Mr Holmes. Twice he said something like, 'This is the sort of boy the Royal Navy can do without.'"

"Hardly surprising under the circumstances," I suggested.

"The identification was in what they call the Parents' Waiting Room, near the head's study. I was asked to look at eight of the cadets as they stood in a row. I remembered that the boy I served definitely had a grey edging to his jacket, like one of the Engineer Cadets. From what I see, not many of them is an engineer, which made it easier. Also, the one I served wore glasses, and he was about so high."

She raised her hand to indicate a height of five feet and six or seven inches.

"And what made you pick out the boy in question?"

Miss Henslowe withdrew again to her defensive line.

"To be honest, people round here always say that they all look alike in those uniforms. I suppose that's the idea. And even two days is a long time to wait when you didn't think at the time there was any reason to remember someone."

"But even so, you picked one out?"

She huffed a sigh at the difficulty of it all.

"There's a difference, isn't there, Mr Holmes? If someone shows you eight cadets and says it's definitely one of them, then you can pick whichever one looks most like. That's how it seemed to be. If they'd shown me two hundred cadets, I might have picked another."

"Or you could have picked no one."

She shook her head.

"From everything that was said, they knew who did it and he was there. Even Mr Carter on Saturday seemed to know which boy it was the navy could do without. I thought the fairest thing was to say I couldn't be sure, but if it was one of those eight, he was the one I picked out. That was fair, wasn't it? At least I got the others out of trouble, didn't I? The headmaster didn't say anything. And on the way out, Mr Carter said that it couldn't have been any of the other seven. They were all at the boats until after three."

"And the boy you picked was Patrick Riley?"

"I told Mr Winter exactly the same as I told you. I was busy at the counter, but this one was wearing glasses and had the grey edging to his jacket."

"Both of which could have been borrowed."

"I suppose they could. But Mr Winter was fair about that. He told me to take no notice of whether they had the grey braid or not. Three had and five hadn't. Then, to begin with, all of them had to stand in line without glasses and afterwards with glasses on. I suppose they borrowed spectacles for the ones that never wore them. Most boys don't."

My heart sank at the prospect of Miss Henslowe in the witness-box telling the world how fairly Reginald Winter had conducted his identification parade. But Holmes seemed entirely satisfied with her and merely asked, "Miss Henslowe, would you do me a very great favour?"

"If I can, sir."

"Would you come to the school now and look at a photograph? I promise that we shall have you back here in no time, but it is of the very greatest importance and urgency."

Miss Henslowe looked at Mrs Franklin. The older sister shrugged.

"Of course she will. Go on, Violet!"

Holmes had timed it to perfection. We arrived in the headmaster's corridor a minute after 8.30. It was the one time of day when Reginald Winter was guaranteed to be absent. I caught an organ groan drifting from the chapel as we passed and then two hundred voices at full volume.

Will your anchor hold in the storms of life,
When the winds unveil their wings of strife?
When the strong tides lift, and the cables strain,
Will your anchor drift, or firm remain?

Somewhat to my surprise Holmes was humming this Evangelical refrain as a tune long familiar to him. I had sometimes pondered over his childhood religion. A tin-roofed sailors' chapel had not been among my imaginings until now.

The main building was silent, and we reached the headmaster's corridor without a challenge. The assistant postmistress was quiet and apprehensive until Holmes stopped before a recent school photograph on the wall.

"Now, Miss Henslowe, have the goodness to examine this. Disregard the importance of spectacles and of uniforms. Taking away those things and suppose that one of these boys, as Mr Winter suggested, must be he who visited you on that Saturday afternoon, which one would it be?"

"I already picked Mr Riley."

"Ignore him. Try again."

She ran her eye along the rows and pointed to another, still bespectacled. Holmes made a note in his pocket-book.

"And just one more."

She repeated the scrutiny and touched the glass where a boy of about fourteen, better-built than the previous one, stood without spectacles or Engineer braiding.

"Very good," said Holmes. "And now if we may, Miss Henslowe, we shall escort you back. You have no doubt been uneasy at the prospect of involvement in a court case with its examination and cross-examination of your testimony, the attendant publicity in the newspapers. I think I may promise you that you will not be troubled any further."

She seemed startled rather than relieved.

"How can you be certain of that, Mr Holmes?"

"Dear madam, I have a long experience of giving opinions in such matters. So far, I have been invariably proved right."

Miss Henslowe moved away and walked ahead of us. Holmes seemed to dawdle. Presently, not far from the door to the courtyard, he tugged at my sleeve, his finger to his lips. I turned and looked at the object of his interest, a far smaller picture framed among several others. It showed a rowing eight from a previous term plus their cox, five boys sitting and four standing behind them, crossed oars mounted on the wall.

At the centre of the front row sat the Captain of Boats, holding a small silver cup. The face might have been the double of the one that Miss Henslowe had pointed out to us a moment before. Yet it could not be the same, for the date on this smaller photograph was five years earlier. Moreover, on a team photograph the names of the members are printed underneath—as they could not be for all two hundred boys.

I recalled the voice of Patrick Riley, talking of his tormentor.

"His step-brother's a cruiser captain and his real brother was here a few years ago. He's at Dartmouth now."

The name below the double of Miss Henslowe's choice was "H. R. Sovran-Phillips."

As we stepped out into the sunlight, Holmes remarked, "Perhaps we shall not be quite as late arriving in Baker Street tonight as I had supposed."

I did not like to suggest that optimism is no substitute for proof.

6

Our last inquiry in the village was at mid-morning. Its venue was the old "Rest and Be Thankful" inn, dating from an age when most travellers went on foot—"Shanks Pony" as the term was in my childhood. They toiled up from the foreshore to the height of Boniface Down, where this homely signboard announced a respite.

As we ducked our heads under the low lintel of the bar parlour and stepped down on to its floor of waxed red tiles, our visitor was waiting, in conversation with the landlady. Samuel Wesley, a grey-haired veteran of the South Coast Railway engine drivers, was not a drinking man. His neat, plain Sunday suit, worn out of courtesy to us, had the discreet badge of a Missionary Fellowship in its buttonhole.

We shook hands and sat down with nothing stronger than small beer between us. Introductions were brief. Samuel Wesley was, as he said, a lover of truth and straight talk. Attempted suicide was "a terrible thing to say about a young man." Unlike Reginald Winter, he was reluctant to say it.

"I suppose you might call it that, Mr Holmes, according to what you saw and how your mind works."

"Quite true, Mr Wesley. And what did you see?"

"Nothing at first, sir, for there is a curve in that tunnel and you don't see the line ahead until you're almost out of it. It was young Arthur, my fireman. He noticed one of the schoolboys running across close to the embankment, as he might run in a game. Then he was lost sight of as he went under the lee of the bank. I was watching the pressure gauges, which can't be read very easily in the tunnel for want of light."

"What would your speed be?"

"Oh, thirty miles an hour at the most, and I daresay more like twenty-five just there. It isn't a place for anyone to do away with themselves."

"But it is accessible to those with suicide in mind."

Mr Wesley took a modest pull at his small beer and shrugged.

"That's true, sir. But Arthur suddenly shouted to me, 'Stop! Brake!' I had my hand on the lever, and even before I'd seen the boy, I'd given it a darn good pull. It didn't take half as long to do it as to tell it!"

"And the train stopped?"

"Not at once. They don't stop at once. What you get first, Mr Holmes, is a bit of a jerk. Then she do slide on the rails. And then she do stop with a big jerk and all the passengers is thrown about."

"And when did you first see the boy?"

Mr Wesley exhaled thoughtfully.

"With the weight of a train behind you it can take the best part of a hundred yards to come to rest. While she was sliding I saw him standing there on the track, looking straight at us."

"Very disagreeable for you," I said sympathetically.

He looked surprised.

"Oh, I never thought we'd hit him, doctor. Not where he was. He'd only to step aside. A hundred yards nearer would have been a different matter, but he could never have got that close.

We came right up to him before she was at rest, but he couldn't have done himself any harm."

"And then?"

"He got off the line, sir. I think he went after another boy I didn't see. Down behind the bank, most like. He shouted at someone. I never saw the other. Arthur thought there was one in the linesman's hut at first."

"Did you think that the boy who had been on the railway line was afraid of the other boy you never saw?"

Samuel Wesley thought this amusing and shook his head.

"I did not, Mr Holmes! Your young chap was smallish but in a mood to knock seven bells out of someone. A terrier! Don't ask me what it was about, though. I got down from the foot-plate to give 'im a piece of my mind but he ran off. I shouted after 'im and asked what the damnation he thought he was doing. I couldn't go and leave the engine standing there, but the whole thing was reported as soon as we got to Ryde. Now I'm told they're going to do what they should have done long ago. Put a proper barbed-wire fence from the linesman's hut to the tunnel mouth. They'll care too much about their skins to try getting over that."

"Whoever they were," said Holmes thoughtfully, "one might have expected them to run down the bank towards the school. But they did not, did they? The first one ran down the bank away from the school, did he not? And your terrier followed him."

"How could you tell which way they ran?" Mr Wesley asked with a laugh. "You was never there, sir."

"No," said Holmes in the same thoughtful tone, "but someone else was."

Samuel Wesley's evidence, which seemed to have been sought by no one but Holmes and me, altered the story of the drama.

To a more distant observer on higher ground, the sight of Patrick Riley running out on to the track in front of an oncoming train might look like an attempt at suicide. At least, it might be conveniently described as that. This more distant observer, perhaps smoking his pipe among the elders and ash saplings by the pond, might not see the second boy with the train blocking his view. After hearing Mr Wesley, however, I could not help feeling that our young client had indeed gone out with a rage to murder rather than an impulse to destroy himself.

As we walked back to St Vincent's, I said, "Tell me, Holmes, how could you know which way they ran? I should have thought it most likely that they would have gone down the near side of the embankment and back to the school."

"Across Reginald Winter's field of vision," he said sceptically. "Unless my brains have turned to sawdust, the unknown boy was one who had determined that he would not be seen during this little drama, while making certain that Patrick Riley should. I can prove that in the next half-hour. If not, on our return to town I shall stand you the most expensive dinner on the menu of the Langham Hotel."

7

Our second interview with Patrick Riley was one of the most difficult that Holmes and I had ever undertaken. I was reminded of nothing so much as the occasion when an injured sparrow stumbled on to our window-sill in Baker Street. It had damaged a wing, and, for my part, I should have thought it best put out of its misery. Nothing would do for Sherlock Holmes, however, but it must be caught. Then it must be installed in a cage with a makeshift splint and fed on bread and cheese until the frail little thing had mended. It was duly released among the trees of the Regent's Park.

I shall never forget the pantomime of catching it to begin with, the twin dangers of letting it fall off the sill to certain death or doing it some terrible damage by snatching at its elusive little body. Cadet Riley was a case in point. One wrong word, one ill-chosen nuance, and we should lose him. As we sat once again at the table in the school sanatorium with its empty beds and sunlight through a mullioned window, Holmes asked, "May we count upon you to tell us the truth this time, Patrick Riley?"

The young face looked startled, first at Holmes and then at me.

"I don't know what you mean, sir."

"I suggest you know perfectly well. You were not going out on that Sunday afternoon to kill yourself, were you? I think we have established that."

"Was I not?" There was such confusion in the response.

"You know you were not. You told us you were far more likely to kill someone else!"

The fourteen-year-old sat and stared at us. Was it that he did not understand the point of the question? Or did he understand it pretty well and not know what to say?

Holmes let a long silence pass. Then he said, very gently, "You must trust me again before I can trust you."

"Yes . . ." His head was down and even sitting at the same table I could barely hear the soft whisper of that single syllable.

"Good!" said Holmes enthusiastically, clapping him lightly on the shoulder. "Now why did you go out on that Sunday afternoon?"

Riley still hesitated and then gave up the game.

"To meet John Porson."

"The boy who lost the postal order? He who had been your friend?"

"Yes, Mr Holmes. They would never have let me go to him, at least on my own."

"Whose idea was it? Porson's?"

"I thought so."

"If they would not let you go out for a walk, do you ask us to believe that they would let you exchange messages with Porson? How could you communicate with him?"

Riley shook his head and then pushed his chair back. Beside his bed was a tin tray, a dark brown thing of the kind familiar in hospital wards. He brought it back to us and sat down.

"Two days before, Mr Holmes, on the Friday, the headmaster's maid—'Mitzi,' we call her—brought my lunch in here. I wasn't allowed to mix with the other boys, so I had all my meals here. When I lifted the plate, there was chalk writing on the tray. The plate had hidden it. Just a message. 'Linesman's hut. Sun 3.30. JLP. RSVP.' That was all."

"John Learmount Porson," said Holmes quietly, "You were to meet him by the railway line on Sunday afternoon at half-past three. What happened then?"

He looked at us as if we should have known better.

"I knew he would help me if he could. If he'd bothered to smuggle a message to me, he must be on my side. Even if he only went to Mr Winter and told him that we were friends and I would never have robbed him."

"And how did you reply?"

"I had nothing that would do for writing on the tray. But with my forefinger I rubbed out the 'JLP RSVP.' I collected the chalk on my fingertip and just managed to make a smudgy 'PR' so that it read, 'Linesman's hut. Sun. 3.30 PR' If it came from Porson, he would be on the look-out for the maid taking back the tray to the scullery. They pile them up there and wipe them over. He must have been able to get at the tray or he couldn't have sent the message in the first place. As for Mitzi, she would never take any notice of a chalk mark like that, even if she saw it. I covered the writing with the plate when she took it away."

To those who knew Holmes well, there was a look of satisfaction on that sharp profile which had not been there since Sir John Fisher first told us his story.

"Good," he said soothingly. "I believe we have got somewhere at last."

"It was my one chance," the boy insisted. "For two days I thought that at last I could talk to someone who would listen to me. Porson would trust me."

"And then?"

Riley looked at us uncertainly, living through all his difficulties again.

"I thought I should never get to the linesman's hut, sir. Any master who saw me leaving the building would stop me. There might not be many boys crossing the field at that moment, but I could still get stopped. It was my one chance, Mr Holmes. You do see that, don't you?"

"I see that, Patrick Riley, plainly enough."

"I could have watched for Porson, but I hadn't got a view from this window of anyone walking across the field. I decided the best thing was to leave it till the last minute and then run. I'd be there before they could stop me. About twenty past three I crept down the sanatorium stairs, always looking ahead and round corners first. There's almost no one about in the middle of a Sunday afternoon. I moved round the edge of the lawn below this window and through the little gate into the main school grounds. Then I ran across the corner of the cricket pitch and into the School Field, as they call it. Even if they came after me and caught me, I might have a minute or two with Porson first. At least long enough to swear to him that I never stole his postal order and knew nothing about it."

"You looked back several times, did you not?" I inquired, "Particularly as you got closer to the embankment."

"Yes, sir," he said uncertainly, and Sherlock Holmes frowned me into silence, "Yes, I did. I wanted to see if anyone was coming after me, but they weren't. I got across the field, then under the wire and up the embankment. I stood by the linesman's hut and looked round, but—"

"But Porson was not there," Holmes said, as if it was the only logical conclusion.

Riley nodded.

"I looked back across the field again, but I couldn't see him coming. It was almost exactly half-past three by then. I even opened the door of the linesman's hut—that's not difficult—to make sure he wasn't waiting inside. That was the only place he could be. His message could have meant that. He wasn't there. Then in the distance I could hear the rumble of a train coming from the tunnel. I was wondering whether to hide, and then—"

"Sovran-Phillips," said Holmes with an air of impatience.

Riley looked at him.

"How could you know?"

"Do not waste my time, young man. It is my business to know such things. Pray, continue."

"He was there on the far side of the line, laughing at me. Or perhaps not laughing, more like sneering. Then I knew of course that the message on the tray had come from him. But if it was a trap, I couldn't think what."

"He would hardly push you under a railway train," I said humorously as Holmes glared at me again.

"No, sir. That's what I would have done to him. I thought he was going to fight but he just stood there, just by the line, talking like Petty Officer Carter. He said people of my type were starvelings and they had no business putting themselves up for Dartmouth or Osborne. Especially if we were no better than grease-monkeys in the engine-room. I hadn't even had a proper father."

Starvelings! If the boy was right, Sovran-Phillips and Winter spoke the same language in every sense of the phrase.

"Tell me," I asked, "what was your father's profession?"

This time Holmes did not glare at me.

"He was a senior cashier, sir, to the Royal Bank of Ireland. After he died, there was only money to keep me here for a year or two. I've always known that the only way I could get to Dartmouth or Osborne would be with a Nomination. That's why I've worked for it."

"Of course," I said.

"Phillips said he could prove my mother was never married to my father—and he would. I'd never get entrance to Osborne or Dartmouth after that, let alone a Nomination. I'd better take my punishment and go home. If not, his brothers could see that I never got to midshipman. And if ever he saw an announcement of my sister marrying, he'd make sure the man would hear how her brother was the boy who stole the postal order at St Vincent's."

"Indeed?" said Holmes gently.

"There was no one else to hear him. He was careful about that. I've got no proof of anything he said. But I decided I'd fight him there and I'd fight my case in court. I'd repeat every word of what he said, whether they believed me or not. He said he'd break my head—"

"But he did not?"

"No, sir. Sovran-Phillips is stronger than I am, but I suppose I was angrier than him. We were on top of the bank, by the line, but he tried to pull away. I could see the train coming from the tunnel. He was hitting at me but I just wouldn't let him go. I was on the track and he was trying to pull away. I said something like, 'I'll fight you here, in front of the train. If I'm killed, I'll hold on tight enough to make sure you go down as well.' I had him by his coat, trying to pull him on to the track. Then he broke clear. I don't think I wanted to kill him exactly—and I didn't want to die. But I was desperate, sir, and I was going to give him a fright he would never forget. I wanted him to know that if ever he hurt my family, I'd kill him by fair means or foul."

It was something of a wild story, but to hear Patrick Riley was to know that he meant it. As he was describing the incident, I calculated that the stationary engine of the train would have hidden the two boys from Reginald Winter's observation soon after it came out from the tunnel.

"And then?" Holmes prompted him.

"I shouted after him as he went down the bank on the other side. By then the train was slowing down and he was out of sight somewhere among the bushes on the other side. That's all I saw, Mr Holmes. I was so mad with hate, I think I could have held him until the engine killed us both."

With a chill down the spine at these last words, I thought of Holmes and Moriarty at the Reichenbach Falls. Such impulses of mutual destruction are no fantasy, even in children. Holmes, perhaps with the same image in mind, said nothing for a moment. The boy blinked a tear or two from his eyes. Then my friend steered us into calmer waters.

"So far we have talked very little about your work. Are you good at it?"

"I was first of my term for engineering and navigation, sir. Only second in mathematics but first in trigonometry again. I like history, but I can't do languages well. If I could get to Dartmouth or Osborne, I should like most of all to be on a training cruiser. They teach torpedo and electrics, gunnery as well as engineering."

"But getting there," said Holmes quietly, "is not the same as staying there, is it? There is a cost."

"Yes, sir," said Patrick Riley quietly.

"Which there ought not to be," said Holmes in the same quiet voice. "Our present system excludes all but a very small fraction of the population from serving the King as naval officers. It admits the duke's son if he is fit but excludes the cook's son if he is fit or not. Every fit boy should have his chance."

Riley stared for a moment, then said, "Did you make that up, Mr Holmes?"

Sherlock Holmes shook his head.

"It was made up, as you put it, by Admiral of the Fleet Sir John Fisher in a speech to the House of Lords almost ten years ago. Word for word. Now let us get back to business. It seems to me that Master Sovran-Phillips, step-brother of a cruiser captain and admiral's grandson, feels under threat from a bank cashier's son and his widowed mother. I find that most gratifying and I shall eat my hat if it is not at the root of all this. All your hopes rest, do they not, on an Admiral's Nomination to Osborne or Dartmouth in the summer examinations?"

He shook his head.

"No, sir. I should never get one now, whatever happens"

"And why should you not get one?"

"Because exams aren't all of it, Mr Holmes. Not as important as the headmaster's recommendation. Not as important as being Captain of Boats like Sovran-Phillips, like his brother before him, or head of term. Not as important for Mr Winter as a boy having a cruiser captain and a head of term at Dartmouth."

There was greater bitterness in this last remark than I had heard from most of our adult clients. We were later to learn that Reginald Winter had blocked many applicants of the "wrong sort" by simply writing such recommendations as, "I know nothing against this boy," and not a word more.

"Very well," said Holmes. "Be so good as to go downstairs and sit in the Parents' Waiting Room. We shall not keep you long, but do not come back until I send for you."

As soon as the boy had disappeared, Holmes turned to me.

"With the aid of Sister Elliston as messenger, we will now have Master R. J. Sovran-Phillips brought before our little tribunal. He has been kept waiting long enough."

8

So we came face-to-face with the terror of St Vincent's. As a villain and tyrant, I confess, he was a great disappointment. Apple-cheeked and blue-eyed, he was large but flabby rather than muscular. His hair was fair and curly. I should have thought him a mother's darling. Perhaps, ten years hence, the curly hair and apple cheeks might ingratiate him in the favours of a young lady with a taste for naval officers of a certain immaturity.

He did not sit down, nor did Holmes invite him to do so. Instead, Sovran-Phillips stood—and remained—at attention. Sherlock Holmes gazed past him at the sky through the latticed window of the sanatorium, and then back at the youth.

"You are R. J. Sovran-Phillips, are you not?"

"Sir!" He almost stamped his feet together as he said so.

"I shall not keep you long. I have only one or two questions. I take it that you know of the present predicament of your term-mate Patrick Riley?"

"Yes, sir. And very sorry I am to hear that the poor fellow has got himself into such trouble!"

The tone was eerily similar to the sleek sympathy of Reginald

Winter. There was abundant good nature in it. But unless Patrick Riley had lied most skilfully, Sovran-Phillips was about to step into an elephant pit of unimaginable depths.

"I am sure you are sorry," said Holmes reassuringly. "And you know, of course, of the ten-shilling note and the sixpenny piece, missing since Porson's postal order was cashed dishonestly?"

"Yes, sir. We all know that."

"Do you indeed?" Holmes looked up, stared him directly in the eyes, and the destruction of Sovran-Phillips began. "Can you tell us how it might be that a ten-shilling note and a sixpenny piece should be found concealed in the linesman's hut by the railway line?"

If Sovran-Phillips was out of his depth and drowning he was no more so than I. How could Holmes possibly know? Arthur the fireman had only thought the first boy might have been in there to begin with. But Sovran-Phillips went beetroot-red with panic.

"Perhaps . . ." he began.

"Yes?" Holmes said patiently.

"Perhaps it is not the same money."

Holmes nodded encouragingly.

"You are quite right that it might be an entirely different sixpenny piece. Notes, however, are drawn new from the bank by certain post offices and their numbers are consecutive. We should be able to check that."

If notes were drawn in this manner it would surely be by post offices in major cities, but Sovran-Phillips was in no position to know it. He stood before us like a lost soul. It was plain that Holmes had hit a target of some importance with his first shot. He let the silence extend, gazing at the youth until our subject could bear it no longer.

"When were they found?" Phillips asked. Had he stopped to think, he would have known this was a question most likely to be asked by the thief. What could it matter to anyone else?

My friend looked surprised.

"I did not say that they had been found. I was very careful to ask you hypothetically how they might get there—not why they are there."

"Then they were not there?"

Uncertainty was almost worse for him than defeat.

"I most assuredly did not say that either." Holmes replied mildly.

"If they are there . . ." Sovran-Phillips was no longer at attention. "Riley must have taken them there, if they are there. Perhaps after he first got them. How else could they be there?"

"That is what we are here to discover. When do you suggest that Riley would have done that?"

"He was there last Sunday afternoon. We have all been told that."

Holmes relaxed.

"You know he was there, do you not? So were you, some time before him, I understand. He would hardly try to hide them with someone else present. Did you see him do so? Be careful before you say you did. You do not yet know they were ever there at all. Perhaps someone else hid them before his arrival. Did you see anyone else going into the hut? No? Did you see other witnesses?

"Sir?"

"One other witness, I should say. Mr Reginald Winter."

The mention of the headmaster as a witness knocked the wind from him.

"Mr Winter?"

"You did not know that he was there? To be sure you did. He really is most grateful for receiving Riley's intercepted message chalked on the sanatorium tray. I daresay your friend Mitzi will enlighten us further when we question her."

That last promise took the breath from him again. The next

ten minutes were an object lesson in cross-examination, never hectoring, always courteous, and terrifying in its unpredictability. This youth had no idea how much Holmes already knew, let alone what the maidservant might say. His confidence was systematically shot through and through. Obnoxious though he might be, Sovran-Phillips made a pitiful figure by the time Holmes had finished, painstakingly stripped of every defence by the masterly bluff of his interrogator. At last his answers were little more than a mumble and a shake of the head. It was visible that he longed to be dismissed, no matter what the result. My friend brought the final silence to an end.

"Master Phillips, I can spare you a few minutes to make your choice. Please do not prevaricate. Did you entice Patrick Riley to the linesman's hut on Sunday to settle scores with him man-to-man? Or did you propose to associate Riley with the discovery in the hut of a ten-shilling note and a sixpence, relying upon Mr Winter as a witness? It will be quite useless to pretend you were not there at the time or that you did not ensure the headmaster's presence. When your plans were thrown into confusion by the approach of the Bradstone stopping train, did you not take the opportunity to start a rumour that Riley had tried to throw himself under the engine, thereby confirming the charge against him?"

There was a long pause, during which the youth's facial muscles moved but he remained silent.

"Well?" said Holmes helpfully.

"I was never near the post office that afternoon, sir. I had no *exeat* permit. Riley must have chanced it without one, He was lucky not to be stopped and asked for it."

"Perhaps not quite as lucky as a Captain of Boats and prefect of his year who was the last person likely to be stopped. Was he not?"

"I have nothing to say."

"Do you not? I daresay that is very wise. We have almost done with you, Master Phillips. You will now accompany Dr Watson to your quarters. There you will produce to him the pad of permits issued to you at the start of every term. I believe each of them, when correctly completed and signed, entitles you to make a visit to the village. You did not go to the village on the Saturday in question, according to your own account. We can always ask the petty officer or master-on-duty for confirmation."

As if he had lost the power of speech, the youth nodded.

"Good," said Holmes encouragingly, "In that case, this term there have been two previous Saturdays and one since. Your pad of permits will be complete except for three torn off, will it not? Off you go, then. Dr Watson is waiting."

A glance at Sovran-Phillips's face told me that his mind was fully occupied with the absence of a fourth permit, no doubt faked for use in case of being stopped with the postal order in his pocket. Had he only had a few minutes warning of this interrogation, he might have destroyed or hidden his pad of permits or at least made up a story to explain the missing one before his mind was thrown into turmoil. But Sherlock Holmes had ambushed him pitilessly and repeatedly in every question.

There is only one description that I can give of the young Captain of Boats as we left the sanatorium. His self-confidence had been comprehensively wrecked after fifteen minutes in the presence of an accomplished cross-examiner. I caught him by the arm to steady him as he stumbled on the winding staircase that led down to the dormitories and reading rooms.

Without a word, he handed me the pad of yellow permits, from which a few had been torn off by this early stage in the summer term. We made our way back, and once again the unfortunate cadet stood before Holmes, who took the pad from me and fingered it.

"Excellent," he said, glancing up at Sovran-Phillips. "These are your record of Saturday afternoon *exeats*, as I believe the word is. You have received three *exeats* so far, I understand, yet four permits have been used. How does that come about?"

Phillips had now recovered sufficiently to say, "A chap can easily get one wrong and have to write it again."

At first it might have saved him, but now it was far too late for this sort of thing.

"I'm sure a chap can," said Holmes patiently, "and you need have no fear. There will be fair play. Mr Thomas Gurrin, of the Home Office, is now retained in this case to make a full examination of all papers and documents. Even to the extent of seeing where a pencil may have pressed down to leave an indentation of its writing on the layer below—on a permit as well as a postal order. We all know, do we not, that a forgery may be traced rather than copied? So does Mr Gurrin. I feel quite sure that a chap may have every confidence in Mr Gurrin. His evidence, in one or two cases at least, has seen men hanged. A chap could not be in better hands. That will be all. Thank you."

And so the witness, whom I can only keep describing as an unfortunate youth, was dismissed.

9

Spithead fell behind us as the paddles of the steamer *Ryde* cut the calm evening water with late sunlight on the grey battleship hulls and dock cranes of Portsmouth ahead. Holmes drew the pipe from his pocket and began to fill it from his pouch. Faced by his deductive power, small wonder that the venomous Sovran-Phillips should have crumpled before our eyes that morning. By tea-time, Sherlock Holmes had been only too pleased to be quit of what he called the spite and snobbery of St Vincent's.

"I would remind you of the first article of our creed," he said casually. "What matters in this life is not what you can do but what you can make people think you can do. In the case of Sovran-Phillips that equation was not difficult. He was bowled middle stump, was he not?"

"The linesman's hut was never searched?"

"Sovran-Phillips enticed Patrick Riley there in the knowledge that Winter would be watching. Phillips did not intend that he himself should be seen. But then he did not intend that a railway engine should be brought to a halt by Riley standing in front of it!"

The breath of a seagull's wing, diving for a catch, caught both our faces.

"Phillips feared that Riley's goose was not quite cooked by the theft alone," Holmes said. "That is what this is all about. Suspicion was strong but not absolute. Suppose, however, that Riley should be seen by Winter on that Sunday afternoon near the hut or, better still, entering it. Suppose that the hut should then be inspected and the money—or an equivalent sum—found there."

"Proceedings which were interrupted by the stopping train from Bradstone."

"Indeed. And circumstances arose which enabled Phillips to embroider a story of Riley waiting to throw himself under the wheels of the engine. A situation which also gave welcome support to Winter's judgement of the boy. It has been evident to me from an early point in our case, Watson, that this had little to do with a stolen postal order. That was the means to an end. Ten shillings and sixpence, though always welcome, is hardly worth risking the rest of one's career for, unless one is a pathological thief and liar. Patrick Riley is no such thing. Sovran-Phillips is a repulsive piece of work but also an ambitious one."

"The Admiral's Nomination?"

"Precisely. Imagine this son of a prestigious naval family, with a cruiser captain for a step-brother, and an admiral lurking in the ancestral shadows. He regards a Nomination as his birthright. The money is nothing to him, it is the prestige. The racing start that it would give to a chap's career. There is only one Nomination for each year at St Vincent's."

"And would he not get it?"

"I am sure Reginald Winter would dearly love him to. His report, as headmaster, would say so. Term prefect and Captain of Boats, like his brother before him. Cricket, boxing, football. The irony is that he might have got a Nomination in any case.

But then there was Patrick Riley. No naval influence, father a bank clerk, a starveling, as they call it. Obliged to win his way by brains or talent. A rather lonely boy whose so-called friends easily turned against him. Organised bully-ragging might break him—and bully-ragging is not discouraged by the likes of Winter, who regards it as character-building. A plausible charge of theft, even if not fully proved, would put him out of the running. By taking his hope of preferment, that also might break him. Confidential dismissal."

"After all," I said, "he would not go to prison, merely to professional disgrace in the Royal Navy. There he would always be the boy accused of stealing the postal order."

"Precisely. Sovran-Phillips and his kind have influence. But the likes of Jackie Fisher value brains and talent. Suppose influence should fail. Riley was the one boy whose mind and enthusiasms could beat Sovran-Phillips—or so Phillips thought. Even Reginald Winter might not be able to save his favourite Ocean Swell."

The little pieces formed their pattern as we took dinner in the Pullman car of the express from Portsmouth to Waterloo.

How easily Phillips might purloin a braided jacket for half an hour and a pair of glasses from the locker of a boy who wore them. How easily he could provide himself with an *exeat* permit of his own devising. The impress of the last one issued would be on the thin paper of his pad. Only the master's initials need be traced. But who would challenge the captain of his year or do more than glance at the *exeat*? Tracing over Porson's permit and the boy's signature, the indentation would be left upon the postal order. He had only to follow this impress at the post office counter. Riley's game with Porson and the "exchange" of signatures had been nothing but a joke and no more than amateur copying. It was Sovran-Phillips who had proved to be the professional thief.

We were later informed that Sovran-Phillips had left St Vincent's as soon as his bags could be packed. This did not surprise me. Even when I escorted him to get his pad of *exeat* permits, I thought he might bolt there and then, out of the nearest door. It was said that he left school on medical advice, consequent on contracting a nervous fever. No proceedings were taken against him. With his departure, it was possible for Reginald Winter to inform the governors that the case had been fully investigated and no boy at his school was involved in it. The money had been found abandoned near the school grounds and restored to its owner.

Their lordships of the Admiralty discontinued their licencing of St Vincent's. Its numbers declined until it ceased to be a school of any kind. The final terms were transferred to Dartmouth or Osborne as age and examination performance permitted. The buildings were purchased by the government and converted into a naval hospital serving Gosport and Portsmouth. Sherlock Holmes received each successive announcement in the *Morning Post* with a shout of derisive laughter at the preposterous evasions by the authorities.

"My dear Watson! This whole affair will have saved more faces than the Day of Judgement!"

Patrick Riley remained at the school only long enough to take the July examinations, in which he distinguished himself. After a meeting between Sherlock Holmes and his brother Mycroft, the boy transferred to Dartmouth for his remaining year as a junior and his entire senior cadetship. We were subsequently informed that he had passed out with distinction as a Royal Navy lieutenant at eighteen years old, in time to serve during the final year of the Great War.

Considerations of money had at first barred his way. His examinations at fourteen produced distinctions in mathematics and navigation, history and algebra. An essay on Athenian naval tactics at the battle of Salamis in 480 B.C. caused our friend Professor Strachan-Davidson to incline his head approvingly. Yet despite these distinctions, the boy had not been supported by Reginald Winter in his bid for an Admiral's Nomination. Happily, he received this preferment directly from Admiral of the Fleet Sir John Fisher without reference to the headmaster. Sherlock Holmes would take no other fee for his advice in the case.

2

The Case of the Ghosts at Bly

1

"What would you do if you saw a ghost, Mr Holmes? Before I go further into a very sensitive matter, I should like to hear your opinion."

Holmes raised one eyebrow a fraction higher than the other. "On the existence of ghosts, Mr Douglas, I can only take refuge in the wisdom of Dr Samuel Johnson. All argument is against it, but all feeling is for it."

We received our young visitor on a bright morning in the spring of 1898. A mild west wind ruffled the awnings of shops and cafes along Baker Street. Below us echoed a bustle of Saturday trade, a rattle of harness, a grinding of wheels against kerb stones, a brisk rhythm of hooves.

I had never heard my friend questioned about ghosts. We had never discussed the matter between ourselves. Our visitor sat back. He studied Holmes's aquiline features and waited.

The Honourable Hereward Douglas had the air of a tailor-made English gentleman, freshly brushed and combed as if he had stepped from a band-box. Taller even than Holmes and quite as lean, he must have been about twenty-five. There was a striking contrast between his smooth black hair, the restless gleam of dark eyes, and a fairness of skin with a youthful blush. Eton College had formed his manners as a schoolboy. Trinity College, Cambridge, had done the rest.

This young paragon won his open scholarship to Trinity in classics, *cum laude*. He then gained a "blue" at cricket, hitting eighty in an hour at Lords, where he led his team to victory in the annual Oxford and Cambridge match. A model of courtesy and elegance, he was any mother's pride and every young girl's ambition. If he outlived his siblings, he would inherit the Earldom of Crome. What had occurred in his privileged young life to bring him to Sherlock Holmes?

"Setting aside Dr Johnson, Mr Holmes, do you believe in ghosts?"

Holmes contracted his eyebrows.

"I shall not dodge your question, Mr Douglas. Bring me the evidence and I will sift it, as a rational inquirer. Probably I shall find a natural explanation. If not, and if all other possibilities are exhausted, I must consider whether these events may not be produced by causes beyond my power to detect. To conclude otherwise would make me a bigot. I may even have to accept, as the song has it, that King Henry VIII's unhappy queen, Anne Boleyn, walks the Bloody Tower with her head tucked underneath her arm. Come to me without such evidence, however, and I must be a sceptic."

"You make a joke of it, Mr Holmes," said the young man reproachfully.

"On the contrary, Mr Douglas, I was never more serious. But now you have roused my curiosity, I beg you will satisfy it. I can act only upon evidence."

Hereward Douglas inclined his head in acknowledgement.

"That is as I would wish it."

"Admirable." Holmes reclined against the back of his chair. "I believe you are turning out to bat for Middlesex against Yorkshire this afternoon. It is now gone half-past ten. Therefore your time is rather more valuable than my own."

Common sense told me that Holmes would never waste his talents on make-believe. Yet he seemed to look for a pretext to involve himself with ghosts and ghouls.

Mr Douglas ignored my friend's cricketing pleasantry. He opened a briefcase and drew out a handsome quarto diary, bound in maroon leather.

"This is a private journal, Mr Holmes, kept by Miss Victoria Temple. It covers events during six months when she was governess to two children at Bly House, the Mordaunt estate in Essex."

Holmes stared at him hard but said nothing. Victoria Temple! Why did I know that name? For a moment I could not place it. My friend had been lying back, as if prepared to be entertained. His eyelids had been almost closed and the tips of his fingers placed lightly together. Now he straightened up and sat forward.

"The Bly House child-murder," he said expectantly. "The trial was last year, was it not?"

Hereward Douglas nodded

"The verdict was insanity, Mr Holmes. Unfit to stand trial. Guilty but insane."

"I recall that. Pray continue."

Mr Douglas became, if possible, still more earnest.

"As you may know, gentlemen, my family's country seat is in Devonshire, near Ottery St Mary. In my second Long Vacation, I came down from Cambridge for the summer. My sister Louise is eight years my junior. Miss Temple had arrived as her governess a month earlier. I found her a delightful and intelligent young woman. It was no fault of hers to be born into genteel poverty, the youngest of ten daughters of a widowed clergyman. His parish lay some forty miles away. My father was patron of the living. My mother knew of the family's misfortunes. She interviewed Miss Temple and offered her the post of governess to my sister. For several weeks we were thrown into one another's company. We talked and strolled together in the garden. During summer afternoons we sat with our books in shady corners of the lawn under the great beeches."

"And there was no more?" Holmes inquired curtly.

The faintest resentment tightened our visitor's mouth.

"There could be no place for romance, Mr Holmes. I am no snob, nor are my people. Yet an alliance with my sister's governess was not what my parents would have chosen for me. In October, I returned to Cambridge. The young lady and I made vows of friendship, shook hands, and parted for ever. Yet during that summer I heard something of how arduous and solitary her life had been."

"How long was this summer idyll before the death of the child at Bly?"

"I knew nothing of that tragedy until after I had left Cambridge. Even then it was merely a paragraph in the *Morning Post* despatched from Chelmsford Assizes. A charge of murder had been brought against Miss Temple, over the death of Miles Mordaunt, a boy of ten, at Bly House. It was alleged she had smothered the child. After judicial argument and medical evidence, some of it from Professor Henry Maudsley himself, a plea of 'guilty but insane' was accepted by the Crown. As is customary, the sentence was indefinite. Miss Temple was ordered to be detained during Her Majesty's pleasure, as the saying is. She was committed to the Criminal Lunatic Asylum at Broadmoor."

Holmes slipped his hands into his pockets and stretched out his legs.

"From a legal standpoint, Mr Douglas, that is the end of the matter, is it not? In English law, an appeal is impossible against a finding of insanity. By accepting such a verdict, those who represent the accused concede that he or she is guilty of the act, though without the necessary intent to make it criminal. I take it that the evidence was not disputed in court?"

"It was not, Mr Holmes. That was the end of the case but not the end of my story. Last winter I was in London, preparing for the Foreign Office examinations. I came home to my chambers in the Albany one evening. My manservant handed me a package. It was addressed to me by Thurlow and Marston, attorneys-at-law of Lincoln's Inn Fields. They had acted for Miss Temple after her trial. The parcel contained this journal, kept during her time at Bly. The entries begin six months before the death of the little boy, Miles Mordaunt. They end with a confused account of his last moments. Miss Temple's narrative must have helped to convince Professor Maudsley and the court of her so-called insanity."

"A curious keepsake, Mr Douglas! What did she hope to gain from you?"

"In their letter, her lawyers told me that she wished me to have the volume. I was the one person she thought might still believe in her innocence. Her own circle of friends contained no one able to exercise influence on behalf of a poor young lunatic."

He stood up and handed my friend the quarto volume. Holmes glanced through it with a frown. He turned to the last page.

"More than two hundred pages covering, as you say, six months. Well, Mr Douglas, I must not keep you waiting while I read it. Perhaps you can help me a little before I do so. What does this volume contain that might have influenced a trial judge or jury?"

Hereward Douglas enumerated the contents on the fingers of his left hand with the forefinger of his right.

"First, their uncle's choice of Miss Temple as governess of the two children at Bly. Miles Mordaunt was ten, his sister Flora younger by two years. Their parents, Colonel and Lady Mordaunt, had lately died in a cholera epidemic in Bengal. The children were left under the indolent wardship of their uncle, Dr James Mordaunt, also known as Major Mordaunt of Eaton Square, Belgravia. He was a retired surgeon-major of the Queen's Rifles. He summoned Miss Temple to his solicitor's chambers in Harley Street and interviewed her alone."

"And she accepted the post?"

He shook his head.

"She felt herself too inexperienced and unequal to such a trust. She thanked him but refused his offer. It seems he had no luck in finding any other lady. After a second invitation, still having no employment herself, she accepted."

My friend made a note on his starched cuff.

"Let us come directly to the ghosts, if you please. Let us also be specific. Who saw them—Miss Temple, presumably? And where exactly did they appear?"

"According to her journal, two apparitions were seen several times at Bly but not together. A man, identified as Peter Quint, had been dead for a year or more. He had been valet to Major Mordaunt, the uncle. Before that, he was the major's batman in the Queen's Rifles. He was seen by Miss Temple at least three times. On a further occasion at night, though she did not see him, she was convinced that the little boy Miles was staring up at him in a window above her. The boy behaved as though he had seen this man. The last time she saw Quint was recorded in the journal just before her arrest. It was at the moment of the boy's death."

"And the second figure?"

"From Miss Temple's description this was identified by Mrs Grose, the housekeeper, as Miss Maria Jessel. That young woman had been the preceding governess. She had gone on a long holiday the year before—it seems she was unwell. She died at her father's home before her return. Her death left the post vacant for Miss Temple."

I glanced covertly at Holmes to see how he was taking this catalogue of make-believe. If he felt any scorn for the ghostly visitors he certainly did not show it. He continued to question Hereward Douglas.

"How did she know these figures were ghosts?"

"Miss Temple had no idea who the two figures might be until she was told. It did not occur to her at first that they might be ghosts, because they were usually seen in full daylight. But as soon as she described the figures, Mrs Grose named them. That lady swore to me that Miss Temple was accurate in every detail. Only then did Mrs Grose tell the young governess that the two people she depicted in such detail were dead."

"Is it not possible that Miss Temple had seen Quint and Miss Jessel during their lives and perhaps mistook two other people for them after their deaths? A trick of light or distance?"

Hereward Douglas shook his head vigorously.

"Until coming to London and to Bly, which is on the other side of the country, she had never set foot outside the south-west of England. So far as we know, neither Quint nor Miss Jessel had any connections or had ever been there."

That was as far as Holmes allowed him to get.

"I have to tell you, Mr Douglas," he said gently, "that it is vastly more probable for Miss Temple to have seen them previously—even if it was when they visited her home county of Devon for some very unlikely reason—than for a man or a woman to return from the grave. However, by all means continue, if you believe it will serve your purpose."

The young man began to look a little downcast and his voice was quiet.

"Peter Quint, the Mordaunt valet, was the first apparition she saw. He was standing by the parapet of the garden tower at Bly, looking down at her across the lawn as a late summer evening turned to dusk. She thought perhaps he was an intruder but she said nothing to anyone. That autumn, seeing him again, outside the dining-room window this time, she complained to the housekeeper and gave the man's description. Mrs Grose told her that she had depicted Peter Quint, down to his stature, the colour and texture of his hair, even the unusual waistcoat that he wore. Only then did the housekeeper tell Miss Temple that Peter Quint had died the previous year."

Holmes watched him carefully as Hereward Douglas continued. "The previous winter, Quint had fallen head-first and smashed his skull open, after drinking late at the village inn. As usual, he had drunk far too much. He was alone in the country lanes on a bitter icy night without a lantern. It seems that he pitched over a large stone in the darkness—went flying, as they say—and broke his head clean open on the jagged flint parapet of a bridge across the stream. Two carters found him dead and frozen next morning. Miss Temple could only have seen his ghost."

"And what did Miss Temple say to his reappearance?"

"Her first reaction, as her journal tells us, was to suppose that the servants were playing tricks on her. Or else that she had seen someone resembling Quint, as you suggest. A brother perhaps. But the man had no brother."

"And the other residents at Bly?"

"They saw nothing. Dr Mordaunt, the guardian uncle, was living in France just then. There were only the servants and the children in the manor house. Dr Mordaunt had sometimes visited Bly before Peter Quint's death, but he had long given up any interest in the place. He thought the house remote and dreary. Unfortunately, it was not his to dispose of. With the death of Colonel Mordaunt, it was held in trust for young Miles, the colonel's only son."

Holmes sighed.

"So Miss Temple's visions of Quint and Miss Jessel are entirely unsupported?"

"Not quite." Hereward Douglas's young face still showed a determination to fight for the unfortunate young woman. "The housekeeper was present the second time that Miss Temple saw Miss Jessel, at a distance of a hundred and fifty feet or so across the lake. The little girl Flora was with them. It is true that Mrs Grose saw nothing, but she had a powerful sense that she was in the presence of an evil force."

"Tell me, pray, how did she sense it?"

"There was an unnatural stillness on that autumn afternoon, Mr Holmes. When Miss Temple first saw Quint, on the tower in late sunlight, she was alerted to his presence by the same eerie way in which the sheep bells fell silent and the rooks ceased to caw. It was as if time and nature ceased when the figures appeared."

"That is really not the same thing as if the housekeeper had also seen the apparition," my friend said reproachfully.

"The children, Mr Holmes!" Douglas had been driven back into his corner but he came out fighting again. "Miss Temple was certain that the children saw the figures, on four occasions at least. Their reactions made it plain."

"And what did the two little ones say about these ghostly appearances?"

"At first she thought they were too frightened to admit them. Then she saw that they were too guiltily excited to confess."

Holmes sucked in his sallow cheeks a little and then breathed out.

"I fear that will be the rock on which your case founders, Mr Douglas. However, let us leave it for a moment. Let me ask you something else. Suppose all this is true. Suppose Miss Temple saw—or even thought she saw—these apparitions. For what reason would two such people return from the dead in order to materialise before your susceptible young friend? She had never known them. She had no interest in them, nor they in her, presumably."

Our visitor leant forward again, eager to dispel a misunderstanding.

"You make my point for me, Mr Holmes. Miss Temple was only a bystander. Their manner and their movements convinced her that their true object had nothing to do with her. Their purpose was the seduction of the two children into the realms of evil and the world of the damned. She had been told repeatedly by the housekeeper, and by servants at Bly, of the malignant and corrupting influence that Quint and Miss Jessel exercised, during their lives, over the two children."

If the rest of the tale was implausible, this was preposterous.

"A power sufficient to commit murder from beyond the grave?" Holmes inquired sceptically.

"No, sir. The little girl, Flora Mordaunt, died of diphtheria in the London fever hospital. Miss Temple was accused of smothering the boy a few days later."

Holmes sat taller, fingers clasped and elbows on the arms of his chair. Hereward Douglas still held my friend's impatient interest, if only by a thread.

"You will read in the journal, Mr Holmes, why Miss Temple was certain that the children saw the apparitions. Miles and Flora were the objects of these evil visitations. It was only some exceptional and special sensibility that enabled the governess to share the visions."

"Neither Master Miles nor Miss Flora remarked upon these ghosts?"

"No," said Douglas forlornly. "Both denied them."

"Dear me," said Holmes lightly. "So you ask us to believe in these appearances because the children—from fear or wickedness—denied them? I am bound to say, Mr Douglas, it is as well for you that you are not, at this moment, bound by the rules of evidence in a criminal court. Pray continue, however. Your narrative is most unusual, if nothing else."

"That was not all!" Surely it was desperation that brought this protest from our visitor. "Miss Temple was certain the children saw for themselves. Do you not understand? They were in league with these visitors! The willing victims! Unless you can accept that possibility, I am wasting my time."

Holmes shrugged.

"In league with them? But for what possible purpose?"

Douglas spoke quietly.

"To be united in death—all four—in a state of damnation to which the children were being seduced. A state for which their corrupted childhood had trained them. There is no other way to put it, Mr Holmes."

I could see from the brightness in my friend's gaze that this folklore of the dead possessing the living was not a mere absurdity to him. Its possibility glimmered on what Robert Browning called the dangerous edge of things. How his rational soul longed to believe!

"By what means were the children to be drawn to damnation?" I asked. Hereward Douglas turned in his chair.

"By self-destruction, Dr Watson. Quint and Miss Jessel were usually seen 'across and beyond,' as Miss Temple puts it. They appeared almost motionless, at a distance, and almost always where they were inaccessible. Death beckoned the children across the deep waters of a treacherous lake—the Middle Deep, as it was called—or from the height of a dilapidated tower. It was as if the two devils summoned their victims to come to them and perish in the attempt. Quint also appeared twice to Miss Temple through the closed windows of a room. Terrifying but, once again, always inaccessible."

"Not tempting her to destruction, however?"

He shook his head.

"No. Taunting her. Doing battle with her for the souls of two innocents."

Holmes met this with the cold inquiry of the logician. Could he believe or could he not?

"If the children should perish, what would that accomplish?"

Our visitor was careful not to give away too much.

"In Miss Temple's mind—and even to the housekeeper—Miss Jessel and Quint were damned, as they deserved to be. Their spirits lusted for the children to share their hellish privations."

This talk of hell and damnation was too much for me. I was about to say so, but Holmes glanced at me and Hereward Douglas resumed.

"Mrs Grose, of course, did not share Miss Jessel's vision of the dead. If she believed in the possibility of their evil presences, it was because she had known the man and woman during their lives. She had sensed the depravity of which they were capable towards the sensitive and imaginative children in their care."

So much for ghosts! A fascination with human evil was now all that kept the ball in play between the two debaters in our sitting-room.

"How exactly did the children die?" Holmes asked finally.

"The little girl, Flora, died first. She was taken ill in London with high temperatures and dangerous symptoms. After a day or two, she was moved to the fever hospital for better care. It was already too late. Her fever turned to diphtheria and she died in the following week. Before this was known at Bly, Miles showed signs of a milder fever but not of diphtheria. There had been something of the kind at school. This was not apparent until a day or two after his sister's death and certainly did not seem to threaten his life. He remained at Bly with Miss Temple. I fear the local doctor was old and ignorant. The boy might have recovered with proper care."

"And what of the ghosts?" I asked cautiously.

"The last apparition of Peter Quint materialised quite suddenly, Dr Watson, in broad daylight at the window of the dining-room. It was the white face of damnation, as Miss Temple calls it in her journal. She seized the ailing boy in her arms to shield him from it."

"But only according to her own journal?"

Hereward Douglas nodded at the volume which Holmes was holding.

"It is there word for word, written just after the event."

"Written to conceal some wrong-doing of her own perhaps?"

"No, Dr Watson. If ever a suspect condemned herself, it was Miss Temple in that journal. She describes how she clutched Miles to her breast to hide from him the terrible vision of Quint on the far side of the glass. In covering his eyes during her hysterical anger at the phantom she also covered his nostrils and mouth. Miles had his eyes tight shut against the horror beyond the window. She admits that he gave a frantic little struggle for light and air. So she allowed the boy a respite but caught him again and pressed him close. She must keep the dreadful eyes from the child's gaze. After that she lost her composure, probably she lost consciousness as well. When she came to herself, at the end of a minute or so, the life had gone from Miles Mordaunt. Miss Temple was staring at an empty window with the dead child in her arms."

"A difficult case to try," Holmes said sympathetically.

"It was, Mr Holmes. Miles was a boy of delicate health, in any case, and underdeveloped for his age. Unfortunately for Miss Temple, the judge ruled at the outset of the case that those who kill must take their victims as they find them. After that, Miss Temple could not put forward this child's weakness as a mitigating circumstance. The servants could only say that they never saw anything but an empty window, where Miss Temple twice saw the features of Peter Quint."

I tried to console the young man.

"A verdict of insanity was her only hope of life. The best way to it was to plead that some form of hysteria had robbed her of consciousness and volition, if only for a moment or two. Otherwise her sole witness was a ghost! A court would dismiss that as sheer fabrication and no defence at all."

The young man shrugged and shook his head. He had done his best against two older and more sceptical listeners but it had got him nowhere.

"I apologise, gentlemen, if I have taken up your time to no purpose. I was bound to do what I could for my friend."

He was an amiable young man, and I tried to make some amends for my disbelief.

"From many years of medical practice, Mr Douglas, I assure you that you have acted honourably and courageously. The sudden loss of reason in a friend or loved one, who has given no other sign of infirmity, is the most distressing form of separation. Far worse than many a mortal disease when it turns a friend into a stranger."

He looked at me, oddly as I thought.

"You misunderstand me, Dr Watson," he said quietly. "I do not come to you for comfort in this matter. I do not ask that you should believe in tales of ghosts or demons. I am no lawyer and certainly not a medical man. I am here because I cannot believe that Miss Temple was responsible for that child's death. A finding of insanity may have saved her from the gallows. Now she lies in a criminal lunatic asylum. But I will take my oath that she is as sane as you or I."

Holmes watched these exchanges, his eyes motionless as a lizard's measuring a fly. He closed the morocco volume which he had been holding open at its final page. Then he stood up and turned to our visitor.

"If you hoped to convince me of the apparitions, Mr Douglas, I fear you have failed so far. However, though you may not think so, I believe you have done enough to persuade me that Miss Temple is no murderess."

"And manslaughter?" Hereward Douglas murmured anxiously.

Holmes looked surprised.

"I should not accept this case merely to agree a compromise over mental frailty. With me, Mr Douglas, the battle is all or nothing."

"Then what of insanity?"

"I have not yet had the pleasure of her acquaintance but I am ready to suppose it possible that Miss Temple is as sane as you or I. Of course, I must inquire for myself. Yet nothing you have told me so far convinces me that she is insane."

"Thank God!" he said softly.

Sherlock Holmes was not given to fatherly gestures but he laid a hand on the young man's shoulder.

"Now, Mr Douglas, you must permit me to read the young lady's journal for myself. I promise you, it will not detain me long. I shall communicate with you by Monday at the latest. Until then, I suggest that you should give your best attention to Lords cricket ground and the match this afternoon."

The tension in our sitting-room thinned and vanished like a drift of cigar smoke. Hereward Douglas was astonished to be dismissed so kindly after bringing us what we ought to have rejected as nonsense. When we were alone I waited for an explanation. After all, Holmes knew about Miss Temple's appearance at Chelmsford Assizes. I had read only a brief press report. He was susceptible to damsels in distress. I hoped his championing of this young woman was not a mere quixotic impulse.

He had turned his back to me and was staring into the grate, his hands upon the shelf of the mantelpiece. He gave a light kick at a burnt log in the fireplace, laid for a chilly evening the day before. Its carbonised crispness disintegrated under the impact. I guessed what was coming.

"I will tell you now," I said quietly, "that you will not easily be granted a visitor's pass to a criminal lunatic asylum like Broadmoor. That is where reprieved murderers are held. Let alone will they permit a private interview with an inmate. At the first mention of ghosts and apparitions, they will probably detain you there as well."

He turned with a smile, the first since Hereward Douglas began his tale.

"Dear Watson, you are right as always. Except in one detail. Before our young friend arrived, I thought it best to establish his lineage from the pages of *Burke's Peerage*. His father is the Earl of Crome. Therefore, should Hereward Douglas outlive his elder brothers and any sons they may have, he will succeed to that title."

"He would rather captain the England cricket team against Australia!"

"I daresay."

"Then how will the peerage help us with Miss Temple?"

"Among other accomplishments, the present Earl of Crome sits on a government committee known as the Prison Board. It is one of his many good works. Certain members are also deputed to attend the Board of Governors of Broadmoor Hospital. I should not be surprised if, by his influence, the hospital superintendent were to permit us to visit one of his patients. Despite my eccentric views, he may even allow me to leave again. You recall that Miss Temple was governess to the earl's own daughter for several months? Mr Douglas spent a summer in her company and has just confirmed that she made an excellent impression on the family."

"You think that will be sufficient?"

"I am confident enough to suggest that you should consult your invaluable copy of Bradshaw's *Railway Guide*. For obvious reasons, the whereabouts of the asylum at Broadmoor is not advertised. It lies near the village of Crowthorne at a little distance from Wokingham. We shall require a morning train from Waterloo. An express, if possible. At Wokingham, we shall easily procure a carriage for the final stage of our journey."

I had feared from the outset that his curiosity would get the better of him. Mr Douglas had won his point. We were to become ghost-hunters.

2

In the course of our partnership, the case of Victoria Temple was the first to bring Holmes and me to the criminal lunatic asylum of Broadmoor. Even as a medical man, I knew of the place only through legends of raving homicides, cut-throat zealots, baths of blood and giggling mania. Its sufferers were confined within fortress walls. They presumably spent most of their lives in strait-jackets or under other forms of restraint. After this sensational reputation, I was quite astonished by the reality.

Had I stopped to inquire, I should have discovered that the inmates of the infamous "Bedlam" asylum in South London had been transferred to an Italianate palace built on a slope of the downs. It rose among fields and hills some thirty miles south-west of London. The incline of a hill had been incorporated in the grounds so that the inmates looked over the outer walls across a landscape of pastureland, farm buildings and copses.

Holmes had been correct. The Earl of Crome, father of Hereward Douglas and former employer of Miss Temple, had secured our passes to the visiting room. I was a medical man retained on Miss Temple's behalf and Holmes was my professional colleague.

Outside the main gate we left the brougham which had brought us from the railway and were escorted up a driveway lined with laurel and rhododendron. It might have been a nobleman's estate. We turned a corner and confronted a rather heavy Venetian campanile, colonnades, handsome galleries and elegant windows. Dr Annesley, the Superintendent, waited at the top of the broad steps.

This was no prison. The outer walls and gates were secure but within the building its inmates had the run of broad corridors, a dining-hall and separate day-rooms for men and women. In two well-lit, plainly-furnished lounges, patients might converse, read or pass their time in hobbies. Men who were for the most part elderly sat talking quietly in pairs at little tables. Others were reading, writing or reclining on side seats with their hands thrust into their pockets, staring into space. How strange that some of these veterans had committed the most pitiless and blood-chilling crimes of the age.

Just before we came to the end of the corridor, Annesley paused. We were beyond earshot of the rooms to either side.

"I will suggest one caution, Dr Watson, and I will give you one warning. Whatever Miss Temple refers to or introduces into the conversation you may discuss as freely with her as your professional good sense indicates. But I must ask you not to question her upon such topics as the so-called apparitions or anything that may be contentious, unless she alludes to it first. I believe you are here to determine whether there may have been a miscarriage of justice."

"I shall do nothing to distress her," I said. "It would be the worst thing in her own interests and our own. Perhaps you would tell me whether what you have just said is a request or a caution."

This serious little man frowned as if I had made a joke in bad taste.

"My warning is this. Whatever you may think of her case, Miss Temple is a tragic and unstable young woman."

"Because she saw ghosts?"

Annesley shook his head.

"Because her relationship with Miles Mordaunt was what a woman's with a ten-year-old boy should never be. She behaved so unwisely that the child boasted of his power over her."

"In what way?"

"According to the housekeeper, they created a fiction that Miss Temple was just twenty-one years old. When Miles grew up they were to be married and he would be the master. Such was the difference in their social standing. Already, when the boy took her out in the little boat on the lake at Bly, he talked of 'spooning' with her and 'squiring' her. Goodness knows where the child got such words from!"

"There was no evidence of vicious conduct?" I asked.

"Evidence? No."

"Harmless make-believe, I daresay," said Holmes brusquely.

"So it might have been, Mr Holmes, had she not encouraged it. She played up to him and allowed the boy to treat her like a female subordinate. In consequence she lost all authority over him. Major Mordaunt was plainly unaware of this. Otherwise Miss Temple's tenure at Bly would have been brief indeed. I merely warn you, Dr Watson, that this is an area of inquiry best left alone. It would not serve you."

"I am obliged to you for that."

We faced the closed door of the visiting-room. Its interior was again plainly furnished, a polished table with a small hand-bell upon it, several leather chairs, a tiled fireplace and prints of landscape views. As we entered, a young woman rose from one of the arm-chairs to greet us.

"Miss Victoria Temple," said Dr Annesley, by way of introduction, "Dr John Watson and Mr Sherlock Holmes."

I had formed a picture of Victoria Temple, looking much younger and more dainty. No doubt a child's death and a criminal trial, even the threat of execution on the gallows, had added to her years in reality. She was tall but a little stooped, brown hair in a bun, her complexion worn rather than lined. She seemed a plain country girl. Genteel poverty had left her to perform tasks which fortunate daughters might delegate to servants. There was something unsteady about her, combined with a look of latent physical strength. Her profile, with the broad points of her cheek-bones, was calm but resolute. In the last resort she would outmatch a boy of ten. As for crime, she looked capable of anything—or nothing.

"I shall leave you together," said Annesley with a pleasant smile. "Perhaps you will take tea before you leave. Meantime, if there is anything you require, you have only to ask."

I took this to mean that if Miss Temple became distressed or "difficult," we should remember the little bell on the table. Annesley withdrew, pulling the door but not quite closing it. The young woman sat down.

"It is good of you to come," she said in the most quiet and reassuring voice I had ever heard. "I am not sure what I can do for you, but whatever it may be, I will try."

I took the seat opposite her at the table, with Holmes to one side.

"I am here as a medical man, Miss Temple. My colleague, Mr Sherlock Holmes, is a criminal investigator. Our sole purpose is to ensure that justice shall be done you."

She looked down at the table, then up again.

"I cannot complain of injustice. I have been kindly treated. As for my medical condition, perhaps you hope that I shall deny my visions. I fear I am a little like Joan of Arc and her voices. I cannot deny what I have seen. It would be so much simpler if I could, would it not?"

I shook my head.

"No, Miss Temple. Only the truth will serve us and you must not depart from that, however convenient it might be."

"But you think me mad? You must, surely?"

Holmes intervened.

"No, madam. If that were so, we should not be here."

Victoria Temple looked at us, her eyes brighter.

"I am better now, whatever I may have been last year. I was ill, distressed, perhaps mad—I do not know. I am still distressed, beyond anything you can imagine. But I am sane. How can I prove I am not mad? They say you cannot prove the contrary, do they not?"

"Then we must prove you to be a rational young woman," said Holmes firmly.

Miss Temple looked at him as if he had perplexed her and she could not think of a reply. At length she said, "They are very kind, Mr Holmes. Ever since that dreadful day at Bly everyone has been good to me—none more so than Major Mordaunt. He still has that title, though since he left the Army he is Dr Mordaunt. He always gave me complete freedom to care for the children. I was to be the mistress of Bly Hall. He felt no inclination for the place, though I believe he lived there with them for a short while after his brother's death. He would never neglect his duties to them. He never forgot them, though he paid others to attend to them. I owe my life to him."

"Very commendable," I said gently.

"When my ordeal came on, Major Mordaunt was living in France. Yet it was he who supported me from there during my trial. I could not believe I had committed murder, though that was what they called it. I knew I never meant harm—but who would believe me? The evidence was all one way, unless I could tell my story well enough in the witness-box. But my recollection was imperfect. I could never have withstood cross-examination by a clever lawyer. What jury would believe my account of the apparitions? Left to myself, I should have been convicted and hanged."

"But thankfully that did not happen," said Holmes reassuringly.

"No, Mr Holmes, it did not, thanks to James Mordaunt. He found a Queen's Counsel for my defence, Mr Ballantine. And Mr Ballantine was on terms with the Treasury Solicitor. There were discussions and I was seen by several physicians—specialists of Mr Ballantine's acquaintance. I do not know how these things are done but it was arranged that the same gentlemen should give their evidence to the court."

"And that the Crown should accept a plea of not guilty by virtue of insanity," Homes said quietly.

I feared the words might distress her, but Victoria Temple seemed indifferent to them.

"Without that, Mr Holmes, I should have been hanged. If Major Mordaunt had not found Mr Ballantine for me—and paid his fee—I should have been lost. I knew so little of the law that I was afterwards possessed by the idea that if ever they believed I had recovered my sanity, the law would oblige them to come for me and hang me. I had the most fearful dreams at first of being woken for that purpose. Dr Annesley and others worked with great patience to encourage me and bring me to my senses over it. And now Mr Douglas, whom I have not seen in all this time, has been good to me as well, persuading you to visit me here."

Then it seemed that the conversation ran into a brick wall. There was silence until Miss Temple herself broke it with a slight wave of her hand.

"Gentlemen, you may talk of whatever you please. The apparitions, Mrs Grose and the others at Bly, the children. Even little Miles. I weep for him, of course, but I am quite all right now. I can speak of him, as I am speaking to you at this moment."

"Very well then," said Holmes quietly. "Tell me, please, before your arrest how many times had you seen Major Mordaunt?"

"Once." She paused for a moment, as if to check her accuracy. "He interviewed me in London, at the office of his solicitor in Harley Street. I was offered the place of the late Miss Jessel. From what I have heard, I was not the first to refuse. You must remember that I had never held a post of this kind. There was no master or mistress in the house, only the servants. My employer would not even be in England much of the time. I was a newcomer and I thought the responsibility too great."

She paused, looked about her, and then returned her gaze to us.

"I feared the loneliness and the lack of company, the distance from my home. There would be no one to whom I could turn for advice, for instructions or decisions. Major Mordaunt made that clear. He had never wanted to be guardian of his brother's children and estate. He preferred that it should be done by others."

"You were to have charge of both children?"

"Only the little girl, Flora, at first. Miles was away at King Alfred's School. He was sent home some time after my arrival."

"For the holidays?"

"No, Mr Holmes. He was dismissed from the school, unfairly dismissed. Dr Clarke, the headmaster, went so far as to insist that his continued presence would injure the other boys. The head would say nothing more than that. I was never able to determine the exact cause. That boy, Mr Holmes, was beautiful in soul and body. He was the type that such schoolmasters dislike. He was too good for them!"

"And what persuaded you to accept the post at last, after you had first refused?" I asked.

"By the time that Major Mordaunt wrote to me again, two months later, I had found no other appointment. I also saw how the increased stipend, which I was now offered, might help my sisters. They were poorly provided for, as matters stood. My mother had now died and my father had few prospects. I had received one or two disturbing letters from home, as to his condition. Therefore I consented."

"Perhaps you will help me to visualise the occasion," said Holmes courteously. "The interview took place in a solicitor's office, simply between the two of you?"

"Correct."

"Major Mordaunt sat on the far side of his desk?"

"Yes."

There was a pause, as if she expected him to continue. When he did not, she looked up and smiled.

"Major Mordaunt is a very charming man, of course, and certainly persuasive. I did not see him for more than fifteen or twenty minutes, but I once told the housekeeper, Mrs Grose, that I had been quite carried away by him. She said, 'You're not the first.' When she first described Miss Jessel to me, I said, 'He seems to like us young and pretty.'"

"A ladies man?" Holmes asked casually.

"I have nothing to complain of in his conduct. He was beyond reproach."

"Good," he nodded, "You never suffered insubordination from the servants at Bly nor any disobedience on the part of the children?"

"Nothing at all, unless you count their denials of seeing the intruders."

"The children's denial of seeing the apparitions?"

"They were intruders, Mr Holmes! Who cares in what form they came?"

So Miss Temple was no mere hysteric who insisted upon ghosts. I found that interesting, but Holmes was impatient and our time with this client was passing too quickly.

"Tell me, Miss Temple, are you a needlewoman or an artist?"

"I crochet and sketch, Mr Holmes. Ah, yes. Of course. I know what you mean. The hospital records will tell you that I do not need glasses for either short or long sight. I see what is in front of me distinctly. That is your point, is it not? Very well. I do not imagine visions, apparitions, or whatever else you like to call them. I can describe what I saw."

"Indeed," said Holmes gravely. "Then tell me about Peter Quint. What did he look like?"

She was a little flustered at this demand but quickly composed herself.

"I first saw him on the garden tower at Bly, standing at the battlements, as I looked up from the lawn. We stared at one another, I cannot tell you for how long. He held a rather unnatural pose, like an actor. Presently he turned and walked to the far corner of the tower out of sight and I saw him no more. He was dressed in clothes that seemed too fancy for a mere valet. As we stared at one another, the world went into a strange silence. The sheep bells and the bird calls stopped."

"So I understand," said Holmes briskly. "However, we will leave the sheep and the birds out of it. His appearance, if you please."

By a glance I tried to warn him against this approach, without Miss Temple seeing me. I need not have bothered. She was quite able to hold her own.

"He never wore a hat," she said, "and so I saw his hair clearly. It was unusually red and tightly curled, red whiskers too. He had bushy whiskers—not a beard—of the mutton-chop kind that a sergeant-major might wear. He had not been a sergeant-major, of course. I understand he was only the major's batman in the Army but followed his master into civilian life, as a valet. He had a long face, rather red, as if he drank too much or was sunburnt from service in foreign parts. His features were straight. His eyes seemed hard as stone. I remember thinking that sapphires so hard would never melt into the sea as they did in Lord Tennyson's poetry! His mouth was wide, but so far as I could tell his lips were thin. He wore—they say he often wore—the same fancy waistcoat. Mrs Grose, the housekeeper, told me that Quint frequently wore garments stolen from his absent master. This waistcoat might be one of them."

"We will also leave Lord Tennyson and the waistcoat to one side," said Holmes. "How far from the tower were you standing?"

"Twenty-five feet, I daresay—perhaps thirty."

"Were you looking straight up at him with your head held back or was it a more level view from farther off?"

"I stared straight at him. At a little distance."

"You must have been at a sufficient distance to see him walk across the platform of the tower when he disappeared. Yet you could tell his lips were thin and his eyes hard? Now then, there were three floors of the house, the tower platform and the battlements—forty feet or more vertically. Add to that your horizontal distance from it. Not less than thirty feet, if you had a view of the direction in which he walked away."

"Perhaps that was so, Mr Holmes."

"As a governess, Miss Temple, I daresay you are familiar enough with the theorem of Pythagoras to teach it to your pupils. Will you take it from me, as a matter of geometry, that such dimensions would put the two of you about fifty feet apart?"

"I must accept that, if you say it is so."

"I do say it, madam. Let us proceed. This man was standing with his face to the east, staring out at you, while the light was dying in the west behind him. His face was red? Was not his face in shadow, though? And could you tell in such poor light, at such a distance too, that his eyes were blue and his lips were thin?"

"Perhaps his lips were not thin. His whiskers hid them, but that was my impression."

I was uneasy at this sceptical cross-examination, but Miss Temple still held her own. She would have done well in the witness-box, after all.

"Your impression alone will not quite do," said Holmes gently.

For the first time, she showed a little irritation with him.

"I saw enough of him in the evening light, Mr Holmes, to know that he was the same man I saw close up, some weeks later, through the dining-room window by lamplight. Mrs Grose and I were setting out for Sunday evening service. The carriage was waiting at the terrace steps and I went into the room just to fetch a pair of gloves I had forgotten. The man who had been on the tower was on the terrace, staring at me through the glass without moving. That night I gave Mrs Grose the description I have just given to you. I was close enough to him for that."

"How far is the church from the house?"

"It is on the estate, about ten minutes' walk, but it was customary to take the carriage."

"And at what time is Evensong?"

"Half-past six."

"This was in early November, I understand, and therefore after dark?"

"It was."

"How many lights were burning in the dining-room?"

"The central gasolier was lit but turned low when we left the room. The wall mantels had been extinguished. They would not be lit until we returned for supper."

"Reflection from the half-lit gasolier, through the window and onto the terrace, was enough to show you the man's features on such a dark November evening?"

"I first ran towards the window, Mr Holmes. He did not move. Then I ran out into the hallway and out at the main door. He had gone. I am no liar, sir!"

This was a more dangerous exchange, but Holmes inclined his head courteously.

"Indeed you are no liar, Miss Temple. A liar would insist that she was far closer to the man on the tower at the first encounter. On the second, she would probably have told me that all the lights in the dining-room were fully lit and shining onto the terrace, where the man stood. She certainly would not have omitted accidentally, as you have done, that there would also be a lamp on the terrace itself—as well as on the carriage—to light you on your way. It must have been bright enough to show the way down the steps to the conveyance which would take you to Evensong."

She looked down with her closed fist lightly to her lips as if she might weep. Holmes forestalled her.

"I have dealt with a good many liars, Miss Temple, and I am so far satisfied that you are a truthful young woman. I cannot yet say that your visitor on the tower or at the window was a creature from the realms of darkness. That you saw a figure of some kind is evident to me."

"Thank you," she said softly.

My friend resumed.

"What else did you see on this second occasion?"

"There was no one on the terrace by the time I reached it, no sign of an intruder. Not a footprint in the earth, not a gate nor door swinging open. Having seen him twice, I still thought he was an ordinary trespasser. It was only after this second appearance that I told Mrs Grose. She replied that I had exactly described Peter Quint—and that Quint had been dead for a year. Until then I had not known our housekeeper well enough to confide in her. I had suspected that this fellow might be a hanger-on of one of the women at the house. Or perhaps the servants were playing a game to frighten me. There is often a grudge against a poor governess. She is in some ways their mistress—able to give them orders—but not truly mistress of the house. They are quick to complain that she has got 'above herself.'"

"They did not complain in your case?"

"No. They were all kind to me."

"Excellent," said Holmes, and his mood changed at once. Miss Temple's answers had unquestionably been straight and true. To me she seemed an honest witness, however deluded. And still there was a simple strength in her. Without that, we might have faced a catastrophe as she gave way under questioning. She now looked at us both and continued.

"Mrs Grose told me how Quint had left the village tavern one winter night and was found dead on the road next morning with a fearful gash across his head. The local coroner from Abbots Langley described the injuries to the jury. From where the dead man lay it was plain that he lost his footing and went headlong. His skull had struck the edge of the parapet over the stream. The sharp ice cut him deeply. After that, Mrs Grose talked to me of the fellow's secret vices, his drinking and his affairs with the village girls. Worst of all, he was too free with Miles. It was outrageous that a promiscuous brute like he should act as the little boy's tutor and guide!"

"And what of Miss Jessel?" I asked.

She paused, as if to gather her strength after the outburst.

"A week or so later I was walking with Flora one afternoon, by the lake. A woman appeared on an opposite bank, the wooded island at the far end. She was too far off for anyone to reach her before she disappeared among the trees again. At first I supposed she must be a servant but then I saw by her clothes she could not be. She was dressed in shabby black mourning, not a maidservant's uniform. Her hair was dark. I thought her beautiful, but in an unearthly way. A beautiful corpse, if there can be such a thing. Make no mistake, Dr Watson, I saw her as plainly as I see you now, but she was not looking at me. Her eyes were on the little girl, Flora. In that moment they became such awful eyes, Mr Holmes, filling gradually with a fury of evil triumph."

"Though she was dead, you thought you knew who she must be?"

"I felt sure, even before I described her to Mrs Grose. I suppose I sound mad to you, do I not? But what was more important, I knew that I was merely a witness. She had not come for me. Like Quint, she had come for the children. Mrs Grose had only told me that Miss Jessel had been as infamous in her lifetime as Quint. In the end, she had gone on a long holiday and had died at her father's home. That was told to Mrs Grose by Major Mordaunt in confidence, for fear her death should upset the other servants."

"And then Miles was sent back from school?"

She nodded.

"We had a season of great happiness, Miles, Flora and I. Music and costumes, theatricals and games. I loved them both, Mr Holmes, because it was so easy to love them. Yet this changed quite suddenly. There were now moments when the children cuddled together and talked of some secret, smiling at me as if to tell me that it was to be kept from me. To be kept from all of us! I swear that was the truth. I knew then that Flora had also seen the figure of Miss Jessel across the lake, just as Miles had seen Quint. The girl had said nothing of it to me—only to Miles. If Flora had been alone, I fear she would have gone without protest, through the veil of death. Thank God I was there."

"Tell me," I asked, "did you ever see these figures indoors?"

"I believe so, though Bly is a dark house with too few windows. A little while later, just as November twilight was vanishing into dark, I crossed the upper gallery of the staircase and saw a man on the half-landing below. If I went down he would have gone before I got there. There were two men on the estate at the time, the gardener and the groom. It was neither of them. I knew that it must be Quint. He stared up at me, as he had stared down from the tower, though I could not tell his face this time. Then my candle went out and there was only a glimmer of cold twilight in the glass above me and a gleam on a polished stair below. By the time I lit the candle again, the figure had gone."

"And Miss Jessel?"

"Several weeks later, from the top landing in the dark, I made out the figure of a woman sitting on a bottom stair with her head in her hands. She seemed to be weeping, like Hecuba in vengeful mourning. The image vanished in a moment. I could not see her face but I know it was she."

"Did you ever see her at close range?" I asked.

"Yes." Miss Temple turned slightly and stared through the window at the roses in the hospital garden. "Feeling a little unwell, I came back early from church on a Sunday morning at the end of November. It was ten minutes or so before the end of the service. The figure of Miss Jessel was standing by my own desk at the far end of the schoolroom, on the upper floor. It was daylight, clear noonday light. She was once more the tragic heroine. For a second, she seemed unaware of me, as though we were in different worlds. This time I was not afraid, Dr Watson. I faced her, filled with anger, and shouted, 'You terrible, miserable woman!' She remained quite still, as if uncertain whether she had heard anything. And then she vanished."

"How did she vanish?" I asked.

The young woman sighed, as if at the impossibility of being believed.

"She was simply no longer there, Dr Watson. How shall I describe it? The brilliant sunlight of that morning came in a beam through the window. It shone directly into my eyes, as if the clouds had suddenly cleared. For an instant I could see nothing but dazzle, like a bad migraine but with no headache. Then the air was black for a moment, as in a faint. Afterwards I could see only dust floating in an empty sunbeam where the woman had been before. I had suffered faintness and mottled dark—a shimmering mottled dark. I stepped out of this and my eyes emptied of her."

"And you had been feeling unwell in church?"

She shrugged and nodded.

"Perhaps I fainted away for a few seconds, but I did not fall. There was a moment like that after I first saw Quint upon the tower. As if some lapse of consciousness for a few seconds had left me standing where I was. Who knows? Cannot a shock wipe out consciousness? That morning, when I came to myself, I was clutching the schoolroom table for support. The last terrible day with Miles was something of the kind."

"Shock may explain it," I said.

"But it will not explain her," she said fiercely, "for that was Miss Jessel in the schoolroom, if Miss Jessel ever was!"

I continued to study Miss Temple. Was she one of those hysterics who expend all their energy in an emotional crisis and then faint into unawareness? "I knew no more," she had said of Quint's disappearance from the tower. Miss Jessel in the schoolroom dissolved into sunlight and dust. A few weeks later, at the moment of her revival in the dining-room, the weight in her arms was the body of the dead boy, of whose precise moment of death she seemed unaware. My friend's voice roused me from these thoughts.

"Tell me, Miss Temple," he was saying gently, "Why were you so sure that the children saw the apparitions? They were not together on any one occasion, were they?"

She was eager to answer.

"They were not, Mr Holmes. Miles saw only Quint—or so I believe. I saw the child standing on the grass in the early dark, looking up at the garden tower as I had done when I saw that man. From where I stood indoors, of course I could see no one. But that child saw someone if ever a child did. I swear it. His little face told a story, betrayed a secret, call it what you will."

"And Flora?" I prompted her.

"Flora saw only Miss Jessel. Yet I swear brother and sister were accomplices, each sharing a secret with the other. Had you seen them together, you would not doubt it. I knew! I was closer to them than their parents had been, than their guardian could be. Ask Mrs Grose! She was there the second time that Miss Jessel appeared across the lake. She was certain that Flora had seen, as I had seen—for she herself felt the presence of that horrible being!"

"Oblige me by describing that second afternoon at the lake," said Holmes patiently. His voice was quiet, but we were now coming to a crisis. Miss Temple looked about her, as though she might be overheard by an invisible presence in that plain hospital room. Then she faced us.

"That was a damp and grey afternoon about an hour before early dusk. I could hear Miles practising in the schoolroom, playing the piano. The Beethoven Minuet in G was one of his accomplishments. Mrs Grose came to me because she was sure Flora had gone out without her hat. Why I cannot tell you—but I could scarcely breathe for fear. I knew the child had gone to that dead woman and that something fearful might have happened already. Mrs Grose and I ran out—down the avenue of the herbaceous borders to the bank of the lake. There was no sign of Flora, but I had a dreadful picture in my mind of the child's face floating under the water by the lily pads.

"The mooring was empty, the little rowing-boat had gone. Flora might have taken it, but there was no sign of her. We walked quickly round past the rhododendrons, where they trail in the water. We saw the boat, moored to a stake. It had gone by the time we returned. I breathed again as I saw the child standing a short way off. She was looking across the water, not at us but at the far bank. I walked up to her and asked directly, "'Where, my pet, is Miss Jessel?'

"She gave me a smitten glare. I followed her eyes across the water. On the opposite bank—more than a hundred feet away with the wild trees behind her—was a wraith in shabby black, rigidly still, a terrible sardonic face. Her eyes were on Flora.

"'She's there!' I cried out to Mrs Grose. 'She's there!' I felt a thrill of joy at producing the proof of it. Surely the housekeeper could see! How could she not? I was not mad, after all! But Mrs Grose was so frightened by my cry that she stared at me, rather than across the lake. I raised my arm, but when she turned to follow the line of my finger it was too late, the vision had faded. From my behaviour, Mrs Grose never doubted that I had seen something. Flora turned upon me and cried out that she saw nothing.

"'I never have! I think you're cruel,' she sobbed. She hugged Mrs Grose's skirts and pleaded, 'Take me away from her.' And that good woman calmed her in the only way she could, saying, 'Nobody's there—when poor Miss Jessel's dead and buried.' What else could she say to a distressed child? It would have been more than her employment was worth! When I pointed again, the figure that beckoned the child across the water had already dissolved in air. My last chance to save Flora had been lost."

There was silence between us in the visiting-room. Holmes changed direction, as if to prevent Miss Temple brooding too long.

"How did Miles take his dismissal from school?"

Miss Temple looked surprised.

"He wanted to go back, if not to King Alfred's then to some other school. That was natural enough. He talked as if I were the child and Flora what he called a 'baby.' He would insist, 'I want to see more life. I want to be with my own sort.' Because he knew I thought him so pure and beautiful, he added, 'Think me for a change bad.' He spoke for all the world as if he were the man and I the child. 'Look here, my dear,' he said, 'when in the world am I going back to school?'"

I could see, like a torpedo through the water, the question that Holmes was about to launch and which must not be asked now. It was a demand to hear of the last terrible moments with Miles. I judged that Victoria Temple's nerves were exhausted. If I did not bring the interview to a halt, she most certainly would. There might be such an outburst as would make any further visit impossible.

So I cut short my friend's inquiry.

"You have done enough, Miss Temple. More than enough in agreeing to discuss these difficult matters so bravely with us. Please believe that we shall do all we can to help you. If we return, it will only be to clarify points of detail. Thanks to you, the great part of the work is done."

From the look that Holmes gave me, he thought our work was anything but done. Yet I knew as a medical man that this inquisition had gone as far as was prudent. Perhaps we should one day discuss with Miss Temple the last moments of Miles Mordaunt. If not, then we must shift for ourselves.

We left our client and pleaded the mandate of Bradshaw's railway time table to avoid a tea-table conversation with Dr Annesley.

As our country carriage rattled back to Wokingham over the uneven surface of the lanes, I said, "Hysteria may explain her loss of awareness on three occasions. Quint disappearing from the tower. Miss Jessel vanishing in the schoolroom. The governess coming to her senses with Miles dead in her arms. It is not always required that an hysterical personality should fall into an outright swoon. And then there is a recovery, a return of the senses."

My friend frowned across the passing hedgerows to the Surrey hills as he spoke.

"'Some unseen mysterious principle again sets in motion the magic pinions and the wizard wheels. The silver cord was not for ever loosed, nor the golden bowl irreparably broken. But where, meantime, was the soul?'"

"Edgar Allan Poe," I said, recognising the quotation. "I am there before you, Holmes!"

"If we rule out apparitions, what are we left with except the fragile psychic mechanism of Miss Victoria Temple?"

He drew from the pocket of his travelling cloak a silver flask, a present from a grateful royal personage in a case of alleged cheating at baccarat. We shared a tot of cognac in place of the tea we had abandoned. My friend watched a carter's wagon edging past us in the other direction. Then he resumed.

"We are left with the detection of a crime. Let us return to the practical question. Why should anyone—living or dead—desire the death of this ten-year-old schoolboy? Why should an apparition bother to entice him to the eternal exile of the damned? *Cui bono*, as the lawyers' dog Latin has it—who would benefit? There, if anywhere, lies the answer."

He tapped his walking-stick thoughtfully against his boot and continued in one of his characteristic monologues.

"Did you not observe, Watson, the most curious omission in this afternoon's interview?"

"I was not aware of any omission."

"Were you not? Really? When Miss Temple arrived at Bly, Miles Mordaunt was not yet there. He was dismissed from King Alfred's some weeks later. His offence was so injurious to the other children that Dr Clarke could not permit him to remain. What offence was so terrible in a child of ten that all his future hopes and prospects must be destroyed in this manner? And why was it left under a veil of mystery? Did not Miss Temple know what it was? A child cannot be expelled from school without a reason! James Mordaunt was evidently in France, and she was the only responsible person available to receive notification. Yet she said nothing of it."

"Why did you not ask her?"

"The fact that Miss Temple chose not to reveal it is far more important to our case than the exact peccadillo of Miles Mordaunt."

He was right, of course. I was left to my own meditations.

"Miss Temple found him beautiful in soul and body," I said presently, thinking aloud, "Except for his refusal to admit seeing the apparitions, which seems to me evidence of his common sense."

He ignored this and returned to his strong practical objections.

"It is time to put the apparitions on one side, Watson. We must not forget that in the first place we are dealing with a recorded crime of homicide. We shall overturn the verdict against Miss Temple only by following the evidence. It is plain to me that our next step must be to establish the cause—and equally important, the circumstances—of Miles Mordaunt's dismissal from school."

I laughed at this.

"An old-fashioned headmaster of King Alfred's like Austen Clarke will not discuss scandal with us! You may be sure of that."

"Happily, I think we may dispense with Dr Clarke's assistance. King Alfred's is situated at Blackdown, within the Douglas family's area of influence. The current edition of *Who's Who*? informs me that it has educated two cousins of Hereward Douglas, Galahad and Lancelot. I believe our client can procure an introduction to a master able to throw light on the boy's disgrace. Your invaluable Bradshaw will suggest a convenient train. This time we shall require the Great Western line to Taunton—and the dining car."

3

Dr Austen Clarke was not approachable. His pride was to have been a boy at the most exalted Victorian school, Thomas Arnold's Rugby. He would never admit—let alone discuss—the expulsion of one of his own pupils. Fortunately our client's elder cousin, Galahad Douglas, had spent four years at King Alfred's before graduating to Eton. He offered to approach its modern-minded history master, William Spencer-Smith.

It was the headmaster who had put all blame squarely on Miles Mordaunt. This ten-year-old had sinned against heaven, in the shape of the school rules, and must go. His continued presence would "injure" the other children. By contrast, the history master, William Spencer-Smith, had argued that the school owed a duty of care towards this troubled boy and that it had failed him.

Galahad Douglas reported that Spencer-Smith would receive us on two conditions. First, our conversation must remain confidential. Second, Dr Clarke must not be told of our visit on any account. I diagnosed Spencer-Smith as an unquiet spirit who was relieved by the chance to talk of his troubles.

We left Baker Street for Paddington Station and the Taunton train on a morning just before the boys of King Alfred's returned from their Easter holidays. At the Somerset market town, a rusty one-horse hackney cab was waiting in the station approach. Holmes instructed the driver to drop us outside the school gates and await our return.

On the edge of the town, the creeper-covered stone of King Alfred's, with its low, crenellated central tower, was a copy of Oxford colleges built two centuries ago. The wide front lawn had been planted with a fine cedar of Lebanon and a stone-cross memorial to the fallen alumni of the Crimean and South African wars. Within the main building lay the Great Hall, class-rooms, dormitories and chapel. The high view from the rear terrace encompassed playing fields, cricket pavilion, with the bleak heights of Exmoor and Dunkery Beacon in the distance.

Here the senior boys lived and worked. The juniors walked in for breakfast from several large houses nearby, each named after a royal dynasty: Tudor, Stuart, Brunswick and Hanover. A note in the margin of Miss Temple's journal informed us that Miles had been a member of Brunswick for two years. His house-master was Mair Loftus, a Cambridge Master of Arts who also taught chemistry.

During the holidays the main building was silent and its grounds deserted. Yet William Spencer-Smith remained in residence. This was his home, for he had no other. We followed the porter up a wide staircase with glimpses of long dormitories and neat rows of beds to either side. At the top landing, a narrow corridor ran off under the eaves of the building. Our guide knocked on a door at the far end and we entered Spencer-Smith's cross-beamed room, immediately below the tiles.

He was a short, rotund man in his thirties with a face that was soft and kindly, his manner nervously evasive. This uneasy disposition was kept in check by quick smiles and rapid talk. I guessed that he was ragged by the boys more than he deserved.

Two broken-down easy chairs, a sofa, a cluttered desk and a length of overcrowded bookshelves made up his spartan furniture. The contents of the room were a match for his shabby jacket and flannels. As we shook hands, a westerly Atlantic wind rattled the old bones of the school at this height. After we had taken our places in the chairs, he came quickly to the point.

"I have agreed to talk of this matter—Mr Holmes—Dr Watson—because I blame myself in part for the outcome. I have thought a good deal about it. Had I argued more vigorously on the child's behalf, he might still be alive. Who knows?"

"But no longer at King Alfred's," Holmes suggested.

Spencer-Smith shrugged.

"Of course he sometimes made mischief. What boy of spirit does not, at his age? The tragedy is that we sent him home just after his parents had died, when we should have cared for him. After all is said and done, he was only a child of ten. We might have saved him from himself. The unfortunate young governess inherited the difficulties we bequeathed to her. To be sure, the dead are beyond our aid, but it is of the highest importance that we should do all in our power for the living."

"Your feelings do you credit," Holmes said courteously, "To put it briefly, Miss Temple is confined in a criminal lunatic asylum. She is there because a verdict of insanity was agreed upon by the Crown and the defence—a convenient decision which now seems grievously in error."

As they talked of Victoria Temple's plight, I scanned the bookshelves. There was little to suggest the history master, but a good deal of mental philosophy, individual psychology and the education of the child.

"You must tell me what I can do," our host was saying. "It is a terrible thing for an innocent woman to be tormented in such a way. Galahad Douglas spoke to me of her misfortune."

Holmes stretched back in his chair.

"Miles Mordaunt was dismissed from school," he said languidly. "Pray tell me why. It was never made clear by Dr Clarke to the family nor to the governess."

Spencer-Smith stared past us as though he saw something at the far end of his long garret room.

"Did he steal?" Holmes prompted him, and the poor fellow shook his head.

I put my own question before he could continue.

"It was alleged that he harmed the others. Was he immoral or depraved in some way?"

"He was not."

"Then what did he do that he must be dismissed?" I persisted.

"He said things."

I was about to ask what these things were. Holmes took another tack.

"To whom did he say them? It is of the greatest importance that we should have witnesses."

"He would never give us their names. One or two admitted it of their own accord. He spoke only to a few boys, I think. To those he liked."

Glancing at Holmes, I saw an impatient tightening of the mouth.

"And they repeated his words to others?"

"Yes. To those they liked. As a special secret, I suppose. Boys of that age are excitable. They love secrets but they never keep them."

Spencer-Smith paused. When he spoke again it was with great deliberation.

"You should understand, Mr Holmes, that Miles Mordaunt was not as other boys. He was with us for two years but he never fitted in."

"He was in Brunswick House, I believe?"

Spencer-Smith nodded.

"He was one of the second-year Brunswicks. Though he was intellectually gifted, he lacked normal physical stamina and agility. Perhaps he had been unwell, in some way unknown to us, before he came to King Alfred's. At all events, he avoided games and sports whenever he could. The others would take a cold plunge at Parson's Pool, where the river bends. He never did. I do not believe he could swim a stroke to save his life. Well now, a boy of that type in a school of this sort either goes under or learns to acquire strength of a different kind. He gains power over the minds of others, unless his life is to be made a misery. He must be stronger in brain than they can ever be in body. That is the key to this child's character."

"And so he said things?" Holmes suggested laconically. "I suppose, in the end, these things came round to you?"

"They did. But it was not I who told Dr Clarke." He looked hastily from one to the other of us. "That was done by the chaplain and another senior master before I could intervene. I should have spoken to the boy first."

"You have no objection to revealing what the child said to his friends?"

Spencer-Smith looked still more uneasy.

"You need not fear that we shall betray confidences," Holmes added quietly.

The history master shook his head.

"I only fear that you may think me ridiculous." He paused awkwardly, then continued. "Miles Mordaunt told his friends that he had received supernatural powers. Others said that he claimed he had sold his soul to the devil in exchange for such powers. I could find no conclusive evidence that he ever said anything of the sort. It was hearsay."

I intervened.

"Surely he was not expelled for hearsay?"

The selling of a soul is utter nonsense to an intelligent adult. Yet it might be terrible for a child of ten to boast of it. The more I heard of Miles Mordaunt, the more I thought the boast was possible. A new intensity in my friend's deep-set eyes suggested that he took this seriously.

"Did he offer his friends evidence of these powers?" Holmes asked.

"He was good at tricks, tricks of all kinds." Spencer-Smith lit a cigarette, as if to steady him for what lay ahead. He shook out the match. "That made some of the others uneasy about him and some admired him. For example, he boasted of his occult power to materialise in two places at the same time. He could produce his doppelgänger, as he called it."

"Where did he hear the word, at his age?"

"I have no idea, Dr Watson. But he proved it to them. In the previous summer, the school photograph was taken on the front lawn, with the main building as its background. The boys wore the short jackets and striped trousers of their 'Eton suits' and stood in long rows, ranged according to height."

He nodded at an assortment of framed prints on the far wall and then continued.

"When the photographs were printed, a slightly-built, fair-haired junior was at the left-hand end of the back row. That was Miles Mordaunt."

"Where was the trick?"

"Behind him, doctor. As I mentioned, the front of the school building was the background. There is a three-sided oriel window in a room to the right of the main entrance door. Within the diagonal leaded lights of its Tudor window, forty feet or so behind the row at whose far end the boy stood, was also the face of Miles Mordaunt. It was a fainter image but beyond doubt it was the same child with the same look of frustrated energy. To credulous junior boys of eight or nine, he offered it as proof of his ability to materialise in two places at the same time.

"A prank," said Holmes dismissively, "I daresay few of his dupes knew that such long photographs are taken in sections and matched together. Miles Mordaunt had only to stand within the window when the process began and then sneak round to the end of the back row before the camera lens shifted its angle."

"With his friends who knew that, he treated it as a secret joke. If they did not know, he made it a demonstration of his psychic powers."

"He was surely not dismissed for such a game!" I said.

"But that was only the beginning, Dr Watson. Next came a series of rumours, dark secrets confided to close friends. He described to one crony how he had drowned his sister's governess when she betrayed a promise. The intensity of his confessions was such that even you might almost believe him, until you knew better. Her death was thought to be a tragic mishap and he was never suspected. There was no truth in this. The poor lady died of natural causes at her father's home, many miles away. She was, of course, replaced by Miss Temple."

"A great misfortune, as it turns out!" said Holmes softly.

"Mr Holmes, there was also a man at Bly, who died in an accident. He was a servant of some kind . . ."

"Quint," I said at once.

"I believe so, Dr Watson. He and the boy were great chums, according to Miles. There were no other males in the household—except possibly a gardener from the outlying estate. Quint, if that was his name, had warned the boy never to let himself be put upon by any governess or female servant. Better drown them like kittens than let them grow to be cats, Quint had said, if the boy was to be believed."

"And that was the worst that Miles said?" I asked.

"Unhappily not, Dr Watson. The boy gathered a coven about him. By closing his right fist, then extending the thumb and small finger, he taught those who swore allegiance to him how to exercise the curse of the evil eye. He confided to them how he had placed curses on those who crossed him and how these had been fulfilled. He always tailored this to misfortunes which had actually occurred, so that he was more easily believed."

I was about to inquire where a child of his age could have picked up such poisonous nonsense, but the thought of Peter Quint provided an answer.

"A boy so young!" I said incredulously.

"Just so, doctor. Children may be capable of the worst imaginings and dishonesties."

I followed his gaze as he spoke. Subconsciously he had led me to a bookshelf and a volume of *Cases at Salem: Drawn from Pleas of the Crown.* How strange to be reminded in this sunlit room of those innocent American men and women sworn to their deaths by children in the famous witch trials two centuries ago.

"He was believed by the junior boys?" Holmes asked.

"Not at first, I daresay. Yet it gave him an air—a reputation for malevolent power. To silence the doubters, he undertook to prove publicly the powers which his demon—Quint perhaps—had conferred upon him."

Holmes sat back with his fingers folded together, missing no word nor nuance of the young master's explanation.

"He performed his tricks, Mr Holmes. I cannot put it any other way. For instance, he claimed that he could see through walls. He could even see into the skulls of others and read their thoughts."

"What was his proof?"

Our host thought for a moment.

"It varied. Several times, to my knowledge, he used a pair of dice. Two boys would go into another room—even into another building—and roll the dice. Miles could not possibly see the result. He told them to take the figure on the left hand die and double it. They must then add five to that answer and multiply the whole by five. Finally they must add the number on the right hand die. Once they gave him that total, even though they had been a dozen miles away, he would give them the precise numbers on the two dice, which he now saw in their minds. He was never wrong. He claimed that he could read their minds as plainly as they themselves. Some of the little boys grew afraid of him. A few began to believe in the things that he told them. Even the seniors grew wary of him."

"A mathematical dodge with a pair of dice!" said Holmes scornfully. "He had learnt it somewhere—from an adult, of course. Who taught him, I wonder? Let me tell you, Mr Spencer-Smith, it is a trick based on multiplication by five. Once his dupes gave him the final total, all he needed to do was subtract from it the square of five. Twenty-five. That would invariably and infallibly give him the numbers on the two dice. So, for example, sixty-two would always equal six-plus-two, thirty-five would always give him three-plus-five. It never fails. It is no more magic nor witchcraft than a recipe for plum pudding! But surely he was not expelled—even for this?"

"No, Mr Holmes. His downfall was the Five Stones murder in the neighbourhood of his home, far away at Bly. I daresay you have heard of it? A mill-owner was driving a cart with a barrel of gold coins, believing that no one knew of his cargo. It was the quarter's takings from several saw-mills which he was carrying to his safe. It was a good deal of money and he had been careful to tell no one of it, as he thought. Unfortunately for him, his route was known to the robber, even if the size of the cargo was not. He was attacked and clubbed to death while crossing the heathland near the prehistoric Five Standing Stones of Bly. Little remains of four stones, but the fifth is still upright. The perpetrators were never caught. For no good reason, it was locally believed that there were five robbers—as there were five stones at the scene of the crime. The fifth, supposed to be the actual murderer, was popularly nicknamed the Fifth Stone."

"I have heard of the crime," said Holmes tolerantly.

"But why was the child expelled from school?" I persisted.

"For what followed, Dr Watson. The master of Brunswick House, Mair Loftus, was not an amiable man. Ill-tempered, strict and pious, he kept his wife and son in fear of him. He was a rasping bully. To all criticism, he replied, 'When I was a junior boy, I feared my master. Now, by God, these juniors shall fear me.' He has since left us. Miles cordially loathed the man and, quite simply, set out to destroy him. For devilment, I suppose, this little boy swore to his friends that he knew a secret about this murder committed near his home. Mair Loftus, all the way down in the West Country, was an accomplice of the Fifth Stone. This housemaster was the receiver of the stolen gold. Little by little, Miles told his friends, the robber brought the gold coins all the way down to Somerset. Loftus changed them at his bank into negotiable notes and even into government bonds. Who would suspect a schoolmaster, especially one with a private income? Miles swore that he had this story from the Fifth Stone himself."

Sherlock Holmes shook his head thoughtfully.

"Wait, Mr Holmes," said Spencer-Smith abruptly. "Brunswick House is a red-brick residence, a home to thirty junior boys. Close to its rear door is a very large, quick-growing Monterey cypress. It should have been felled years ago but now its base is quite four feet across. Miles assured his friends that if they put their ears to the bark and listened very carefully, they might hear whispering. With the breezes from Exmoor and the Bristol Channel in the branches, it was not difficult for some children to convince themselves and their friends that they heard whispers.

Perhaps they could not make out the words. But rumour runs like fire through a community of small boys. If two or three believed it, the rest were not to be left out."

Holmes sat back, finger-tips tracing patterns on the padded leather arm of his chair.

"According to Miles Mordaunt," Spencer-Smith continued, "the proceeds of the robbery had been worth a fortune. The Fifth Stone still visited Mair Loftus, to trade gold for bank-notes. In a hollow within the base of this giant pine—a small kiosk, as it were, with underground access—the two conspirators met to negotiate the disposal of the booty. The power of seeing into rooms and minds, which Miles had already demonstrated, enabled him to detect what was going on. It was a yarn straight out of a penny dreadful."

"Pray continue," said Holmes softly. "You have my complete attention."

"Mair Loftus had always acted as if his duty was to keep the boys in awe of him. This child showed an extraordinary adult subtlety and intelligence. Because most of the boys shared his loathing of Loftus they were eager to believe that they also heard the whispering of words in the trunk of the old fir tree. After all, they had seen Miles Mordaunt's occult powers demonstrated elsewhere."

"And now they believed him in this case?" I asked.

"It was as if there was another personality within him, Dr Watson," said Spencer-Smith sadly, "or perhaps one that had taken him over. To hear him speak, to watch his mannerisms, was to believe that an adult was imprisoned in the body of an underdeveloped child of ten."

"And in due course these stories of Mr Loftus reached Dr Clarke?" Holmes inquired.

"They came to the chaplain first and thence to the headmaster. They were absurd!"

"His parents," I said suddenly, "were they dead by this time?"

"The news had barely reached us. I understand they had both died during a single cholera epidemic in India. Because the news was received just as the decision to dismiss their son from school was taken, our action seemed the more heartless. Now here is another curiosity for you. The boy himself appeared quite unaffected by the loss of his parents. It was almost like a liberation, a confirmation that he had left childhood behind him."

"It is a moral oddity perhaps," I said, "but not unknown to medicine."

"Not entirely an oddity, Dr Watson. Colonel Mordaunt's regiment had been in India for most of the child's life. Miles cannot have been close to his parents in any case, though our rules required him to write to them every week on Sunday afternoon. He can rarely have seen them. Perhaps he had come to resent their desertion of him, as it may have seemed to him."

"What arrangements were made for him after their deaths?"

"Of course he was his father's heir as lord of the manor of Bly, though he would not come into the property until he was twenty-one. The guardian of both the children and trustee of the estate was automatically his uncle."

"And he was . . ." Holmes prompted him.

"Colonel Mordaunt's only brother, Major James Mordaunt, an Army surgeon-major in his youth. I understand he had seen service in India and Afghanistan. He remains a bachelor with no pretensions to marriage or fatherhood, as I was told—certainly not to practicing medicine any longer. When their father died twenty years ago, Colonel Charles Mordaunt inherited Bly, as the eldest son, but the major was also provided for. He lives sometimes in a fashionable area of London but mostly in France."

"Then what became of Miles and Flora?" I asked.

"Major Mordaunt did his best, while their parents were in India. He had no true interest in them. I do not recall that he ever visited Miles here. I cannot even say whether he ever saw the children. At any rate, when we sent the boy away, Major Mordaunt had already employed Miss Temple as governess for the little girl. The major insisted time and again that he did not want to be bothered over the children's upbringing. She was to deal with any contingencies as she saw best. Whatever was needed, she had only to ask the lawyers for money."

"So she has told us," said Holmes.

"I argued with Austen Clarke, Mr Holmes, believe me I did. Miles should not have been dismissed from the school. He should have gone to one of the other houses, away from Mair Loftus. We should have helped and cared for him. His so-called necromancy was the silliest nonsense, but the emotional disturbance within him was terribly real. Dr Clarke simply replied that the boy had plotted to destroy the authority of Mr Loftus, to make his position in the school untenable. Subversion of that kind could not be countenanced."

"Tell me," I asked, "was Miles seen by a physician while he was at King Alfred's?"

"He was, Dr Watson. For a week or two he was confined in the school sanatorium with catarrhal pneumonia, an inflammation of one lung which yielded quite readily to treatment. Every boy returning to school at the beginning of each term has to bring a certificate, signed by the family physician, to confirm that he is not suffering from any disease—contagious or otherwise. Miles Mordaunt was not physically robust, as his appearance would suggest, but since then he always seemed buoyant and in high spirits."

"Was he seen by a specialist at the time?"

"I recall that his uncle arranged for him to be seen by a chest specialist in London. It seemed that the boy had made a complete recovery."

Holmes put his hand on the arms of the chair as if about to stand up. Then he paused.

"Can you can tell me, Mr Spencer-Smith, how news of the boy's expulsion was conveyed to his family?"

A hint of frank bewilderment passed across the history master's face.

"Why, Mr Holmes, Dr Clarke wrote a letter to Major Mordaunt, as the boy's guardian, after he had discussed the matter with the rest of us."

"That is not quite what I meant. Dr Clarke did not presumably tell the major that Miles was harming the other boys—and leave it at that?"

Spencer-Smith seemed relieved at the explanation.

"Certainly not. These occasions are happily rare, but the headmaster is always very specific in his reasons. I believe he does this to forestall argument. He naturally cited the harm caused by Miles to the other boys and the undermining of the housemaster's authority. I think you will find that Dr Clarke even reported the substance of the puerile slander so that Major Mordaunt would see that it was impossible for us to keep the boy. I believe there was a temporary dispute of some kind over the amount of school fees which were owing. Major Mordaunt eventually settled the bill."

Holmes relaxed again. He stood up and held out his hand.

"We will impose on you no longer, sir. You have been most patient."

It was now Spencer-Smith who hesitated.

"One more thing, Mr Holmes—a curiosity, perhaps! We had not done the boy justice. I wrote to Major Mordaunt. If he sought another school for Miles, he must call upon me for support in the strongest terms. I am not without influence in other places. He need not fear the outcome."

"And Major Mordaunt responded?"

"His letter thanked me in charming and gracious terms. He would accept my offer in due course. For a while, however, he would entrust the boy to his new governess. The rest you know."

Holmes took the master's hand again.

"You have been most generous with your time and advice, sir."

"If poor Miss Temple is innocently condemned, I am at your service."

We made our way down the narrow corridor and the staircase. Our ancient cab, spattered from the local lanes, was waiting for us. My friend said nothing until we were sitting in a compartment of the London train and the low-lying Somerset pasture-land, still water-logged from spring rains, was slipping past our window. At length he spoke.

"Mr Spencer-Smith has all the trappings of the schoolmaster, does he not, Watson? A man among boys but a boy among men. I fear he and Miss Temple have told us all that they are likely to tell. By-the-by, did you observe a curious detail at the end of our conversation this afternoon?"

"What was that?"

"Major Mordaunt preferred that his nephew should be taught by a governess at Bly, rather than educated at one of our great schools, which Spencer-Smith's offer would have made possible."

"It was too soon after the boy's dismissal. It would have come in time."

Holmes relaxed.

"I wonder. Then that leaves only Bly as the key to the puzzle, perhaps in the hands of the worthy housekeeper, Mrs Grose. I fear we must return to Miss Temple's ghosts."

Two passengers took seats within earshot. He drew his silver cigarette case from an inner pocket. Then he opened a slim mathematical treatise on the enigma of the Riemann hypothesis and spent the rest of the journey to London in a cloud of meditation.

4

None of this persuaded me to believe in Victoria Temple's "apparitions." She was an honest witness, but I had treated too many hysterics and neurotics in twenty years of medical practice to regard such visitations as anything but a disturbance of troubled minds. Like Scrooge in his dream, I would dismiss a nocturnal ghost as nothing but a piece of undigested cheese.

Yet if any place could persuade me of hauntings, I suppose it would be the landscape of Bly. Even the governess's journal of her six months' residence had not prepared me for its air of the remote and the abandoned. Where the ghosts were said to have walked, we were warned that several wooden steps inside the garden tower were now missing. We soon saw for ourselves that the lakeside structures were in decay. A sense of isolation was pervasive. Yet the railway line with restaurant cars and morning newspapers was only five miles away across the fields. There was a village just a mile off and several nearby farms to the north-west.

Our carriage turned from the country lane into a gravelled drive, running over flat pasture through an avenue of tall lime trees. After the traffic and street cries of London, this seemed like the last place on earth. The housekeeper, housemaid, dairy-woman, groom and gardener had done nothing but keep the place tidy for the absentee Major James Mordaunt. But his interest in it had long withered. He had no taste for riding to hounds or weekend parties. Bly's empty rooms, dark corridors and crooked staircases, its stables and yew-tree walks, needed a family complete with attendants. Without them, it was dead.

The house had been built three centuries ago for some Elizabethan Master-in-Chancery or Baron of the Exchequer. Its first owners had been too occupied in the London courts to come down here often. Bays of leaded windows rose handsomely from lawn to rooftop. Yet the prison-grey stone, enclosing its gravelled forecourt, looked no better than cement rendering. This plain front and tall chimneys gave it a barrack-like appearance.

Sherlock Holmes left our driver and strode to a wrought-iron gate leading to the territory of the apparitions: the gardens, lakes and terraces at the rear of the house. Here the dead had "materialised" in full daylight.

The grounds were a pleasant contrast to the dreary front. Their wide lawns were particularly fine. The first was set with oval vase-shaped yew trees, regular as pieces on a chess-board. Beyond it, over the drop of a ha-ha, a broad meadow lay picturesquely detailed beside a willow vale of river trees. Cattle grazed or rested in the shade of ancient oaks.

All that remained of Miss Temple's drama was a child's swing, hanging disused from the canopy of a great cedar tree. A rusted garden roller stood under the boughs of a beech, as if pushed to that point and abandoned for ever. Poignant symbols of two young lives brought to an untimely end! Thankfully, they were not evidence that the cursed spirits of Peter Quint and Miss Jessel now held the children's souls in pawn.

According to Miss Temple's journal, that evil pair manifested themselves on the top of the tower and across the lake. Here they had beckoned the children to destruction, through the gates of hell. Even to catch oneself thinking like this showed the effect of the place on a rational mind.

The lawns and the alleys behind the house ran down to a long ornamental lake, the chief feature of the grounds. A small river fed its waters, controlled by a bank and an iron sluice at the far end. The banks were shaded by ash and sycamore, beech and oak. Level with the rippling surface, stretches of tall rhododendrons in purple bloom trailed their tendrils and scattered their petals among the shallows. Through gaps in the trees, the hills of summer shimmered in a sunlit distance.

This placid lake was large enough to have an island with a dilapidated garden pavilion among its trees. Much of the shimmering surface of the water was covered by clusters of cream water-lilies, some in masses twenty feet across. They looked treacherously like a planting that might support an unwary footfall. Silence and stillness were broken only by a dance of yellow hover-flies in the warmth of the May afternoon.

Despite my scepticism, I recognised our governess's account of the quietness which accompanied her visions. Clouds hung motionless as a stage-set against blue sky. Hardly a falling leaf or a breath of air marked the passing of that calm afternoon.

What a perfect place to fabricate a haunting! What effect must these surroundings have had on a young woman's morbidly nervous temperament! Suppose Maria Jessel or Peter Quint now stepped out before us from the trees on the far bank, a hundred yards away. We were too far off to interrogate them or even to describe them in detail. They would have time to fade—or more probably tiptoe off-stage—before we could reach them.

Holmes paused. From where we now stood Miss Temple had twice seen a handsome young woman, waiting motionless in shabby mourning. My companion interrupted my thoughts.

"I believe, Watson, we may allow ourselves a circuit of the lake. It cannot be more than a mile."

I drew my watch from my waistcoat pocket.

"And what of our engagement to take tea with Mrs Grose?"

He waved this away

"As I intended, we have almost an hour in hand. It will be easier to absent ourselves now than later. I should prefer to examine the shore of the lake by full daylight."

It proved impossible to follow the water's edge at all points. Where rampant overgrowths of tall rhododendrons in luscious bloom prevented this, the footpath took an inland detour for a hundred yards or so. To a photographer or an artist, the view across the water to the far bank might be charming. To me it still remained a place strangely without sound or movement.

Within the hour we came full circle. Our walk ended at a small overgrown area of the bank, boarded over in part as a makeshift landing-stage and otherwise surrendered to weeds. A wooden cradle several feet long supported a delicately-built rowing-boat. It had lost much of its white paint, though its interior looked sound and dry. I doubted whether it had been launched for some months, perhaps not since Miles Mordaunt took Miss Temple "spooning." A stake driven into the shallows at an angle trailed a filament of thin rope, but nothing had been moored there recently.

Holmes broke the silence.

"If Miss Temple is correct in her supposition, Flora rowed alone to the point from which Miss Jessel was seen. When the governess and housekeeper walked back with the child, the boat had gone. The ghostly Miss Jessel cannot have taken it, for she was on the other side of the water. Who then?"

"Miles Mordaunt," I said caustically. "No doubt the young master had wearied of practising Beethoven's minuet! The whole thing is nonsense."

And yet the gardens of Bly House still affected me. Why? I caught myself wondering whether children may not after all be the victims or agents of evil spirits—living rather than dead. Ghosts do not impress me, but I am readily convinced of the existence of human depravity, pitiless and all-devouring in its malice. If you were to argue that such evil influences may somehow survive the death of the body, I would listen with an open mind.

But if Miss Temple truly experienced a vision, reason suggested that she alone was the target. Why else did these alleged apparitions confront her when the children were not present—from the garden tower on a summer evening, at the dining-room window by November lamplight, perhaps even indoors? I looked at my watch again and was cross with my thoughts. Even to think in this way was a sign of reason yielding to tomfoolery.

At one side of the alleys and borders, stretching from the rear of the house to the lake, dusty brick walls divided smaller gardens into a series of enclosures, almost like large open-air rooms. Each enclave of trim grass, pink tea-roses and trailing plants concealed a gardener's store, or a tool-room, or a potting-shed. The structures themselves were abandoned. The potting-shed contained only a scattering of brown leaves and a few pieces of parched earthenware. The spades and jars had gone from the hooks and shelves of the gardener's store, leaving only two fruit-boxes of broken wood.

Holmes examined each forlorn outbuilding until he stood finally at the door of the tool-room with its brick lintel, walls of stone and flint and slate roof. I waited, turning my back and ostentatiously admiring a rough-stone pillar with a figured rustic vase of the seventeenth century on its summit.

Holmes said, "Keep watch for a moment, there's a good fellow."

There was no one to be seen in any direction. How should there be? He took the handle of the tool-room door and turned it. This time it was locked fast. Had it opened, I believe he would have lost all interest. The need to lock this shed when all of the others were open naturally stimulated his curiosity. He opened his pocket-knife and inserted the point of the smallest blade into the keyhole. I tactfully studied the tiger-lilies and agapanthus, enjoying the warmth of the spring sun on my back. Presently I heard a snick of metal and the door of the stone shed creaked open.

"How intriguing, Watson! Tell me what you make of this."

I walked across. The shed had a square small-paned window at its far end. The shelves on either side were bare. On one wall a pair of brackets held two light oars or sculls. It was impossible to be certain but, from the webs strung about them, I should not have thought they had been used for some time.

"Locking one shed which is empty, while leaving the others open," he said to himself, "Not a profound mystery but inviting a question. Why?"

"Hardly a mystery at all!"

"Then let us call it merely the charm of the inconsistent," he said with a smile.

He began to inspect the dusty and cobwebbed interior surfaces. The roof-space had been tightly boarded to provide a ceiling below the slates. He stretched up, doubled his fist and thumped the planking. I heard nothing but a faint reverberation of the wood. The stained and dusty glass of the little panes looked out directly at the lake. He took his reading-lens from his pocket and examined closely the corners and edges of the small glass squares with their mad erratic dance of little flies bred by the sun.

There was nothing here for us. He opened his knife again and turned round.

"And now, Watson, we must be on our way or we shall find our hostess waiting."

We stepped outside and he used the knife blade once again to lock the door behind us.

As we crossed the lawns in silence I thought that the gardens had allowed my friend very little opportunity of putting on one of his erudite performances. He rather liked to begin a visit with something of the kind, like a tenor exercising his larynx before the rise of the curtain. As it was, we left the territory of the apparitions behind us and turned to the homely prospect of afternoon tea.

5

Our cab still waited in the gravelled courtyard. A woman of sixty or so was talking to the driver. Holmes had dressed formally for this visit and he now doffed his black silk hat.

"Good afternoon, madam. You are Mrs Grose, I believe? I am Sherlock Holmes and this is my colleague Dr John Watson. We arrived a little early and have been admiring the glories of your garden. The penstemon, the tea-roses, the agapanthus, the sedum and sweet peas are charming. Your tiger lilies are splendid and your cedar trees are a glory."

Blushing with pleasure, she dropped a half-curtsey. Mrs Grose was a comfortable figure in dark grey dress and white cap. Her face had filled out with age, but the grey wide-set eyes and handsome features suggested that she had been a "stunner" in her youth. A comfortably furnished room was set apart for her on the first floor. Presently we stood in its window, looking down on the geometry of the garden.

"What is on the island at the end of the lake, Mrs Grose?" I inquired

She chuckled.

"Not much, sir! Mostly covered in trees and bushes now. So overgrown you'd very likely hitch a foot and break an ankle. There was a summer house, so called. Hard to see it for the overgrowth now. What the man Quint called the temple of Pros-er pine. Whatever that may be!"

"Pro-ser-pine," said Holmes pedantically. "The goddess of hell."

She pursed her lips.

"Well he should know, Mr Holmes, because that's where he is now. Good riddance to bad rubbish, as they say."

Our hostess shivered but continued her explanation.

"Master Mordaunt, father to Mr Charles and Mr James, built it as a pleasure pavilion, when he came home from Asia. Fitted it up with chairs and cushions, even a piano of sorts that went out in sections on a cattle raft. In those days, they had music and lanterns on summer evenings. But they tired of it all even before the father died. With Mr Charles in India it was left to rot. Then Mr James did nothing to it but wouldn't have it touched, though it had gone so shabby and the raft might have cleared it. I daresay he had some plan of his own."

Mrs Grose put a certain emphasis on this last remark. I guessed the housekeeper and I were thinking of the same plan. Two lovers naked together in perfect safety, as they could never quite be in the house itself. Once the major had taken the only boat to the island, there would be no spies and no interruptions.

"Tell me, Mrs Grose," said Holmes quietly, "are the stone sheds in use at this end of the lake? They appear abandoned, which seems a waste."

"They want taking down and clearing away likewise," she said with a knowing smile. "All the tools were moved last winter when they built the new kitchen garden to the other side of the house. Major Mordaunt was spoken to about it but he had no more interest than his brother used to have. They'll fall down before they're took down. You can't run a house like Bly with an absentee master, sir. And that's what both brothers have been."

With that, it seemed she had been as indiscreet as she was prepared to be. As we sat down, a silver tray was brought in by a maid. She studied Holmes and me as eagerly as if we were exhibits in a zoo.

Mrs Grose poured tea and said, "Master James being in France, as is usual with him in spring, I took on myself to receive you gentlemen here. He hates being bothered and I know as much about the place as he does. Anything that attracted sightseers would be disagreeable to him. If Miss Temple's visions became gossip, we might have folk coming to stand and stare, when summer's here."

"And Major Mordaunt would not care for that," Holmes said firmly.

"I should think not!" She looked at him as if they were sharing a joke. Then she became solemn. "To be fair, though, when Miss Temple was in trouble, he did everything for her. He was away in Paris at the time but he never begrudged a penny of what it cost to save her from prison—or worse. Still, he'd rather those ghosts should be delusions of her poor frightened mind than horrors for the world and its wife to come tripping after."

"And Miss Temple?" I inquired.

Her pause told me that she disliked this question more than the ghosts.

"Of course, sir, we all hope she'll be well again and they'll set her free."

Holmes listened, his left thumb under his chin and two fingers curled across his mouth. Then he lowered his hand and took the tea-cup. "What about you, Mrs Grose? You are not a believer in apparitions?"

She put down the pot and spoke carefully.

"Not exactly, sir. But I was by the lake with Miss Temple and

Miss Flora, the second time Miss Jessel was supposed to appear. The little girl had gone ahead of us. Perhaps she unhitched the boat and rowed to where we found her. She was alone. The boat was almost out of sight, tied to the fence where it comes down to the water."

Holmes nodded, saying, "Miss Temple described seeing Miss Jessel on the far bank, beyond the Middle Deep. On the island. Flora, I believe, was positive she saw no one. You neither saw nor noticed anything?"

"Saw? No, sir. Noticed? It felt for that moment as if the world had stopped. As if you might look at your watch five minutes later and find the time just the same as when it all began. Everything motionless. Just like the figure of Miss Jessel herself was said to be."

"How long did this last?"

She looked at him awkwardly.

"That's just it, sir. I couldn't say."

"Of course not," he said courteously. "And what else?"

"Looking at Miss Temple, I'd take my oath she saw something. Or perhaps she only thought she saw it, but she was not making up a story. Like when she saw Quint at the dining-room window, just before evening church. I never saw anyone then but I was afraid without knowing why. Even Miss Temple said I was white as if I'd seen a ghost myself."

"Was she afraid of these apparitions?"

"Angry, more like."

"And you were there with the children present?"

"Only when Miss Flora was with us by the lake. Just once."

"Of course," said Holmes kindly. "Flora was there, before you and Miss Temple. We shall never know what may have passed between her and the vision of Miss Jessel before you both arrived."

"Something happened to that child, Mr Holmes, while the

world was so quiet and still. Something she was glad of. I stood to one side but Flora was with Miss Temple. And Miss Temple was pointing her to look across to where there was a gap between the bushes on the far bank. I couldn't see because of a rhododendron bush immediately beside me."

She paused, glancing towards the window with the garden view beyond, recalling her thoughts. Then she spoke firmly.

"Miss Flora vowed she never saw anything. But I know children. That child was too upset for nothing to have happened. She clung to my skirts, crying to be taken from her hateful governess! When we were alone together the poor little mite told me horrors. What she heard Miss Temple had said and done at other times. How Miss Temple was in league with the dead, if you please! You may be sure she got that from Master Miles and his loose talk. And she talked scandal of Miss Temple misbehaving with the master! How could she when he was in France? But that child's words shocked me, sir. I can't think where she picked them up, not even from her brother."

Holmes nodded, as if all this was to be expected. To me, such talk of a league with the dead reeked of Miles Mordaunt.

"After the incident at the lake, you took the same route back?" I asked.

"We did."

"And you passed the boat which the little girl had moored there?"

Mrs Grose stiffened, as if caught in an untruth.

"No, sir. We went through the gate in the fence but the boat had gone. Most likely, Master Miles took it while we were further on. It's a little thing, convenient to handle."

Holmes returned to his ghosts.

"At other times, did Miss Temple herself think the children behaved as if they had seen Maria Jessel or Peter Quint, even though she had not?"

She looked from one to the other of us.

"I know children! These two were up to some mischief or other. I'd catch them whispering and laughing together. They'd smile at us, as if they knew what we were thinking. As if saying they'd have their way with us and nothing we could do would prevent it."

It was almost exactly what Victoria Temple had said to us. Perhaps she had got it from Mrs Grose.

"But, so far as you know," Holmes asked, "they did not misbehave behind your backs?"

She looked a little awkward.

"I never told Miss Temple, Dr Watson. They used to creep after her, making a noise, sniggering and mewling. But she'd look round and they'd just be sitting there with their books or games, good as gold. As soon as she looked away they'd start again It was as if they wanted to make her think there might be an animal hidden close by. As if it might be calling for her."

I thought of Quint's policy of drowning kittens so that they should not grow into cats, and my spine tingled. Perhaps sensing something of this, Mrs Grose added, "It was nothing to Miss Temple, sir. She never condescended to notice it."

Without thinking sufficiently, I asked a question that sounded ill-judged as soon as it was spoken.

"If it was ever necessary to drown unwanted kittens on the estate, would Miles have been allowed to do it?"

Mrs Grose gave a soft, surprised laugh.

"Bless you, sir, no! A child? Never!"

"Who then?"

"If ever it came . . ." She paused. "Quint the handyman. Who else?"

That was the last thing I wanted to hear.

"And the boy might be there with him?"

"There was no reason for it."

"But he might let the boy be there as a special favour?" I persisted.

I caught her sudden realisation, quickly masked by a grimace of distaste.

"Oh," she said awkwardly, "it might happen. Anything like that might happen."

Holmes interrupted.

"What did the children talk of between themselves? Did you ever overhear them?"

She shook her head.

"Miss Temple swore they talked of horrors, hearing the voices of the damned. She only saw visions of Quint and Miss Jessel, but the children might hear their voices as well. Just as a dog or a cat can hear sounds a man can't."

I had blundered a moment ago and now I must intervene on behalf of common sense.

"Suppose that there were no ghosts, Mrs Grose. Suppose the two figures were common intruders, as Miss Temple first thought. Could they not stand where she could see them but you could not? Could not trespassers reach the places where she saw them, without being challenged?"

The cautious soul reckoned this up. Then she replied.

"Anyone can come up the drive or over the meadow. They might be seen and asked their business—or not. Keeping to the path through Bly woods, they need not be seen."

"And indoors?"

"Miss Temple told me she thought she saw Quint and Miss Jessel on the stairs in the dark. But without a candle she'd never see who was below her. And they'd be gone before she could get down there."

"And the garden tower?"

"The first time she saw Quint he was on the tower. An intruder might get there through the house. The wooden stairs badly want mending, have done for ages. But no one goes up there, so no one bothers. And no one locks the doors by day. Except for Miss Temple and the children, there'd hardly be anyone about when the servants were below stairs. We'd only be upstairs to lay fires, make beds, polish furniture and the like. And serve dinner, of course."

Holmes intervened courteously.

"On a Sunday morning in November, Miss Temple came home early from church. She thought she was alone in the house and went into the schoolroom. Miss Jessel was standing at the far end by her desk. Miss Temple recalls shouting, 'You terrible, miserable woman!' In an instant the figure dissolved to dust in a beam of sunlight. Our friend lost all sense of where she was until she came to herself a moment later. The same loss of consciousness occurred when Miles died in her arms."

"I think she had what they call 'drops,' Mr Holmes. It was spoken about by doctors at her trial. But you know that already, sir. More than that I can't tell you."

Time was pressing and I was determined to hunt out the evil genius.

"What of our other ghost, Peter Quint? Why did no one like him?"

She wrinkled her brow.

"He was low, doctor. Low and mean. Too free with the maid-servants. Much too free with Miss Jessel—and she with him. Too free with the boy, worst of all. Major Mordaunt was squire while his brother was in India. But the major was seldom here. He gave his valet the run of Bly. I've seen Quint, with my own eyes, wearing smart clothes or fancy links and chains that I knew to be his master's. He went like a gentleman in stolen clothes to be handy with the parlourmaids or village girls. Even a little piece where his hair was gone at the front. Call that a gentleman!"

"And his dealings with the children?"

"He never came near Miss Flora. I saw to that. Master Miles was God's angel, until Quint came here. That fellow taught him to talk to women."

She paused as if I had not caught her true meaning.

"To talk to women like a man, not a child" she insisted. "A boy of eight or nine, if you please! Quint taught him things a boy shouldn't know until he's a man."

"And what of Miles's dismissal from school?" my friend interposed.

"Whatever wickedness the child took to school, sir, he got it from Quint. He was in that man's company from breakfast to dinner!"

"And Major Mordaunt? Did he not know the boy was dismissed from school?"

"That was a bad business, Mr Holmes. Major Mordaunt should never have acted as he did. The headmaster wrote to him that Miles was dismissed. When the major saw Dr Clarke's writing on the envelope, he never opened it. He sent it on to Miss Temple with a note saying the headmaster was a bore. She was to deal with it, whatever it was. Probably school fees owing. She could arrange that with the lawyers. He was just off to France, if you please!"

"So he did not know that the boy had been dismissed?"

"Not then, sir. Of course, Miss Temple wrote to tell him. Then to cap it all, as we found out too late, Miles used to open her letters to the master while they were lying on the hall-stand here to be posted. He read this one and destroyed it. I once heard him say outright that he wouldn't have a servant-girl—that's what he called her!—sneaking to his uncle. Before the major got wind of all that had happened, the poor child was in his coffin."

"Thank you," said Holmes encouragingly. "Now, if I may impose on you for the last time, how did Peter Quint die?"

Her face reflected an aversion to this repetition of the man's name.

"Miles was still away at school. Miss Jessel was here as governess to Miss Flora. I shan't forget that night. Quint used to come out of the village inn, always the worse for drink. It was a winter midnight with the roads like glass. He must have come a real cropper on the ice. In the darkness he came down with a proper smash. Went flying into the wall of the little bridge that crosses the stream and cut his head open on the stone-work. That lane leads nowhere but up to Bly House. So he was only found next morning. The blood from his wound had frozen and he was dead."

"There was an inquest?"

"Of course. What could it say? Accidental death."

Holmes's eyes suggested it might have said a good deal more.

"And by then Quint had corrupted the boy?"

Mrs Grose stared at him, straight and hard, as if prepared to reveal something she had kept locked in her heart.

"That man was a fountainhead of corruption, Mr Holmes!" The good woman paused, self-conscious at such a chapel-preacher's phrase. Then she continued. "I may not have seen the ghosts, Mr Holmes, but as soon as Miss Temple described the figure on the tower, I knew who it was. Dead or alive! His eyes were the worst. He caught yours and never let them go. His were hard as jet and black as hell. You couldn't wait to look away and give him the satisfaction of staring you out!"

Holmes nodded again.

"And what of Quint's conduct with Miles Mordaunt?"

"He acted like the boy's tutor more than a valet. If Master Miles was bad at King Alfred's, Quint made him bad before the child ever went there. Miss Temple thought the boy an angel, even though he came back in disgrace. Quint was dead by then, of course. She told me both children had an unnatural beauty, an unnatural goodness. Something from another world. But I heard Master Miles tell her once that he was bad. Then he laughed at her, as if he was telling her there was nothing she could do about it. He was the master—her master."

"Very well," said Holmes patiently. "How was Miles bad when Quint was still here?"

"I warned the boy that he was a gentleman's son and not to put himself under a menial. And what do you think? Miles turned round on me and swore Quint was a gentleman. Quint had been a soldier. Quint knew something of the world. I was the 'menial,' if you please, the scullery-maid. That was the very word he used to me—this boy of eight or nine, as he was then! After that he lied and was impudent—and Quint protected him. I could do nothing with him. That's how he came to be sent to King Alfred's. To make him knuckle under."

"And when he came back in disgrace?"

"He was worse! He got his way with Miss Temple by smiles and bossing. As Quint would have done. As if Quint was whispering to him, dead or alive. He courted his governess, this child, like a grown man. He had Quint's way with women. What was it he called her one day, talking to me? Words I don't just recall, Mr Holmes, but they gave me a shudder."

"Indeed," said my friend indulgently.

The sunlight moved from the lawn and cedar tree at the side of the house. Mrs Grose seemed about to tell us something we should not care for.

"I would not harm Miss Temple, sir, but I must speak the truth."

"The truth will not harm her, Mrs Grose."

"The foolishness was on both sides, sir. If Master Miles courted her like a grown man, she behaved like his obedient sweetheart. He could do what he liked with her and she would forgive him. She never seemed sure of herself with him. Out of her depth, you might say."

"You need not fear that it will damage her case, Mrs Grose," said Holmes quietly. But he showed no inclination to inquire further.

I recalled Dr Annesley mentioning Miles Mordaunt's boast of "spooning" with his young governess. I had felt uneasy, though reassured on meeting her. The fragile emotional balance of this young woman had been the sport of predatory children—as well as of her own "ghosts" in her imagination. Why did the little ones taunt her with their mewling of cats behind her back? Why had the boy boasted falsely to his cronies at school of having drowned his governess? Why were kittens to be drowned before they could grow into cats? Thanks to Holmes, I had read a little of the new psychopathology. Professor Krafft-Ebing would surely diagnose psychopathy in the mind of this child. A boy dreamed of murder giving him a power over women, which his lack of manhood still denied him in any other form.

Our time was almost up and I roused myself from contemplating worse horrors than any so-called ghost. There were questions I must ask, as a medical man.

"Mrs Grose, will you tell me about the deaths of the children?"

She nodded calmly. No doubt she had been questioned at the time.

"Flora was taken ill in London?" I prompted her.

"A week or so after the upset by the lake, I took the poor little soul to her mother's sister, Lady Camerton in London, away from Bly and its ghosts. But at Apsley Square the child grew feverish. Two days later an infection began in her throat and lungs. She was moved to the fever hospital. Then it became full-blown diphtheria. We thought she got it in London or travelling there. Now it seems both children probably caught it from the same source of infected water. The major wanted the best for her. But, most of all, he had wanted Miles kept away from Flora's illness."

"You returned alone to Bly from London soon after the little girl died?"

"And Master Miles was gone by then. What a dreadful business that was! But they never thought of diphtheria in his case for there was no time. It was Miss Temple who smothered him in her madness. I grieve for her but it must be she who did it."

"Can you be sure?" Holmes asked.

"Until the post-mortem they never knew diphtheria was in him—just feverishness. He'd had lung fever at school and thrown it off. He could have thrown off this. What happened that last day, I can only tell you as it was told to me. Master Miles was a little poorly but quite well enough to come downstairs. That counted against Miss Temple at her trial. They even talked of which new school he might go to."

"And the rest," Holmes interposed, "is in Miss Temple's journal."

"So I understand, sir. They were in the dining-room talking of another school, when she saw Quint at the window. Just as she did before Evensong a few weeks earlier. She tried to stop Miles seeing that evil man. She was strong as a field-girl, governess or not. She held him tight, felt his pulse race with fear. He was white as chalk and cold sweat running from him. So I was told."

Holmes kept his eyes on his notes as Mrs Grose continued. Then he said, "She says that she seized him and felt his heart flutter, not that he gasped for breath. She tells us his face looked ravaged by those eyes glaring through the glass. She too felt sick and faint. At the window was a spectre of damnation. She fought with that demon for the child's soul."

The poor woman lowered her head and there were tears in her reply.

"Perhaps she fought the evil beyond the glass—but more the evil in the child, for evil there was. If the boy died for want of breath, I swear she could not know it. And when she went under, in her faint, she thought she heard Miles cry out, 'Peter Quint—you devil!' Who did he mean was the devil—she or Quint? Either way, she held him tighter to protect him. Better he should die in her arms, I suppose she thought, than go to damnation with Quint. But when she came to herself, that devil had gone and the child's soul with him."

After a moment's respite, Holmes spoke again.

"It grieves me, Mrs Grose, that we can bring you so little comfort. But let there be justice for Victoria Temple."

"I hope so, sir. This has been an unlucky house. Masters and mistresses coming to grief. You'd never think it on a sunny afternoon like this. Sir Guy Mordaunt hanging from the cedar tree after his young wife's death. Harry Varley the poacher swimming the lake by night. The weed in the Middle Deep got his legs and held him, the poor fellow jumping like a trout for air but always pulled back, until he could jump no more."

"You may depend on it, Mrs Grose, that I shall do all in my power to set Miss Temple free. When we meet again, I hope she will be with us."

The poor woman looked a little flustered.

"I don't think you'll see me again, sir. The house will be shut up in a day or two. There's only me, the maid and the agent's man at the gate-house."

"Then where will you go?" I asked politely.

She brightened at this.

"To my son. At Cwm Nant Hir, the valley of the long river, a sheep farm, among the mountains of Wales. I won't miss Bly without the children."

At seven that evening we joined the London express. In the restaurant car, after dinner, two glasses of brandy stood before us. Holmes sighed.

"What would Professor Sidgwick and the Society for Psychical Research make of all this?"

"What the Court of Criminal Appeal may think is surely more to the point."

Trailing white smoke and steam across ripening cornfields, we rushed towards a slim gothic spire against a darkening sky.

"Odd that diphtheria was ignored by the defence," Holmes continued thoughtfully, "with the threat of a wilful murder verdict still possible."

"Diphtheria could not have gone far enough to cause death on its own. It merely weakened the child and made suffocation that much easier. That is all."

He brooded on this for a moment, his lean profile reflected in the darkened window of the carriage. Then he brightened up.

"As always, we must bow to the evidence. I shall attend Somerset House tomorrow morning, to view the death certificate of Miles Mordaunt. I believe we must test your presumption that diphtheria could not have gone far enough to kill him on its own."

It was dark across the marshes. The bright, square illumination of the carriage windows flashed on hedgerows and embankments as we thundered into the night.

6

The powers of memory exhibited by Sherlock Holmes would have been worth a whimsical monograph of the kind that only he could write. How any human being could have so encyclopaedic a recollection of so many divers facts was beyond me, and I no longer sought the answer. Once he had tried to explain it by saying that the only thing necessary was a passion for knowledge which made it impossible to forget. Then he tried to define it as a system, in which knowledge of one thing led by association to two more—and so on by geometrical progression. It seemed far simpler to accept that once his indomitable memory learnt a fact, he never forgot it.

None of this prepared me for the next day's bombshell.

On the morning after our return from Bly, I was later than usual coming down to breakfast. Holmes was seldom an early riser and I was not surprised to see the *Morning Post* unopened. But his knife, fork and plate had been cleared away. Therefore he had gone out even before the paper was delivered. Once the game was afoot, as he called it, there were nights when his head hardly touched the pillow before he was up and about again.

I finished breakfast and was reading the county cricket scores in *The Times*. The rasp of a wheel rim against the kerb indicated that a cab had pulled up. Slow and hollow hoofbeats signalled the driver's return to the Regent's Park rank. I waited to hear Holmes's key in the lock and his footsteps on the stairs, while I followed the report of yesterday's match at Bath between Middlesex and Somerset. As time ran out—ten to make and the match to win!—Hereward Douglas had hit a stylish half century for the visiting team.

Why was there still no sound on the stairs? I got up and drew back the curtain a little, looking up and down the street for any sign of Holmes. He was a hundred yards away, towards the park, in conversation with half a dozen of the ugliest little ragamuffins I ever saw. Four boys and two of their sisters, no doubt. This unsightly group was a detachment of his "Baker Street Irregulars," as he called them. They were his spies in enemy territory. While they watched and listened, gathering intelligence or shadowing a quarry on our behalf, our opponents never gave them a second glance. He was either describing the details of their next assignment or arguing over their extortionate demands for payment.

The prestige of working for Mr Holmes, the Baker Street Detective, always carried the day with these little bandits. Several coins now passed from his purse to the tallest boy of the group. The balance would follow upon completion of their task. He turned back and strode towards the freshly polished brass of Mrs Hudson's doorstep.

Vigorously, as if he had just woken from a good night's sleep, he came up the stairs two at a-time and into our sitting-room. Action and activity were his great restoratives. His cap went skimming onto the hat-stand. He threw himself down in his fireside chair and greeted me with a broad smile. Then he drew a sheet of paper from his breast pocket.

"We have it, Watson! I shall be surprised if a competent Queen's Counsel cannot argue Miss Victoria Temple out of Broadmoor by next week."

He produced a sheet of paper.

"What is that?"

"A transcript from Somerset House. Their doors were open at eight-thirty and I was the first applicant across the step. This is a transcript of the death certificate of poor young Miles Mordaunt—or rather the details which I have copied from it. Still appended to it was a post-mortem report."

"How does it help Miss Temple? She has already admitted killing him. If she was so deranged that she did not know what she was doing or did not know it to be wrong, she will remain insane but guilty under English criminal law."

"I shall take the liberty of calling that into question."

"How?"

He sighed.

"Because she never killed anyone. The great pity, Watson, is that I was not invited to attend Miss Temple's trial. I could have saved the lawyers on both sides so much trouble."

On these occasions, he was quite insufferable.

"What trouble, for God's sake?"

"She was found guilty of suffocating the child. But the post-mortem evidence here shows that the primary cause of death was cardiac arrest. Not suffocation."

"Cardiac arrest at the hands of Miss Temple? What of it? All deaths—including all those occasioned by murder—end in cardiac arrest. The question is how they are brought about!"

He beamed at me and clasped his hands.

"Like everyone else, I had first believed Miss Temple's confession in her journal. She hugged a delicate boy tightly enough and long enough to suffocate him. Without her intervention, any slight initial diphtheritic infection would not have killed him at that point and might well have yielded to treatment. Her conduct was what the law calls the *novus actus interveniens*, the new act which changes the course of events."

This legal subtlety was merely an irritation and I told him so. His smile grew a little warmer as he continued.

"Our simple rustic coroner never went further than the story in her journal. Miss Temple had confessed to murder, therefore it must be so. My dear Watson, I have also been through the post-mortem report of the fever hospital, separately and minutely. As a result, I am quite convinced that Miss Temple could not have murdered Miles Mordaunt because the child she hugged to herself was already dead. There were too many mind-doctors at her trial and too few specialists in contagious diseases."

He had a trick up his sleeve, but for the life of me I could not see what.

"It will not help her, Holmes! Let us suppose she frightened a delicate child violently enough to cause heart failure. By legal precedent, it is unlawful killing to frighten a victim to death, even by impersonating a ghost. What else is her nonsense of an evil spirit at the dining-room window but such an act?"

He relaxed his smile.

"The boy was in the very early stages of diphtheria."

"We already know that. The very early stages would not kill him. They will certainly not exonerate Miss Temple."

He shook his head indulgently.

"I believe, my dear friend, that an item of your medical training has escaped your memory for a moment. It certainly eluded the simple country physician at Bly. The equally simple coroner's jurors were content to believe Miss Temple's confession in her journal. Accordingly, they returned a verdict of homicide against her."

"What is your alternative?"

"Curiously, while diphtheria may take its course over several days or a week, it can also kill at once and without warning. It can even kill without any previous symptoms."

This was too much.

"I have treated diphtheria for twenty years and I have never met with such a case!"

He stood up without replying and walked across to the long bookcase, extending from floor to ceiling. Its rows of scrap-books and volumes of reference made up his library.

"Nor, perhaps, have you ever heard of Professor Stresemann. If you are not too weary after yesterday's journey, let me show you the relevant section in his admirable volume on forensic pathology, *Das Lehrbuch für Gerichtsmedizin*. Among others, he cites two recent cases of patients feeling a trifle feverish, as Miles Mordaunt did. Like him, they were not apparently suffering from any serious or specific illness. The idea that they were in the grip of diphtheria would have seemed alarmist. They resembled precisely the reported state of Master Mordaunt. Nothing was done. Both victims were found dead a few hours later with no previous suspicion that they had contracted the disease."

"Impossible!"

He drew his volume from its shelf and continued his explanation as he turned to the page.

"The only reason, my dear fellow, that you have never known such a case is that diphtheria was not diagnosed. Like the boy, Stresemann's cases were in the early stages of the infection which might still have yielded to treatment. A diphtheritic deposit had gathered in the throat but that would not have had time to be fatal. However a further autopsy revealed unexpected diphtheritic deposits in the bronchi. These deposits travelled suddenly and rapidly from the throat down the bronchi, the congestion created by this then causing cardiac failure. Everything in the case of the poor child at Bly corresponds with Professor Stresemann's description and findings."

Not for the first time, my friend's random erudition was a cause of personal annoyance. I tried to cut him short,

"A delicate and under-developed child of ten was seized by a healthy and well-built woman in her twenties, certainly capable of overpowering him and depriving him of air."

He shook his head.

"There is no evidence of that whatever except in her journal, which Miss Temple completed in the short period before her arrest and with her mental balance in question. She is no diagnostician and would not know the first thing about a diphtheritic deposit. She convinced herself that she must have smothered the child and worked backwards from there! It was diphtheria which killed him!"

"You think so?"

"She came round from her hysterical *absence*, as the French call it. The live child she had been hugging before was now dead in her arms. Therefore she concluded that she must have caused his death. Oh, she believed it, I am quite sure. Having passed judgement on herself, she then did her best to get herself hanged, as if seeking expiation. Her journal and her statements are totally uncorroborated. To say the least, she wrote the final pages in a state of extreme mental confusion. She sincerely believed that the boy's soul had been carried off by Peter Quint as an agent of the devil. It was her fault, for which she sought punishment. Such a confession should never have been allowed in evidence! Miles Mordaunt was in all probability dead from a blow to the heart by the dislodgement of diphtheritic deposits before she took him in that last embrace."

"Impossible to prove!"

He handed me Stresemann's book.

"Impossible to disprove, rather. Ironically, the post-mortem evidence does not incriminate Victoria Temple. If she had never kept that journal, she might not even have been a suspect. If you do not object, however, we will keep this to ourselves for the moment."

"While Miss Temple remains in Broadmoor?"

"For the shortest possible time. As the great military strategist Clausewitz remarked, a wise commander fights the right battle, at the right time, and in the right place. That moment is approaching but it has not quite arrived. There is still murder at the heart of this case but it is not the murder of Miles Mordaunt and certainly not of his little sister."

"Who else can it be?"

He was not yet to be drawn. For much of that day he sat in an easy chair smoking his pipe, or droning on his violin, or lounging with a handful of Boxer cartridges and his hair-trigger revolver, elaborating with bullet pocks our patriotic *VR*—for *Victoria Regina*—on the opposite wall. Life, it seemed, was returning to normal.

It was almost dusk. Streaks of late sunlight across the carpet were deepening to a tawny orange. There came an erratic hammering at the front door, followed by a scampering on the stairs. His Baker Street Irregulars had returned. He took half a dozen sheets of paper from them and studied the contents. Then he threw back his head and began to chuckle. The chuckle grew to laughter, as if at the most preposterous tale he had ever read.

He was still laughing as the six young scamps, each clutching a half-sovereign, scrambled back down the stairs and disappeared, shouting, into the street.

7

If Holmes was right—there was an end of our case, ghosts and all! How absurd it was for him to continue talking about murder! Who the devil had been murdered, if it not little Miles Mordaunt? And who could have committed murder upon the child if not Victoria Temple? I suggested facetiously to my friend that perhaps he believed the apparitions had murdered one another. He looked at me seriously and with a nod of approval.

"As to that, Watson, you may be closer to the mark than you realise."

The next day—and the day after that—I saw nothing of him between breakfast and dinner. This was not unusual when he had a case in progress. From time to time during our investigations there would be days of absence without explanation. Despite my impatience, I confess that they had sometimes brought about the sudden and triumphant conclusion of an inquiry.

After dinner, he showed no appetite for conversation. When the meal was over, he rang for the housemaid to clear the plates and dishes. To avoid interruption, he transferred himself to a plain wooden chair at his disreputable work-table with its stained surface, bottles of malodorous preparations and untidy piles of paper. Now he began to read, not with laconic amusement, as he read the newspapers, lounging by the fire. He devoured books and articles so quickly that one could hardly believe he had read them at all. His lean angular features were drawn in a grimace of concentration. From time to time, he made a pencil note in the margin of a volume or on his starched white shirt-cuff.

I made a pantomime of yawning, looking at the clock—and so to bed. As I passed, I noticed the titles of the books at his elbow. One was a treasure in any collection, Reginald Scot's *Discoverie of Witchcraft.* Published in 1584, it was still in its primitive sheepskin binding. Stamped in gold on polished calf, was the *Ars Magna Lucis et Umbrae.* It had been given to the world in 1645 by a scholar of the occult and the arcane, Father Athanasius Kircher. Even that formidable Jesuit could have known little more than Sherlock Holmes by now about the art of light and shade.

I waited for him to resume idling about the house, playing the fiddle, and reading in a desultory fashion. Despite his promise of an early solution to the mystery, a week passed. Then it seemed his work was over. He breakfasted late and went nowhere. At four o'clock that afternoon, he put down his teacup and spoke from behind the evening paper.

"If you have nothing better to do this evening, Watson, you may care to be my guest."

There was an irony in his tone that made me uneasy.

"You have not joined a club? You of all people!"

"Certainly not. I am not inviting you to dinner, my dear fellow. I have already alerted Mrs Hudson to feed us by seven o'clock." He folded his copy of the *Globe* and pushed aside the tea-plate from which he had been eating richly buttered toast. "Our destination is not a club. I might call it an intimate theatre or perhaps a learned society, which it is hoped you will join. That is the pretext for your attendance."

"What society?"

He stood up and filled his pipe with tobacco from the Persian slipper.

"You will recall the murder at the Yokohama Club two years ago and our efforts to save Mrs Edith Carew from the gallows? That case persuaded me to keep abreast of matters which apparently defy scientific explanation. I associated myself some time ago with the Hermetic Order of the Golden Light."*

"A bunch of crack-pots!"

He shrugged.

"I have attended several meetings, at the first of which I was initiated. In consequence, my membership gives me the entrée, as a distinguished guest, to almost any séance in London, genteel or fraudulent."

So that was it!

"This is still about those confounded apparitions, is it not?"

He occupied himself with a lighted match, drawing smoke from his pipe. Shaking out the flame, he looked across at me thoughtfully and said,

"We are to be in Kensington by eight-thirty this evening. If all goes as I intend, I shall present an apparition that will put to shame Peter Quint and Maria Jessel. By the way, old fellow, in these arcane circles I am known only as Professor Scott Holmes."

"A séance in Kensington, to which you will be going under a false name and title?"

It was one of the rare occasions when I saw him wince. He said, "It is commonplace for members of such societies to

* "The Case of the Yokohama Club" in Donald Thomas, *The Secret Cases of Sherlock Holmes,* Carroll & Graf, 1998.

adopt a *nom de plume*. I employ two of the names conferred on me at the baptismal font. I am, after all, William Sherlock Scott Holmes. I may surely decide which I shall use? I already have some reputation in the occult world, uncompromised by my career in criminal investigation. To go as Sherlock Holmes would cloud the issue and startle my hosts."

"Ghosts!"

"Oh, let us call them spirits. It sounds so much more polite."

"If they did not manifest themselves to us at Bly, you may be sure they will not condescend to appear in West London!"

"There I think you may be mistaken."

"So you expect to raise Peter Quint or Miss Jessel from the dead?"

"My sights are set higher—on an Egyptian courtier of the Eighteenth Dynasty."

This was far beyond a joke. I scented real danger and made one more effort. I spoke quietly and, as it seemed to me, sensibly.

"Holmes, we have done our duty to Miss Temple. A favourable outcome to her case is in sight. Do you not see that if we are now known to dabble in nonsense of this kind, we shall make complete fools of ourselves? We have nothing to gain from it and everything to lose. If the story gets around, as it is bound to, we shall be lucky if we have a single client left."

There was a disconcerting merriment in his dark eyes.

"You must not come, old chap, if it will embarrass you. I have undertaken to conduct a most important experiment and I am obliged to be there. It is only my second visit to this suburban villa and its clientele. I had not been there at all until I called to make myself known and to offer my services last week. Happily, my fame as Scott Holmes went before me. So I made a promise. Now I have a reputation to preserve—or lose."

Before I could reply, he walked from the room and closed the door gently behind him. I heard him stride up the next pair of stairs. There were sounds of banging about in the attic. He was up there for more than an hour, before coming down with a brown leather hatbox and a large basket, better employed for a riverside picnic. He was formally suited, as if he might be attending a recital or an opera.

Without a glance in my direction, he took a flimsy telegram form across to the bureau and began to write. I could not read the words of the message from where I sat. When it lay folded on the table, I was able to glimpse a name on the envelope, "Inspector Tobias Gregson" and the address "Criminal Investigation Division, Scotland Yard." He had once assured me that Gregson was the smartest member of the Yard's detective force. This, at least, gave me some reassurance.

He rang for Mrs Hudson's Billy, gave the lad a coin and despatched him with the electric message to the post office at Baker Street Underground station. Sitting down, he yawned, opened the evening *Globe* once more, and appeared to give no more thought to his plans for that evening. All attempts to entice him into conversation failed.

As a medical man I was trained in scientific habits of thought. I had always regarded spiritualist mediums as dupes or swindlers. Their séances were surely meetings of deluded believers preyed upon by avaricious charlatans. I had good reason to abhor the heartless exploitation of grief by wraiths of ectoplasm or greetings from the after-life. The reader must remember that I had lost my own young wife seven years earlier. Hints from well-meaning friends had nudged me towards the possibility of communication with the dead. The closer I came to the magicians, the more strongly was I repelled.

As I gazed towards the park trees at the end of our street, I had no doubt that Sherlock Holmes had produced a diagnosis of diphtheria which must soon establish the innocence of Victoria

Temple. Having won his case, why should he care about the poor young woman's hysterical visions?

Just before eight o'clock, Mrs Hudson's long-suffering Billy was sent to call our chosen cab off the rank. In the thickening summer twilight, we pulled out along the Marylebone Road towards Sussex Gardens and Hyde Park. A last golden glow darkened along the cream terraces of the Bayswater Road. Lamps were lit in the little shops of Kensington Church Street.

Our destination was Sambourne Avenue, a secluded street of double-fronted villas, built ten years earlier in mellow red brick with white-painted gables. They rose three storeys above the broad tree-lined thoroughfare, each with a spacious area and basement below. These were substantial homes with bay windows and conservatories. By contrast, they made our old-fashioned quarters in Baker Street appear cramped and gloomy. Yet I felt no envy. Suburban houses of this type too often attract rackety people with more money than sense.

Our brown-whiskered cabman, whom I now noticed for the first time, unloaded the leather hatbox and picnic hamper. I know most of the drivers on the Regent's Park rank, but this one was unfamiliar. Perhaps he was not a regular, just a supernumerary who must work when he could. It seemed he was obliged to take his child with him on the cabbie's perch, as if having no one else to look after her. In response to his knock, the hatbox and hamper were taken in by a manservant at the door of the basement kitchen. Holmes turned to our postillion.

"You will wait, my man. I may be some time. You shall be well remunerated on my return. If it should be a long visit, I shall ask them to give you and your little girl something in the kitchen."

The wiry, gnome-like fellow began to grumble.

"I don't know so much, guv. I brought you here fair and square. I can't spend all evening sitting about with no chance of another fare."

"Very well," said Holmes impatiently. "Take this and get refreshment for yourself and the child at the coffee stall off Kensington High Street. No beer—no gin! And be back here no later than an hour from now."

He handed the man a shilling. We left this Jehu muttering to himself that "proper toffs" would have treated him more handsomely.

The whole of this pantomime was witnessed by a maid in a plain cap and apron. She had come to the front door in response to Holmes's ring at the bell. We went up the glossily-blacked steps and were admitted.

To begin with, I thought we had come on the wrong evening. There was not a sound to be heard, even though it was half-past eight. The maid led us down the hallway to a baize-covered door. There was far more depth to this house than I had supposed, covering a larger area than appeared from the street.

We crossed a dark-curtained and over-furnished reception room. Its olive-green walls were hung with oil-painted figure-studies of women, done in a questionable taste. So much for spirit portraits! A black-leaded fire-place was lined by hand-painted Dutch tiles of a similar nature. Above the mantelboard with its green leather and brass-headed nails, the wall was fitted with shelves displaying curious little terra cotta figurines and Chinese jars. On the mantelshelf below, an ornate gold-and-enamel Buhl clock backed by a mirror ticked time away with a soft uneasy beat.

All this nick-nackery seemed contrived to impress upon the gullible that they were entering a world of exotic possibilities. There was a hint of the improper without anything that could be defined as downright objectionable. One breathed deceit and depravity in that curtained space, almost hinting at bizarre rituals or white-slave scandals. By contrast, a business-like alcove contained a plain chair and a small table with an upright telephone upon its stand. All in all, the place looked like the parlour of a very select and expensive house of ill-repute.

A varnished scrapbook-screen concealed the far end. As we stepped round it, I saw the reason for such silence. We were on the threshold of a spacious and plain-walled music-room, to judge at least from the modest-sized Bechstein grand piano, wheeled aside and folded up against the wall. In its place, fifteen or sixteen faces looked up at us earnestly from their chairs. They were gathered round the oval of a large table covered by a crimson velvet drape. Above it, a brass gasolier with vine-patterned branches was burning low, casting a stark but limited radiance on the ceiling. In the shadows at either side, a further platoon of guests sat on upright chairs along the walls, waiting their turn to be called like patients at a dentist's surgery. There must have been thirty or forty, all told.

In the dim background, a rounded archway opened into a darkened conservatory with a vaulted roof of glass panes. Palm branches and white orchids gave off a cheap illusion of night in the mystic East.

At the head of the table, immediately opposite us, sat a woman whom I suppose I must describe as the mistress of ceremonies. Her appearance would have been overdone even on a vaudeville stage. The rouge alone might not have called attention, had not her hair been a little too auburn, her lips a little too rosy. She wore a wide-brimmed picture-hat of blue velvet, set at a slant like a mushroom. A patterned décolletage covered her neck and shoulders, almost transparently, above a bodice of lilac-mauve silk. This extraordinary ensemble was completed by black elbow-gloves, leaving exposed the coloured imitation gem-stones on her fingers.

A semi-circle of playing cards, which she had apparently been studying with the aid of a lorgnette, lay before her on the crimson velvet of the table-cloth. To either side of these a skull and a stuffed raven on a plinth stood guard. A small plaque by the raven identified her as "Madame Rosa, Clairvoyante." It would not have surprised me in the least to learn that she had a police record.

Flanking this personage sat two women, evidently there to do her bidding. One I judged to be in her fifties, a plump and respectable-looking body. The other was younger, her black velvet hat coming coquettishly to a peak at one side. I thought her a pretty witch. A half-veil obscured her features, but I heard her addressed as Miss Shelley.

Had our mission not been of possible importance to Victoria Temple, I should have burst out laughing, turned on my heel, and left. According to Holmes, this was not the first time he had been here and so I gave him the benefit of the doubt. Madame Rosa favoured us with a slow nod and indicated a pair of vacant chairs in the shadows.

I will not try your patience by a full account. I was less interested in Madame Rosa than in the men and women who came to sit under her spell. Their dress and manner were sober, they behaved with decorum. Most of them might easily have changed places with a congregation at Sunday Evensong in one of the more fashionable churches of Knightsbridge or Chelsea. Even so, several were no doubt accomplices of Madame Rosa, masquerading as inquirers after spiritual truth.

Our evening began with a "photographic" séance and all the tricks of that trade. The gasolier was dimmed to a feeble glow and the spirits of the dead were summoned by Madame Rosa. She had a rather peremptory manner, like a schoolteacher calling the roll of her class. We saw no sign of the immortals, though a mysterious tapping was said to be proof of their presence. A tame photographer, his lens facing the conservatory, exposed a series of glass plates. His head was under the usual black linen hood as he did so. In order that he should not be accused of exposing his plates in advance, one of the newcomers was invited to take up any position or pose of his choice in the view of the lens.

I intervened at this point to ask that this person should also hold my copy of that evening's *Standard* newspaper, which I had brought to read in the cab. I requested that its headline on the front page should be displayed in the photographs. "MR CHAMBERLAIN'S BIRMINGHAM SPEECH—FULL DETAILS." I was rather disappointed when Madame Rosa agreed at once. Her spoken English was entirely correct but coloured by a slight French accent. Miss Shelley, the pretty witch, took the paper from me and handed it to the witness.

Presently, we observed the development of the glass-plate negatives in the conservatory sink by infra-red light. Who could doubt that spirits had been with us? Each image included the man holding my evening paper with headlines of the Colonial Secretary's speech at Birmingham. But in the photograph the walls of the conservatory were decorated with cabalistic inscriptions and "spirit portraits" done by invisible fingers. Madame Rosa closed her hands together, prayer-fashion, giving thanks for these messages from beyond the grave. None of the graffiti and portraits were visible to our unaided sight. No mortal hands could have painted them there while so many witnesses were watching. To my chagrin, my newspaper had merely strengthened the imposture.

Alas, the wondrous inscriptions and portraits are explained by simple truth. It was known to Holmes and me, doubtless to Madame Rosa and her photographer, but apparently not to anyone else present. The fact is this: quinine sulphate painted on a surface is invisible to the naked eye but will appear on a photographic collodion image. Whoever staged this little drama in Kensington knew that many of the guests at the séance waited in an agony of hope for spirit messages from their departed loved ones. They would not have thanked Holmes or me for undeceiving them. Does the owner of an old master painting thank the art historian who proves it to be a forgery?

On other prints from the glass plates we marvelled at phantasmal spirits in angel robes, smiling upon the flesh-and-blood witness holding my evening newspaper. Alas, how easy it was for the cameraman, while his head was under the hood of black linen, to insert a "ghost transparency" in front of the glass plate to be exposed. Or perhaps it was possible to effect a double exposure. Since Holmes made no comment, I kept my peace. Perhaps I over-estimated the importance of the occasion. Docile though the onlookers appeared to be, they may have come for no more than the fun of the fair, as if to Jasper Maskelyne's stage "magic" at the Egyptian Hall in Piccadilly.

In a finale to the first part of the performance, half-a-dozen spirit messages were miraculously revealed in chalk on sealed slates. Madame Rosa was quick to remind us that the late William Ewart Gladstone, Prime Minister until four years earlier, had been a believer in this art.

To the initiated, the trick is simple enough. Two blank classroom slates in wooden frames are hinged and folded to face inwards to each other. The moistened surfaces of the wooden frames are coated with white adhesive powder and pressed together. They are also locked together and sealed with a stamp on melted red wax. The metal die which has stamped the seal is then placed where everyone can see it. Any interference with the slates appears impossible.

On this occasion, the gasolier was extinguished altogether to effect a "dark séance." Madame Rosa in her sumptuous décolletage sat holding the locked plates in her lap. We were invited to close our eyes but even with mine open I could see almost nothing by the dying glow of the gas mantels. Our hostess sat apparently motionless. She could certainly not have held a pen nor a stick of chalk.

After five minutes of invocations, the gaslight was turned up. We were able to confirm that each seal was unbroken and the lock secure. It had been impossible for our hostess to separate the two slates. Miss Shelley was then commanded to break the wax seal, open the lock, and ease apart the two gummed frames. As the light fell on the first slate it showed a faint but perfectly legible inscription in white chalk. It was written unevenly, as if with difficulty from a great distance. "Your darling little Charley still waits for you where the special flowers you loved are for ever in bloom."

All but one guest stared at this, knowing the message was not for them. When the words were read out, however, I saw that it was Miss Shelley on her upright chair who turned her face quickly away and inclined her head. She was surely hiding her tears and my instinct told me that her grief was not a trick. I had made a mistake in her case. Because she sat next to Madame Rosa and performed small tasks for her, I had assumed that my pretty witch was one of the conspirators. I was wrong—she had been one of the dupes.

The public had not yet read the warning against slate-writing by Count Perovsky-Petrovo-Solovevo of the Society for Psychical Research, first contained in a private letter to Sherlock Holmes. A few years later, this Russian nobleman exposed the deception to the world. When two slates are to be fastened hermetically face to face, some of the white adhesive powder is left unmoistened. It is allowed to fall "accidentally" and harmlessly into a corner where the slates join. Even if it is noticed, the guests think nothing of it. In truth the mixture contains sufficient chalk to inscribe a faint but legible message—and enough iron filings to respond to the attraction of a small but efficient electro-magnet.

The right hand and fingers of the medium are easily concealed beneath the slates. Skilfully palmed, a miniature magnet attracts iron filings in the powder within the thin slate. A small amount is gathered during the dark séance. With a magnet as "pen," words are inscribed within the slates through their underside. It takes a little practice but, as I find from experiments, a birthday-party conjuror can master the technique. The effect of "spirit-writing" on the susceptible and willing, when the seal and the lock have plainly not been tampered with, is apt to be sensational.

I glanced covertly at Miss Shelley, whose composure was now quite recovered. I wondered about her little Charley and the place where the flowers they loved were for ever in bloom.

Madame Rosa had approached Sherlock Holmes, as if to signal that his turn had come. He walked slowly into the conservatory. A curtain was drawn across after him. I still had no idea what his hatbox and picnic hamper might contain or what his supernatural magic might be. He had not told me. In my present mood, pride had kept me silent.

8

In the next few hours, the mystery of the ghosts at Bly moved to a conclusion. Its crime had little to do with diaphanous spirits or celestial voices but much to do with bludgeons and blackguards. Before the continuation of Madame Rosa's pantomime, there was a brief interval while we each took a cool glass of lemonade from the sideboard. I kept my eye on Miss Shelley as she carried a tray among the guests. I was right. She was here to serve, not to command.

Holmes had disappeared behind the curtain and I knew not a soul in the room. Some had a sheepish air, as if half ashamed of having come. The rest put on confident smiles, ready to treat the whole thing as a West End show. For entertainment, they could not have done better with the Davenport Brothers or Monsieur Houdin at the Alhambra. To Madame Rosa and her confidantes, every simple-minded convert would return a profit.

Excited chatter broke out here and there but most of us kept ourselves to ourselves, sipping the cool sweetness of the lemonade. When we were called together, the curtain was still closed across the arch of the conservatory. The music-room became the darkened stalls of an intimate theatre. The blacked-out conservatory was our stage.

Madame Rosa stood before us in the gloom. She promised that an attempt would now be made by "the eminent Professor Scott Holmes" to invoke the spirit of the Lady Teshat. This obliging ghost had materialised at several London séances and answered questions put to her. Absolute silence and concentration were necessary. Our distinguished visitor came to us from the Hermetic Order of the Golden Light. His experiment carried the approval of the Society for Psychical Research. That, of course, was a downright lie.

For good measure, our hostess promised that the professor would stand well back among the onlookers. He was anxious that no grounds should be given for suspecting ventriloquism.

With a rattle of brass rings, the curtain was at last drawn back. It was difficult to see very much, though I could make out the unmistakable profile of Holmes against starlight in the conservatory windows. At that moment, he was not looking at the stage but facing his audience. His large round hatbox of polished leather was somehow fixed open upon its side on a table so that we gazed into its depths. As I grew used to the darkness, I saw by dimly reflected light that it contained an object of some kind. Perhaps it was a simple block of wood but shaped like a human head. It might be an artificial head, for no body could be attached to it. Every side of the isolated hatbox, as well as the space above, below and at the rear, was on view to some part of the audience.

The voice of Sherlock Holmes commanded attention with quiet authority.

"Two vast and trunkless legs of stone
Stand in the desert. Near them, on the sand,
Half-sunk, a shattered visage lies. . . .

And on the pedestal these words appear:
'My name is Ozymandias, King of Kings;
Look on my Works, ye Mighty, and despair! . . .'"

They listened to that voice as they had listened to none of Madame Rosa's nonsense. If a man might work magic, it was surely the owner of that compelling delivery. His power of address and his sense of stage "presence," acquired in his youthful theatrical career, had never left him. Now he turned to the conservatory, for all the world like a pagan priest before an altar.

The outline of the thing in the hatbox was clearer. The face itself, if it was a face, gave off a slight luminous glow. His voice came again.

"Speak to us, O, Spirit. Tell us who you are and whence you come."

There was no response, but it was—surely it was—a severed head that the box contained. A head perhaps long defunct and long interred. Well, I suppose it is not hard to contrive a trick like that. The eyes appeared closed and the mouth sagged open a little. In other respects, the profile was reminiscent of the magazine engravings of Queen Nefertiti in the Egyptian museum at Berlin. Yet this complexion was wizened by the dust and decay of centuries, as real flesh must be.

"Open your eyes," said Holmes in gentle command. "Open them."

The intent silence was broken by a sharp gasp from the audience as the head in the hatbox slowly raised its eyelids. The light had intensified. Yet its pale glow must come from within the box. How? It was a small head, perhaps a child's, but life-size. As it grew clearer, the colours appeared more natural. Then it seemed that the image wavered, as if we might be watching it though the flame or smoke of a temple altar.

"Greet us with a smile," said Holmes more easily. He spoke with some relief, as if he had not been confident that the spirit would answer his summons.

There was another murmur from the onlookers. This head, isolated from anything outside the hatbox, assumed a faint smile. The truly startling thing was that the smile was as natural as that of a girl walking in the park and meeting a friend. The apparition—for now I caught myself thinking this pernicious word again—was three-dimensional yet somehow insubstantial. If it was a trick, which surely it must be, how the devil was it done? This was no static magic-lantern display of glass plates. It was as far beyond slate-writing and spirit photographs as an express train is beyond a horse and cart.

From where I sat, the outline of Holmes's gaunt, motionless profile now seemed carved in ebony against the faintly-reflected night sky of the conservatory and the dimmest illumination from the hatbox itself. I looked again at the shrivelled face of a woman who was still young. Holmes resumed quietly but with the same directness of command.

"Tell us, O Spirit, who you are and whence you come."

The following pause was so long that I was sure he had failed. But this was merely a tribute to his sense of theatre. At last she replied and stilled every movement among Madame Rosa's guests. No one had expected to hear a voice from beyond the grave, unless by an obvious trick of ventriloquism, which this could not be. The natural movement of the spirit's lips ruled out such a dodge. It was a young voice, the tone flat and almost indifferent, as if the words belonged to someone else and were of no concern to her. Even Holmes could not have imitated it. Her reply came with a great effort, distantly and with an intolerable weariness.

"I am called the Lady Teshat, daughter of the Eighteenth Dynasty, a child who will never be a woman. My service is to the god Amun of Thebes who is named the Hidden One. My master is Ozymandias, King of Kings. I am cast out for my fault, condemned to walk the future without rest, an exile through time in the courts of a Grecian underworld and the groves of a Roman Avernus."

Most of them surely knew the thing was a trick but enjoyed the fun. Perhaps a few could scarcely believe what they heard but longed for this preposterous muddle of mythology to be true.

"Why do you answer our call?"

Her reply was little more than a whisper, yet not a syllable was lost.

"I bring words I do not understand to a world I do not know. I come to a woman who is a stranger to me. She is the mistress of two lovers, one dead and one still living. The blood of the dead lies upon the hands of the living."

"From whom does the message come?"

"He who is the master of the message was once a servant. He was called among you the Fifth Stone."

I caught my breath at this, recalling Spencer-Smith's account of Miles Mordaunt. I followed every word as she spoke again.

"He was a servant to her other lover who still lives, who with his mistress shed the blood of this rival. The hidden murder of her first lover calls out for vengeance. The violation of an inheritance calls for retribution. Through me the secret of the guilty one shall be known."

"Give us your message."

"The blood of a lover and the soul of a dead child call for blood in return. An inheritance is betrayed. This very night is the time of reckoning. Their enemies are close upon the killers. The only safety lies in flight. Within the hour their lives are forfeit unless she to whom I speak can bear a warning to her lover who lives unaware. Let her warn him before the sands of the hour run out. The blood of the dead lies on the hands of the living. The avengers have their scent."

But how was he doing it—a live head in a hatbox, answering back!

"How shall she know that your message is for her?"

"Her lover who lies dead was that Fifth Stone. His death was also her crime. Her life, like that of her paramour, stands forfeit to the executioner."

That was more like it, I thought—eight o'clock on a Monday morning, side by side in the execution shed of Newgate!

"Whom does the Fifth Stone signify?" Holmes asked.

"His name is not my language but a Roman title."

The Fifth Stone! The Roman title, in dog Latin, was Petrus Quintus. Plain English made it Peter Quint! Any school-miss could put the two halves together! But now the face was fading—or rather disintegrating—as the flame-light died. Petrus Quintus! An absurd but effective mangling of tongues. The image flickered, thin as a ghost, and breathed its farewell.

"Let her carry the warning before it is too late. . . . Let her remember it is not sweet with nimble feet to dance upon the air. . . ."

Here and there I caught a gasp from the onlookers. This very month I had bought a copy of a book which had been reprinted five times since Christmas. It was talked of and quoted everywhere, *The Ballad of Reading Gaol.* Dancing on the air with nimble feet was its description of a hanging in a common English prison-shed. To judge from the look on Miss Shelley's face, she recognised the lines too well.

By the time the image fell silent, it was as if I had been told a story that ten minutes earlier I could not even guess at. Around me the others were clapping vigorously, as if at the Palace of Varieties or the Egyptian Hall. A few sat motionless, not knowing what to think. The gasolier above us was brightening, illuminating the depths of the hatbox. Where the head had appeared lay nothing but a pile of ashes. The trick had carried such conviction that I caught myself almost believing its unearthly mystery. I forgot for an instant that all this had come from the fertile genius of Sherlock Holmes.

I stood up, looking over the heads of others to see the gaunt figure of Holmes slipping through the curtains before they closed again with a rattle of rings. Perhaps the audience thought this was a pause in his demonstration. To me, his movements indicated that speed was of the essence. I shouldered my way after him. What I saw behind the curtain explained a good deal.

He was deftly but calmly fastening the hatbox, which showed no trace of dust, head or flame-light. A girl of fifteen or so was wiping greasepaint from her face with a towel. Under the paint, she was surely the cabman's child! Behind a projecting wall that hid one side of the conservatory from the séance parlour of the music room, the black metal cube of a compact but powerful magic lantern, fitted with a red lens, stood on a kitchen trolley. It was capable of focusing a concentrated beam of light upon its subject. In front of its lens, a bowl of cooling water still gave off steam. I saw at once how the beam had been angled to illuminate a plain kitchen chair from which the cabman's daughter had risen. An inspection of the hatbox would no doubt reveal a sheet of glass fitted to fill its opening and capable of being tilted at an angle. I thought at once of Dr Pepper and knew the answer to this splendid illusion!

Let me explain. Twenty years earlier, I had been despatched from medical school to Aldershot for my Army training. There I saw an evening performance of *The Haunted Murderer* at the Hippodrome, which serves as a garrison theatre. In this theatrical novelty, the source of light was hidden from the audience. I learnt that it was a powerful lamp backstage shining on an actor in the wings. This bright image was then reflected by a sheet of plate glass, fastened at an angle on the darkened stage.

The principle of the illusion was the reflected "ghost" of himself which, for example, a traveller sees when staring out into the darkness from a railway train at night. What appeared at the Aldershot Hippodrome, through the invisible slant of plate glass on the darkened stage, was a much stronger and lifelike "ghost" of the subject. As in the railway carriage illusion, the figure seemed to float in air at some distance beyond the glass. By careful stage lighting—or the lack of it—the spectre at Aldershot moved and talked like any other actor but was insubstantial as a cloud. The play on that evening was produced by the great John Henry Pepper himself. At the climax of the drama, the villain was confronted by this apparition of his better self.

The Kensington spiritualists had just seen a refinement of Pepper's trick, perfected by Holmes for the occasion. This soon became known as Colonel Stodare's "severed head" illusion and held theatre audiences in awe over the years! Unfortunately, it could not explain events at Bly because it would never work in daylight.

I glanced at the operator of the magic-lantern and saw the same wiry build and sardonic features as those of our cab-driver. Before I could say so, Holmes turned to me as he finished buckling the hatbox.

"Look sharp, Watson! We have flushed her from cover. You may depend upon it, she has dreaded this moment for the past year and more. I trust you enjoyed my little deception, my mastery of occult claptrap."

"She? But who is she?"

He ignored this and strode to the door.

"Gregson and two plain-clothes men are watching the street. A constable has the rear of the house in view. Our driver this evening, by the way, is only an amateur cabman but a professional wizard: 'Professor Hermann' of the Adelphi Theatre's Phantasmagoria."

"Otherwise known as Tom Rathbone and pleased to meet you, sir," said this new acquaintance, shaking my hand.

"And this," Holmes added, with a graceful gesture towards the young woman "is the soi-disant 'severed head,' his assistant and daughter, Miss Clarissa. An accomplished little actress. Now, let us be on our way."

We went out through the kitchen door and up the steps to the street, leaving Rathbone to follow with the hatbox and basket. Holmes led the way to our cab, now drawn up in a darker stretch between the lamp-posts. From the interior, a tall fair-haired man in a dark suit craned forward. By the light of the carriage-lamp on his flaxen hair and on his clean-shaven but unnaturally pale face, I recognised Inspector Tobias Gregson.

"Good evening, Mr Holmes. I'd be obliged to you for some explanation of what is going on. What am I to tell the commissioner when he asks where all his fine brave policemen have got to?"

Holmes stepped into the cab and took his seat opposite the inspector. Rathbone was back on his perch but the vehicle did not move. Holmes glanced in the mirror at the view of the street behind him.

"To begin with, my dear Gregson, this is about murder. We seldom deal in smaller currency. And then it's about a brutal robbery by one of the most ruthless footpads that our underworld can boast. And if that won't do, it's a matter of the walking dead."

"Indeed!" said Gregson quietly. "And where's the Belgravia division in all this? My instructions are that any message given to an officer by an infant calling itself a Baker Street Irregular goes straight to Mr Holmes. Chief Inspector Lestrade's orders, sir, but I don't like what I can't understand!"

"One moment," said Holmes quietly. "Sit and watch quietly

for two more minutes. Keep your eyes skinned for a young lady who has just had the shock of her life. A poor young creature whose every thought is shadowed by the coarse touch of a rope round her neck, a strap round her wrists and a trap-door under her pinioned feet. I trust that will do for the moment."

"More than enough, sir!"

"Six pairs of eyes have been watching Eaton Place for the past week," Holmes added, talking to Gregson but never taking his eyes from the mirror. "As a rule, my young friends are more concerned to avoid the police then to approach them. With my blessing, they have come to an understanding with the constables who patrol that beat—and with their sergeant. Let us leave it there. The lady in the case is our first concern."

I took my turn.

"She won't fall for your stage magic, Holmes! Only a complete fool would be taken in by that."

"Watson, you are, as so often, entirely correct. I count upon her disbelieving it. Have you not grasped it? That is the whole point. What she is therefore obliged to believe is that her closest and most dreadful secret, supposed to be known only to her lover and herself, is running loose all over London. I added the lines from Ozymandias for her benefit. They happen to be the work of the man she claims to be her natural great-grandfather and whose name she bears."

"Shelley!"

He did not reply. Instead, he tapped sharply on the roof with his stick. The cab jerked forward.

From my seat in the far corner of the darkened vehicle, I could see two figures who had emerged from the house of the séance. One was the manservant who had taken in Holmes's hatbox and hamper on our arrival. The other, fluttering to and fro in urgent expectation of a cab, was my pretty witch, Madame Rosa's handmaid.

The servant raised his hand. Tom Rathbone reined in the horse. We came alongside the pavement, behind another cab, apparently called for Miss Shelley. Holmes opened our door and got down. He walked across to hold open the door of the cab in front, and courteously doffed his hat to the young woman.

"Professor Scott Holmes!" Her voice was startled and not pleased.

"We are at your disposal, Miss Shelley—or should I say Miss Jessel?"

She stood pierced by shock, unable for a moment to reply. My friend continued in the same quiet voice.

"I must confess that I am more often known as Sherlock Holmes. You may have heard of me."

The breath had been knocked from her but she now managed a whisper.

"You are mistaken, sir! I am Miss Shelley!"

"Indeed you are," said Holmes sympathetically. "More precisely, however, you are Maria Shelley Jessel. Are you not?"

Miss Jessel—the ghost of Bly if anyone was—looked about her. The cab whose door Holmes held open was plain and black. Its driver wore a dark high-collared tunic. On the off-side, two women in black uniform clothes stepped down and walked to where Holmes and his new acquaintance stood. This pair could only be police matrons, accompanied by a duty constable.

Holmes left our quarry with them. He returned and slid across the buttoned leather of the seat to the corner where he had been sitting.

"Scotland Yard, I think, Gregson," he said thoughtfully.

9

Several floors above the river and the Victoria Embankment there is a plain green-walled office at Scotland Yard. When it is in use, a uniformed constable stands outside its door to prevent interruptions. Few sounds are overheard from within, except occasional rage or weeping. The walls are lined by plain wooden cupboards. A hat-rack stands by the door. At the centre is a wooden office table, with three upright chairs on each side and one at either end. At the quarters of every hour, the boom of Big Ben echoes like a funeral drum from the nearby Houses of Parliament.

Tobias Gregson sat at one end of this table. To his right, Holmes and I were side by side. Opposite us was Miss Shelley. A police matron accompanied her, sworn to silence by the Official Secrets Act of 1889.

The chair that Miss Shelley occupied had accommodated Dr Neill Cream the Lambeth Poisoner, Oscar Wilde at the time of his downfall and more recently Ada Chard the baby farmer. Even Montague Drewitt had sat there, the man whom the late Commissioner, Sir Melville Macnaughton, swore to Holmes and me was "Jack the Ripper" but could never quite prove it. To me, this plain official room had a far more sinister ambience than all the haunted landscapes of Bly.

Miss Shelley had not yet asked for an attorney to represent her. Gregson had not charged her and so perhaps she hoped that she did not need one. Perhaps she did not even know that she was entitled to one. She must have hoped that, once the matter of her name was cleared up, she would be free to go. Too soon she realised her mistake but, all the same, the inspector got nowhere with his questions. Our suspect no longer denied that she was Maria Jessel but she did not admit to anything else.

During a pause, Holmes broke in upon the interrogation.

"I fear you are not cut out to be a criminal, Miss Jessel, let alone an accessory to murder," he said sympathetically.

"I have no idea what you mean, sir."

"Have you not? You face arrest and detention, perhaps much worse. What will become of your child in that case? Please do not shake your head at me, madam. We know you have a child."

I knew no such thing—nor, to judge from his expression, did Gregson.

"I do not understand you, sir," she insisted, "I have nothing to do with you. I do not know why I am here. I certainly do not know why you are!"

Holmes became her friend.

"Come, now! While you were governess at Bly you became the mistress of Major James Mordaunt, did you not? It is not an uncommon thing between a young governess and an unmarried employer. There may even be a prospect of marriage. After some months, however, it became inconveniently evident that you were carrying a child. The prospect faded."

She lowered her eyes but still shook her head.

"The truth is best," Holmes said coaxingly, "What better solution was there than to tell Mrs Grose you were going home for a long holiday—and then let it be known, through your employer himself, that you had died during this absence? Believe me, it is a common enough subterfuge resorted to by young women in such a predicament."

He had taken a terrible gamble in jumping to this conclusion. Yet the expression on her face convinced me he had hit the answer at his first shot. She shook her head again, but he went on in the same quiet voice.

"The story of your death would satisfy Mrs Grose—and she in turn was bound by a promise that the other servants were not to be told for fear it would upset them. She would not question the truth of the report, if her master did not. So now that the two children are dead and Mrs Grose has gone to live with her son in Wales you might even return with Major Mordaunt to Bly—unless he has other plans for you. If there were a few people who had heard a mere rumour of your death, and if they chanced to see you now, they would simply know that such tittle-tattle could not have been true."

She kept her face lowered, pressing her handkerchief to her mouth. Holmes sighed.

"You would be perfectly safe to the end of your life, unless questions were asked. Unfortunately, even a novice criminal investigator would go first to Somerset House to find your death certificate. There is none, is there?"

She stared at him, visibly paler, eyes reddened. My friend continued.

"What there is, however, is a birth certificate. It registers a male child, Charles Alfred Jessel, born several months after your departure from Bly. He is Jessel on the certificate and his mother's name is Maria Shelley Jessel. His father's name and occupation are blank. James Mordaunt did not think enough of you to give your child his name. Is that it?"

How I pitied her! Her teeth were clenched on the hem of the

handkerchief, as if she might tear it! But then she looked up fiercely—and her silence broke.

"I do not want his name!"

"Do not? Or did not?" Holmes asked gently, "Think carefully, I beg you. The difference may be the thickness of a hangman's rope."

"Did not!" she burst out, "James Mordaunt had gained power over me. He had got my child, not I. It was put away where neither he nor I might see it. Those were his terms."

"Because it was not his child, was it?" Holmes suggested coaxingly, and once again my heart missed a beat at this dangerous leap in the dark. But I saw from her expression that he had hit the bull's-eye twice in a row. His voice softened. "Mordaunt would not take you from Bly to live with him in Eaton Place, so long as there was this reminder of another man under his roof."

It was so simple! The secret love of James Mordaunt for Maria Jessel was as dead as the two children of Bly. Yet some other man's child remained the means by which he still commanded Miss Jessel's obedience.

In the next half-hour we heard how Charles Alfred had been sent to a nursery school in Yorkshire, if baby farms for unwanted children can be called nurseries. Paid for by money drawn from the Bly estate, James Mordaunt kept it out of sight and mind at this private institution It was an establishment founded at Greta Bridge by William Shaw, twice sued by parents after children had gone blind from infection and gross neglect. Little Charles Alfred remained there, in pawn for his mother's obedient behaviour.

I took my chance.

"Do you tell us, Miss Jessel, that Mordaunt had such a hold over your affections that you would consent to this dreadful thing for your child?"

"I think not, Watson," Holmes interrupted gently, as our

suspect began to weep. "Neither affection nor passion holds them now. Fear of discovery is the bond."

He turned to her again.

"You had best tell us, Miss Jessel, what happened on the night that you—or more probably Major Mordaunt—killed Peter Quint at Bly House. That is to say when the father of your child, then still unborn, was killed."

He could not be certain of so much! He seemed like the gamester who risks one throw too many because his feral instinct senses a winning streak.

She looked up in tears, her hair straggling a little, and Holmes resumed.

"Was it the jealousy of your two lovers—servant and master—that caused the quarrel?" The pitiless voice was hardly more than audible. "Was it Mordaunt's discovery that you were carrying Quint's child—or was it something more? Did Quint strike you, for some reason, and did Mordaunt then deal him a murderous blow in return—across the skull with a blunt instrument? You left Bly for your so-called holiday a day or two later, did you not, wearing a convenient travelling veil to hide a swollen mouth or a bruised cheek?"

There was no reply, only a relentless sobbing.

"Peter Quint was a brute," Holmes continued quietly. "Did you perhaps strike in your own defence? You are not powerfully built, Miss Jessel, but even you might catch him from behind while he was sitting in a chair. Even you are strong enough to smash a poker down on his head. If one blow did not do it, you dared not let him recover and strike back. Blow must follow blow. Quint was a powerful man. He could kill you and your unborn child with a stroke of his arm or a swing of his boot. You had no alternative but to repeat those blows with force enough to cause that dreadful wound. Such a wound as might be mistaken for a flying impact against a stone parapet! To strike again and again for fear he should live and retaliate!"

At that instant, Holmes illustrated such violence by bringing his fist down on the table with a reverberating impact and Maria Jessel cried out, "No! Oh, no!"

But all sympathy had drained from my friend's voice.

"To carry him to the bridge that winter night offered a desperate escape. But you could not have lifted him. Mordaunt could. I have examined the inquest papers, the photograph of the body where it lay. Your hobble-de-hoy country coroner saw simply what he expected to see. I know rather more of blood and fatal wounds—and I have read the medical evidence. Peter Quint bled too little, even on a winter night, to have died at the bridge. The dead do not bleed as freely as the living—and he had almost stopped before he was placed there. I could prove, if I had to, that he lost too little blood at that place—even in the ice and cold."

"No!"

What did this denial mean? That Quint's body was not carried to the bridge or that she was not involved in his death?

"Oh yes, madam," Holmes persisted. "He was killed elsewhere and laid in the freezing darkness to be discovered next day when the medical evidence would be less clear. A man with medical knowledge, well within the competence of Surgeon-Major Mordaunt, could easily assist in misleading the coroner."

Our poor butterfly was pinned and wriggling.

"Quint walked back to Bly that evening," Holmes continued quietly. "At Bly he died from a blow—or blows—to the head, dealt by one or both of you. Mordaunt, let us say, carried or drove the body to the bridge. It would be frozen by morning. The correct time of death would be judged from when he left the inn. He was a drunkard who appeared to have died a drunkard's death. Why go further? If he died at the bridge, you and Major Mordaunt were both safely at Bly House when it happened."

He did not hurry her. At last she looked up.

"James Mordaunt," she said. "I could not do it! I had not the strength."

Her tears had stopped with the suddenness of fright, but her face was as wild-eyed as a fury of Greek tragedy.

Holmes was gentle with her again.

"I believe you did not do it, Miss Jessel. I believe I could prove that, if you will help me. But I can do nothing until I know why you assisted Major Mordaunt to drive Miss Temple almost out of her mind."

In these three sentences her persecutor offered to become her champion and lit the way through her despair. She looked at him uncertainly and then burst out:

"I did not want to harm Miss Temple! Why should I? But Quint had told secrets to little Miles. Secrets that James Mordaunt assured me might destroy us both, if they went further. The little boy betrayed them innocently when he said things at school. We did not know this when Miss Temple first came and Miles was still at King Alfred's. But we could not risk what he might say to her if she remained."

In similar words, Spencer-Smith recalled how Miles "said things" to the other children.

"Secrets about the evil eye and the selling of souls, perhaps? Crime and criminals? Power over others?"

She nodded without looking up.

"The boy worshipped Quint like a father."

"Go on, please."

"Such secrets would destroy us, if ever Miles was questioned about them!"

I saw my friend take a breath before his next question, as if the croupier's wheel was spinning once more.

"Destroy you and Major Mordaunt?"

She answered with her eyes and now I saw the whole truth, even before she told it. Maria Jessel was calmer. She addressed Holmes in a quiet monotone.

"If Miles believed that Quint was dead, James Mordaunt feared the boy might not hesitate to tell the man's secrets. But Miles would do nothing to hurt Quint if the man might be alive in some form. If we could make the boy and his sister believe that Quint and the dead governess could somehow linger at Bly." She dropped her voice to a whisper, "Even as ghosts. Miles loved tales of terror, as children do. He believed all that Quint had told him."

Inspector Gregson intervened cautiously.

"Did Major Mordaunt suggest to you that if the secret of Quint's murder was known, he would hang for his crime and you as his accomplice? Is that what it comes to?"

She looked at Holmes, as if for authority to answer. He gave a single nod.

"Yes, sir," she said. "He suggested that threat to me—only once."

"So Peter Quint and you, the dead governess, must appear at a convenient distance?" I asked. "Upon a tower or across a lake?"

"Half a moment," said Gregson, lifting his hand. "The boy would know the difference between Quint and his uncle in disguise, even at a distance."

"Of course," said Holmes casually, "and that is why Miles was never to see him, except possibly once at the window of a tower in the dark. Miss Temple was to identify him, with Mrs Grose's assistance. Major Mordaunt could carry off an impersonation for the benefit of Miss Temple, who had never seen Quint himself. The same build, the same clothes, the hair-piece of unusual red and the whiskers. For good measure, Flora saw the real Miss Jessel and knew she could not be mistaken. If Miles Mordaunt truly believed in the powers of darkness, then from all he heard he must have thought his prayers had been answered."

"Apparitions?" Gregson asked anxiously.

"Only Miss Temple was to see apparitions of both the so-called Quint and Miss Jessel. If Mrs Grose confirmed the descriptions, there was powerful temptation for Miles to believe. Small wonder that the children talked excitedly together of little else but hauntings. They no doubt compared secrets about the two friends whom they must protect, even in death. We cannot be sure that it was Mordaunt whom Miss Temple had seen at the solicitor's office. She had never met him otherwise."

So much for ghosts!

"The timing fits," I said hastily, "There were no apparitions in the first months of Miss Temple's residence at Bly. They began only after Miles had been expelled from King Alfred's for his story of the Fifth Stone. With all his poisonous nonsense about devilry and fraud, the boy was a perfect victim for deception."

Holmes turned again to the prisoner.

"Tell us, Miss Jessel!"

She spoke clearly but quietly, as though still in a state of shock.

"Once or twice James Mordaunt went to Bly on his own after Miss Temple came there. I do not know why or what he did there. He took me three times, after Miles was sent home from school. I had not been there otherwise since I left to have my child. Twice we slipped across to the island. I was to stand where Miss Temple should see me. I did not expect Mrs Grose to be with her but I moved back, out of her view."

"And Flora was there?"

"James Mordaunt knew she would be sure to tell Miles. When I was governess, the island had been a special place for the master and me. Once we had taken the boat, no one else could cross and surprise us together. There is an old pavilion. They call it the Temple of Proserpine. We used to go there secretly when I was at Bly. After I left, he was always kind when we went back there, kind as he used to be. Kind for several days afterwards. He was different there, as if he knew it was his home."

"And if you had refused to act your part in this masquerade?"

"If I did not behave sensibly, as he called it, the story of Peter Quint's death would come out in the end. He could easily escape to France, Spain, even to South America. He had the money. I should be left behind. What he asked of me was not much. I need only make Miss Temple believe his nonsense and leave us alone. I had no idea he might kill Peter Quint. I knew nothing of the Five Stones until after that. I was only to help him create a story of a poor mad governess and Miles, her besotted little admirer."

Gregson's expression suggested that much of this was double-Dutch to him. With the curiosity of a medical man, however, there was one question I must ask.

"What of the Sunday? When Miss Temple came back early from church? What happened then?"

"It was an accident. We went early from Abbots Langley, on our way to Cambridge, to fetch some papers from his tower room, while all the people were at church. He came to me in the schoolroom when he saw Miss Temple walking back. He said that we should give her an experience she would never forget. It would keep her nose out of our business, that was the expression he used. If I heard her on the staircase, I must simply step through a narrow door at the far end of the schoolroom. The tower steps lie beyond. That was to be our escape. He went out to look again and then returned."

Holmes intervened.

"Did Mordaunt have anything in his hands when he came back to the schoolroom?"

She sounded surprised that he should know.

"Why, yes. He was holding a mirror, four or five inches across, from his Army days in India. He showed it to me once before. It was what he called a field heliostat. I presume he kept it with his other souvenirs."

"A square, plain-glass signal-mirror, in other words," said Holmes approvingly. "From the Himalayas such a device has been known to flash Morse code messages as far as sixty miles. Small wonder if it blinded Miss Temple like a migraine, even in mild October sun!"

"He had not planned it," she said, "but when the opportunity came he knew just what to do. That Sunday was like a day in summer. From behind the lace curtain that screened the oriel balcony where he waited, he caught the sun in the glass—he had been trained to do that—and shone it directly into her face. It almost blinded her but not before she caught a glimpse of me. I heard her cry out, 'You terrible woman!' or something of the kind. She was fumbling or stumbling. There was a bump. Perhaps she fell, but I had gone out through the low doorway to the tower steps. I did not see what happened."

Big Ben began to toll ten o'clock. Gregson had been patient during all this. Now he leant forward to our prisoner.

"Well, miss, act sensibly and you may have the means of getting free from this brute. But as Mr Holmes says, you must help us and you must do it quick-sharp. Tell us straight. Why should Mordaunt want Miles to believe in Quint's ghost?"

The look of exasperation in Holmes's eyes at the inspector's intervention is beyond description.

"To shut the boy's mouth!" he said impatiently. "Peter Quint turned to robbery—after he left the Army and before Major Mordaunt picked him up from the gutter and made him his valet. Is that not so, Miss Jessel? Quint was the Fifth Stone in the most important of your unsolved robberies and murders. Gossip has it there were five robbers to match the Five Stones. Evidence suggests there was one—Peter Quint. Robber and killer!"

Gregson glanced at Miss Jessel and then stared at Holmes again.

"How could a boy of ten know all this?"

Holmes glanced at his watch and then at the inspector.

"Quint treated him like a comrade in arms. It flattered the valet to entertain this child with stories of women and crime. Miles grew proud of the only man who seemed like a father to him. In a drunken or foolhardy moment, Quint boasted in some way of the Five Stones robbery. Soon after that Miles went to school. Boys of his age love to brag of their fathers. He showed off what Quint had taught him—selling his soul, the trick with the dice, the evil eye. He even talked of drowning his prim young governess because Quint said such kittens should be killed before they became cats. In the end Miles embroidered this tale of his friend by naming him as the Fifth Stone, but not as Quint. In revenge for some fancied ill-treatment, he also cast his abhorrent housemaster, Mair Loftus, as the gang's receiver who changed the stolen gold coins for bank-notes."

"The story of a major robbery told in masquerade," said Gregson softly. "Then the receiver of the gold was not Mair Loftus, was he, Mr Holmes? He was our man James Mordaunt!"

To look at Maria Jessel just then was once again to know the answer.

Before Holmes could reply, there was a knock at the door. A uniformed constable entered and presented a blue police telegram to Tobias Gregson. The inspector read it and then looked across the table at the police matron.

"Remove the prisoner!"

When Maria Jessel rose, it was obvious that she was shaking. She lost her footing as she crossed to the door but the matron's arm steadied her.

Gregson handed the form to Holmes. For my benefit, the inspector explained.

"When we arrived here, Dr Watson, I wired a request to the Royal Mail inspectors. Any communication sent to Major

Mordaunt of Eaton Place to be delivered but its contents to be reported to me. After what she heard at the séance, I rather expected Miss Jessel would slip a message to her friend. She might care nothing for him, but his danger was just as much hers. This was despatched by telephone from Sambourne Avenue shortly before we detained her. To Major Mordaunt. 'The Fifth Stone is known. Cross at once. I will follow. Watch for me on the other side.'"

Holmes beamed at him.

"Cross at once, indeed!" Gregson said with satisfaction, "Watch for me on the other side! I shall wire every police-post at every cross-channel port. He fancies himself safe on the Continent, does Major Mordaunt. But not a man shall leave for France nor the Hook of Holland tonight without giving an account of himself. I fancy we shall have him, Mr Holmes!"

Holmes stared at him.

"Well done, Gregson! You are ahead of the game this time and no mistake. I prophesy there will be no stopping you!"

Even Gregson caught the irony in this. He looked as if he did not quite know how to reply.

"Of course, you do not know what your man looks like by now," Holmes continued cheerfully, "but do not let that discourage you. Suppose him to be thick set with mutton-chop whiskers and piercing eyes, or something of that kind. You will have him the minute he tries to book his passage."

Before I could intervene, there came a second knock at the door. It was the young uniformed constable again, looking far more flustered than before and short of breath.

"Telephone call to your office, Mr Gregson. Compliments of duty inspector, Belgravia. A gunshot was fired in Eaton Place five minutes ago. No report of injuries but no further information. A service revolver by the sound of it."

10

Before Tom Rathbone returned the picnic hamper and its contents to Baker Street, Holmes had rescued his long grey travelling cloak and close-fitting cloth cap. The effect of these was to make him look taller and leaner than ever. We were now both dressed for the occasion as the footsteps of the CID officers clattered ahead of us like a troop of cavalry down the stone steps which led to the transport bay of Scotland Yard. For the benefit of Gregson, Holmes called out,

"You have the instinct of a marksman, Mr Gregson."

"We don't carry guns on duty, Mr Holmes. You know that."

"You miss the point, my dear fellow. After Miss Jessel's warning to him, we may take it that you now have Major Mordaunt as a target on the wing."

"Or with a bullet through his brain," I suggested, too quietly for the inspector to hear.

Gregson glanced over his shoulder. Here was my chance.

"Twenty years ago, Gregson, our man fought in a successful guerrilla war across Afghanistan, under Major-General Sir Frederick Roberts, as he was then. So did I. His regiment, the

Queen's Rifles, scouted over the most hostile terrain you can imagine. Leaving a dark house, hidden by shrubbery, on a moonless night would be child's play."

"Take no notice of Watson, inspector, you will have your man!"

Gregson withdrew into a suspicious silence, no doubt brooding over the interruption of his questions to Miss Jessel. We followed him to the Embankment Gate of Great Scotland Yard. The quarters of half-past ten droned through the air from Parliament and a light rain began to fall. The inspector hoisted his bulk into the black cab that had brought Maria Jessel from Kensington. It bore us past Westminster Abbey in the lamplight and into the dim reaches of Victoria Street, its shops and offices unlit. A scent of oranges and peaches from the greengrocers' stalls of the South Coast Railway hung in the mild rainy air at Victoria Station.

Mordaunt had caught himself in a trap of his own making! Quint and Miss Jessel had certainly earned the reputation that Mrs Grose gave them. What the good housekeeper did not know was that with every arrival of Mordaunt at Bly, the young woman must slip from the embrace of a menial into the arms of her master. The vicious passion of Quint and the arrogance of Mordaunt were well matched. For a master to seduce a governess was a cliché of fiction. For the young woman to be the mistress of a valet at the same time—carrying that valet's child!—foreshadowed catastrophe for all concerned.

Twice in my professional career I had encountered a man and woman drawn together by such animal attraction and held together by a crime. Yoked together in fear, passion grown cold, there was as much love then as between two ferrets confined in a sack. Mordaunt and Miss Jessel had nothing to hold them but a memory of Quint and a sick fear of the noose. The master hardly dared let the young woman out of his sight. He was secure only through Charles Alfred, held as an innocent ransom in the cruel confinement of William Shaw's baby farm at Greta Bridge.

The conclusion was plain as a proof in geometry. There could now be no safety for either party except through the death of the other. But how might that be accomplished?

We crossed Buckingham Palace Road and came to the cream fronts and garden shrubberies of Eaton Place.

These villas and mansions seemed quiet enough, but I made out half a dozen helmeted figures among the bushes. Those who had been on observation earlier had no doubt dived for cover as soon as they heard the gunshot. There was still confusion. Several uniformed men were arguing as to whether there had been one shot or two—or possibly even three. A stationary cab on the adjoining side of the square contained two or three plain-clothes officers, no doubt issued with police pistols.

The disturbance had drawn residents and passers-by to their vantage points. On the next street corner a knot of sightseers had gathered from the saloon bar of the Royal Clarence Hotel. Several wore the brown-and-white-check overcoats of rat-catchers or racing tipsters.

Within its shrubbery, Mordaunt's villa was immediately opposite us. Heavy curtains had been drawn across the tall ground-floor windows. There was no sign of light or movement.

"I never knew a suicide who bothered to turn the lights off before despatching himself," Holmes said thoughtfully.

As a military man, I found the concealment of the police officers deplorable. An old soldier like Mordaunt with Indian service in his blood would spot their first movement from behind his darkened windows. Alerted by Miss Jessel, startled into action, he would not miss a single movement.

In the drizzle of the spring night, Gregson led us up the front path between dripping laurel branches. Two plain-clothes men flanked us. The man next to me had the flap of his jacket loose.

His hand was close to a Mauser "Zig-Zag," so-called because of its quick-reloading position. Gregson pulled the doorbell. It jangled somewhere in the basement but there was no response.

"Who did he shoot," Gregson muttered to me, "if not himself?"

"We cannot assume he is dead," I whispered. "He may be lying wounded—and armed."

The inspector reached for the black knocker of the front door. Its thump reverberated through the house. If the fugitive was there, we were giving him ample warning. Our plain-clothes men now crouched to one side. Only Sherlock Holmes stood upright, immobile and sceptical.

Gregson motioned to one of the uniformed men. The constable drew his truncheon and shattered the nearest sash window close to its catch. The others held back and waited, but still there was no response. The man edged his arm through the broken pane and drew the catch. Nothing moved in the darkened room. Gregson stepped forward and eased the window-frame upwards until there was enough height to step across its sill. Holmes and I followed with the plain-clothes detail.

We stood on a carpeted floor in the dimly-reflected lamplight from the street. By the aid of a constable's lantern I saw only what I had expected. An immaculately-papered room was furnished by two silk divans and matching chairs of inlaid wood, more elegant and appealing than the interior of Bly. Gregson pushed open the hall door. Reflected light fell on the curve of a silent staircase. We followed cautiously up the carpeted steps. Once again I thought of my own revolver lying uselessly in its Baker Street drawer.

As we came level with the landing, a patch of light showed where a bedroom door was not quite closed. Without seeming to push past Gregson, Holmes reached the landing first. He edged the door a little, then flung it wide.

We were on the threshold of a dressing-room. Behind its

velvet curtains, a pool of electric light fell upon the leather inset of a dressing-table. Gregson and his men continued to search by the subdued light of dark lanterns.

"Curious," Holmes murmured. "As we came in at the lower window there was still an air of gun-smoke—quite acrid. Up here it is clear."

I could smell another odour and was trying to put a name to it. It was a spirituous tang. Not medical but almost like confectionary. I thought, absurdly, of theatrical whiskers.

"I believe we have the measure of him," Holmes continued, in the same quiet voice. "Mordaunt must choose between the hangman's art or his own hand. Miss Jessel has left him no other choice. Beware the selflessness of passionate love as it takes on a merciless egotism. I should not care to be in this poor devil's shoes."

By now, I was creeping back down the stairs behind one of the plain-clothes men. We crossed the hall and cautiously entered a ground-floor sitting-room at the rear to light the gas. These windows looked out onto a small garden behind the house. The man ahead of me stumbled in the semi-darkness, cursed, and then spoke with some awe.

"It's a body, doctor!"

And so it was. In a moment, the light went on. We found ourselves looking down at the body of a pure white greyhound, shot cleanly through the skull. This poor creature was added to the haphazard menagerie of evidence.

"A man who thought more of his dog than of any human being," said Holmes over my shoulder, "would not leave it to the mercy of the vivisectionist or the curiosity of holiday crowds. A most interesting pathological type. But I think the dog had a greater part than that."

"What part?"

"Imagine the scene. A shot rang out. Policemen jumped for

cover. Some of the bystanders hurried towards the scene. Some were running away, some running towards. Darkness everywhere. The poor beast's death created a skilful diversion. I swear our man was through this rear garden and across the road while the echoes of the shot were still dying. You must not forget your regimental field-craft, Watson. When surrounded, make your break during the moment of maximum confusion. As for that scent upstairs—"

"I noticed it."

"Spirit gum, which will turn the smooth-shaven hero into a bearded ogre for a brief period. Recall the mutton-chop-whiskered figure on the garden tower, my dear fellow."

One of the plain-clothes men had found a bureau open. There was no passport nor money. That was little enough for one who was leaving never to return. Where was the rest to come from?

A glance from an upper window into the darkened road showed a dozen uniformed officers standing about forlornly. The companions of the Royal Clarence had made their way back into the saloon bar, discussing the drama with agreeable earnestness.

Presently we stood with Gregson at the black-painted iron-work of the front gate. The inspector had already ordered wires to be despatched from Scotland Yard to the police posts of the English Channel and the North Sea.

"Every port sealed tighter than a rat's eyeball," he assured us.

Before my friend could comment on this, he was interrupted by an urchin who seemed to stand no higher than his waist and whom Gregson was no doubt about to tell to "Hop it, smart!"

"Please, sir! Mr Holmes, sir, if you please."

Holmes looked down and his features relaxed.

"Why, Smiler! Smiler Hawkins of my intrepid militia!"

The infant took heart at this.

"If you please, Mr Holmes, I was left to watch when the other two went to have their supper."

"Be off with you!" said Gregson sharply, making as if to cuff the child's ear.

"But I saw him, sir. The cove as was in that house! Face-to-face. I saw him go."

"A feat which the combined forces of Scotland Yard and the Belgravia division failed to accomplish," said Holmes amiably. "All things considered, Gregson, I think we had better listen to what this budding thief-taker has to say."

Gregson seemed about to grumble but then stood back.

"Tell us, Smiler," Holmes encouraged him. "What happened?"

"There was a shot, sir. All of a sudden it came, from behind the house. Everyone ran for it. Mostly into the bushes."

"Including Major Mordaunt, I fear."

"I seen him yesterday, sir. At the front. Not close up but wearing the same clothes as tonight. He came out from the back this time, except everyone else was running and hadn't time to notice him."

"What did he look like, when you saw him face-to-face this evening?"

"Not much of a gent, sir. Just a common overcoat wiv them little brown checks. Thick-built, he was. Not as tall as you. Reddish hair and whiskers."

"Wore a hat?"

"Greyish topper. Not a real gent's black silk."

"Bald, would you say?"

Smiler looked as if the idea had only just occurred to him.

"Yeah, could have been. As likely as not. Hard to say under a topper."

"Where did he go?"

"He come out of that back lane, where the tradesmen go, just after the gun was fired, and joined at the end of all the others.

Walking fast rather than running. You'd think he was running wiv 'em rather than running away."

"Precisely," said Holmes quietly.

"I only saw where he went because I was watching close to that back lane. Cool he was, as if he might be in command. He sloped up to the bunch standing by the Royal Clarence. Mingled wiv 'em and went into the bar when they did."

"A pity you did not manage to keep him in view!" said Gregson bitterly.

"Oh, but I did, sir. I couldn't come away to find you at first or I'd have lost him."

"Not there now?"

"No, sir. He came out again through the other door of the Clarence, the public bar. Then he walked so smart I could hardly keep up with him. Straight down to the King's Road and hailed a cab. It was a minute or two before one came along, otherwise I'd never have caught the order he gave the driver."

"Well?" said Gregson aggressively. "Lost our tongue, have we?"

"Oh no, sir," said the infant innocently. "I heard him. Liverpool Street Station. He even give the platform. Platform 12. I could have hopped on the board at the back, crouched down and gone wiv 'im. But then I wouldn't be here to tell you, would I, sir?"

"Was he carrying anything?" I asked.

"Naw, sir. Not to speak of. Little attaché case. Nuffing more."

Holmes reached down and patted the uncombed head. He drew a sovereign from his note-case.

"Well done, Smiler! If Mr Gregson knows his onions, you may find yourself in the detective division a year or two from now."

"Thank you, Mr Holmes! Thank you very much, sir."

This infant prodigy scuttled off, gripping the coin in his right hand.

"Platform 12!" said Gregson vindictively. "Harwich! Hook of

Holland! The overnight crossing! In three or four hours, Major Mordaunt could be outside territorial waters. Tomorrow he might be on an express train to anywhere in Europe. Try bringing him back from Spain or Italy, where there's no extradition treaty!"

"You have alerted Harwich, as well as the Channel ports?"

"I wasn't born yesterday, Mr Holmes. He'll do as his lady friend advised, and she knows it. He'll be waiting for her on the other side. He can't leave her loose to talk."

"You will not catch him at Liverpool Street, however," said Holmes, pocketing his watch. "The train for the Hook of Holland ferry left Liverpool Street ten minutes ago. If memory serves, there is no other tonight, except the mail train at ten minutes to midnight. Passengers are not carried upon it."

This might be unwelcome news, but before Gregson could say so, Holmes suggested blandly, "All things considered, you had best telegraph Chief Inspector Lestrade to meet us at Liverpool Street—Platform 12—in half an hour from now. He has just about got enough time."

The unease on Gregson's pale, dyspeptic features suggested to me a fish rising reluctantly from the bottom of an opaque and stagnant pool.

11

No express could now overtake the Harwich ferry train. In any case, not even Scotland Yard could command a pursuit train to be added to the busy railway traffic in the middle of the night. As for other forms of transport, when these events occurred some thirty years ago, the motor car was a tortoise by comparison with the slowest train. The aeroplane was not even a show-ground curiosity. Communication by a telegram or "wire" might convey a message almost instantaneously—but it could only be received at certain fixed points. Beyond them, it was delivered by hand. Once we set off by night in pursuit of James Mordaunt, we must depend on our own wits.

Fortunately, Sherlock Holmes had a connoisseur's knowledge of the oddities of the British railway system. During the hours of darkness, there were trains which cross-crossed the country without being listed in Bradshaw's passenger time table. Many were supervised by the railway police on behalf of Her Majesty's Royal Mail. They included "high-value-package" coaches, kept out of bounds to the travelling public.

From Smiler Hawkins's information, Mordaunt must have

intended to catch the eleven o'clock ferry train from Liverpool Street to Harwich, for the overnight crossing to the Hook of Holland. Or did he merely want us to think this, the more easily to throw us off the scent? The 11 p.m. was the last passenger train on the Harwich line and we had missed it already. Our thoughts turned to the 11.50 East Coast mail train. Its vans carried the bulky canvas post-bags from the City of London sorting-office to King's Lynn in Norfolk, via Chelmsford, Colchester, Felixstowe, Harwich and Great Yarmouth.

By good fortune, Lestrade was duty commander of the Criminal Investigation Division at Scotland Yard overnight. As Holmes suggested, Gregson turned to his sergeant with orders to alert the chief inspector and request his presence urgently at Liverpool Street.

"A further wire to be sent to Harwich," Gregson added, calling the man back. "The ferry train is to be met at the docks. All passengers to be checked. Look for a thick-set man with red hair and whiskers, wearing a brown-and-white plaid coat. Possibly carrying or wearing a grey hat."

"You think of everything, my dear fellow!" said Holmes admiringly. I looked at my friend uneasily.

Gregson ignored this compliment and beckoned the police van which had brought us to Eaton Place. A moment later its two horses were moving at a gallop across Belgrave Square, down the Strand, up Ludgate Hill and past St Paul's, towards Bishopsgate Street and the East Coast mail. We passed the illuminated face of Liverpool Street Station clock-tower, whose hands pointed to twenty-five minutes to midnight. Gregson glanced at it and checked his watch. A moment later the inspector got down from the van in the station forecourt and strode towards the office door of the railway police.

Under the glass canopy of the departure platforms, the lamp lit air was filled by columns of steam and the boom of engines in motion. Holmes and I headed for Platform 12, where the mail train appeared as a set of six security vans with very few windows, all of them barred. Inside it, as the powerful locomotive rattled through the night, workers in brown overalls and arm-bands stood at long tables. Deftly and casually, they would sort envelopes and packets from the canvas bags into bundles for delivery to the towns and villages of East Anglia. At every stop along the line, another squadron of bags would be hoisted out onto flat trolleys.

At the iron-railed gate of the platform, a lean ferret-like man in an Inverness cape, his air furtive and sly, was already standing by the gate. Scotland Yard was nearer to Liverpool Street than Belgravia had been. Chief Inspector Lestrade held out his hand in greeting.

"Well, Mr Holmes! Should I thank you for giving us Maria Jessel? A most contrary lady! From all that's happened, Mordaunt ought to be a dose of poison to her. Rum thing is, she won't say a word against him now. What she's hoping for? Do you know?"

"Her freedom, I suppose," said Holmes unhelpfully.

Lestrade pulled a face.

"I don't see it. What's she after?"

"Justice, if you prefer it." My friend looked at me, his back to the chief inspector, and raised his eyebrows as if in despair of him.

"Then why won't she ditch him and have done with it, sir?"

Holmes swung round on him.

"I believe, Lestrade, I may go so far as to say we shall learn the answer to that by tomorrow morning. Meantime, I have two requests to make."

The Scotland Yard man's eyes narrowed a little.

"Yes? Such as?"

"Your colleague Gregson is on a somewhat different track to

us. He fancies Mordaunt will make a dash for the Hook of Holland."

"And how do you propose to remedy that, Mr Holmes?"

"By assuming that Mr Gregson is mistaken. The ferry train is not half-way to Harwich yet. Colchester is the last stop before the docks, I believe. Put aboard two plain-clothes men for the last leg of the journey. Give them Mordaunt's description, as we have it. He can hardly change it much in full view of the other passengers. By this time of night there will be only a final handful of travellers still making for the docks. Just let your two men search the train unobtrusively between Colchester and Harwich for anyone who might be Mordaunt. From the police post at the docks let them wire the result of their search to every station-master along the route."

Lestrade's eyes widened.

"You think he might not be on the train after all this?"

"Let us say I think it very unlikely that they will find him on it."

"Then you're the only one who does!" said the chief inspector humorously. "After he bought a ticket for the docks!"

"Just as any man would who wanted to throw off the pursuit. As for other opinions, I am well used to being in a minority."

I was quite sure that Lestrade's inclination was to refuse us, but he mastered his feelings after a few moments' thought.

"Very well, Mr Holmes. You have done us a good turn in finding Maria Jessel. We owe you a favour. You shall have two men at Colchester. And your other request?"

"A little more ambitious. I require Inspector Alfred Swain of the Essex Constabulary Criminal Investigation Branch, his sergeant and a dozen good uniformed men to meet this mail train at Abbots Langley. Mind you, Lestrade, it must be Alfred Swain."

I thought there was going to be a pitched argument over this. What possible reason could there be for a detachment of police to meet a train on which Major Mordaunt could not possibly travel? He would surely be at Harwich by then! Our Scotland Yard man drew his plaid cape more tightly round his shoulders and spoke quietly.

"I hope you know what you're doing, Mr Holmes. I do so hope you do. As for Alfred Swain, I suppose you know his story? He had to leave Scotland Yard for a country posting. A matter of personal differences with his commander."

"Differences with Superintendent Toplady that I might also have had, were I in Swain's place." Holmes became more coaxing. "My dear Lestrade, Mordaunt is no ordinary criminal. I believe you are playing for higher stakes than you suppose. On the evidence you have, the major could reduce Maria Jessel's story to thin air, the vapours of feminine spite. Who are your witnesses? A poor mad governess now lying in Broadmoor and a cast-off mistress who must almost admit to murder herself in order to catch him. I fear you would seize him only to let him go again."

Lestrade fell silent for a moment. Then, he said, "Meaning what in particular?"

"Your supposition is correct but your timing is in error. Mordaunt will make a sudden bolt for the Continent. However, he will not do so—he dare not—until he is certain that nothing is left behind to betray and therefore destroy him. Your evidence remains precarious. I warn you that you must catch him in the act or you will not catch him at all. With due modesty, I believe I am the only person who can accomplish that."

"Do you indeed?" Lestrade straightened up and looked at him hard. "You don't think much of yourself, do you, Mr Holmes?"

Holmes ignored this pleasantry.

"Take him too soon, Lestrade, and what have you got? Can you even prove that Mordaunt killed Quint and that it was not some other man of Miss Jessel's acquaintance whom she now protects? Can you prove that Mordaunt carried Quint's body to the bridge and left it there? You know you cannot. Even the verdict of the coroner's court stands against you. You may suspect it but you can prove nothing. Leave that to me!"

Lestrade appeared to chew his lip. It was now 11.45 by the illuminated clock-face above the platform.

"A man as clever as you say Mordaunt is will not wait around to be caught by you, Mr Sherlock Holmes!"

A little twitch of impatience pulled at Holmes's mouth.

"I venture to think he is a little less clever than I shall be."

The chief inspector paused and the illuminated clock jerked forward to the next minute on the dial.

"In that case . . ." Lestrade began hesitantly.

"In that case, you must make Mordaunt hang himself. It can be done but it must be done now."

"How?"

"Leave it to me! Get me Alfred Swain!"

Lestrade looked long and hard at the clock again, while Gregson ran across the forecourt towards us. Something unpleasantly like a smirk distended his thin, pale face. He drew a sheet of paper from his pocket.

"A man positively answering the description of Major Mordaunt, as given to us by your young friend this evening, purchased a first-class single ticket to Harwich at approximately five minutes to eleven."

"Oh really?" said Holmes indifferently. "Well he would, wouldn't he?" He turned again to Lestrade. "I must positively insist upon the two requests that I have made. One is of no use without the other."

Lestrade peered at him through the steam-laden railway mist.

"He bought a ticket to Harwich, Mr Holmes—not Abbots Langley!"

"Which is why he will not be going to Harwich," said Holmes in some desperation.

We were standing beside a first-class passenger coach with a guard's compartment which formed the rear of the mail train. Holmes gripped the handle of the locked door. It was evident to me that he had no intention of letting go of it and that he must be dragged down the platform if the engine moved. There was a reproving shout from the station-master, who was standing with his whistle raised near the locomotive. Lestrade began to flounder. He gave a short nod and let out a hard breath.

"Very well, Mr Holmes."

The station-master's whistle blew, hard and sharp from the front of the train. The uniformed guard at the rear replied. Without another word, Lestrade walked off towards the overnight telegraph office. He showed all the enthusiasm of an aristocrat of the *ancien régime* keeping an appointment with the tumbrel.

Holmes patted the brass handle of the carriage door.

"Ours, I believe."

The guard opened the door with a bolt-key and we took our seats. My friend settled himself into a window corner. There was a final sharp note from the guard's whistle and the first rhythmic blast of steam ahead of us. We rumbled sedately through long soot-lined tunnels under the tenements of Whitechapel and Shoreditch. As we gathered speed among the sleeping suburbs of Hackney and Stratford, Holmes offered us his cigar-case.

"There is nothing so deceptive as an obvious fact," he said, as if to himself. "It is truly extraordinary the extent to which people believe whatever they are told. They see what they expect to see. My own profession would be impossible if they did not. However it also enables villains like James Mordaunt to live easy and reputable lives."

"Lying does not convict him of criminality," I said patiently.

"It is not in itself a criminal offence, Watson. Yet how easily Mordaunt was believed! Miss Temple, the new young governess, expected to be interviewed by Mordaunt. She never doubted it was he. Who knows? Perhaps it was he—or perhaps a paid impostor. At Bly he merely informed Mrs Grose that the previous governess, Miss Jessel, was dead. The good woman would hardly demand to see a coroner's certificate! They agreed not to upset the lower servants by telling them. Why should she doubt her master?"

"And then?" I asked sceptically.

Holmes returned the slim cigar-case to his pocket and lit a match.

"Mordaunt assured Miss Temple that he had no interest in Bly or the children. The lawyers would see that she had ample funds for whatever was needed. She had only to ask. He preferred to spend most of his life in France, with an independent income from his property there. The rest of the time he lived at leisure in Eaton Place."

Tobias Gregson looked increasingly uneasy during all this.

"And you know better, do you, Mr Holmes?"

A brief grimace suggested the answer.

"The world believed James Mordaunt to be a man of substance in fashionable Belgravia, but more often to be found abroad in Biarritz or the Boulevard St Germain. He never seemed short of money."

"And do you know better, sir?" Gregson repeated, leaning forward.

"It is my business to know better," Holmes remarked airily with a wave of his cigar. "One or two servants at the Beargarden Club, to which he belonged, knew him better. Before his brother's death in India, the major was a most unlucky gambler. One man, in particular, also recalled him as an habitué of certain establishments where none of us would care to be seen. There was a whisper of a subpoena to summon him to the trial of Mrs Mary Jefferies during the white-slave scandals stirred up by W. T. Stead and the *Pall Mall Gazette* some years ago. Fortunately for him, that came to nothing. He had covered his tracks. Even so, he soon exhausted a younger son's inheritance. In consequence, his pretended indifference to Bly masked a determination to get every penny from the estate."

Gregson managed to look both sceptical and uneasy.

"That's a new one on me, Mr Holmes. All his wealth was a put-up job?"

"The fashionable world—and the money-lenders—must be made to believe he could afford his losses. So they did. They thought him nothing but a rich fool. In truth, his inheritance was so emaciated that he acted as a criminal receiver to his former batman. That batman, Peter Quint, had become his valet after being discharged from the Army. But it was not sentiment that kept them together. Unhappily, Quint committed murder in the course of the Five Stones robbery for which Mordaunt was to act as receiver. They were both parties to the crime. Mordaunt could not withdraw, for if Quint was caught he promised to drag down Mordaunt with him."

"But what of France," I protested, "and the property there?"

"According to information gathered in Belgravia by our young friends, Mordaunt was seldom absent from Eaton Place. I have established that the house he lives in was never owned by him. There was no property in France. He was there briefly, because it was safer to change stolen gold into respectable banknotes and bonds in Paris than in London. So long as he appeared as an Englishman of substance, he could do it. It must be he. A ruffian like Quint could never have crossed the doorstep of Rothschilds or the Crédit Lyonnais."

The black chimneys of North London had fallen behind us and the lamps of villages were a pin-point scattering in the dark. Gregson sat back with a sigh.

"I still say, Mr Holmes, you will need more than tales of

servants from the Beargarden Club or the likes of Mrs Jefferies and her young ladies."

My friend smiled at him sympathetically.

"There was more than one document in the Court of Chancery, for those prepared to dig a little. They related to actions pending against James Mordaunt for substantial sums. Gambling debts may not be recoverable at law. Unpaid rents in Belgravia are another matter. Happily for our man, his brother Colonel Mordaunt then died in India. James Mordaunt became trustee to the estate and guardian to the two children. Miles could not inherit until he was twenty-one—eleven years more Meanwhile, as if by magic, Chancery actions were withdrawn and bills were paid. The guardian of Bly avoided ruin by the skin of his teeth."

"Eleven years in which to pilfer the estate!" I said.

"Eleven years in which to remove a delicate child from this world to the next. Otherwise the embezzlements must come to light. Mordaunt would inherit the estate in his own right if Miles should die before him. Ironically, a few tiny diphtheritic bacteria made all his scheming unnecessary."

Gregson shook his head.

"If there was eleven years to do the deed, Mr Holmes, he seems to have been in a bit of a hurry to get it finished."

"No, Gregson. I should say he had been planning unhurriedly for a year or two. It was the behaviour of Miles at King Alfred's school that shook him. The boy's stories of the Five Stones robbery and a murder. How many people had Miles told the story to? How long before someone who heard the tale put Peter Quint's name to the facts—and Quint's name involved his master? There must be no more stories. The boy must never leave Bly for school again. Hence Mordaunt's eccentric preference for having him taught at home by his sister's governess."

We roared through a deep cutting between fields.

"So Mordaunt sought out Miss Temple?" I asked sceptically.

Holmes chuckled.

"My dear Watson, murderers are opportunists far more often than they are planners. He needed a governess for little Flora. Why not one who was emotionally frail and naturally compliant? That was why he rejected so many. With Victoria Temple, he saw at once what might be done. He interviewed no other candidate afterwards. Though she refused at first, he paid highly for her services two months later."

"I suppose you can be sure of that, can you, Mr Holmes?" Gregson asked cautiously.

"Two weeks ago, I visited Appleford's Scholastic Agency, by whom Miss Temple was sent. I explained that Major Mordaunt had recommended them. Could they offer any other young lady whom the major had chosen to interview after Miss Temple's first refusal?"

"And did they?"

"Not at first. They insisted the matter was sensitive and confidential. However, they checked their lists. Then they were quite ready to tell me that Major Mordaunt had not interviewed any other candidate during the two months between Miss Temple's first refusal and her acceptance of the post at an unusually high salary. The major had rejected the offer of a dozen candidates for interview in the meantime."

Tobias Gregson and I stared at each other as the iron bogey-wheels of the railway coach rattled over the points of a country junction. The inspector sat forward and said earnestly,

"In a nutshell then, there could be no doubt in the children's minds that Maria Jessel was real—if a ghost can be real—because she was truly Miss Jessel at a convenient distance. Mrs Grose never saw the so-called ghost of Quint. But she identified Quint from Miss Temple's description of someone else disguised as him. In the little boy's mind, if the first vision was real, how could the second not be?"

"In a nutshell, if you insist," Holmes said sympathetically, "James Mordaunt is no fool. His cunning in the arts of camouflage and disguise was no doubt sharpened by war against the Afghan tribes. But it was his knowledge of human hopes and fears that helped him most. All that he did at Bly was certainly done with skill and subtlety. Miles believed the truth his sister and his governess told him. Both had seen Miss Jessel. One had every reason to believe she had seen Peter Quint. More important than that, Miles believed what he wanted to be true, that his hero still haunted Bly in some form or other. His real father was nothing to him. The boy could dispense with both his parents rather than lose Quint. Do not underestimate, Gregson, his passionate longing for these stories of the apparitions to be true."

"Once upon a time all the world waited for King Arthur to come again," Gregson said with a laugh. "This must be a small matter compared to that."

Holmes smiled at him.

"Very neat!"

"A further point," I told Gregson. "Mrs Grose tells us that the man Quint resembled his master sufficiently in his height and his girth for him to steal Major Mordaunt's clothes when he went to the village inn. According to Mrs Grose, there was also a hair-piece that Quint wore from vanity. It was not listed among items at the supposed scene of his death, though he had been wearing it at the inn—no more than two hundred yards away. I understand it has never been seen since. It argues, of course, that he did not die at the place where his body was found."

"And Miss Temple, gentlemen?" Gregson inquired. "Which was she to be? The mad governess who put the boy to death by suffocation or in some accident upon the lake?"

Holmes shrugged

"My dear Gregson, you must not step into a trap. A fall from the ghostly tower perhaps, precipitated by a vision of the beckoning dead. Or Miles 'spooning' on the water with his infatuated governess, a boating accident at the weir or the sluices of the haunted lake. The drowned lovers lifted from the Middle Deep in one another's arms. None of it impossible. But Major Mordaunt would not plan such catastrophes. He need only wait for an opportunity to present itself."

Conversation died until Gregson leant forward again earnestly.

"If you want my opinion, Mr Holmes, this case could still go all wrong. Maria Jessel won't destroy Mordaunt. Not if it means leaving her child abandoned to a baby farmer."

Holmes looked a little self-conscious.

"You are quite right, Gregson. I confess I have kept one detail to myself until now. I believe Maria Jessel no longer fears for her little boy."

"And why might that be, sir?"

"Charles Alfred Jessel died a fortnight ago during a routine epidemic of scarlatina at William Shaw's nursery school in Yorkshire. Not two years old."

Gregson stared at him.

"Why did you say nothing when we questioned her?"

"I am a cold-blooded creature, Gregson. Silence suited my purpose."

"But does she know of her child's death?"

"I believe she must know. Hence, perhaps, her interest in the spirit world and her grief that Little Charley waits for her where the flowers they loved are in bloom. However, the entry of the child's death will not yet be in the Somerset House registers. For that reason, she presumably thinks we do not know. That was important to her this evening. She would not wish us to guess the incalculable depth of her hatred for Major James Mordaunt."

"Neither can ever be free of the other," I said, "until that other is dead."

Holmes drew out his watch and glanced at it.

"Let us deal with first things first. What will hang Mordaunt is the discovery of evidence, unless he can destroy it before we find him. And that is why he cannot make a bolt for the Continent yet."

"Then where, Mr Holmes?"

"My dear Gregson, you may proceed to the docks at Harwich, if you wish. Watson and I must leave you at Abbots Langley."

"For Bly?" I exclaimed. "In the middle of the night? We have already been there by daylight and seen for ourselves."

"We have been there and, I fear, not seen for ourselves."

He closed his eyes, thinking, not sleeping. As we lost speed before our arrival at Abbots Langley, he looked up and pulled his coat into place.

12

In his plain clothes, Inspector Alfred Swain of the Essex Criminal Investigation Department had a quiet and scholarly look. He stood six feet and a couple of inches in the neat tailoring of a charcoal grey suit, with a slight benevolent stoop. He was thin and clean-shaven. His light blue eyes seemed to doubt politely everything he saw. There was an equine intelligence and gentleness in his glance. The sole ornament to his dress was a gold watch-chain which looped across his narrow abdomen from one waistcoat pocket to the other. I recalled that he and Holmes had met before, most recently in the case of the Marquis de Montmorency Turf Frauds. Following certain disagreements with his superintendent, Swain had been banished from Scotland Yard to the fields of Eastern England.

"Mr Holmes, sir!" He shook my friend's hand in a more cordial manner than Gregson or Lestrade would ever have done. As I was introduced I remembered Holmes's description of him as the best fellow Scotland Yard ever had. A self-educated man, Swain had read Sir Charles Lyell's *Principles of Geology* and Tait's *Recent Advances in Physical Science* as easily as Lord

Tennyson's *Idylls of the King*. By dint of early rising on the first day of sale, the young inspector had bought a first edition of Mr Robert Browning's translation of *The Agamemnon of Aeschylus*.

Such was our guide to murder! His mild eyes surveyed us.

"A telegram for you, Mr Holmes, which you won't much like. Neither Major Mordaunt nor anyone who could be him—in any disguise—was seen between Colchester and Harwich on the ferry train."

So much for a bolt to the Continent! Holmes gave Gregson a smile so sharp that it was hardly a smile at all. Then he turned back again.

"You are mistaken in one thing, Mr Swain. I like it very much. And what of passengers leaving the train here?"

Swain gave an awkward sideways nod of his tall head.

"Major Mordaunt would find it hard to pass in disguise round here. He's not been seen, not before the ferry train and certainly not since."

"Then that's that!" said Gregson irritably. "By playing games, we've lost him!"

In his indignation he spoke across Holmes directly to Swain.

"I think not," said Holmes quietly.

"Then how—"

"One moment."

Conversation was impossible as the engine of the mail train uttered its long shunting blasts of steam, pulling the jolting sorting-vans towards King's Lynn.

Instead of replying to Gregson, Holmes turned to Swain and took the inspector's lamp.

"If you please, Mr Swain."

Swain let it go. With his grey cloak wrapped round him, Holmes patrolled the edge of the platform, shining the lamp across the dark iron rails to the platform on the far side. He turned to the station-master.

"When was the last train tonight from the far platform?"

"Ten-fifteen, sir. Always the last. After that the gate is locked and the way over the footbridge is closed as well. You don't want that side, sir!"

"On the contrary," said Holmes under his breath, "it is the very thing I do want and mean to have."

He drew his cloak tighter around him, still holding the police lamp. The station-master had just time to cry, "You can't do that, sir!"

But Holmes had done it. In a swirling leap he was down from the platform onto the iron rails where the mail train had stood. Three strides carried him across the double tracks. One hand at waist height on the opposite paving and a lithe upwards swing bought him, crouching, onto the far platform, breaking every railway by-law on his way. The station-master could only watch as Swain, Gregson and I followed more cautiously. Holmes was staring at a cream-painted wooden wicket-gate that led to the station yard and a darkened road. It would serve well enough to enforce ticket collection among law-abiding passengers. He unwrapped his cloak and handed it to me, took two long-legged strides, and cleared the top bar effortlessly. He landed heels-down on the soft earth beyond.

Presently he called back to us.

"In the dark, no one would see him drop down on this side while the train was stationary. From other sets of footprints—the depth of their impact—this has been a popular escape route from railway premises by those who feel disinclined to buy a ticket."

Swain was inspecting the wicket-gate.

"You might have saved yourself the trouble, Mr Holmes. Someone kicked this fastening loose after it was locked tonight. Anyone could walk out of here."

"Very well, Mr Swain, then we will begin our advance upon

Bly, if you please. Let us take a roundabout route. If Major Mordant is on foot, as he may be, or if he is lying low, we must not alert him. It is almost five miles. With the use of a vehicle, we may still count on getting there first."

So began our journey in the dark. A black van stood in the lamplight of the cobbled yard outside the country station. Its horses were restless in the chill. A sergeant and six uniformed men of the local division were waiting. A second sergeant and a constable had gone ahead to reconnoitre the gates and approaches of the house. With Holmes, Gregson, Swain and myself, there were twelve in the van. Gregson was of equal rank to Swain. Yet without speaking a word on the subject, Holmes had made the country policeman his second-in-command.

Mordaunt, if it was he, would be an hour ahead of us but on foot. I calculated his route as a trek across rough ground in the dark. The summer night was damp and much cooler by the time we reached the deserted gate-house of Bly, its long driveway between lime trees leading to the main courtyard and house. Sergeant Acott saluted his inspector and spoke softly.

"No sign yet, sir. He must either cross the road from Abbots Langley or take the lane from the village. He hasn't done either yet—and both are being watched. What's more, he could hardly penetrate these woods without a light—and we haven't seen one."

"Major Mordaunt served with scouting parties of the Queen's Rifles in the Second Afghan Campaign," said Holmes quietly. "You will not see him. We shall not get a sight of him until he reaches us."

A few stars were out. The landscape was almost dark except where the tallest trees and the hedges caught what light there was in the sky. We passed on foot through a strange white-on-black world like a photographic negative. Acott with his constable remained at the gates as we approached the forecourt of the empty house.

Holmes and I knew the lie of the land as well as any of the others. Acott posted another two men to keep surveillance on the house. Four more were to lie low at different points in sight of the lake. With one lantern between us, its shutter almost closed, Holmes and I with Swain and the sergeant followed the shadows of the rear lawns until we came to the locked stone structure of the boat shed in its walled rose garden. Among these smaller formal gardens, Holmes took a general survey without making a sound or casting a shadow. I followed him to the door of the stone shed, whose simple lock he had picked with his pocket-knife on our first visit. He tried the handle and found it still locked.

"Excellent," he said softly to one of our uniformed constables. "Stand out of sight by the corner of the wall. If anyone should approach, alert us. You will have time to get round the far side of the wall. I do not think he will come this way now, but we must know at once if he does."

Not five seconds later the lock clicked and the door eased open. Here was the same stone interior, facing the dark lake. The grimy window panes still danced with their mad race of little flies in a dimmed blade of lamplight. It was impossible to risk the reflection of a lantern on the white-washed stone interior.

"He will not come here now," Holmes repeated softly. "He has been. See for yourself, Watson. A man who would keep pace with the scouts of the Queen's Rifles on campaign must cover forced marches over the worst terrain of barren hills. He would cross the fields from Abbots Langley to Bly at night as light-footedly as a huntsman with a pack of beagles. He has quite literally stolen a march upon us."

"How can you be sure?"

"Look up there on the brackets. The oars have gone. The boat that looked as if no one used it can be used after all. But only by the man who can get at its oars. Only by the man who could open the lock on this shed. Therefore, only by Major Mordaunt. I daresay Miss Jessel might purloin the key, but she is otherwise engaged."

In the uncertain starlight we followed the path taken long ago by Victoria Temple, Mrs Grose and Flora on the afternoon of Miss Jessel's apparition. It now occurred to me that Mordaunt was certainly armed. He had used a gun to put down his dog. No gun was found in his house, therefore he still had it with him. I had not packed my Army revolver because I had not supposed I should need it at a spiritualist séance! Gregson had not stopped to draw a handgun, knowing his plain-clothes men in Eaton Place would be carrying their police pistols. Holmes seldom bothered with firearms. As for "Mr Swain" with his poetry books and his geology! I doubted if he knew one end of a gun from the other. Our manhunt might yet turn into an awkward business with an armed and determined fugitive.

We moved cautiously over dew-soaked turf towards the lake's edge. The lily pads showed pale in the starlight. About five minutes later I saw the place on the bank where the shell of the white boat in its cradle would have been, if it had still been there. It was presumably concealed, for there was no sign of it on the water. Could Mordaunt have crossed to the island already, for that was presumably the "crossing" that Maria Jessel had meant? Holmes had been right about that.

A rift in the night clouds struck a starlit gleam from the lake and lightened the background. The surface of the water was a flat calm. Ahead of us the shore was a sweep of lawn to the water, trees massed together further on. A plantation of beech and spruce rose behind the laurel and overhanging rhododendron. I made out the irregular silhouette of ash trees and sycamore standing high, sometimes reaching out low across the water for twenty feet or more. The shoreline would soon become inaccessible as the bank with its tree roots dropped steeply and unevenly to the lake. The path ahead of us now turned inland, skirting this wide shrubbery and coming back to the water's edge well beyond it.

"There is nothing for him here," I muttered obstinately. "He should make for Holland or France."

"Let us not jump to conclusions."

"If he gets here, Gregson will have him. You may depend on that."

"I do not depend upon it. In any case, Gregson will do no such thing. I should intervene if he attempted it. Major Mordaunt must lead the dance a little longer."

A cloudbank rolled across the stars again. We neither saw nor heard an alert from the constables posted to keep watch. But if we could not see any sign of Mordaunt, there was as good a chance he could not see us.

Several minutes later Inspector Swain caught us up again.

"Messenger from Bly village, Mr Holmes. About an hour ago, a man crossed the little bridge where Quint's body was found. No one's come back that way and no one's come up past the gate-house. I'd say he went through the trees, about twenty minutes before us. Being so far ahead, there's a good chance he didn't see anyone following. Our men have orders to close the shutters on their lanterns, lie low and watch. You and I can move ahead."

As a cloud covered the sky above us, we edged across the grass to the first lakeside trees. A half-moon had begun to rise beyond the firs, shedding a cool but fuller light on the water. This was where the path curved inland: rhododendrons and tree trunks made the water's edge impassable. I must do my companions and their Essex policemen the justice of saying that neither movement nor glimmer betrayed their presence. Swain had trained them well.

It was either Holmes or I who tipped a two- or three-pound

stone with a foot and caused a splash below the bank. There was no response. As we stood quite still, however, a white shape like a large fish or a small whale slid out under the overhanging foliage. Mordaunt, for surely it was he, was just visible, stooping a little in the shadows and hauling at a length of cord. Reflected moonlight brightened and the cord became the painter of the boat which had once been lying in the wooden cradle.

Mordaunt had launched this craft easily. I caught the slippery suction of his boots in soft mud as he pushed it out and boarded it over the stern. He took his seat in the bow, his silhouette clear against a moonlight glimmer on the water.

Was this the fairy craft which had taken Miss Temple and the boy "spooning" on the lake? Moonlight made it seem daintier than the hull in the cradle, but I knew it was the same. There was room for an oarsman in the bow facing a pair of passengers in the stern with a picnic-hamper behind them.

Such a scallop might be moved easily and lie concealed under the overgrowing shrubs and trees, as this had been. Neither the gardener nor the groom would use it or even see it. With its oars locked in the shed and the key to the shed in his pocket, it was in Mordaunt's sole possession. Perhaps no one else had crossed to the island since the death of little Miles. Perhaps Mordaunt crossed every week without being seen, though there seemed little reason for that.

This was our first sight of Major James Mordaunt. In silhouette at the oars he was burly, quite strong enough to push the craft out from under a muddy bank into the shallows and pull himself aboard. He paused suddenly in mid-stroke, as if he might have heard something. Not an owl hooted, not a badger stirred the undergrowth. Our presence had put such sensitive night-dwellers to flight. Mordaunt might yet pass among us without knowing it!

How long would the silence last? There was a startled sound

above me, the heavy wings of a restless wood pigeon displaced by our movements. That alone could betray our presence if the sound carried. Worse still, I caught the crackle of bracken in the uncleared copse, not trodden underfoot but pressed aside by one of Swain's men. Surely Mordaunt would not miss it?

But he was pulling out from the rhododendron bushes and tree trunks, forty feet at least beyond us. Hauling on the sculls with his back to us, he was turning out into the Middle Deep, heading for the island.

I felt Holmes's cold, hard grip upon my wrist.

"The Temple of Proserpine! No one else has the means of getting there so long as the oars are under lock and key."

I said nothing. Instead I recalled Mrs Grose's story of Harry the Poacher trying to swim the Middle Deep and dying in the treacherous embrace of the water weed. There was no danger of that. Without a boat we could do nothing. If Holmes was right—and if it took Swain an hour or even less to summon a boat on a cart from Abbots Langley—we had seen the last of such evidence as Mordaunt intended to destroy. What would be left—except Miss Jessel's word against his?

Tobias Gregson was, as they say, munching his teeth with frustration just behind us. I caught his muttered curse upon the wooden-tops, as Scotland Yard was apt to call its country cousins. Holmes ignored this. But Gregson was soon beside us. Indeed he was edging forward too far, where the tree trunks grew almost in the water and the mud of the bank ran into silt. It seemed as if he was trying to get level with Mordaunt and almost into the man's view.

If Mordaunt did not notice these movements, it was perhaps because something seemed amiss with him or his boat. The light of the short summer night was still poor, but the man's outline remained clear enough to show that this figure at the sculls was making heavy weather of it. He was labouring as though his strength was failing him. Almost a hundred feet out among the lily pads, the boat was moving slowly and, worse, responding sluggishly. It was going nowhere. I could see no reason at first. Water weeds may drag down a human body but they would hardly snare a boat as tenaciously as this. Perhaps it had run into impenetrable pads of water lilies. Surely he would know his own waters well enough?

To my astonishment, it seemed he was trying to stand up. The boat did not rock under his movements, as one might expect. Its bulk was lying too low in the water. He had an oar in one hand and was trying, vainly, to find the muddy bottom of the lake. Was his aim to move the little craft like a punt into the shallows? Perhaps it was by standing up that he caught a sound or glimpsed a movement on the bank. The mid-summer night had begun to lighten further towards dawn. I made out a plantation of horse chestnuts whose candles now stood white in the mist.

Holmes was immobile as a graven image, his tall, spare figure with his back to the broad trunk of a beech, the edge of the lake at his toes. In the darkness, he would have been just out of line with our fugitive. But the distance between the two men was no longer quite dark. I could make out enough of Mordaunt's wraith-like figure to see that he was gripping or waving something in his free hand, an object which he had taken from his pocket. His manner of holding it convinced me that it must be the gun with which he had shot his dog. We later learnt that it was a Webley Mark 4 service revolver.

No one had been prepared for this. It would be an hour or more before we could have armed officers in place, let alone launch a boat on the lake. Mordaunt on his island with this revolver and a pocketful of .455 cartridges could keep us where we were for the next day and night.

Then, in one startled moment, I understood the feeling of

those who claim to have jumped out of their skin. From several feet behind me came the crack of a voice carrying the certainty of command.

"Major Mordaunt, sir! Your attention if you please!"

The authority of that voice was such that the outline of the man upright in the boat seemed to stiffen to attention as if obeying a command. But he was bringing his right hand up. A roar from the Webley echoed like a ricochet across the misty surface of the water. I heard its bullet chip the bark of the beech trunk about eight inches from my friend's left shoulder. Mordaunt had heard Swain but seen Holmes, the grey cloak against the darker tree trunk. Holmes remained perfectly still, as if resigned to martyrdom. Every policeman near us was now lying flat with the exception of Inspector Alfred Swain, whom I had supposed to be more at home with the *Agamemnon* or the *Idylls of the King* than with armed conflict.

"Put—your—gun—down, sir!"

The same crack of authority rang out but Mordaunt's arm was coming up again. Holmes did not move and there was not even time for me to jump forward and knock him flat. Yet Quint's murderer was a marksman who would not miss him a second time. With a terrible sickness I heard a hoarse explosion and saw the human figure spin round and catapult into the water.

Then the tall, quiet man whose face had suggested mild equine intelligence, whose private hours were spent among dead fossils and what his superiors derided as "School-Miss Poetry," lowered his arm. He gently wrapped the grey barrel and the black stock of the Smith & Wesson .32 handgun, an ejector target revolver, in a piece of lint and handed it to Inspector Tobias Gregson.

"Have the goodness to take care of this, Mr Gregson," said Alfred Swain quietly. "There must be an inquiry. The weapon is signed for but it is best that it should be in your custody now."

During some thirty seconds, in the gloom before dawn, this ghastly drama of life and death was played before us. Mordaunt had put himself a hundred feet beyond any aid that we could give him, even if he were still alive. To save Sherlock Holmes, Swain had shot with the care of a man who knows he must hit his target with a single bullet and the confidence of one who is certain he can do it. Could he be sure of killing Mordaunt instantly? Had he done so? The major's body went under at full length. There was a pause and then his head reappeared, hair streaming wet from his scalp. His arms threshed and he snatched at a frail wooden scull that had floated free.

Sergeant Acott waded in a dozen feet from the slippery bank until the water was almost at his chest.

"Get back, Mr Acott!" called Swain, "The mud is like treacle out there. You won't come out of it."

I thought again of Harry the Poacher in the Middle Deep. The weed clung tighter each time the poor fellow jumped breast-high from the water like a fish, gulping air, Mrs Grose had told us. The weighted mass that was festooning him pulled him back each time until he could jump no more. At the moment Mordaunt seemed upright, as if standing. But he could not be standing, where the floor of the lake was twenty feet down. Then he was on his back with arms spread out, snatching at air. Gregson and those about him talked busily of what to do. Holmes and Swain knew that there was nothing. The fugitive sank, motionless and expressionless. Perhaps he was dead already. The water settled and lay still. The drowning man appeared no more. Whatever the damage from Swain's bullet, it had cut short his struggles.

"If ever a man took his own life, it was Mordaunt," said Holmes philosophically. "Once he saw we were here, he knew he was done for. Trussed up for the assizes and the execution shed. In his place, I too should have fought it out."

Alfred Swain showed only the calm that is often a consequence of shock. He stood in his plain, neat tailoring with the watch-chain across his waistcoat and gazed out over the misty lake as the daylight grew.

"The boat, Mr Holmes," he said gently. "I believe we shall find that the boat will repay examination."

13

As the sky warmed into a pale yellow summer dawn, we stood like men awaiting a funeral *cortège,* solemn but without a show of personal grief. Two labourers appeared. One of them carried an iron winding-handle which opened and closed the sluice at the far end of the lake. When opened, this would lower the water by several feet, into a stone channel down to the Bly river. By mid-morning, a wide band of dark clay along the banks lay uncovered. The rumble of water down the chute had fallen to a murmur.

The treachery of the Middle Deep was plain. A floor of mud sloped gradually from the bank for ten or twelve feet. Abruptly it became steeper. At the lake's centre, the undercurrents that were created by diverting the river water had created a weed-filled ravine. Somewhere in the cold depths of this Major Mordaunt presumably lay in a clinging shroud of water weed.

A flat-bottomed wherry had been brought up from the Bly river on a trailer. It had been launched and now lay in position above the Middle Deep. The rope of a drag stretched out behind it. Inspector Swain's commander, Superintendent Truscott, seemed to take pleasure in predicting that to trawl such contours as these would be a long and difficult job.

Contrary to my expectations, Mordaunt's waterlogged boat had not sunk entirely. It wallowed becalmed with the rim of its hull just above the surface. The little craft was light enough to float when waterlogged, where a heavier and more business-like ferry might have gone straight down. The two men in the wherry had attached a line to the rowing-boat's painter and paid it out to the others on the bank. Like competitors in a tug-of-war, Alfred Swain's constables took the strain and heaved the submerged hull gently into the shallows from which the water was receding.

"Don't count on seeing Major Mordaunt for a day or two, Mr Holmes," said Truscott morosely, stamping his feet and rubbing his hands as the boat was hauled in. "You can't drag a lake bottom as steep as that one. Best let him pop up of his own accord. They all do so, sooner or later, once the gas starts to lift them. It won't do for the coroner, though. That's the difficulty."

He walked off towards Sergeant Acott, presumably for the satisfaction of repeating to him what he had just said to us.

I had not seen Alfred Swain for more than an hour. He was no doubt in conference with the local coroner. A gravelly-bearded man in a dark suit, driving a horse and trap, certainly had the appearance of an officer of the court.

An inquest could come to only one conclusion. If ever there was a case of justifiable homicide I supposed it must be this. Mordaunt had proved himself an experienced shot, even in the half-light. His first aim had missed Sherlock Holmes by only a few inches. He had been given two chances to lay down his revolver and had declined both. Without Swain's presence of mind and unexpected marksmanship, my friend would have stood no more chance against the second bullet than a duck in a shooting gallery.

It transpired that Alfred Swain was the only man to have drawn a firearm—and the last whom I expected to be carrying one. At eleven o'clock that morning he reappeared at last, riding a grey mare. Behind him a farm wagon carried a boat not much larger than Mordaunt's but somewhat more sturdy. Such craft were generally on call to country police forces for use in rivers and reservoirs. The consequence was that each force had to take what it could get.

Two long planks were drawn down from the tail of the wagon to the mud of the bank.

"Mr Holmes!"

"Mr Swain?"

Swain walked closer.

"We can cross to the island, sir, if you would care to go. Before the county sheriff and others get here, perhaps you—and Dr Watson, if he wishes—would like to see for yourselves."

"Major Mordaunt's private kingdom?"

"If you were to do it, Mr Holmes, I think it had best be done without further delay."

In plain English, once Superintendent Truscott's guests arrived from Abbots Langley we should have as much chance of investigating the pleasure island as Adam and Eve had of returning to Paradise. What debt from the past did Alfred Swain owe to Sherlock Holmes that it should be repaid so amply now?

"There are boots on the wagon, gentlemen."

We sat on a felled tree trunk and pulled our waders on. Our ferry boat was in the water. Supported by constables at either arm, we edged down a slippery plank and clambered over the stern of the hull. Swain took the opposite seat as oarsman in the bows.

The inspector was a quiet man by nature, son of a Dorset village schoolmaster, as Holmes later told me. It was still hard to say whether he was shocked or serene in the aftermath of Mordaunt's death. As we were crossing the calm lake, he spoke softly—to us or to himself.

"What possessed him to stand up in the boat? Surely he knew he would swamp it!"

It seemed to me an eminently sensible comment, but that was all by way of conversation until we reached the island shore. We waded across some fifteen feet of mud before coming to a crude plank slipway. I thought that a man who brought a woman here would probably have to carry her ashore, establishing an intimacy from the first step. However, if anyone had been here for many months, there was little sign of it. A path had been trodden long before between laurel bushes and yew but the banks of brambles and nettles in flower were now badly in need of clearing.

The so-called Temple of Proserpine was no more than a few minutes' walk from the water. With its single gable, it suggested a garden bungalow on an Indian tea plantation. Shutters were locked over the glass panels of its two double doors and there was a fixed window at either side of them. It might very well have served as a cricket pavilion, its front quite forty feet wide. Most of the original top coat of white paint had peeled away, leaving a cream undercoat with patches of bare, silvered wood.

Such was Mordaunt's rendezvous with his female companions. Perhaps it was also a conveniently secret spot where he met Peter Quint to trade gold for bank-notes. So long as he had the only key to the shed where the oars were kept, he was master of either situation. This lawn was where Miss Temple had first seen Maria Jessel. I thought how easily a tragic boating accident might have been arranged for Miles and his governess as they wooed their ghosts!

Swain made no objection when Holmes opened his useful pocket-knife to deal with the lock. Then he drew apart the shutters and opened the glass doors. Dappled sunlight through the glass revealed a dilapidated lounge equipped with bamboo furniture and scattered cushions. It was flanked by two smaller rooms on each side. The whole place was a tribute to the colonial tropics, familiar to three generations of the Mordaunt family. Against the far wall stood an upright Broadwood piano in tortoise-shell lacquer, no doubt a memento of lanterns, parties and music on summer evenings! Holmes touched the keyboard casually. Half of the notes were now dumb and several of them sank down, never to rise. It had served no purpose for many years.

"One hesitates to condemn any musical instrument as beyond saving," said my friend casually, "yet I fear this must be so."

Before I could say that Mordaunt should have jumped at the chance to have the wreck dismantled and removed on the cattle raft, as Mrs Grose described it, my companions moved on.

A smaller room with two wall-mirrors and a miniature dressing-table had presumably been set apart for female guests. Another, on the far side, had a leather chair and a table—perhaps this was the counting house where Mordaunt and Quint exchanged coins for bank-notes. A shelf in the adjoining room held a flame-darkened primus stove and rusted tins labelled for tea, sugar and coffee. Holmes made a little routine of opening the drawers in the furniture and closing them without finding anything of interest. Or so it seemed. Standing in the mirrored room with his back to Swain, he "palmed" a small bottle from the dressing-table drawer. It had a cosmetic or theatrical look about it.

I could not see that there was anything here for us. Only the broken-down piano, retained for no obvious use, seemed worth my friend's inspection. Holmes stooped and used his pocket-knife blade to loosen a screw under the keyboard so that the pedal-board might be lifted out. This revealed only the iron frame with its strings and the pedal mechanism. Straightening up and lifting the top, Holmes then peered down into the musty space of felted hammers and treble wire. Shaking his head, he closed the lid and turned away.

As though it were a last resort, he dropped down on one knee and unfolded his pocket magnifying-glass to examine the wooden floorboards just in front of the two foremost casters.

"Most curious," he said quietly, folding the glass and returning it to his watch-pocket. "Unless the instrument is lifted a little, the weight on the casters is bound to mark floorboards of softwood timber as it is moved over them. In this case, it seems that the right-hand caster alone has been moved repeatedly in a brief arc. Put more simply, someone who had no companion to help him lift the weight from the boards has had to pull the right-hand side of the piano from the wall on numerous occasions. Two men would have been able to lift it clear of the boards. Why did he always do this alone—and so often? It is a small matter but well worth our attention. This particular model of the Messrs Broadwood has a very substantial iron frame. Perhaps, Mr Swain, you would be kind enough to assist me."

The inspector eased his right arm and the edge of his shoulder into the narrow gap between the back of the tall piano and the wall.

"You will find, Mr Swain that there is a hand-hold about half-way down. I shall lift from under the keyboard."

Holmes drew the piano carefully forward. The floorboards at the far end groaned as the left-hand brass casters ground into them. A few seconds later the right-hand end of the upright piano was at a slight angle to the wall, revealing the back of the instrument.

The structure was not solid, as I had supposed. A fine wire mesh on a wooden frame fitted into the back of the instrument and was screwed into place. It required only the loosening of half a dozen screws to remove it. This was done easily with the edge of a penny coin.

Once the mesh on its frame was lifted out, I doubt whether, even among pianists, many knew that their instruments had a concealed recess below the strings. It was large enough to hold a book or even a small painting, though its original intention was presumably to house furniture polish, dusters, methylated spirits and all the essential cleaning materials for rosewood, brass, ivory and ebony.

When I saw what lay in this recess I knew we were on the right road, though I could not yet tell where it led! It was a large steel key. Only the man who put it there would ever have looked for it in such a place or even have known that such a recess existed. It was plain at a glance that the key did not fit any door or item of furniture around us. In the first place, it was too old.

I guessed that it had not been made in the last forty years. It was about four inches long, the oval of its handle decorated with filigree work of mid-century. Holmes held it in his hand and intoned two lines from his store of street literature.

"My name is Chubb, that makes the Patent Locks;
Look on my works, ye burglars, and despair."

Then he gazed about him.

"Up there, I think," he said presently. "There is nothing down here worthy of it."

An inspection-trap was recessed in the centre of the main ceiling, giving access to a loft or roof-space. It seemed the only place where there might be a lock to match the key. Holmes stared at it.

"A curiosity of the deviant mind, Mr Swain, is that a man who works to frustrate detection invariably draws his pursuer onto a trail pointing the way he has gone. As if the poor devil wanted to be caught."

"I can't see that here, Mr Holmes."

"Can you not, Mr Swain? Of the garden sheds, only one was locked. How could it fail to attract interest? It contained a pair of sculls. Had it not been locked, they might not have signified. The need to make the only boat unusable by all but one person gave them importance. No one could cross to the island without Mordaunt's authority. On our arrival here, what do we find? A piano whose voice is defunct, which might have been removed on several occasions but was kept here by his orders on at least one occasion. The damage to the floorboard indicates that the only function of the poor voiceless instrument was to be moved to and fro at frequent intervals, making the right-hand side of its back accessible. It beckons the investigator to that hiding place behind the covering of metal gauze."

"But if you are correct, Mr Holmes—"

"I am, Mr Swain. One more thing, however. No matter how thoroughly this room might be searched, the piano with its iron frame could be moved only by someone with sufficient strength."

"Excluding Maria Jessel and, for that matter, Victoria Temple," I said suddenly.

"Precisely. Now, if you please, gentlemen, there remains the inspection hatch."

"We had best proceed quickly, sir." Swain glanced at the window, as if expecting Superintendent Truscott's shadow to fall across it. "I can hold you standing on my shoulders if you can balance there, Mr Holmes. You could easily reach the ledge of the hatch. I am a little younger and therefore can bear your weight easily."

"Younger, and therefore had better stand on my shoulders," said Holmes peremptorily. "The greater strength will be needed in pulling up through the hatch."

"As you wish, sir."

With a balance that might have graced a circus acrobat, Swain crouched on my friend's back in stocking'd feet as Holmes straightened up. The inspector's soles and heels moulded themselves to the changing posture until he had only to lift his hands and push the white-painted trap aside. He pulled himself up and slid into the roof-space.

"A main beam and a rope attached to it, Mr Holmes. He probably pushed the trap up with a pole and hooked the rope down. He might nudge it closed afterwards and take the pole with him. Stand away a little, if you please."

A length of knotted rope swung down, hanging level with our knees. It was a simple device that every scouting party in rough terrain would be familiar with. In my training for Afghanistan, I should have thought nothing of climbing it. Now I was not so sure.

Holmes stepped in front of me.

"Wait a bit, Watson!"

He took the rope between his hands, locked his feet on the lowest section and swarmed up as if he had done nothing else all his life. I followed, standing on the knot and holding as high as I could.

"Grip tight and hold, sir," said Swain quietly. Then I was guided by either arm to the safe flooring of the attic. Light through a rear dormer window was quite enough for our investigation.

Disused garden furniture made up the lumber, except for a military travelling chest of dark, varnished elm. This was some four feet long by two feet wide and eighteen inches deep. Its dark lacquer was scratched and worn, as if from campaigning. At the centre of the lid, in a scroll of dim red letters, I read "J. Mordaunt, M.D., Netley." How well I knew that design! It was almost a twin to the one which accompanied me to Netley barracks as a newly-qualified physician beginning my regimental training, twenty years before.

Holmes was on his knees, inspecting the keyhole with its

old-fashioned ornamental plate. It was surely a match for the key. My friend scrutinised the floorboards at the front of the box.

"No one has opened this for some months. Possibly not since Miss Temple's trial."

"You are sure?" I asked.

"Once the poor young woman was locked away in Broadmoor, believing gratefully that Mordaunt had saved her from the gallows, the evidence ceased to matter to him. See here. There is an infestation of woodworm—furniture beetle—in the rim of the lid. The eggs are laid in existing holes by the adult beetle during the autumn, usually in September. The larvae eat their way out in the spring—April or May, as a rule. The powder—the frass—is undisturbed in this case. Mordaunt thought he had all the time in the world. That was very nearly the truth. Casual neglect of this sort—postponing the destruction of evidence—has proved fatal even to some of the great criminal minds. Mordaunt was not remotely of that first rank."

He turned the key and raised the hinged lid. The interior had been divided, as usual, into shelves or trays which could be lifted out in turn. It was by no means full. The upper level contained a leather case for a razor, another for two silver-backed hair-brushes and what I can only describe as cosmetics, to judge from a faint odour of the barber's saloon which emanated from the dark bottles. A second layer held two silk shirts, a port-wine cravat and a green waistcoat with a pattern of fleurs-de-lis. Such a style, once fashionable among young men at Oxford and Cambridge, had not been seen for ten or fifteen years, except on such occasions as Miss Temple confronting Peter Quint through window-glass or upon a garden tower.

The deepest tray had room for a jacket and breeches of brown Norfolk cut, equally suited to gamekeeper or village squire. The clothes were a perfect match for those "borrowed" by Quint to be handy with the village girls, as Mrs Grose put it, and to adorn

Miss Temple's vision. From among the hair-brushes and treasures of the dressing-room, Holmes picked up the reddish brown brush of a small fox, or so I thought.

"A hunter's trophy!" I said casually.

"My dear Watson! In all your medical experience, did you never see such a piece, affected by men who have lost their own hair?"

I never did. But I was looking elsewhere.

"Look in the box, Holmes."

"You have truly not seen a wig such as this one—unmistakably of Quint's colour, as it was described to us?"

"Look in the box!"

He stopped and looked down. There it was. The case was leather. It might have held a large-sized pair of field-glasses, but its shape was square and not long. The leather was stamped with a War Department "crow's foot" and a simple inscription: "R. J. Begbie & Son, Woolwich, Field Heliostat, Standard Issue."

It was surely the glass that had blinded Miss Temple as she came face-to-face with Maria Jessel. Only James Mordaunt would have been likely to conceal it among the costume pieces for his masquerade as Peter Quint. And who but Quint's murderer would be in possession of the hair-piece worn by the man that evening in full view of a score of people but missing from the body when it was found a stone's throw away?

Holmes returned the items, locked the box and gave the key to Alfred Swain. The young inspector must now take the credit for these discoveries on the island. Holmes was insistent upon that. As we crossed back over the Middle Deep, he repeated for Swain's benefit, "It is the most humble inconsistencies which are frequently the evidence of major crime. I commend the thought to you, Mr Swain."

Swain bent his back to the oars and said, "I have never doubted it, sir."

"Good. When you make your report, let it be terse and to the point."

"Indeed, Mr Holmes."

"The facts are these. The world knew it was Peter Quint's body lying dead on the bridge that winter night because Major Mordaunt told them so. After that, what remained of Quint became the property of the coroner's officer and the anatomist from Chelmsford. They knew him only as a corpse. They did their duty meticulously, every item of evidence was accounted for. They did not inquire for a missing hair-piece. Why should they? They knew nothing of its existence. Those villagers who merely saw his body laid out would hardly be surprised if it was not still in place. Yet its absence, a stone's throw from where he was seen wearing it, further suggests that he cannot have died at the bridge—therefore not in an accidental fall. Miss Jessel has told us the truth if anyone has."

"Then it just amounts to the hair piece, Mr Holmes?"

"What it amounts to, Mr Swain, is that Mordaunt killed Quint. Within a day or two, Maria Jessel left for her holiday, during which her death was reported. She was carrying Quint's child. Thus we have one singular incident coming close to the heels of another singular incident. So close, in this case, that she and Mordaunt were privy to them both. It does not make her party to Peter Quint's death. There is nothing against her on that but her unsupported statement. There is conclusive evidence against him."

That afternoon, Mordaunt's boat was pulled on to dry land. Several fittings, including both oars, had floated clear as it settled in the water. The oarsman's seat had gone and two of the footboards across the bottom of the shell were detached. Superintendent Truscott was occupied elsewhere and Swain stood over the wreck. While we waited for the hackney carriage to take us to the train at Abbots Langley, Holmes carried out a discreet inspection.

With the two footboards gone and the hull drained, the cause of the catastrophe seemed clear. Mordaunt had not thrown the boat out of balance by standing up or as his pistol recoiled.

"The plug in the drainage hole at the bottom of the hull was forced in by a rush of water," said Holmes casually. "See for yourself, Watson. That is quite apparent as the cause of the boat settling in the water."

I cast myself as the schoolboy oarsman I had once been.

"In a boat of this sort, the plug is hardened cork and conical-shaped so that an inward pressure of water would force it all the tighter."

"Indeed it would," he said placidly, "unless it had been tampered with."

"Tampered with? How?"

"Look at the convex shape of the drainage hole. If a bung were mutilated, or reversed, or in any way loosened, it would yield to the pressure of water and sink the boat. This craft certainly did not tip over or flood as a result of Mordaunt's antics. It foundered under a weight of water below the footboards. The bottom of the boat had been flooding gradually ever since he pushed it out into the shallows. As the weight increased, his progress became slower, precisely as we saw."

I stared at it and shook my head.

"Come, Watson. It may simply have been removed. If I were the killer, I should prefer if possible to fit the plug so that it would not give way completely until he got above the Middle Deep. A reversal of its position, ideally. I doubt that the major had bothered to take up the boards and inspect the bung when he had the hounds at his heels. Even if I am mistaken in that, at a glance it would seem intact. Especially in the half-light."

I had stopped listening to him. Was this the plan Mordaunt had laid?

"It sounds to me, Holmes, more like the boating accident that might have overcome Miles and Miss Temple as they yielded to a beckoning ghost. Perhaps, by some evil irony, his own method was turned against him."

But Sherlock Holmes had already turned away and was indicating the waiting carriage

It was half an hour later when we paid off our driver in the cobbled forecourt of the railway yard at Abbots Langley. The express was not due for twenty minutes. As we stood talking on the platform in the sunshine I was aware of distant hoof-beats, a rider approaching at a canter. The sound died away and presently the tall neatly-suited figure of Alfred Swain came down the steps of the bridge. So far as he could ever be, he seemed a little excited.

"They've found him, Mr Holmes! Major Mordaunt. Just under the ledge of the Middle Deep. The bullet had clipped him at one side, enough to knock him into the water. After that, it seems he drowned!"

14

Sherlock Holmes adjusted the curtain of the dining-car window against a strong afternoon sun as the coaches of the London train eased forward. With a sigh, he lowered himself into his seat and waved a hand towards the distant landscape.

"I am bound to think occasionally, Watson, how pleasant it would be to retire from all this sort of thing. To seek out a fold or a ridge of the Sussex Downs and live entirely for oneself. I can almost taste at this moment the clean salt air across the Channel waves and over the chalk cliffs. Yellow gorse in the thickets, the sheep bells and the restful murmur of bees in warm summer evenings."

"You would go out of your mind, Holmes, without a case to investigate."

"I should devote a small part of my time to critical monographs on speculative topics. The ironies of justice, for example. I should choose as my cast those murderers who have gone to the gallows when the victim whose wealth they coveted would have died of natural causes a few months later in any case. Or the artless cracksmen in 1884 who went to great lengths in planning to break the safe of the City and Suburban Bank, only to find on arrival that another gang were already in possession of it on that same night. The subsequent battle between the two sides woke the entire neighbourhood and resulted in the arrest of all concerned."

"I take it that you would include the Bly House murder in this catalogue of ironies?"

"Possibly. Major Mordaunt is a perfect example of the man who uses all his talent to plan murder, in this case to kill his nephew Miles, only for nature to do the job before he can."

"And the murder of Quint?"

"Quite lacking in irony. As the immortal Robert Browning described his own Roman murder story in *The Ring and the Book,* an episode in burgess life, nothing more."

"And the death of Major Mordaunt himself?"

He looked at me innocently. I prompted him.

"The sabotage of the boat."

"Let us call it the curiosity of the boat!"

"If the cork bung had not burst inwards and the craft had not begun to founder, Mordaunt might have clung to the wreck. The bullet wound was not fatal. He might have been pulled ashore and his wound dressed."

Holmes shrugged.

"To save him for the hangman and possibly to take Maria Jessel with him. He would not thank you for that."

I was not to be deterred.

"Once she knew of her child's death she would be a fury from the gates of hell. She has that build and that temperament. You have seen her. A fit young woman who could easily walk five miles to Bly from the station at Abbots Langley—and five miles back. She had been his partner in deception—if not murder. Ten-to-one she knew where the boat was hidden from their days together when she was his governess. She knew, at any rate, that he alone had access to the oars. If anyone used that boat to cross to the island now it would be he. By adjusting the bung, she had a perfect opportunity to ensure that the next time he used it would be his last. Even if a servant had seen her walking through the woods at Bly—she would have been reported as another apparition of the living dead. That would have been believed by no one. We know better!"

He gazed across the flat fields and shook his head in admiration of the theory.

"Knowledge is not proof, Watson. You also forget the part our client must play in any further investigation. Miss Temple would not thank you for putting her through the public ordeal necessary to convince a jury that Maria Jessel drowned Major Mordaunt. I will grant you that the message she sent from our séance was intended to destroy him, not to save him. But you can scarcely expect her to admit it now. We must leave it there."

He beckoned the steward of the dining car.

"Her child is avenged," he continued. "The sole witness who might implicate her in the death of Peter Quint is now dead. Let it rest there."

He paused to order a pot of Earl Grey with cinnamon teacakes. Then he added, "When the contents of the military travelling chest are examined, the murderer of Peter Quint will be identified beyond question and Alfred Swain will earn the commendation that Scotland Yard always denied him."

It was now almost two days since we had seen our beds. He stifled a yawn and stared from the carriage window across a ripening cornfield scattered with poppies. Then he looked back at me with a certain disapproval.

"The hunting instinct is strong in you, Watson. I have to tell you that if Miss Jessel is still in custody when we reach London, I shall advise her that she is entitled to legal representation. I shall also inform her that a competent Queen's Counsel might go before a judge in chambers and, upon the present evidence, apply successfully for a writ of *habeas corpus*."

"And we shall say nothing more of the boat?"

"I think Maria Jessel has suffered enough. I, at least, will take no further part against her." He turned and looked at me with exasperation. "For God's sake, Watson, I will not hound that young woman in order to please Tobias Gregson! Sometimes I must be judge and jury in the case I have established. I know you would not have it otherwise, old fellow!"

Then he stretched out his long legs as far as the carriage seats would permit and was asleep before our steward returned with the tea-tray.

Next day, when we were safely back in Baker Street, a wire from Lestrade confirmed that Major James Mordaunt, late surgeon of the Queen's Rifles, had "popped up" from the lake at Bly as Superintendent Truscott had predicted. An autopsy was undertaken and an inquest was to be held in a fortnight's time. Holmes and I had been witnesses to the man's death and our attendance was required. I had no wish to see Bly again and was not best pleased that the court would convene in its manorial hall rather than at the Abbots Langley coaching inn. In case the jurors might need to view the scene, the house was thought to be more convenient.

There is a good deal of press interest in any case where a police officer has shot dead a suspect. The coroner, Dr Roderick Allestree of Chelmsford, strove to repress sensationalism. He instructed the jurors to find a verdict in the death of Major James Mordaunt—and no more. At the first hint of ghosts or previous murders or robbery at the Five Stones, he called the inquest to order. How did Major Mordaunt die? That was all.

Alfred Swain was first exonerated and then commended. He had fired to prevent the certain death of Sherlock Holmes. His marksmanship was impeccable and his bullet was found in the arm that held Mordaunt's Webley pistol. The wound alone would not have been fatal, even without immediate medical attention. The major had drowned.

Ranged with plain wooden chairs, the dark manorial hall of Bly was oak-panelled and high-windowed but a little smaller than I had expected. Despite Dr Allestree's best efforts, it was hard to separate the death of Major Mordaunt from the question of whether Peter Quint died in consequence of foul play at his hands.

Maria Jessel was probably saved by the manner in which Holmes gave evidence. He endured cross-examination by a legal bumpkin, Mr Mossop. This fellow had been hired by the Quint family to keep a watching brief, in case something might now be got by way of damages from the Mordaunt estate for the death of their relative. Mossop evidently believed that the implication of Maria Jessel—even if only as an accessory to crime—might open the way to a financial settlement of some kind with the Mordaunt estate.

It was a poor case, but it also put her in danger of criminal prosecution. As Holmes remarked beforehand, a conviction of Miss Jessel as accessory required a principal crime of murder to be proved, which seemed impossible with Mordaunt dead. However, if Mr Mossop hoped to succeed in getting his clients bought off, an indictment of some kind against Maria Jessel would open the way.

Mossop's cross-examination of Sherlock Holmes was the keystone of this attempt. The process evoked an image of a short, stout gunboat popping its cannon at a well-armoured and deftly-manoeuvred battle-cruiser.

"Mr Holmes, as a criminal investigator, you will concede that facts pointing to the role of James Mordaunt in the death of Quint point also to Maria Jessel as an accomplice? In the light of present evidence, a verdict of accidental death upon Peter Quint can hardly be sustained."

Dr Allestree stirred himself to intervene. Before he could do so, Holmes fixed his eyes six inches above the top of Mossop's large head and asked, "You do not mean that question literally, do you, Mr Mossop?"

Dr Allestree sat back expectantly. An uneasy look came over Mossop's reddening features, the face of one who senses some irretrievable error but cannot yet identify it. A large pit had opened and his adversary was nudging him gently towards it. Allestree intervened, as if to save him for Holmes to deal with.

"I think, Mr Holmes, we must do Mr Mossop the courtesy of assuming that he means what he says."

Holmes, in formal morning dress and white tie, made a short bow to the coroner. As the jury looked on, it was greatly to Mossop's disadvantage that he had thought a Norfolk tweed jacket would be good enough for a country court. He looked as if he might have been sent to Bly to carry the luggage for Sherlock Holmes. My friend was careful to look into the jurors' eyes as he spoke, cutting out his adversary altogether.

"Were I fortunate enough to be retained on Miss Jessel's behalf, I should undertake her case with complete confidence in the young lady's innocence."

That tripped Mossop very neatly. The jurors, who seldom took their eyes off the famous detective, heard that the great Sherlock Holmes believed in the young woman. After that, my friend could have said anything. What followed was conclusive.

"To see Miss Jessel is to know that she has nothing like the strength required to strike that terrible blow to Quint's head, let alone to carry the body of a full-grown man half a mile over icy paths to the river bridge. If she did neither of those things, what part did she play in this crime—whose very occurrence remains unproven?"

"Major Mordaunt—"

"Quite so. Major Mordaunt was a well-built veteran of active service. He had escaped suspicion as accomplice to robbery and murder at the Five Stones. Quint was the only man who might still betray him. He and he alone had cause to wish that man dead. Major Mordaunt, now being dead himself, cannot be prosecuted. I have such faith in British justice that I do not believe any case against Miss Jessel would get past a local magistrate's court, let alone a red judge at the Old Bailey."

"Thank you, Mr Holmes," said Dr Allestree, but my friend bowed again.

"It would be impertinent in me, sir, to suggest that this court should not take Mr Mossop's question seriously. I, however, cannot."

There was absolute silence among the jurors, and for a dreadful moment I thought they might applaud him. Mr Mossop sat down. In a few sentences, Sherlock Holmes had backed him into a corner and tied him into knots. The greatest criminal investigator of the age had announced to the world the innocence of the young woman whose liberty was at stake.

Dr Allestree rubbed salt into Mr Mossop's wounds by reminding us that the sole issue was the death of James Mordaunt and the conduct of Alfred Swain, who had undoubtedly precipitated it. I hoped for "misadventure" or even "justifiable homicide." Guided by the coroner and puzzled by the medical evidence, the jurors returned an open verdict.

I stood up and turned round. At the back of the court were two figures, sitting decorously apart. Maria Jessel wore a black veil of mourning. I could not imagine what had brought her to Bly. Despite Inspector Gregson's memorandum, the Treasury Solicitor recommended no action against her. Peter Quint had died in the County of Essex, and Alfred Swain had argued against a prosecution. As for the boat, how a bung came loose was a matter of pure conjecture, and no evidence could be found to connect her with this. The one item that now appeared to prove her innocence beyond question was a message from her on the night of Mordaunt's death loyally warning her lover of the danger he was in.

The second figure behind me wore no veil. It is always within the Home Secretary's discretion to release a prisoner from Broadmoor—and that discretion had been exercised several days before. Proceedings to set aside the verdict of "not guilty by reason of insanity" on Victoria Temple were more complex and might be argued delicately throughout the summer term by the Lords Justices of Appeal. There was no doubt of the outcome.

Holmes and I congratulated our client. We listened encouragingly to her plans for buying a small house on the Devonshire coast, near Lynmouth, and joining a friend who ran a little school there. We congratulated Alfred Swain, whose integrity and marksmanship had carried the day.

Holmes was in demand for a further half-hour. He congratulated Superintendent Truscott on resisting a prosecution of Maria Jessel. In truth, Truscott had been all for it but was outmanoeuvred by Swain. Holmes, in his most affable manner, also suggested that reputations would suffer if the debacle of Victoria Temple's case were to be followed by another. He intimated that Edward Marshall Hall and Rufus Isaacs had already offered their services to the young woman without fee. Isaacs was a demon in cross-examination with no great respect for the constabulary. Miss Jessel was troubled no further.

I took a final circuit of the lake. Summer warmed the immaculate lawns, the cedar canopies and alleys running to the water. The lake was full, its yellow pads of lilies stretching to rhododendrons in purple view. The sounds and the sense of habitation died away. I stared again across the Middle Deep to the shore where Miss Temple had seen Miss Jessel.

It was perhaps fifteen minutes' walk back to the house. As on that previous occasion, there was an unaccountable stillness. As I listened, I heard not a sound of a bird—nor a sheep. I had surely been walking back for much longer than fifteen minutes. It was almost a relief, as I passed opposite the clearing of the apparitions, to hear the call of a bird and see the lake move. That call came again, but not quite at the same pitch or of the same duration. Of course it was an animal, not a bird.

It seemed best to step out and be going, but that curious call rang again. It was surely a cat's cry. But it could not be. No cats could get to the island. How would they live there? It was damned nonsense—but it was a cat if it was anything. Then I thought of the mewling of the children as they stalked Victoria Temple. Damned nonsense, to be sure. If there were no cats on the island there were certainly no children! But in the warm summer gardens the air was cold. That was the breeze on the lake, no doubt.

A cat's wail may be long and even undulating, but it does not break, as this one did, into a sob. This was distant, treble, plaintive, the hiccupping rhythm of a human motor that will not start. Very well, then there must be a children's picnic on the island. It was entirely probable on a summer day and a preferable explanation to any other.

There was no boat, but even so . . . The sobbing rose louder and fell again. It broke as infant tears, then into a laugh. It was someone playing a joke! Who? And how? Another laugh, chuckling, derisive. In that case, reason required that children were playing a trick as Miles and Flora had played one with Miss Temple. That was all. But Miles and Flora had been alive—and now they were certainly dead.

All I had to do was to walk steadily along the remainder of the lakeside path. There was nothing to impede me, and every step brought me closer to the company of Holmes and the others. But to welcome safety in this way was to give in to the thing again. As I walked, the sobbing or chuckling, which had fallen behind, now seemed to keep pace. I hope I am no coward in such matters. Twice I swung round—and saw only motionless water-lilies and the high white clouds still as a stage-set against the blue summer sky.

The lawn was in front of me now and the gate to the courtyard. The Tudor garden tower with its ruined staircase rose warm and still at my side. This was where the whole thing had started and it proved to be no more than an easy cheat by James Mordaunt. No apparition could linger here now. I paused and listened. The calls and cries, whatever they were, had gone. How could they be more than country children sounding closer than they were—the effect of the wind carrying sound through branches and over quiet water? But now there was no wind, it was still again. The birds and the sheep were silent once more, for all the world as if they were listening to the silence.

I was level with the brick tower and I kept a dignified pace as I passed towards the courtyard gate. I was not to be hurried. I could look where I liked and hold my own. But I did not feel the need to look up at those battlements. Whether it was because I disdained to do so or because I preferred not to, I must leave to the reader to judge.

3

Sherlock Holmes: The Actor

A FRAGMENT OF BIOGRAPHY

A number of my readers will be familiar with the fragments of biography which I have recalled in illustrating the cases of my friend Mr Sherlock Holmes. As we enter the world of the London theatre—"gaslight and greasepaint," as he used to call it—I must say something of his youthful stage career. It was very brief, beginning in 1879 and ending in the early spring of 1881, shortly before we first met.

I only once saw the tall, spare figure of Sherlock Holmes upon a stage. The audience had left the auditorium of the Royal Herculaneum more than an hour before. The curtains had been drawn open again to reveal the set. The lights had gone up and, by the battlements of Prince Hamlet's Elsinore, stood Holmes, tall, hawk-like and angular. In the white tie and tails of his evening clothes, he was in conversation with the stage manager, Mr Roland Gwyn. Beyond earshot were two stage-hands, one or two actors with minor parts, and two officers from the Metropolitan Police. Inspector Hopkins of Scotland Yard was in plain clothes. Superintendent Bradstreet of the nearby Bow Street police station wore the frogged jacket of the uniformed branch.

A few yards away, one of the greatest actors in England—in the world, indeed—lay dead in his dressing-room.

Let us leave that great tragedian lying there a moment longer, while I explain our involvement in what I have called "The Case of the Matinee Idol."

If ever a man was a born actor, it was Sherlock Holmes. Early in our friendship, he employed masterly disguises as a cabman and as an elderly nonconformist clergyman, in our case of "A Scandal in Bohemia." I remarked to him at the time that the stage had lost a great actor when he turned his back upon it in order to become a specialist in crime. To my surprise, he took the comment seriously and at once began to compare himself favourably with the great performers of the day. Holmes never suffered from false modesty. He thought he would have encountered little competition on the London stage—except perhaps from Irving and possibly from Sir Herbert Beerbohm Tree. But that was all.

This will sound absurdly boastful to those who know little of his life before our meeting in 1881. Indeed, few of his clients or acquaintances at Scotland Yard, let alone his enemies, ever had any idea that he once lived and worked in the company of such theatrical giants as Sir Henry Caradoc Price or popular character actors like "Captain" Carnaby Jenks. On half-a-dozen occasions, as an understudy, he even played opposite the great Sir Henry Irving himself.

My companion's longest theatrical acquaintance was with "Caradoc," as the mercurial Welshman was universally known. By 1890, Caradoc Price's Royal Herculaneum Theatre in the Strand was a by-word for the boldest and the best. In his own estimation, at least, this flamboyant actor-manager was the greatest Shakespearean of his day.

A few weeks ago, having decided to give this story to the world, I made my way once again up the steep stairs of the

Baker Street attic. Among dust and cobwebs in that lumber room stand such souvenirs as the fine silhouette profile of the Great Detective, designed and fashioned by the renowned theatrical artist of Grenoble, Monsieur Oscar Meunier. When it was set against the curtain of our sitting-room after dark, those looking up from the street were convinced that it moved as the angle of the light changed. It was first used to bring to justice the notorious Colonel Sebastian Moran, and several times persuaded Holmes's enemies that he was at home when in truth he was many miles away.

At the far end of the loft was the cumbersome tin trunk, which had belonged to my friend since he left home in his teens. Its hinge moved a little stiffly and the black lacquer was somewhat chipped. Yet the documents and legal parchments it contained were as crisp and alluring as ever. Each represented some *tour de force* of his analytical reasoning.

Here and there I noticed packets of letters, tied with tape and pencilled "Miss Ethel Le Neve *in re* H. H. Crippen for murder," or "Society for Insuring against Losses on the Turf," or "The City of Paris Loan Frauds." Elsewhere, barristers' briefs, black-letter legal parchments, had been marked by Holmes's scribble. He had written on *Rex v. Dougal*, "The Case of the Naked Bicyclists," and on *Regina v. Temple*, "The Bly House Murder." The notorious Siege of Sidney Street by Russian anarchists, which brought gunfire and insurrection to the London streets, was annotated rather whimsically as "The Mystery of the Yellow Canary." News of a missing canary was indeed the first clue to the conspiracy.

Holmes had been too busy until the last day of his life to find time for putting such a mass of papers into order. Fortunately, I knew what I was after and soon came to a stiff white envelope, about eight inches by ten. From this I shook out several theatrical programmes. The first was for McVicker's Theater,

Madison Street, Chicago. This ornamental structure had been rebuilt after the great fire of 1871 in that city. The cover of its programme for November 1880 announced "The Sassanoff Shakespeare Touring Company of London." The drama to be played was *Romeo and Juliet*. Romeo was performed by Henry Caradoc Price and Juliet by Anna Weld. Among the supporting cast, the character of Mercutio was acted by "William Sherlock Scott Holmes." At the Broad Street Theatre, Philadelphia, the programme for the Sassanoff company advertised *Othello*. The hero was once again personified by Caradoc Price and Desdemona by Miss Weld. The part of the hapless dupe Roderigo was taken by a young supernumerary, Carnaby Jenks, and the villainous Iago by "W. S. Holmes."

These four actors played turn and turn about in *Macbeth* and *Twelfth Night* at the Lafayette Opera House in Washington, and *The Merchant of Venice* and *Hamlet* at the Garden Theatre in New York. From time to time they performed in front of university audiences at Princeton and Yale. Henry Caradoc Price invariably took the leading role, but "W. S. Holmes" seemed content to be Macbeth's porter or Shylock's servant, Hamlet's Horatio or any of Falstaff's unsavoury cronies.

I once asked Holmes why he had abandoned his career as a consulting detective and turned his back on forensic chemistry for a year. Was it merely to set off on this theatrical jaunt to America—as it seemed I must call it? He looked at me as if I should have known that he had not abandoned anything. It was imperative for an ambitious young "consulting detective" to add a thorough knowledge of acting and disguise to his other talents. In the end, as he boasted in the case of Colonel Moran, he could walk and crouch in such a manner as to take twelve inches off his height for several hours on end. His American tour was not a flippant diversion but the burnishing of an essential weapon in his armoury.

Nor did he abandon criminal science. He began in 1879 only as a part-time actor in London, almost two years before our first meeting in the chemical laboratory of St Bartholomew's Hospital. By day he was the self-taught student of scientific method. Every evening he attended the Lyceum Theatre, sometimes as a "supernumerary" spear-carrier, often as a "walking gentleman" without words to speak, occasionally as an understudy. After one or two small speaking parts it was evident that he had a voice of command and could silence an auditorium by his presence. He was allowed to understudy the part of Horatio in Irving's production of *Hamlet.* At least twice during that time he was called upon to act the part. In later years he could truthfully boast that he had played Horatio to Irving's Hamlet. It was a play for which he nourished a lifelong enthusiasm.

As for Caradoc Price, later to be a household name, he was first of all among the most promising of Irving's young men. Then, by resorting to the money-lenders, he bought for a song the effects and good will of the bankrupt Sassanoff Shakespeare Company. Within a week he announced to his friends that this "company" would seek its fortune in New York. He invited them to join him. You may judge the speed of his success by the fact that he repaid his entire loan within a year. Unfortunately, this convinced him that money would always be as easy to make.

Holmes seized this chance to see something of the New World. With the rest of the company, he spent about eight months there. Upon their return to London, the lease of the Herculaneum Theatre in the Strand had fallen vacant. Caradoc Price used his growing reputation to borrow or beg every penny needed to take it on. Not long afterwards, following a visit by the Prince of Wales and a supper party, this enterprise became the Royal Herculaneum Theatre.

Sherlock Holmes parted company with his theatrical friends on their return from America and went back to the chemical laboratory at St. Bartholomew's Hospital. There I found him in the spring of 1881.

He never lost touch with the arts of the theatre. His impersonations of "Captain O'Malley," when investigating the Camden Town murder, or Peter Piatkoff the Anarchist during the siege of Sidney Street, were so lifelike that I met him on both occasions without recognising him as my closest friend.

It was not a matter of gumming whiskers to his face or assuming a theatrical tan. That would have done little. His personality would hold any audience because for that moment he was the very person he presumed to be. At the door of our lodgings I confronted the foreign ruffian who swore destruction to "Meester Sharelock Hoolmes," as he called him. I never doubted that this was the terrorist Piatkoff, called "Peter the Painter," until he burst out laughing in the unmistakable tones of my friend.

Of all the figures from Holmes's brief theatrical career with whom he grew acquainted in the Sassanoff Company, Henry Caradoc Price became by far the most famous. Even so, I do not think they met after 1881. A dozen times or so in the next ten years, Holmes and I sat in the stalls of the Royal Herculaneum, spellbound by the Celtic wizardry of Caradoc as Hamlet or Shylock or Falstaff. Yet there were no backstage visits and no admiring letters.

Because we must now come to the death of this great Shakespearean, it is necessary for me to say something about his life.

Those who recall the London theatre of thirty or forty years ago will need little reminding of Sir Henry Caradoc Price. At the height of his success, when his performances as Hamlet or Richard III were sold out long in advance, it was enough to speak simply of "Caradoc." He was seldom out of the spotlight, whether as Bernard Shaw's "vibrant and melodious hero," as the younger critics thought him, or Andrew Bradley's "meretricious showman," as he appeared to the purists. Caradoc did not hesitate to adapt the words or the actions of Shakespeare's plays for his own purposes, often to superb effect. At the same time, he was not known for his humility. "The Bard of Avon may be a greater artist than I," he replied to his detractors, "but I stand upon Shakespeare's shoulders."

Caradoc's past was as romantic as any stage production. It was even said that his greatest performance had been as the central character in his own life. He had come from childhood destitution. Born in South Wales, among the collieries and blast furnaces of Merthyr Tydfil, he was an "underground" pauper child in the coal mines of the Dowlais ironworks. At seven years old, he was employed to guard an "air door," against the danger of an explosion from fumes and flame. He liked to recall how he fell asleep one day from weariness during his ten-hour shift, after the rats ate his bread and cheese.

The supervisor, whose belt the children feared, caught him sleeping. Happily, this ogre was in company with Sir Josiah Guest. Sir Josiah owned the ironworks, collieries, railway, even the ships that carried his railway lines and wagon wheels round the world. Yet this liberal-minded patriarch had also been Member of Parliament for the Welsh industrial town since electoral reform in 1832.

Sir Josiah founded a school where the children of the collieries and blast furnaces might receive an education. Caradoc Price was one of its first pupils. By eleven years old, he had a "voice" and could sing. His father was blacksmith at the ironworks forge and both parents attended Bethesda Welsh Congregational Chapel. The family sat every Sunday before the pulpit of Rhondda Williams and his evangelists. The boy listened and, alone on the mountainside, practised their rhetoric.

England's new young monarch and her consort invited the children of the Dowlais school to Windsor Castle. Caradoc sang Felix Mendelssohn's "On Wings of Song" before Queen Victoria and Prince Albert. Each child was rewarded with a gold sovereign, which the future Sir Henry Caradoc Price wore on his watch-chain to the end of his life. The Prince heard the child piping "O for the Wings of a Dove," and recognised an artist. By His Highness's patronage, the boy was elected to a scholarship at the Royal Academy of Music.

The beauty of the childish voice did not survive the onset of manhood. But while his singing became mediocre, the speaking voice with its resonant inflections of the Welsh pulpit grew captivating. It had a rich, melodious tone in which critics claimed to hear the range of a cathedral organ. Better still, he could calm or excite an audience by a word or a gesture. He had only to stand upon a stage and look at them for the house to fall silent. When he spoke, one could hear a pin drop. By twenty-five, his natural feeling for words and a love of language marked him out. Robert Browning, himself the greatest living author of poetic drama, wrote that "No man could possibly be as wonderful as Caradoc Price seemed in the person of Falstaff or King Lear."

At thirty he was lessee of the Herculaneum, one of the three fashionable theatrical houses in the Strand. He had probably borrowed far more money than he could ever repay but it made him one of the great actor-managers. Even his debts were equalised after the tercentenary revival of *The Spanish Tragedy* by Shakespeare's great rival Thomas Kyd. Reviewers swore that the like of Caradoc as the mad hero Hieronymo had not been seen on the London stage since Edmund Kean, seventy years before.

After the last performance, he rose as Sir Henry Caradoc Price. Among his rivals at that time, only Irving had been so honoured. As a Knight of the Order of the British Empire, Caradoc was also one of the first men invited to record his voice upon the new wax discs of Thomas Edison. He showed little gratitude.

After listening to the result he replied to the inventor, "Sir, I have tested your machine. It adds a new terror to life and makes death a long-felt want."

Now he could afford to be popular. Comedies like *The Corsican Brothers* by Alexandre Dumas and such sentimental melodramas as Du Maurier's *Trilby* or *The Bells* by Leopold Lewis ran at the Royal Herculaneum month after month. He threw down the gauntlet to Irving, a few doors away at the Lyceum, and the Gatti brothers at the Adelphi. "When I pass before the theatre and read my name in such large letters," he once remarked, "I blush—but I instinctively raise my hat." He was armed against all criticism. A notice above his dressing-room door read, "Every man is a potential genius—until he does something." Elsewhere he answered those who denounced his "tampering" with the text and setting of Shakespeare, "A critic is merely one who uses dead languages to disguise his ignorance of life."

There were by now many people who had reason to dislike Caradoc—or even to detest him. A mental crisis seemed to derail him after ten or twelve years of fame He was more apt to take an evening off and let his understudy appear for him. He would be content to play King Claudius where once he must be Hamlet.

In money matters, his voice acquired a confident and jovial insincerity. It had the reassurance of a rogue who made common cause with you because his interest and yours were the same—and you were exhilarated to have him on your side rather than against you. Even those who subsequently counted their losses smiled at one another in the knowledge that they had Caradoc as their ally.

Saddest of all, he and Lady Myfanwy, the Celtic princess of his youth and the wife of his middle years, had grown apart from one another. Caradoc was apt to forget, as Holmes put it politely, where he should be sleeping. Yet he remained loyal to his childhood and his Welsh birth, if to nothing else. It was a point of honour that he should live in Hammersmith, only because it was the nearest London borough to Wales, a hundred and fifty miles away.

With the coming of the mass circulation newspaper and the monthly "society" magazine, far more people read about Caradoc than ever saw him on the stage. His photograph also appeared in the weekly sporting papers with their love of gossip and scandal. He was always ready to comment on any subject the reporters might put to him. Unfortunately, this opened the door to the most acrimonious public exchanges. The tongue that had been so mellifluous on the stage was apt to grow venomous in private quarrels.

Caradoc Price was a pitiless enemy, never more so than in his final vendetta with Oscar Wilde after 1890. The quarrel between the maverick Welsh actor and the egotistical Irish wit began during a long run of *Hamlet* at the Herculaneum. Robert Reynolds, a sycophant of Wilde, stole one of his master's witticisms and applied it as the headline of his review of Caradoc's characterisation of the Danish prince. "Price Without Value," as the heading called it. Reynolds attacked what he called the vulgarisation of text and scene which Caradoc had inflicted upon Shakespeare's play.

It might have ended there, for Reynolds did not say much that other journalists had not said already. Unfortunately, Wilde himself visited the Herculaneum during the run of the play. By this time the great Welsh Shakespearean had grown thick-set. Wilde was witty in the circle bar. Worse still, he became louder as his companions fell respectfully silent around him. He intoned Hamlet's famous speech, "Oh that this too, too solid flesh would melt." It was "the lament of a man who can act the Prince of Denmark only by courtesy of the corsetier." This pleasantry ran round until it hit its target. Caradoc recognised Wilde as his antagonist and flayed him as an example to others. To the sporting journalists he confessed, "I employ the services of a corsetier and perhaps should not. Wilde does not—and most certainly should—a middle-aged man who abandons his sex and casts himself as Salome."

This would have been bad enough. Caradoc in his present mood apparently thought it fell short. He remarked to a wide circle of his own admirers at a green room supper after a performance of *The Second Mrs Tanqueray* that "Mr Wilde's tragedy is to become the creator of laughter on the public stage and of sniggering in private conversations." He was too close to the mark, and the endangered playwright dared not retort on such a subject. Within a few days, Caradoc's epigram was quoted in the gossip column of *The Winning Post*. A fortnight later his portly antagonist was arrested at the Cadogan Hotel on charges of indecency.

Wilde's plays closed and his books were withdrawn but Caradoc would not leave the wretched man alone to his destruction. He harped on Wilde's physical appearance, assuring his Herculaneum audience, after a curtain call, "The London theatre has suffered a heavy loss in Mr Wilde. He has left a gap which it will be hard to fill." There was little laughter and a long silence of embarrassment. Even death was no reason for mercy, at least in private conversation. "Mr Wilde has been such a bore all his life that it is no wonder the grave should yawn for him."

In his later years Caradoc lost friends and made enemies. It was hard to say how many friends he lost or how violent were the enemies he made. People in the theatrical profession were simply frightened of him. Among his admirers, the laughter at his jibes grew hesitant and the silences became longer. Holmes knew more than I did, but to me it almost seemed that the poor fellow had become an obsessive, if not demented.

He always drank more than was good for him. Backstage, at

the green room banquets which followed his performances, he presided as tyrant and buffoon before his own actors and a host of theatrical celebrities. Here he was in his element. The characters of men and, worse still, the reputations of women who had resisted his charms were publicly flayed in his harangues for the benefit of gossip columns of *The Winning Post* or *Town and Turf*. Private lives were turned to public laughter all over London. Once, notoriously, the soul of his partner in romance had been so brutalised in his onslaught that she could no longer face her family or friends. Mockery followed her everywhere. She was found several days later, having opened her veins in the bath like a dishonoured matron of the Roman world. It was a brave man who stood his ground against Caradoc and a still braver woman who defied him to do his worst. Yet he remained the great tragedian of his day

I thought of all this as I gathered and checked the details for the present narrative. I returned the Sassanoff programmes to their envelope. I took out one or two other documents and letters. Then I closed and locked the tin trunk again. As I went back cautiously down the attic steps, I recalled the comfortable New Year's Eve when the whole thing began. How close and vivid it seemed as I held the papers in my hand—and yet what a different world it had been to the one I was living in now, so many years later!

4

The Case of the Matinee Idol

1

Now I must lead my reader back to Baker Street and the beginning of our adventure. New Year's Eve is a time I shall always associate with the headline "Royal Herculaneum Mystery" on the newspaper placards. Snow had fallen every day since Christmas, and by nine o'clock on that last evening of the year the view from our sitting-room had all the impressionist charm of Camille Pissarro's Paris streets.

Lamp-lit shops were open late and warmly lit. Each window was illuminated like the stage of a little theatre. The smiling doll-faces and tinsel of Mr Pollock's Toys, the warm patterns of Indian cloth in the Marylebone Linen Company, the solid rounds of Stilton and Cheshire cheese on Mr McIver's marble slab, gave a cosiness to the chill of the year's last night.

Holmes and I were in evening dress. We had accepted our annual invitation to an early-evening reception at the Bohemian Legation, from which we had just returned. Years before, Holmes had rendered a considerable service to the "Count Von Kramm," otherwise known as Wilhelm Gottsreich Sigismund von Ormstein, King of Bohemia. It was a matter of extortion concerning a certain photograph in the possession of Irene Adler of New Jersey. No woman ever affected Holmes so acutely. He abominated official receptions of all kinds, but I believe there lingered a dying hope that she would one day make her appearance at the legation in search of him.

I stood at the window and smiled at the thought. Two muddy gashes of carriage tracks, carved by cabs and twopenny buses, brewers' drays and bakers' vans, disfigured the white sheet of snow. The clear chimes of nine o'clock carried through the crisp air from the steeple of Marylebone Church. The northern sky towards Hampstead and Highgate was gently luminous with reflected snow-light. A few years later, we recalled the events of this New Year's Eve and the beauty of that winter scene with its tranquil light from the sky. Holmes then became reminiscent and murmured slowly to himself,

Serene and bright,
And lovely as a Lapland night.

The lines struck me as an ideal opening to the tale of the Herculaneum mystery. For reasons which the reader will discover, its publication was to be delayed, but I was anxious to have it "on paper."

"I say, Holmes! That would do very well at the beginning. Are they your own lines? Or some modern poet whom we might acknowledge?"

"I do not think, Watson, you would care to acknowledge them. They belong to George Joseph Smith, the so-called 'Brides in the Bath' murderer. They describe his only surviving wife, in his final letter to her. It was written a few hours before they stretched his neck on the gallows at Pentonville. You may recall that that particular tragedy owed something to my own modest abilities. Of all psychopathic personalities, Smith remains for me the most intriguing. I suggest a more suitable epigraph."

For the present, removing his coat and slipping into his mauve silk dressing-gown over waistcoat and trousers, he draped himself along the sofa. With a bottle of Bollinger sparkling between us, we toasted the year to come.

It was some time later when the bell of the street-door rang. At that hour, it would hardly be a call for our landlady, Mrs Hudson. Holmes stood up at once. Hanging his dressing-gown on the back of the door, he resumed his dress coat. From the hallway I caught a murmur of voices, one of which was Mrs Hudson's. There was a quiet footfall on the stairs and a tap at the door. With some sense of despair, I guessed that our plans for ringing out the old year and ringing in the new were at an end.

Our good lady appeared.

"A young gentleman, Mr Holmes. He brings you a message concerning Sir Henry Caradoc Price."

She spoke with all the importance the name demanded. Holmes frowned.

"Caradoc? What can he want? It is a year or two since I heard from him!"

He took the envelope and I glanced over his shoulder at the messenger. This was no urchin of the Baker Street Irregulars. Perhaps fourteen years old, he wore a dark, velvet suit, as if he had come from his first evening party in Portman Square. Holmes scanned the single sheet of paper. His long aquiline features were without expression.

"Dear me! Dear me!" he said with a sigh. "Who would have thought it?"

He handed me the sheet of notepaper with its printed heading: "Sir Henry Caradoc Price KBE, Royal Herculaneum Theatre." I read what followed.

My dear Holmes.

We have not communicated for some years. I beg you to come at once to the street entrance of the Royal Herculaneum. Bring whatever "investigating equipment" you usually carry. I am in the most dreadful fix of my life.

As the newspapers will tell the world tomorrow, Caradoc Price was killed this evening in front of a thousand witnesses. I fear the papers must also tell the world that I did it. The Bow Street police and the house surgeon from Charing Cross Hospital have been summoned. They are close by and will be here soon. It is imperative that I should speak to you before the arrival of the detective officers from Scotland Yard. If this is delivered to you at once by the theatre call-boy, you may just be in time.

I implore your assistance, for old acquaintance sake.

Carnaby Jenks.

"For old acquaintance sake!" Holmes said with a groan "Appropriate for a New Year's Eve joke, is it not? I do not, however, treat this as a joke, despite the thousand witnesses. I recall Jenks as a histrionic egotist. Wherever he is, trouble attends him—and spreads to those around him."

I glanced at the paper again.

"Caradoc Price was a Knight Commander of the British Empire!"

My friend adjusted his cravat and wrapped himself in his plaid overcoat.

"Brother Mycroft assures me that Mr Gladstone was determined upon the award before he resigned his premiership," he said as he fastened the buttons. "Indeed, the Grand Old Man shed tears during Caradoc's last performance as King Lear. Everything was forgiven the old scoundrel when WG made his recommendation to Her Majesty. Public hostilities and scurrilous innuendoes, not to mention irregular romances, were overlooked. So were two famous backstage fist-fights with other actors."

"Fist-fights?" I pulled on my pumps with a shoe-horn.

Holmes reached for a silver-topped stick.

"Do you not recall his Arthurian drama, *Sir Gawain and the Green Knight*? He and Rosemount Phipps in suits of woollen stage-armour were to argue on either side of the famous round table. Phipps was to smash his fist down with such strength that his half of the table broke off and fell to earth. The property manager had prepared and positioned it for Phipps's half to fall at a mere tap, the other half being reinforced. Before the curtain rose Caradoc contrived to turn the table round."

I remembered the story now, but Holmes continued with a chortle.

"Phipps brought his mailed fist crashing down—and nothing happened. He struck four times with increasing force and desperation—at which point the wrong half of the table fell off. There was giggling in the stalls and a fist-fight with Caradoc behind the scenes. Rosemount Phipps was a young man of promise and he left the company next day."

He turned to the velvet-suited messenger, who waited with insolent impatience.

"And now, sonny, we will proceed to the cab, which I assume you have ordered to wait."

A quick movement of the boy's eyes confirmed that he did not care to be addressed as "sonny."

"Yes," he said gracelessly.

"Then perhaps we may reach the Herculaneum before Lestrade or his cohorts take possession of the premises."

The malevolent stare of the velvet-suited infant did not falter. He had been watching his chance to put an oar in.

"Murder," he said with childish satisfaction. "That's what they say it is."

Holmes remained unruffled.

"Do they? Do they say that? The wonder is that it has not happened long before. However, I suppose it is of some importance that we should go and see if they are right. Be so good as to fetch the black bag on the floor by the hat-stand, and carry it out to the cab."

We followed the sullen child downstairs, climbed aboard the waiting hansom and set off at our best speed for the Strand.

The wheels jolted uncomfortably over the packed snow of Baker Street and Oxford Street, onwards down Regent Street and into Pall Mall. Conversation was curtailed by the presence of the velvet-suited Mercury. In the end I decided to ignore the little shaver.

"I do not recall, Holmes, that we have ever before had a client who killed his victim in front of a thousand witnesses. Short of slaughtering Caradoc in a Roman arena . . ."

"I never cared for Caradoc as a man, Watson. However, I never liked the histrionic pip-squeak Carnaby Jenks much more."

As we passed down Regent Street I guessed this was no hoax. A small group of sightseers stood at the window of the London Stereoscopic Company. An array of famous figures was on show. One in particular attracted these idlers. I had passed it the day before and knew that it was a sturdy, self-confident image of Sir Henry Caradoc Price. It had been snatched by a sly street photographer. Caradoc in top-hat and tails had been walking down Piccadilly when a removal man passed him, staggering under the load of a grandfather clock. The great tragedian, according to the caption under the photograph, was saying to the man, "My poor fellow! Why not buy a pocket watch?"

West End street-rumours of murder at the Royal Herculaneum

had no doubt brought these window-gazers to peer at the illustrious victim. Our cab crossed Trafalgar Square to Charing Cross. The sky of a Lapland night now glowed pale above Nelson's column and Landseer's lions.

Our cabbie reined in his horse, weaving into the lamp-lit traffic of the Strand. To our left, at almost equal distances, stood the white façades and Grecian columns of three famous theatres. The first was the Royal Herculaneum. Beyond it rose the Lyceum and the Adelphi. Though it fronted on the Strand, the "Herc's" rear doors and windows looked on to the narrower and more squalid cobbles of Maiden Lane.

Long before we reached the front of the building, the posters on its tall hoardings were legible. They proclaimed "Sir Henry Caradoc Price" in lettering about two feet high and "Hamlet" in much the same size. "William Shakespeare" was somewhat reduced. At the foot of each bill a small and discreet announcement confirmed that on Mondays, Wednesdays and at afternoon matinees the part of Hamlet would be played by Mr Carnaby Jenks. Sir Caradoc would still be seen, playing the less taxing role of King Claudius. New Year's Eve was a Wednesday. The curtain would rise at 6.30 in order to liberate the patrons in good time for their midnight festivities.

The octagonal lamps of the portico shone white and stark, though the carriages with the patrons of the boxes and the front stalls had departed an hour ago. Through the glass doors I glimpsed four men in the foyer. They stood by a broad flight of marble steps, carpeted in red, which led to the dress circle and the boxes.

Carnaby Jenks, thin and angular, was waiting by the pay-box next to a uniformed constable. I had seen him only two or three times on the stage, but he was watching for a chance to step forward and open the door of our cab as soon as we arrived. With his dark, tousled hair, the neurotic energy of his walk and a look of latent anxiety. He would not be at his best under police questioning.

Holmes stepped down, a tall figure who just managed not to knock off his hat in the process. He stood on the pavement, which had been scraped and cleaned but sparkled with ice. Looking at the pale, bony actor, he produced the sheet of paper and asked sharply, "Jenks! Will you please explain this message? Is it a Caradoc joke?"

At that moment Jenks looked like a tramp in fear of a savage dog. He had just been able to pull on a jacket and trousers in place of his stage costume, but his hair was awry and the orange tan of stage make-up had been imperfectly wiped from his features.

"Thank God you have come, Holmes! I am in earnest! You are a true friend, if ever there was. Caradoc is dead. I appear to have killed him."

"Really?" said Holmes in the same sceptical manner. "Are you under arrest then? It does not seem so."

"I may very soon be arrested. They will not let me out of their sight, but I have declined to answer any questions."

"That is, no doubt, why they will not let you out of their sight," I said helpfully. Holmes dismissed this with a half-wave of his hand.

"I must have a chance to talk to you first," pleaded Jenks. "Caradoc is lying dead in his dressing-room. Cyanide! That can only be murder. Surely?"

Holmes seemed almost relieved to hear it. It certainly clarified the situation.

"After such a message, Mr Jenks, I was not expecting anything less. I assume you did not literally kill him with your own hands?"

"But it seems I did! Quite literally! On the stage! Do you suppose that I should have sent for you otherwise? I gave him poison—cyanide."

Holmes turned to the two men whom Jenks had been watching over our shoulders. In any event, we were about to be interrupted by a tall, broad-shouldered man with wide eyes and bold features. He wore the peaked cap and frogged jacket of a senior officer in the Metropolitan Police uniformed branch. I recognised him without difficulty. He was not a detective, but we had first met Inspector Isaiah Bradstreet at his office in Bow Street police station. It was many years before, during an investigation given to the world as "The Case of the Engineer's Thumb." He seemed larger now, but his face had altered very little.

"My dear Bradstreet," Holmes said, extending his hand, "the crown upon your epaulette is new to me. I shall take great pleasure in addressing you henceforth as 'Superintendent.' I had not heard of your promotion."

"Thank you, Mr Holmes. It is recent. As to the present case, I was the first to be called, Bow Street being just round the corner from here. I was on the premises ten or fifteen minutes after the body of Sir Caradoc had been discovered. Six constables accompanied me to guard the scene of the crime and Sergeant Witlow to keep the gentlemen of the press at a distance."

"Six!"

From the hiss of his voice and the dismay on his face I knew that Sherlock Holmes was imagining the damage that might have been inflicted on the evidence during the past hour by six pairs of constabulary boots and hasty hands. Bradstreet went on as though he had not heard the sharp monosyllable.

"We need to be well-manned on these occasions, Mr Holmes. You know how lurid stories can spread. There is strong public interest, Sir Caradoc being who he was."

"Murder is apt to be lurid," said Holmes blandly. He then favoured Superintendent Isaiah Bradstreet with the quick, humourless smile which conveyed that he considered his time was passing to no useful purpose.

The superintendent performed a half-turn towards the marble-balustraded stairs.

"Gentlemen, may I introduce you to my junior colleague from Scotland Yard?"

Sherlock Holmes had assumed a rather contemptuous look, but then, to my relief, his face softened. This junior colleague was a young man in quiet tweeds and cravat. One might take him for a schoolmaster or a confidential clerk. He was slightly-built by comparison with Bradstreet, yet he seemed taller than he was by an upright and obviously military bearing.

"Introductions are not necessary," said Holmes more affably. "Inspector Stanley Hopkins and I are well-acquainted."

So they were. Bradstreet was a moderately intelligent uniformed officer but not the most amenable. By contrast, Stanley Hopkins had been our companion in several recent cases. He was of a younger generation and had always shown great respect for the methods of Sherlock Holmes. He was not ashamed to act at times as though he were my friend's pupil, inviting opinions or advice. He would even ask for assistance during investigations in which we had no part. Those of my readers familiar with our inquiries in "The Case of the Missing Pince-Nez" or "The Case of the Abbey Grange" will not need to be reminded of him. If Carnaby Jenks was in trouble, I should prefer Stanley Hopkins to our cocksure friend Lestrade or his more quick-witted colleague Tobias Gregson.

Hopkins came forward with hand outstretched.

"A pleasure to see you again, Mr Holmes. It seems as if this case may be rather in your line. Not quite as straightforward as we first thought."

I do not believe Bradstreet cared much for this. Though he was in command, the young detective officer seemed to be cutting him out. Hopkins continued his explanation.

"Dr Worplesdon, the young houseman from Charing Cross Hospital, was here in ten minutes or so. Just across the road. He diagnosed an apoplectic seizure or something of the kind. Mr Bradstreet, more familiar with unexplained deaths, was the first who caught an odour of bitter almonds. Dr Hammond, the police surgeon, later confirmed it. An accident seems unlikely. And not many people would choose prussic acid as a means of taking their own lives. That leaves murder. All the same, sir, we should value your view and Dr Watson's."

"I should not readily challenge a police surgeon of Dr Hammond's experience," I said generously, hoping to bring all sides together.

Holmes took off his silk hat and white scarf, placing them on a marble-topped programme-table. Bradstreet stepped between my friend and Hopkins. The superintendent was smiling now, perhaps acknowledging the tribute which Hopkins paid him as the discoverer of bitter almonds.

"Naturally, Mr Holmes, we cannot countenance anything irregular—anything that is not correct procedure."

Holmes was not the least put out.

"My dear Bradstreet, I would not have it otherwise. I am only here because Mr Jenks has requested me to act for him. To be fair to him, he first sent for you and young Dr Worplesdon. Mr Jenks is now, however, my client—unless and until he tells me otherwise."

Jenks let out a long breath, almost like a gasp. I really think he had believed Holmes might turn him away. His facial muscles relaxed.

"In any case," my friend continued, "I cannot believe it would be irregular for me to view the evidence and form an opinion—and of course to share my conclusions with you."

"I daresay Dr Hammond has done our work for us," I added soothingly. "Our views will very likely coincide with your own,

Mr Bradstreet. I do not think that we seek to do more than confirm the evidence."

Stanley Hopkins added his pennyworth.

"Since Mr Holmes and Dr Watson have an interest, sir, the sooner their views are known to us, the more speedily we shall make progress."

I felt this harmony was too good to last. Bradstreet, however, agreed that Holmes might be told the facts and allowed to "look around." Yet the superintendent still seemed to fear, as the old saying has it, that Holmes might get a spade under him and assume command of the investigation.

"The play being *Hamlet,*" said Hopkins confidentially, "it had reached the final scene with Mr Jenks deputising as Hamlet tonight and Sir Caradoc playing King Claudius. As you know, sir, in Shakespeare's story Claudius poisons one of the two goblets of wine that are brought in. But his tricks are turned against him. Queen Gertrude unknowingly drinks the poison. In revenge, his step-son Hamlet forces the King to drink from the poisoned goblet before running him through with a rapier."

"How many times have I acted that in youth!" said Holmes wistfully.

"Indeed, sir. In Sir Caradoc's production this final scene is set on the terrace of Elsinore castle behind the battlements. Usually I believe it is an interior hall. Hamlet drives the King to the battlements, holds him over on his back, forces him to drink from the goblet and stabs him. He rolls him over so that King Claudius falls to his death on the rocks below. That is to say, he falls on to two inclining mattresses about three feet below, out of view of the audience. Very dramatic, they tell me. A little variation that has proved popular with the public."

Jenks said not a word during this. I thought the poor fellow looked ill. He was deathly pale, and the bright gaslight caught a sheen of perspiration on his face. For a moment I wondered whether he might not have been poisoned as well! He straightened up but said nothing.

"I saw the production last season," Holmes was saying quietly to Hopkins. "You describe it admirably. May we assume that Sir Caradoc picked himself up from the mattresses and made his way off-stage to his dressing-room? Over the next ten minutes or so the performance would have been concluded and followed by the usual series of curtain calls. In my youth I played this last scene frequently. I believe that the time from the death of the King to the final curtain and then the usual compliments would take up about a quarter of an hour."

"So it would seem," said Bradstreet, "that Sir Caradoc had a private sitting-room and a bedroom in the Dome of the theatre. Its balcony overlooks the Strand. However, he would have gone straight to his dressing-room, in the passage behind the stage. He did not appear for the curtain call."

"A cause for alarm?" I asked. Hopkins shook his head.

"It had happened several times of late, doctor, when he was merely playing King Claudius. Once the performance was over, his dressing-room door appears to have been locked on the inside. Not usual but not a cause for alarm. There was nowhere else he could be—alive or dead."

"And Mr Jenks was on stage until the end of the play?"

"He was. It ended about quarter to ten, after an early start for New Year's Eve. There was the big green room supper for the cast at ten-thirty with guests, speeches and compliments. They thought Sir Caradoc was preparing his speech. A real piece of spite that could be, even about his friends, let alone Mr Wilde, George Alexander and his rivals. His actors dreaded it, but he was their paymaster. With his dressing-room door locked, it seemed he was not ready to be disturbed just yet."

"Then he was out of sight for about three quarters of an hour in all?"

"Quite so, Mr Holmes. No one thought it necessary to give him a knock until about ten minutes past ten. There was no response. In the end, one of the cast opened a sash window from the street outside. There are bars, but the window can be raised for air and to give a view into the room."

"Someone looked and saw him dead?"

"He was lying on the floor, sir, by the chair of a small desk that he kept in there for business purposes. The dressing-table and mirror are in the adjoining bathroom. It looked as if he must have toppled from his chair. They managed to get him onto the sofa. He was lying there when I came with Dr Hammond, the duty police surgeon."

"And Dr Hammond spoke of cyanide?"

Bradstreet had been waiting to get his word in.

"Dr Hammond concluded it was prussic acid, Mr Holmes. I had previously suspected it. You might say Sir Caradoc had it on his breath. The goblet he drank from was still on the stage and was examined. It had the same odour as he did. Thank God it was reserved for his supper and no one else had touched it. I suppose that would have put anyone else off drinking from it. And that's how the case stands, sir."

"I think it may stand a little differently," Holmes said equably. "I am sorry to disappoint you of a public spectacle. However, I should be very surprised if Sir Caradoc allowed anything to pass his throat at the moment of his stage death. I cannot imagine a more certain recipe for choking oneself than swallowing during a struggle. In any case that particular goblet is also used in the scene by Queen Gertrude. Sometimes by Hamlet as well. Lady Myfanwy Price is in good health, I take it? And at this moment we see Mr Carnaby Jenks standing before us, suffering no ill effects."

The superintendent's voice sounded a little husky, but he cleared his throat.

"I don't follow you, Mr Holmes."

"Mr Bradstreet, I enjoy the quite unfair advantage of having understudied and played that final scene many times. Two goblets of wine are brought in and set on the table, prior to a duel between Hamlet and Laertes. The first goblet is drunk from by Queen Gertrude and, in some productions, by Hamlet. King Claudius is also forced to drink from it when Hamlet kills him. The second goblet is the important one. It is brought in at the same time. Only the King drinks from it. He drinks twice before the duel of Hamlet and Laertes—as many times as you like while he watches them fight. I repeat—he alone drinks from it. Only Sir Caradoc was affected by poison because he drank from this second goblet. The first goblet, which Mr Jenks forced him to drink from, was safe."

There was a moment's silence before he concluded.

"At the risk of spoiling a good story, the audience did not see Mr Jenks poison Sir Caradoc, unless the goblets were switched at the end, which is not suggested. The poisoned wine in the second goblet had already been drunk by Sir Caradoc several minutes earlier. That was when he would have been poisoned. I concede this does not necessarily acquit my client. Indeed, he would have had ample time to tamper with the wine. As Hamlet, he is not required for an entire half-hour or more before the final act, for Hamlet has sailed to England."

Carnaby Jenks favoured him with the ghastly stare of a man who has been acquitted of picking pockets only to be arrested again on a charge of murder. Holmes remained unruffled. He turned to the superintendent.

"As young men in the Sassanoff Company, it was Sir Caradoc and I who played Hamlet and King Claudius alternately—box and cox about, as they say. One man cannot play the Prince night after night. Yet we could not afford an evening with no performance. I soon noticed that when it was his turn to play the smaller part of King Claudius, Caradoc ordered real wine in his goblet, and there was very little left by the final curtain."

Carnaby Jenks broke forward—I cannot describe his gesture in any other way. He was still pale and moist, despite the evening chill.

"I had nothing to do with his death, Holmes! You must see that! You must all of you see that! Why should I kill him? Tell them I would not!"

Holmes gave the shrug of a reasonable man.

"I should imagine you loathed and feared Caradoc quite as much as the rest of us used to do—and no doubt with equally good reason. I was his companion on stage but I did not care for him."

They stared at one another, unblinking, as if neither would be first to turn away. The two policemen watched. A flicker of white gaslight shone on the marble and the red carpeting of the foyer. Holmes broke the silence,

"Did you like Sir Caradoc, Mr Jenks?"

Carnaby Jenks blinked. He echoed his interrogator.

"Like him?"

"That is the question. Many people did not. I should like to hear your answer."

"He had changed for the worse—"

"Excuse me, that was not the question," said Holmes patiently.

Quite unaccountably, it seemed to me, Jenks lost his temper. "You call me your client, Holmes! You have no business to cross-examine me like this in front of—"

"Do you think the Criminal Investigation Division will not cross-examine you presently? If it comes to court, do you not think you will be cross-examined by men who will tear to pieces any answer based on hesitation or equivocation? I prepare my clients for what must come. I do so now in your case."

"How?"

"You played the part of Hamlet, did you not? I will remind you that the wine, when it was poisoned, was presumably standing in a goblet waiting to be carried on to the stage early in the fifth act. Prior to that, Hamlet—that is to say Carnaby Jenks—does not appear in the play for above half an hour. There is not a single member of the cast who appears to have had longer access or better facility for using poison than you did. That is a serious matter and I beg you will give your attention to it!"

For a moment it seemed as if Jenks could not find the voice to reply. Then he spoke quietly but with a flash of true melodrama.

"Sherlock Holmes, I have trusted you. I always thought of you as my friend. Are you determined to get me hanged?"

Holmes consigned him to the company of Superintendent Bradstreet with the gesture of one dismissing a beggar.

"Contrary to your assertions this evening, Jenks, we have never been close friends nor confidants. However, that is beside the point. The probabilities are equally balanced that you are an innocent fool or a consummate deceiver. My task is to determine which. I have no doubt that I shall do so before the night is over. Meanwhile, you will greatly oblige me by not making your case any more difficult than it is. I suggest that you keep your mouth shut, difficult though you may find it."

2

After such treatment, Jenks might have been relieved to be led off by Superintendent Bradstreet and the uniformed constable. Stanley Hopkins spoke quietly,

"We've had a chance to question the theatre people, sir. Between ourselves, I think you had better know what Ophelia and Horatio heard your client say a week or two ago."

"Indeed?"

"They were both present in the green room when Mr Jenks opened a note from Sir Caradoc. Apparently it informed him that after the end of the month—today that is—he would no longer play Hamlet in the matinees. The part was to be taken by a new understudy, who needed the experience. Mr Jenks's wages, prior to his departure from the company, would be reduced accordingly."

"How unfortunate," said Holmes indifferently. "Such a fact will tell against him when motives are weighed up."

"Yes, sir. Other witnesses report Mr Jenks having once used some choice descriptions of his governor. Your client concluded by saying, 'I would murder him with very great pleasure. He will find what it is to drive a man to a point where he has nothing to lose.' Something of that kind."

Holmes sighed at the impossibility of defending such a buffoon. Hopkins tried to console him and made matters worse.

"Of course, it's only words, Mr Holmes. It proves nothing. Still, you know what lawyers can do with that sort of thing in court. I thought you'd better know."

"You did right, my good Hopkins, and I am indebted to you. I suppose the note he read to himself really did contain notice of dismissal and that Jenks was not just having us on?"

"That hadn't crossed my mind, sir. But why have us on?"

"Why does Jenks do anything? The quirks of an old character actor who makes his whole life a drama. For the moment let us put aside questions of motives for killing Sir Caradoc and concentrate on who had the opportunity. From what I am told, he must have faced a battalion of enemies. I do not even think we could exclude Lady Myfanwy. If all I hear is true, ladies have killed for much less."

"Opportunity, Mr Holmes?" Hopkins reminded him hopefully

"Quite. I will confine myself within Mr Bradstreet's limits but I should be greatly obliged for a tour of the evidence. Perhaps, standing where we are, it would be best to start with the auditorium."

Holmes and I followed Stanley Hopkins up the red-carpeted marble steps which led to the varnished doors of the dress circle.

The interior of the Herculaneum was little different, except in size, to a dozen horseshoes of red plush in the West End of London. The same curving seat-rows and pillars, cream and gold paintwork rising from stalls to gallery. As we stood at the back of the dress circle, the stage curtain was open. We were looking down at the set which Caradoc had commissioned for the final act of Shakespeare's most famous play.

I understand that William Shakespeare gave no stage directions for the setting of this scene. Caradoc had copied a famous design by William Telbin at the Lyceum production in 1864. Instead of a hall with thrones and galleries, he had staged the denouement on the battlements. Perhaps I should call it a broad terrace edged by the battlements. We looked out across what seemed to be a considerable drop towards a cyclorama of distant sea. There were two throne-like chairs and two long baronial tables. One table was strewn with the remains of a banquet. From where we stood, I could see a pair of pewter goblets of Elizabethan design.

Centre stage, a uniformed London constable stood at ease. Two more men had been posted in the wings and another in the gangway of the stalls. The Herculaneum was as securely in the hands of Bradstreet's officers as a conquered city might be. Hopkins spoke quietly to Holmes, though not so quietly that I missed anything of the exchanges.

"I've had half an hour to look round, Mr Holmes. There's one or two things that you won't find in the evidence. Mr Squire, the stage-door keeper, liked Sir Caradoc. That puts him in a minority. He says that if you want to understand the great man, remember one thing. Our hero discovered at fifty that, contrary to what he had always told himself, he did not love his fellow men. By fifty-one, he saw no reason why he should."

"The ruin of youth," Holmes said philosophically. "Even when he was thirty, I predicted as much."

"Indeed? He lived a solitary life in the Dome. Lady Myfanwy went up there only when necessary. I had a look just before you came. It had a sad feel, Mr Holmes. Panelled walls with scenes from his productions, others embellished with fancy mottoes. 'He who takes in too much wine gets drunk. He who takes in too much water drowns himself.' That sort of thing. 'It is better to drink a little too much than much too little.' He certainly drank more than was good for him, which perhaps he didn't do when he was younger."

"On the contrary he did, Hopkins. Its effects were less apparent then. What of his ladies?"

"Lady Myfanwy was never sure where he was at night. I'm not convinced she any longer cared. He was a matinee idol, after all. When he was younger, there were so many women writing for a lock of his hair that they say he kept a young man just to grow hair for him. I can't find that there was anyone in particular at present. In the past few years, a young country virgin or a woman of the city streets seems to have been all the same to him."

"What a falling off was there," said Holmes, looking about him. "He was no angel at thirty, but the melancholy seediness which you describe had not quite engulfed him. Who will lament his passing?"

Hopkins shrugged.

"Not many, sir. Some will lament the death of his spirit several years ago. Few will regret the passing of the man himself now."

"My dear Hopkins! There is a tone of poetry in your diagnosis!"

The young inspector shook his head.

"The wrong diagnosis, Mr Holmes. Thanks to your client, a thousand people will read the papers and believe they saw Sir Caradoc drink poisoned wine in his struggle with Carnaby Jenks."

Holmes gripped the red plush of the circle barrier and stared at the blue cyclorama of the stage.

"All theatre is illusion, inspector. Jenks is no more than what he makes himself for the passing moment. Was real wine always drunk?"

"They say Sir Caradoc was never in liquor when he played Prince Hamlet. He liked a decent bottle to fill his goblet if he was only King Claudius. After all, it was the last scene and the play almost at an end. If you ask me, the only thing he liked better than drinking was the reputation of drinking. To hear them talk, you'd think most people came in the hope of seeing him fall down drunk on the stage."

"Where did this bottle of wine come from?"

Hopkins took out his notebook and flipped over a page.

"The bottle was brought in as usual, at about ten to nine by a waiter from the Cafe Boucherat in Maiden Lane, just round the back. It was a Nuits St Georges 1885. Because it was a numbered bottle, the time when it was drawn was noted in the stock book. Restaurants do that to prevent pilfering by their staff. It was uncorked and sniffed by Monsieur Boucherat, the proprietor. It certainly wasn't poisoned then."

"And the waiter?"

"Never out of sight of the cafe until the bottle was passed to Mr Squire the stage-door keeper. Sir Caradoc took it from him and filled one of the pewter goblets in his dressing-room. The other one had something like ginger cordial for Hamlet and the Queen. Very often they had nothing at all and just pretended to drink. Caradoc put the goblets on the stage manager's table in the wings at about nine o'clock or just after. Roland Gwyn, the stage manager, had all the properties for the last scene in place by five minutes past nine. They were under his eye after that and he doesn't strike me as a murderer. The goblets were carried on-stage by two footmen during the last scene at about ten past nine or very soon after."

"Then we are invited to believe that the poison must have been added to the goblet of wine by sleight of hand? In a split second between about nine and ten past?"

"So it seems, Mr Holmes. If you take that time, I expect there must have been moments when no one was looking. Even after Mr Gwyn took charge. Presently, King Claudius on the stage calls out, "Set me the stoups of wine upon the table," and that's when the servants carry them in. The King stands at one end of the long table and the Queen with Hamlet at the other. The goblet put down for Sir Caradoc was the only one with real wine in it and within his reach."

"Hopkins," said my friend delightedly, "you have made the play your own!"

Again, the young man blushed slightly with pleasure.

"I'd rather make the case my own, Mr Holmes. But there's no other way that I can see how it happened."

"And very probably you are right. We have only to find who could have put poison into the goblet in the wings. We may still exclude the stage manager, I suppose?

"Unless I've lost all sense of innocence and guilt, sir. For all his theatrical connections, Mr Gwyn's pride is being a deacon of the Welsh chapel in the Tottenham Court Road."

"How very singular. I believe we may also exclude Sir Caradoc, unless this was a suicide of truly melodramatic originality. That is a theory to which I do not incline."

"And what if he noticed an odour of almonds in the goblet as he drank, Mr Holmes?"

"He might take it for just that, an almond odour in the goblet. All wines smell of something or other. Certain red wines pride themselves upon a nutty flavour, do they not? In any case, he would be swallowing already, as his part requires, and it would be too late. He may have thought the wine had been spiced or was sour. He would complain to the Cafe Boucherat afterwards but he must drink. For all his vices, Caradoc would not halt a performance of *Hamlet* in the middle of the last act. Whoever killed him no doubt knew him well enough to be sure of that."

"As I understand it, sir, the performance would require him to drink two or three draughts during the duel, as well as two before it, which was the way he usually played the part. We reckon, at least a third of a bottle of wine in all."

Holmes nodded and the inspector added,

"Then there was the make-believe of Mr Jenks forcing him to drink from the other goblet and rolling him over the battlements. It seems Sir Caradoc played his part to the end. As for what came next, Mr Holmes, we calculate he could be in his dressing-room—with or without the door locked behind him—a minute or so after coming off the stage."

"What was his routine?"

"As a rule he never called his dresser, Alfred Cranleigh—a loyal old fellow—until he had relaxed for fifteen or twenty minutes. He needed to 'calm down,' as he called it. That was when he had his regular cigar. He'd read the evening paper while he smoked. After that, he would call for Cranleigh. Tonight Cranleigh received no call and would never have gone into the dressing-room without one. Sir Caradoc might have had company on his sofa, if you believe what you hear."

"How was the alarm raised?"

"The play probably ran for ten or fifteen minutes after he came off. Plus, of course, the curtain calls, compliments and little speeches. No sign of him. I'm told he disliked being present when anyone else was applauded as the hero. He'd even started talking of playing Claudius under a *nom de plume*. A joke, I expect."

Hopkins fell silent and I took my chance to establish the order of events.

"He left the stage at about twenty-five minutes past nine. After the final speeches and the curtain calls, the performance was over by quarter to ten. No one saw him until his dressing-room was opened. Why did they become suspicious?"

"Why, doctor? He never missed his chance to perform at the green room supper on New Year's Eve. It was to be at half past ten, and by just after ten there was still no reply to knocks on his door. Lady Myfanwy had tried once or twice by then. The door was locked, but they checked that he hadn't gone up to the Dome. Where else could he be?"

"And this was some three-quarters of an hour after he came off the stage?"

"If you put it like that, Mr Holmes. Lady Myfanwy lost her patience. She seems to have been sure he was in there. There was certainly a light on. Harry Squire the stage-door keeper said it was shining out into Maiden Lane. The windows are frosted glass so that's all you can see. He might have been taking a bath—or he might not have been alone. There is that sofa in there, Mr Holmes. . . ."

"So I understand."

"The trouble was, sir, if they used the pass-key to open the door, everyone was crowded in the main passage waiting to see what was going on. And all the world would hear about it."

"I assume this was not the first time that the problem had occurred?"

"Once before, Lady Myfanwy had gone outside into Maiden Lane which runs along the back of the building. After what she saw when she opened the window, there had been all hell to pay, if I may use the expression. She did so again tonight. The dressing-room windows are at street level, of course. That's why they have iron bars on the outside to keep out sneak-thieves. Being sash windows, they are also fastened by a catch at night when the stage-door keeper goes round last thing. During the day they are free for ventilation. The bars still keep intruders out."

"There was no interference with the bars?"

"Perfectly secure, Mr Holmes. Lady Myfanwy put her hands through the bars and raised one of the windows to see if he was there. Supposing he was in the adjoining bathroom, she could call out and he would hear her. What she saw was Sir Caradoc dead on the floor."

"And what was happening on the stage all this time?"

"No one was on stage just then, except passing to and fro. Fortunately the goblet hadn't been touched. It was kept for Sir Caradoc to finish his wine at supper. No one would have dared to drink it meantime!"

"When does Dr Hammond suggest that he died?"

"It must be by about ten o'clock or soon after. That's all anyone can say at present. It could easily have been half an hour earlier."

"I know something of poisons," I said hastily. "Prussic acid is notorious for acting quickly. Contrary to popular belief, however, death is not always instantaneous. If it were, presumably Sir Caradoc would have died on the stage. The victim may not be aware of what is amiss for ten or fifteen minutes. Even so, I should be surprised if he was alive at ten o'clock. How was he found precisely?"

"The doublet and hose from his costume were hung over a chair. He was wearing his green silk dressing-gown but the tasselled cord was lying halfway between the desk and the door, as if it had dropped there. The key to the door lay close by it. Sir Caradoc was on the floor by the desk, looking as if he had toppled from his chair. Lady Myfanwy first thought he must have suffered an attack or a fit of some kind. She ran back and the door was opened with the pass-key. Everyone could see that he was dead."

"Face convulsed and bloated?" I asked. "Wet around the mouth?"

"Just so, doctor. Dr Worplesdon was called at once. Mr Gwyn, the stage manager, sent to Bow Street police station to report an unexplained death. After Superintendent Bradstreet arrived, he put through a call to the Yard. Being duty CID inspector tonight, I was here about twenty minutes later with Dr Hammond. So far as location goes, Mr Holmes, I'd say this was about the most convenient murder I've ever known."

"A little too convenient," said Holmes sardonically.

"Mr Gwyn ordered that nothing should be touched—on-stage or off. Very helpful. Both goblets were still on the table. As soon as Dr Hammond smelt the second one, the look on his face said everything."

"An exemplary investigation, Mr Hopkins. How conveniently the obvious facts present themselves to us. That is the one thing which causes me to treat them with suspicion. If you do not mind, I should like to see the scene of the crime for myself. It may help to point us in the right direction."

"The stage, sir?"

"Dear me, no, Hopkins. The dressing-room."

3

I had never before been "behind the scenes" of a great theatre. A baize-covered pass-door at the right of the dress circle led to the dressing-room passage at the rear of the stage. Sir Caradoc's room was about half-way along. By the standards of my own profession, this secret interior of the theatre was inexcusably higgledy-piggledy. It was a cross between a woodworker's shop and the deck of an old-fashioned sailing ship.

We passed ladders and rolls of carpet, an upright piano, heights of blank, dark wood. There were structures of canvas and ply-wood painted as chairs, tables and armoires—make-believe furniture that could almost be lifted with one hand. Here and there we managed not to stumble over counterweights of rope and iron that supported scenery as a guy rope supports a tent. The main curtain was still raised. Through a gap we glimpsed the set, looking strangely small from this angle, and the darkened auditorium of a great theatre beyond it. The angled mattresses below the rear of the set remained where they had been. Nothing appeared to have been moved since Caradoc Price tumbled onto them.

The dressing-room passage itself was distempered in cream above and dark green below, a black dado running its full length. At its far end was the stage-door which came out near a corner of Maiden Lane. As we approached it, I noticed a young couple coming towards us. I had the strong impression that they had stepped outside for a moment, perhaps to find privacy for a conversation. They were both in their early twenties. She had the youthful flaxen beauty of a Dutch doll. He was tall and lean, with a certain fair-skinned handsomeness.

The young man's grey herring-bone overcoat and calf-skin gloves suggested that he had not long arrived from somewhere else. His care, as he kept one arm about her in almost brotherly comfort, caused him to walk with a slight stoop. When they came closer, the girl's simple beauty was blemished by flushed cheeks and reddened eyes. She had been weeping but was doing so no longer. Yet this theatrical tragedy had struck her with a shock that looked like fright. Poor child, I thought, how ill-prepared she was at such an age. Her escort's folded arm remained comfortingly round her shoulders and he had the look of one who is lost.

We stood back as they passed us and went into one of the dressing-rooms further on. I turned to Hopkins.

"Poor girl looks most dreadfully shocked. What was Caradoc to her?"

"She was Madge Gilford to him," he said casually. "The young man is her husband, William. They were married a year or so ago. Mrs Gilford is Lady Myfanwy's dresser and general wardrobe mistress. During the last scene tonight, I understand she was with Lady M. in the wings until her ladyship went on-stage. The goblets were carried on about a minute and a half later. They were in the stage manager's care before that. I think we may rule out young Madge and Lady M. from our list of suspects as never being within reach of the bottle or the goblets.

Madge was, in any case, one of the charmed inner circle devoted to Sir Caradoc. A young woman with no experience of sudden death is apt to take it hard, sir."

"Most interesting," said Holmes. "And her husband?"

"William Gilford came to collect her from the theatre as he usually does. He did not arrive until after the wine had been drunk on stage and the play was ending. We know pretty well when he got here. He stopped to speak to Harry Squire at the stage door. He asked Mr Squire where the play had got to, the timings being earlier on New Year's Eve. Mr Squire said the last scene had gone on. And he reminded Mr Gilford to move about on tiptoe, if he had to move about at all. The worst sin in these theatres, Mr Holmes, is to make a noise backstage during the performance. They fine them for it."

"As I am aware from my own experience. Then it seems you must rule out Mr Gilford and his wife from any part in this crime?"

"I should say so, Mr Holmes. William Gilford is a polite and well-educated young gentleman of charitable instincts. He has no personal connection with the theatre, though he is often here to take his wife home. He makes his way to the wardrobe room and waits for her there."

"What is his profession?"

"I understand he was a Cambridge man, sir, Natural Sciences Tripos. Unfortunately he had to leave college after a year, when his father died. They say he proposes to read for the bar. By day he is an almoner at the Marylebone Hospital. On two evenings a week—Monday and Wednesday—he teaches Latin for an hour to working-class men and women at the university settlement in Whitechapel."

"Toynbee Hall?" I said in some surprise. "What do they want with learning Latin?"

"To discover that they can do it, sir—and do it as well as anyone else," said Hopkins with a suggestion of reproach. "Following his classes this evening, Mr Gilford was present at a teachers' committee meeting. We have the names of half a dozen most reputable witnesses. He was with them until about five minutes before nine o'clock. An express train could not have got him here from Whitechapel in time to poison a goblet of Nuits St Georges '85 before it was taken on to the stage to be drunk by Sir Caradoc."

Caradoc's dressing-room was just ahead of us but the view through that open doorway was blocked by the bulk of Superintendent Bradstreet standing with his back to us. As he moved aside, I thought that this interior with its desk and chair looked more like a medical man's consulting room than an actor's retreat. One of the two sash windows of frosted glass had been raised a little for ventilation. The dressing-table with its make-up and wigs was just visible through the open door of the adjoining bathroom.

Turning aside I saw a crimson sofa. The bulk of the great actor, seen close up with his leonine mane, pocked cheeks and hairy nostrils, lay stretched out in death. He still wore the green silk dressing-gown wrapped round him.

Goodness knows I have seen enough dead men in my time. Yet whatever his failings I could not ignore the solemnity of that moment. This disfigured flesh was all that remained of that wonderful voice which until an hour or two ago had filled a packed auditorium with the most sublime words in our language. Now its resonant and subtle music was silent for ever.

Bradstreet turned to Holmes. The superintendent was carrying several sheets of writing-paper in his hand.

"I am not required to show you these, Mr Holmes. Indeed I am probably in breach of duty for doing so. However, it may save us all time and trouble if you see them now. They are samples of your client's correspondence, found upstairs in the Dome by Lady Myfanwy. She has handed them to us."

I read them over my friend's shoulder. Certain lines stick in my memory but the four documents themselves now lie in the tin trunk of the Baker Street lumber room.

> *You have taken away the parts and plays I made famous for you. I am Romeo or Hamlet only when you cannot be bothered, I am paid like a supernumerary. I cannot live upon this. I starve at the Herculaneum and you will not recommend me elsewhere. Your talk of naming me to the Actors' Benevolent Society was a lie! They have never heard from you. You would do well to remember that if I am to perish, I have nothing to lose.*

The others were in the same vein, mingling threats with entreaties. What an unsound mind was here!

> *For God's sake help me now! Next week will be too late! I shall have nowhere to go from here. At my age I cannot start again. I would take what I can get, but who will take me?*

Had Jenks been given his marching orders after all? We came to Caradoc's behaviour with his female admirers—if they were such.

> *You wretch! You have paid well to discover the profession my sister was reduced to by men like you. For how many innocents have you left your street-door unlocked and your private stairs open?*

A final mad outburst would surely help to persuade a jury to put a rope round the foolish fellow's neck.

You hell hound! You Judas! You have now cut me out of engagements by threats of blackmail. How dare you blackmail a fellow actor? Next time I ask you for a reference it will be at Bow Street police station, where my lawyer will expose you. If I die on the Newgate gallows, you will be to blame. It would be a price worth paying. I would advise you to take my letter to Scotland Yard this time.

"Curious," said Holmes with remarkable unconcern. "And how have these most remarkable specimens come to light? What is their provenance?"

Bradstreet tried not to smile at the neatness of his triumph.

"Among Sir Caradoc's papers in the upstairs desk—unanswered correspondence, as you might say. There is no date, but I should imagine they are quite recent—probably arriving one a day. They would certainly suggest a motive, if nothing else does. Perhaps Mr Jenks thought that Sir Caradoc would tear them up or throw them in the fire. Unfortunately for him, he was wrong."

"Have you questioned him about these pages?"

"Mr Jenks refuses to say anything about them until he has spoken to you in confidence, sir. Perhaps you can advise him of his own best interests, Mr Holmes. I believe we shall soon have finished our investigations here. Then he must come with us—or show us why he need not."

"I presume you have not found any replies from Sir Caradoc addressed to Mr Jenks?"

"No, sir."

"Where is my client at the moment?"

"In the sitting-room of the Dome. He is accompanied by two of my uniformed men, Sergeant Witlow and Constable Royston. He maintains his innocence but refuses to discuss any further questions. He says he will swear to his innocence upon Holy

Writ—but he will not deal with me. You must make what you can of that, sir. I assume you wish to see him before we take him elsewhere?"

"Presently, Mr Bradstreet. Seeing him at once would complicate my own investigation. First, I should like to examine certain evidence for myself."

"And so you shall, sir. Would you like to begin with the stage? That seems to be where the root of this mystery lies."

Holmes's mouth tightened with impatience.

"I think not. I have seen quite enough of the stage."

I was surprised by this. So far as I could see, we had hardly been near it.

Holmes was saying, "I have no doubt that your police surgeon's analysis of the contents of the goblet will confirm his suspicions. A fatal dose of prussic acid is the least that we can expect. However, I would appreciate a few minutes to survey this dressing-room."

"There is a plain mortuary van outside, sir," said Hopkins quietly. "It was waiting only for Mr Holmes to see the body. Sir Caradoc could be moved now."

"Thank you," said Holmes courteously. "Sir Caradoc will not inconvenience us. Let him remain, if you please."

Bradstreet was visibly concerned that my friend's requests should be so modest and apparently irrelevant.

"There really is not much in here, Mr Holmes. His key to the door was lying on the carpet, close to the tasselled cord of the dressing-gown. The evening paper is on the desk. It seems that he usually read it after the performance, while he smoked his cigar. I believe he liked to do the puzzles which they print at the back. It relaxed him."

Holmes brightened up at this. Bradstreet continued.

"We have not touched nor moved the ash-tray, nor the half-smoked cigar lying in it. Still, it may save you time if I tell you that there is no trace of poison that Dr Worplesdon or Dr Hammond from Scotland Yard could detect in the cigar or its ash."

"Nor I," said Stanley Hopkins apologetically.

"Capital!" said Holmes enthusiastically, "I wonder if these two medical gentlemen have chanced to read a slight monograph of mine, printed in 1879, 'Upon the Distinction between the Ashes of the Various Tobaccos.' It would be of the greatest assistance to them. Unfortunately, at the time, I was insistent that it must be illustrated with colour plates. I was therefore obliged to defray the cost of having it privately printed. In consequence it now changes hands at a premium and has become something of a rarity."

The two policemen shook their heads sympathetically.

"No matter," said Holmes amiably. "If you would be so good as to leave us, we shall not keep you very long."

Bradstreet hesitated, but Hopkins forced the issue by walking into the passage at once. The superintendent followed reluctantly and Holmes closed the door behind them.

4

"Bradstreet is the giddy limit, Watson! He may only be a uniformed man but that does not preclude the exercise of a little common sense or logic. Hopkins, however, may go far."

Sherlock Holmes stood over the desk. A gold-inlaid green leather blotter was filled with pink paper that showed not a mark. Roughly folded across it lay that evening's *Globe* newspaper. A silver cigar-cutter had evidently been used and then put to one side. The white china bowl of the ash-tray was about half full of grey dust. A quarter or so of a partly-smoked cigar lay balanced upon its rim. A box of yellow Vesta matches was beside it, one of them used and discarded with the ash. The paper band of the cigar lay among the dust. This ash-tray itself was a distinctive but not uncommon souvenir, embossed with "Royal Herculaneum Theatre" in crimson round its edge, and with a gold Prince of Wales crown where the two ends of the legend met.

Holmes picked up the *Globe* and turned its pages. Nothing took his fancy until he reached the end. A blank strip had been torn from the margin of the final page. There was no indication of its use. He looked about him, scrutinised the top of the desk and then turned to me.

"Be good enough to see what you can find in his dressing-gown pockets."

"His pockets?"

"Certainly. In his predicament, assuming he tore it off, that is where I should put a slip of paper. It is missing and it is not on the desk or on the floor. His pockets are the only other place that would probably have been within reach during his last moments. We are meant to believe that he had already staggered towards the door to open it and found he could not do so. He lost the cord of his dressing-gown and dropped the key as he struggled back to the chair. He was not a fool. He knew he was in mortal torment. It seems he tore a strip from the back page of the paper. Why? Surely to write a message. He would not spend the last seconds of his life playing newspaper games."

"To leave his last testament?"

"Look in those pockets. The right-hand one. I do not recall he was left-handed."

Averting my eyes from the dead man's contorted features and crimson-blotched cheeks, I slid my hand into the right pocket. Holmes was correct, of course. There was the stub of a pencil and a crumpled scrap of paper that anyone else might have thrown away. Why was it not on the desk? I handed it to my companion. The writing of the dying man spidered into illegibility but Holmes seemed to make sense of it easily enough. He had recognised that the subject was a nonsense poem of a kind well-suited to newspaper competitions. When we first met I had noted that his knowledge of literature was esoteric but extensive.

"Holmes! What the devil is this trumpery?"

"A riddle well enough known to those like Caradoc who particularly enjoy such mysteries. It dates, I believe, from the reign of Queen Anne. I imagine that the *Globe* newspaper has made use of it in the recent past on its puzzle page."

"But what use?"

To three-fourths of a cross. . . .
Two semi-circles. . . .
Next add a triangle. . . .
Then two semi-circles. . . .

He held it in front of him and completed those lines that I had not been able to decipher. I stared at the finished text.

To three-fourths of a cross add a circle complete;
Two semi-circles a perpendicular meet,
Next add a triangle that stands on two feet,
Then two semi-circles and a circle complete.

He spread it on the desk.

"Very well. Let us see what we have. 'To three-fourths of a cross add a circle complete.' Now that indicates the letters T and O, does it not? Then we have, 'Two semi-circles a perpendicular meet.' What can that be but the letter B? There follows an instruction. 'Next add a triangle that stands on two feet.' What a picturesque description of the letter A! And last of all. 'Two semi-circles, and a circle complete.' That can only be the letters C plus C plus O. Put it all together and you have TOBACCO."

"What has tobacco to do with it?"

"What, indeed? And why should he thrust it into his pocket?"

"So that it should not be found," I said.

"No, Watson. So that it should be found later on, when his pockets were turned out. It must be hidden for the moment. In his last moments, he seems to have guessed that his enemy would return to this room to make certain changes in the evidence. He could not leave his scrap of paper where that man—or woman—would find it. Such a person would be alert for it on the desk or even on the floor. But with only seconds to spare, the killer would not dare to waste time in struggling with the dead weight of a corpse, searching the clothes for something which was probably not there anyway."

"And yet to search him might make all the difference."

"Balance that against the difference between slipping out into the passage unseen or walking into the path of a witness. In other words, the murderer's second visit was almost certainly during the curtain calls and speeches when the dressing-room passage was empty and the keeper of the stage-door had his eyes on the little crowd of worshippers who gather there each night for a kind word or an autograph."

"But neither Worplesdon nor Hammond found any contamination of the cigar."

"Of course not. That is the whole point."

He had drawn his folding lens from his watch-pocket. He opened it and sat at the desk, peering through the glass at the remaining length of the cigar and then at the match which had been used to light it. There was also a crumpled paper band which had been stripped from the cigar before lighting it. He gave a quiet sigh of satisfaction, like one whose expectations have been justified. Without another word of explanation, he eased a fresh match from the box and, for what seemed like an age, gently sifted the cold ash.

If there was no poison in the room, I could not see how we should find anything of interest here. The flakes of pale grey ash at the tip of the dead cigar looked a perfect replica of those in the ornamental porcelain bowl. Holmes continued to poke cautiously with the unused match, stirring so lightly that hardly a fragment of ash fell out of place. Presently he uttered another long and relaxed sigh, as if he had been holding his breath in a trance throughout this process.

"As I supposed," he said to himself.

"Prussic acid?" I asked uncertainly. "Cyanide?"

He looked up at me in despair.

"Of course not, Watson! That is the last thing we shall find here! You underestimate our adversary, whoever he or she may be."

"Do you mean that Caradoc was not poisoned here?"

"I did not say that."

"But if there is no cyanide here, how can he have been poisoned by it in this room? The door was locked and he did not go out. And if there was no cyanide in the wine, how was he poisoned at all?"

"I deduce that there was no cyanide in the wine during the final scene of the play," he said softly, "But there is now. Be patient and watch."

I looked on but I could not see that he was doing anything other than before. The ash below the surface was not even much different in colour. A little darker, perhaps, but the colour of different burnt leaves from a single cigar will almost always vary a little.

"Look," he said, easing up a flake of ash which seemed to have a mere thread of spider's web hanging from it.

"What is it?"

"A burnt stalk. This cigar is of premier extraction." He paused to flatten out the red and gold band. "'Real Feytoria Reserva,' a Portuguese importer and a Brazilian leaf of the highest quality. Believe me, such a superior weed does not contain the stalk of the tobacco leaf. That is the mark of an inferior brand, what is called in the trade 'bird's eye.' You will see tiny white flecks here and there. You understand me?"

"The ash in the bowl has come from elsewhere?"

"Much of it has. On its own, that is conclusive of nothing, but it is indicative of a good deal."

I could not see the logic of this.

"Surely the bird's eye may have been deposited either by Sir Caradoc at some other time or by some other person?"

He folded his glass and slipped it into his watch-pocket again.

"Cranleigh would have left a clean ash-tray. I am sure that Caradoc smoked his usual cigar this evening after settling down in his chair with the newspaper. He came in, changed from his doublet and hose, putting on his green silk dressing-gown. However, I do not think he bothered to lock the door after him. People were not in the habit of disturbing him, and, in any case, he was on his own. As I say, he smoked a cigar. What he did not do was to smoke this cigar."

I saw at once what was coming but I was not quick enough to say so.

Holmes continued.

"A Real Feytoria is a long and expensive cigar, such as Caradoc affected. It is not a sixpenny, twenty-minute cheroot. He would never touch those. I should not wish to pose as an expert merely because I have written my little treatise upon the subject. However, I may tell you that a Real Feytoria would probably last a smoker for at least fifty minutes or an hour. There is not enough ash in the bowl to account for that. Someone who knows little about the joys of smoking has bulked it out with the ash of bird's eye, but it is still too little."

Now I took my chance.

"Caradoc probably did not live for anything like thirty or forty minutes after leaving the stage. He was found then but he had not answered any knocks for most of that time. In any case, he could not have smoked so much of the cigar before that."

"Well done, Watson. As so often, you are there before me.

After Caradoc's death, his adversary returned. The contaminated cigar was taken and this remainder was substituted. Someone has cut off a large portion of it and lit what remained. It was left here for us to find."

I tried to pin down a flaw in this.

"Suppose Caradoc had started his cigar earlier, let it go out and lit it again after he left the stage at the end of the play."

"It would seem, Watson, that Shakespeare wrote *Hamlet* with the primary purpose of thwarting you as a detective. If you will look at the last hour of the play, there is hardly a point where the King is off-stage for long enough to tempt a sensible man into ruining a good cigar. In any case, why would the dresser Cranleigh bring his master a bowl half filled with the ash of bird's eye? No, my dear chap, let us settle the one remaining point."

"Which is?"

Holmes got up from the desk.

"Caradoc drank his wine a few minutes before he left the stage. Suppose, after all, it contained prussic acid. How long would he live?"

As the reader may imagine, the answer to this question is that one cannot tell until the victim has been anatomised. Perhaps it may be impossible even then. In the course of our detective partnership, I had pursued a little research into the art of poisoning, including cyanide, rare though it is. Dixon Mann in his *Forensic Medicine and Toxicology* and Garstang in *The Lancet* of 1888 talk of those who have taken a fatal fifth of an ounce of hydrocyanic acid and survived for an hour and three-quarters. I noted that, in 1890, the *British Medical Journal* described a woman who accidentally swallowed an ounce of cyanide in the form of powder but was able to "rush" upstairs, report the fact, obtain treatment and survive.

In the light of all this, I could offer only my doubts.

"Holmes, we must judge from the facts. If the wine was poisoned, Caradoc was obviously not one of those who succumbed in a couple of minutes, or else a thousand people would have seen him die on the stage! Perhaps that was the public revenge that Carnaby Jenks hoped for. Failing that, any dose swallowed in his wine could not have been sufficient to be immediately overwhelming. He was able to get back here at least five minutes later."

"Would he still have been alive half an hour after drinking the wine—even if the poison was present only in a small dose? Alive just before ten o'clock?"

"I think not. It is most unlikely, though not impossible. My friend Mr Knott of Lincoln's Inn is editing the trial of England's most famous poisoner, Dr William Palmer of Rugeley. In that case the defence rested on the survival of his victim for an hour and a half. That man had taken poison which should have killed him in no time. As for Caradoc, it was not impossible that he was alive until ten o'clock—but without treatment, most, most unlikely."

"We may allow that he might have begun to feel unwell a few minutes before his sudden death?"

"If he survived for even ten minutes or so after taking the poison, his collapse might not have been as sudden. He would perhaps have felt the effects more gradually."

"Time enough to call for help? Or to write a few lines with failing legibility?"

"Very likely."

He stared at me and said in that coldly rational voice, "Then he was poisoned in this room, not on the stage. That is the only solution which fits the facts. Forget the miracles recounted in *The Lancet* and the *British Medical Journal*. Sitting in this chair, he breathed in the fumigation vapours of rat poison from his cigar before he knew what he was doing. He lived just long enough to tear a strip from the newspaper and scrawl a dozen words or so upon it. He did not have time to get up and struggle to the door. Someone else placed the key and the cord where they were found."

"The murderer?"

"He or she had ample time to return after Caradoc's death, perhaps verifying through the window from the street that he was dead. Time to change the evidence and leave—dropping the dressing-gown cord by the door to muddy the waters. There was probably time for all this before the play ended and the actors reappeared. It was the murderer who locked the door upon leaving. It need not have been locked before. Caradoc's own key was used to close it. Then the man or woman went out into the street, raised the sash window and tossed the key over by the door. If I were the criminal I should also have left one of the sash windows open a little to clear the air."

He paused and then added emphatically,

"Neither Bradstreet nor Hopkins is to hear anything of this."

"But surely Dr Hammond found poison in the wine?"

"How easy for anyone to slip it in when the play was over and the goblets standing unnoticed! There was no poison when Caradoc drank it. That is the key to this case. That is the fog that Bradstreet and Hopkins have got themselves into."

"And Dr Worplesdon and Hammond?"

His face softened.

"My dear old fellow, we have indulged in a pleasant little fantasy in which Caradoc was one of those rare souls who survive cyanide poisoning for half an hour or more because the dose was a low one. A thousand people will believe it because they think they saw it happen on stage. Bradstreet and Hopkins believe it because the wine was certainly poisoned by the time they arrived. They could find no poison anywhere else. Worplesdon and Hammond also believe it—save the mark!—

because he was dead of cyanide poisoning when they got here and it must have come from somewhere!"

"Then where is the remainder of the poison now?"

"You may depend upon it that all which remains is safely inside Caradoc. You will look in vain elsewhere. Whoever had it last put a little of it in the wine on-stage after the curtain came down but before Caradoc was examined. That would have been simple. While Bradstreet and Hopkins have been plodding through their so-called investigation, an unknown hand has had an hour and a half in which to tip the remainder of the powder or the liquid down a sink or even into the sewer in Maiden Lane. I think you may be certain that not a grain nor a drop is left in this building."

"And what of our client?"

Holmes did not often scowl but he did so now.

"I do not know whether Mr Carnaby Jenks is playing a game with us, or with the police, or with someone else. I propose to find out—in very short order."

"You think he is a poisoner?"

"He is certainly an unscrupulous liar and a less accomplished actor than he thinks he is. That is what will hang him, if he persists in it."

5

We found our way through a door in the dressing-room corridor to a narrow flight of wooden stairs. The walls of this stairway were hung with sketches, prints and signed photographs of those who had trodden the boards of the Royal Herculaneum during its years of fame. I noticed Johnstone Forbes-Robertson, Herbert Beerbohm Tree, Mrs Patrick Campbell, Madame Modjeska, Squire Bancroft and Madame Bernhardt. After a right-angle turn the stairs led to the door of the famous Dome. To one side, a passageway and a further flight led downwards to the street-door of these domestic quarters.

Holmes paused and nodded towards them.

"How are the mighty fallen, Watson. This route was designed when the Herculaneum was last rebuilt, half a century ago. In those days theatre-going was not quite respectable. This was a private entrance to the box used by Queen Victoria and Prince Albert. They came repeatedly to see the great William Macready in *Macbeth* and *King Lear*."

If Holmes was remarkable for nothing else, his knowledge of

buildings in London, even of their private rooms and passages, would have secured him a modest fame.

He did not knock at the door. When we entered, Jenks was sitting in a chair and Sergeant Witlow in another. A uniformed constable stood behind the prisoner. Their attitudes suggested that there had been no conversation for some time.

Witlow stood up as we came in, and Holmes said brusquely, "Sergeant, Mr Hopkins assures me that a cup of tea is waiting for you and your colleague in the green room. Perhaps you would be good enough to leave us with Mr Jenks. I shall not keep you long. I promise you he will not evade us."

"Very good, Mr Holmes."

Holmes and I stood in silence as they left. Then my friend turned to Carnaby Jenks, shrunken, as it seemed, in his chair.

"Mr Jenks, this case is not yet three hours old. I may say already that you are the most difficult client I have ever had to deal with. If you are quite determined to put the rope round your own neck, then tell me so and I will go back to my bed in Baker Street."

Jenks raised his eyebrows in an actor's expression of surprise.

"I don't follow you at all, Mr Holmes."

"Do you not? Are you a lunatic?"

"You know I am not!"

"Then why have you concocted at least four demented notes and addressed them to Sir Caradoc Price?"

"Can the police put me in prison for sending notes to him?"

"Listen to me, Jenks! I was most careful in my choice of language. I suggested that you addressed them to him—not that you sent them or that he received them."

I was surprised to see that the distinction between "addressing" and "sending" rattled Carnaby Jenks far more than the threat of the gallows had done. If he had launched a plot, he now seemed fearful that it was out of his control.

"I sent them," he said peevishly, "Every word was justified. It has been getting worse by the day. I saw long ago that he kept me on here only for the use he could make of me. He knew that at my age I would never be employed elsewhere."

"In what way does he use you, except to employ you?"

Unless he was a more accomplished deceiver than I supposed, Jenks was truly angered now.

"By promises betrayed, sir! That I should have leading roles in my own right. Even that I should be his successor. But I was a leading man only when it suited him to have a quiet evening or to escape a matinee performance. Never when a play was reviewed or the theatre was full and I might get a benefit. I wrote to him. What would you have me do?"

There was no pity in my friend's response. The dark gaze of Sherlock Holmes as he leant towards the chair seemed to fix Jenks like a butterfly upon a specimen board.

"What would I have you do? The very thing you have avoided doing since I arrived this evening. Tell me the truth. I am not here to be made a fool of."

"What truth?"

Holmes straightened up and shook his coat into shape.

"In the first place, that you are not responsible for the death of Sir Henry Caradoc Price but that you have gone to every length imaginable to convince the police that you must be."

The thin nervous frame quivered once and Jenks blinked at him, like a schoolboy under reprimand. Then the pale nervous temperament in him flared up again, his face reddening and his voice almost a gabble.

"I am an innocent man, sir. I will not have my words twisted. I know the law. I have my right to silence against the police. If they believe I am guilty of some crime, let them prove the fact. It is no duty of mine to help them."

"My further suggestion," said Holmes quietly, "is that this intrigue does not touch you alone."

That also shook him. He could not see how Holmes might think it on such evidence—let alone know it.

"We will leave that for a moment," my friend went on, "but let me first assure you that stupidity hangs more men than wickedness alone."

Sherlock Holmes sat down in the elbow chair with his chin in his hand and a finger across his mouth, as though performing a calculation of some kind. At length he looked up.

"These notes to Sir Caradoc, they speak of other things. When did you send them?"

"On various dates. Not in the last few days."

"He does not seem to have mentioned them to anyone. They also have a remarkable uniformity in their calligraphic style. What have you to say about that?"

"Nothing. Neither to you nor to anyone else."

"A Home Office examiner will almost certainly tell the court that they were probably written on a single occasion. Presumably to be planted among the dead man's papers."

Carnaby Jenks said nothing—but he listened more intently than almost any man I had seen questioned by Holmes.

"From the time the house surgeon and the Bow Street police were alerted until they got here must have been fifteen or twenty minutes. You are a literate man, Mr Jenks, and I have a certain knowledge of handwriting. Whenever these notes were written, they were written very quickly, as the tailing script confirms. They are fluent in thought as well as script. In total, I should say they could all be written in about seven minutes."

A sudden look of dread at what was coming glimmered in Jenks's eyes. He repressed it with an effort. Holmes continued.

"You had time enough tonight to write those fragments before Dr Worplesdon and Mr Bradstreet arrived. Sir Caradoc

Price had just been found dead in his dressing-room! Everyone was down there. Your way to his desk in the Dome was clear."

"You may believe me or not as you please."

It was the last gasp of a runner crossing the finishing-line.

Holmes attempted to refresh the conversation.

"What of the blackmail, Mr Jenks? You say in the notes that you were blackmailed by Sir Caradoc. How and when?"

Once again, Jenks blinked as if someone had slapped his face.

"I cannot discuss it."

Sherlock Holmes sighed.

"In any court of law, Mr Jenks, a judge will direct you to discuss it. And, believe me, the nature of the blackmail you allege is one of the first facts a cross-examiner will require."

To see the perspiration on his forehead was to know that something had indeed gone terribly wrong with his plan. But then suddenly it seemed as if all was well again.

"I did not say that I was the direct victim of the blackmail."

"Did you not?"

"I said it was an actor whom he blackmailed. Indeed, it was the sister of whom I had spoken and through whom we were both blackmailed."

"Your sister? Your sister whom you say he ruined?"

Jenks's words came in a rush but he spoke like a man now standing on firm ground.

"She worked to be an actress at first, Mr Holmes. After he corrupted her, he threatened to make her name notorious throughout the streets and theatres of London unless she submitted to his further demands. He included me in these threats, if I made trouble for him. He would make the details of her downfall a joke and a smoking-room story in every club. To use his own words, she would crawl back to her burrow and dread the light of day. That was what I meant by blackmailing a fellow actor."

"Was it?" said Holmes, looking past Jenks with a distant scepticism. "It did not sound like that in the note but pray continue."

"She and I were his victims."

Holmes continued to stare at the curtained window.

"It seems," he said thoughtfully, "that we are back to where we were five minutes ago. I repeat, Mr Jenks, you will be meticulously examined—and cross-examined—about this sister. You say in your note that Caradoc ruined her. Doubtless she now walks the promenade bar of the Empire Music Hall in Leicester Square—or something of the kind. Does she exist? Think carefully before you answer."

"Yes."

"As your sister?"

"What does the title matter?"

"For the purposes of this case, Mr Jenks, you may take it from me that it matters."

"Molly has always been kind to me when I have met her with one of the men she calls a 'husband' on her arm. Five shillings or ten, a guinea even, when the scoundrel here would not sub me for a day or two. He laughed and said he had no money in his pocket but he never went short."

"And do you propose to inform the police of all this? I shall not tell them, of course. I imagine they will find out anyway."

But he had done too good a job. The brain of Carnaby Jenks, rather than his voice, seemed paralysed. He bowed his greying head in his hands. Then he looked up.

"I must think," he said feebly. "You must let me think."

"Very well. Wait here with Dr Watson. I will fetch Sergeant Witlow. In your present frame of mind, it would be best that you should continue to refuse all questions. I suggest you also retain a solicitor to advise you."

Holmes stood up.

"You will not abandon my case?" Jenks pleaded.

Sherlock Holmes turned round again, ignoring the question.

"One more thing, Mr Jenks. Do not think of escape while I am out of the room. It is all that is required to put a noose round your neck. In any case, my colleague Dr Watson carries his Army revolver on these occasions. He knows how to use it and will not hesitate to shoot you through the leg at your first attempt. You will not be the first fugitive he has brought low."

"I have nothing to run from," Jenks muttered morosely. "I am innocent, damn you all."

Holmes went out and there was silence again. I thought of my revolver, oiled and wrapped in lint, lying in its Baker Street drawer. Our client turned away from me, sitting in profile. The silence continued. After what seemed far too long there were voices on the stairs. We left the sullen figure of the suspect in the custody of Witlow and his constable.

As soon as we were out of earshot, I turned to Holmes.

"This comes of having a client who can act one part after another!"

He ignored the remark and took my arm.

"Interesting, Watson. Most, most interesting. Did it not strike you?"

"Did what not strike me? That the man is a pernicious fool?"

"I left a trap open and Jenks fell into it slap-bang. The world believes Caradoc was poisoned on the stage at about quarter past nine and that the poison was added to the wine shortly before. Previous to that, Hamlet *alias* Jenks was off-stage for half an hour with a better opportunity than most people of contaminating the goblet during that time. He knows it. Very well. What is the first thing a criminal would say?"

"I suppose he might say, 'I cannot have done it. I was elsewhere at the time.' That would be a complete answer."

"Exactly! Jenks has not once offered an account of his movements at any time during that half-hour. I have been very careful not to press him. He has not even said, for example, that he was in his dressing-room. Yet he is on the verge of a murder charge. Surely a man in that situation would offer an alibi, if he had one. It is the first refuge of the criminal and the innocent man alike. Jenks says nothing of his activities in that half-hour between about twenty to nine and ten minutes past."

"As if he wanted to be the suspect."

He stopped and nodded at me, relieved that I had understood at last.

"That hits the target."

"Then where was he?"

"Precisely!"

6

Five minutes later, we were standing in the doorway of the green room. Holmes spoke just loudly enough for me to hear.

"There is a limit to the wanderings of a man standing in the Royal Herculaneum with thirty minutes or so at his disposal. My topographical knowledge of this area of London is extensive. I have hunted over it a good deal. You will recall that we used the Lowther Arcade as an escape route in our final encounter with the late Professor Moriarty. After chasing 'Poodle' Benson round the Charing Cross Hotel and its neighbourhood during the Turf frauds, Villiers Street and its surroundings remain detailed in my memory."

"Do you have somewhere in mind?"

"If I were Jenks and proposed to build my defence upon an alibi at the last moment, I should not do so if the theatre was my location. It is too uncertain and people might easily confuse one day with another. Where was he then, during his respite of half an hour or so? A man with half an hour to spare will not risk a walk of more than ten minutes or so in each direction. That reduces our area of search considerably. At nine o'clock in the evening, where could one be certain of having being seen and remembered? The number of places open at that hour of night will not be many. Offices, banks and commercial premises will be closed. It must also be somewhere he goes to in theatrical costume. That limits it severely."

"A public house?"

"Indeed, but which one will accept actors in costume?"

"How many are there within ten or fifteen minutes' walk?"

Holmes chuckled at his own cleverness.

"There is only one for an actor—where his profession gathers, even in its stage finery. The old Garrick's Head in Bow Street, the assembly room where the late 'Baron Renton Nicolson' of blessed memory was accustomed to stage his disreputable 'Judge and Jury Show' in defiance of the magistrates and the police. It has always been a favourite with the theatrical fraternity, even in my day."

We put a best foot forward and reached the old hostelry in good time. Even at this hour of night, the long bar was crowded like a fancy-dress ball with the costumes and talk of actors who had fled the theatre for the tavern. We were the only two in mufti. Holmes shouldered his way through the noisy crowd and accosted the landlord, who knew him at once.

"Evening, Mr Holmes, sir."

"Compliments of the season, Mr Roscoe. You have not by any chance seen our friend Mr Carnaby Jenks tonight? My colleague and I appear to have missed our rendezvous with him."

Roscoe's face split into a humorous beam.

"I should say you have! He was away from here by nine or just after. Hamlet he is tonight. He was over here for his interval as usual. Mr Jenks doesn't care for the way the old 'Herc.' is going. The less he sees of the place and its governor, the better he feels."

"How long was he here?"

The man gave half his attention to us, the rest to the glass he was filling.

"Ten minutes at least, perhaps fifteen. Not more. Just his usual glass of mild and bitter."

"He never meets his sister here, does he?"

The landlord stopped filling the glass and shook his head.

"Not that I know of, sir. Comes alone. Goes alone."

Holmes held a gold sovereign between finger and thumb.

"You may drink our health, Mr Roscoe, when you are less occupied."

"God bless you, Mr Holmes, sir. Indeed I shall. Much obliged, gentlemen."

We walked back to the Herculaneum stage-door. In the cold New Year of the darkened street I said, "That is surely just about as complete an alibi for the so-called poisoning of the wine as he could wish. It is almost too good to be true."

"At the time, Watson, I believe he did not know that he would ever need an alibi. When Caradoc was found dead, however, he saw that he could build a defence upon it. Let us see just how strong that defence may be."

7

The bells of the Old Year faded from the steeple of St Martin-in-the-Fields. Across the roofs and down the streets from Trafalgar Square the chimes of midnight followed. Sherlock Holmes brooded in the same elbow-chair of the Dome sitting-room, across the table from Carnaby Jenks. I truly believe that the ageing actor thought he had seen the last of us for that night. He was quite unprepared for our return and a resumption of the questioning

"Let us agree that this performance has gone on long enough, Mr Jenks." Holmes paused and then turned his face casually to our client. "Tell me something of young William Gilford. He figures in your drama, does he not?"

Jenks sat bolt upright, as though he felt a knife in his back. He almost spat the answer.

"No he does not! Who has been talking to you?"

"You have been talking to me, Mr Jenks. If anyone has given away your secret, it is yourself. Mr Gilford is a member of your family perhaps?"

"He is no relation to me whatever."

But there was a look of panic that had not been there before. What the devil was Holmes up to?

"A member of your family was the term I used. Someone for whom you might care as if he were a brother or a son."

"How can you say that? I have no son, and he is far too young to be my brother!"

Holmes ignored the answer. He nodded slowly, as though he understood and sympathised. This generally preceded bad news for the person he was talking to.

"A little while ago, Mr Jenks, I said that I had never had a client like you. Forgive me. That was not quite accurate. I had one a little while ago. His name was Dr Hawley Harvey Crippen."

Incredulity and distaste contended in Jenks's reply.

"Dr Crippen!"

"Even so. All the world knows Dr Crippen. I believe I could have saved him from the gallows, had he not prevented me. To be sure, he was responsible for the death of his vulgar and cantankerous wife, but that death was a medical accident, not murder. Such a fact would have been hard to prove in any case, but there was a witness present who might easily have saved him."

"Miss Ethel Le Neve?"

"Indeed, his young mistress. A charming, unspoilt girl. I am pleased to find you a reader of the sensational press, Mr Jenks. Unfortunately, had the case still gone against Crippen, despite her evidence, she would then have been indicted as his accomplice. Therefore that gallant little gentleman was determined to face the gallows himself, rather than imperil one who was so precious to him. Do I make myself clear? Are you a gallant little gentleman?"

Our client, if he remained such, stared back without replying. Holmes resumed.

"Dr Crippen went so far as to draw suspicion upon himself

deliberately in order that he might save her. That is a matter of history. Alas, the law took him at his word, as it does in such cases. He now lies in quicklime under the prison wall at Pentonville. Be careful how you play the game of life and death with the law, Mr Jenks."

This rattled him to the marrow. Whatever his game, I cannot believe he thought it would lead him to a felon's grave.

"Very well," he said quietly.

"From the moment you boasted that a thousand people had seen you kill Sir Caradoc Price, I was reasonably certain that you intended to lead us astray. Guilty men do not make such boasts."

Jenks shook his head but said nothing. Holmes resumed.

"Now then, sir, you know the play of *Hamlet* quite as intimately as I do. Anyone familiar with the last act knows that the goblet the King first drinks from is not drunk from by anyone else. It is the second goblet, used to poison the Queen in the story, that the hero forces him to drink from at the end. Lady Myfanwy had used it already and has suffered no ill-effects. You knew when you sent your message to me that you could not have poisoned Caradoc."

"That means nothing! In the shock of it all, I confused the goblets!"

"Wait, please! My inquiries this evening also reveal a complete alibi for you at the Garrick's Head, covering the time when poison would have been put into either goblet, had it been used on stage. You have not spoken of that alibi—even to me. You assumed, correctly, that the police would check any alibi that you give them but they would not search London to find one on your behalf. To that extent, your scheme was moderately clever but not fool-proof."

There was still no response. Jenks stared back, like a ferret in a cage.

"Moreover," said Holmes gently, "you allowed your hastily-written and abusive letters to be found in this room. Had you had more time, you would have dealt more skilfully with your allegations of blackmail."

"There was blackmail!"

"Indeed, I am sure there was, but not quite as you describe it. Now then, in my experience the first thing a suspect would do, on hearing that Sir Caradoc had been found murdered and knowing that he had fifteen minutes before the police arrived, would be to sneak up these stairs and search this room for those threatening letters. They were easy enough for Bradstreet to uncover."

"I did not think of it!"

"No," said Holmes, "you did not think of retrieving them because they had not been sent. What you thought of was to write these venomous little notes—unless you already had them in waiting—to sneak up here and plant them among his papers. You knew they were bound to be discovered."

"Prove it!"

Holmes laughed amiably,

"Why should I bother? You had previously announced before members of the cast that Sir Caradoc had cheated you of your matinee benefits and given you notice. I daresay that was true. As a result, I am told, you said you would murder him with pleasure. Did he cheat you, by the way?"

"He did!"

"Do you still have his letters to that effect?"

"I threw them in the fire. It seemed the best place for them, at the time."

"What a pity. Conveniently, Caradoc is no longer here to prove you wrong. Many people had cause to dislike him. You, it seems, were the only one with cause to wish him dead."

"What of that?"

Holmes shrugged.

"Unlike Dr Crippen, your alibi may save you as soon as you summon Mr Roscoe of the Garrick's Head to the witness-box. If the case goes that far. What you will have done meantime is to make nonsense of the police investigation. In the end, of course, you may prove to be the one person who certainly cannot have poisoned Caradoc's wine. The critical time would be between a few minutes to nine o'clock and five minutes past or so, when Roland Gwyn took possession of the properties for the last act. Until ten past nine or even later you were not near the stage. From then until the final curtain, by which time Sir Caradoc was certainly poisoned and very probably dead, you were on public view in the final scene."

Holmes gave him a moment to come to his senses and then concluded.

"In the light of all this, I think you may dispense with my services, except in so far as you may be charged with obstructing the police investigation."

Carnaby Jenks struggled to his feet.

"Sit down, if you please, Mr Jenks!"

Jenks sat down. Holmes became reminiscent.

"In my experience, when a man or woman takes on the guilt of another in this fashion, it is to protect a close member of the family or a lover. Madge Gilford appears hysterically distressed over the death of Caradoc. William Gilford seems anxious but remarkably composed."

"There is no reason that he should not."

"One moment," said Holmes courteously. "William Gilford also has an alibi. It is supported by very respectable teachers at Toynbee Hall and by the stage-door keeper here. The goblet of wine was already on the stage when he arrived at the theatre. It is evident that he could not possibly have tampered with it before it was taken on."

"Then I do not understand what all this is about."

"It is about perfection, Mr Jenks. Gilford's alibi is almost too perfect. And you have added to its perfection, if such a thing were possible. Why would you do that? Why these scribbled notes? Why the silence over an alibi of your own that you could have produced so easily? Why the boast in your note to me that you had killed Caradoc before a thousand witnesses? You see?"

I offered up a prayer that Holmes was not about to reveal what we had discovered in the dressing-room. I need not have worried.

"You are surely drawing suspicion upon yourself in order to protect someone else. I conclude that you took action at once, on hearing of Caradoc's death and before knowing of Gilford's alibi. The notes must be written and in place before the arrival of Bradstreet and Hopkins. Who were you protecting? Are you quite sure you cannot tell me the relation in which William Gilford or his wife stands to you?"

There was a terrible silence and the poor fellow seemed to wrestle with his soul. The pulse in his throat told me that we were near the truth.

"What will happen?" he whispered at length. "What will you do?"

"I am not a policeman, Mr Jenks. You have summoned me here to help you. Unfortunately, you have made my task extremely difficult. I have believed almost from the first that you have brought me here to shield someone else. Young William Gilford, I daresay, and possibly Madge. Now, will you tell me what he is to you? You are walking the plank and you are almost at the end of it. The parish records or the register of Trinity College should yield the answer I seek. I would rather have it from you. Now!"

There was a long pause. At last the answer came, the first calm words the haggard player had spoken.

"Very well, Mr Holmes. I know nothing of Caradoc's death. The truth is that I was born out of wedlock. William Gilford is more then thirty years my junior but his grandfather adopted me for reasons I will not specify. When the young people came to London a year or so ago, Madge Gilford was very much taken with the theatre, which I had shown her. It was a new thing to her, a child's fairyland. She was too genteel for it, but at the request of the couple, I found her a place here as wardrobe mistress. William was the breadwinner but Madge was quick with a needle and something like this would occupy her. It seemed innocent enough. I thought it would be safe. That is all I have done."

Then, to my dismay, Carnaby Jenks began to weep.

"And your sister, to whom you refer in your letters?" Holmes inquired gently.

Jenks shook his head without looking up.

"A dear friend, that is all. One who helped me and who has suffered by that evil man. I will not say more. Roland Gwyn, the stage manager, is the person who can tell you, if he thinks it right."

This time, I knew that Jenks would keep his vow of silence. He was shaken but resolute. Sherlock Holmes was always of the opinion that Jenks intervened that night, when Caradoc was found dead, in fear of what he thought young William Gilford might have done, rather than from knowledge of it.

So it was that we made the acquaintance of Roland Gwyn. He was a man of short but wiry build and greater strength than might appear. I think he was no more than forty, but like Caradoc, he had made his way to London from the Welsh valleys of collieries and blast furnaces. The two men had met, and Gwyn's practical turn of mind as a stage-hand soon commended him as a manager.

We stood with him on the deserted set of Elsinore which had still to be dismantled.

"Tell me, Mr Gwyn," said Holmes quietly, "you probably

know best of all where everyone is at every moment and what they are doing. Is that not so? You can help me—if you will."

"And why should I not, sir?"

"Perhaps, first of all, you could clear up two points for me. How long had Sir Caradoc been the lover of young Madge Gilford? And how long had her husband known of this?"

I thought it must be a shot in the dark, but looking at Gwyn, I knew it had found its mark. The poor fellow went pale but he came back fighting.

"William Gilford knew nothing of it, sir. Because there was nothing to know."

He had never expected such questions, I am sure, and there was a fatal hesitation between his two replies. Holmes let him know it but he spoke reassuringly.

"Mr Gwyn, by answering my second question first I fear you have given the game away. Your first instinct was to say that William Gilford did not know, not that the thing had never happened. You would not last long against Inspector Hopkins. Even Mr Bradstreet would catch you with some such trick."

Gwyn stared down at the boards of the stage.

"I know nothing of that, sir. I could not tell you."

Holmes went on in the same even-tempered voice.

"I think you could, Mr Gwyn, but I will not force you. Do you know of me? Do you believe I am an honest man?"

"Everything I have heard of you, Mr Holmes, makes me believe that. When we shook hands a moment ago, your grip was the grip of an honest man."

"Will you believe me when I tell you that those two young people shall be safe with me? That they shall come to no harm through me? That I may yet save them for one another?"

Unlike Carnaby Jenks, Roland Gwyn was a straightforward man by nature. It was easy to see the passions of doubt and hope contending in his strong features.

"Come," said Holmes, "If you tell me, I can help them. But I cannot help if there are facts and evidence of which I am unaware."

What on earth was this? For all the world it sounded as if he was offering to compromise a police investigation.

Roland Gwyn sat down on a gothic chair that had been placed for King Claudius or Queen Gertrude. He stared up at us.

"I will tell you something," he said, "and then you must decide. William Gilford is the son of an attorney in the town of Carmarthen. I knew the family, though not well. William was a scholar at Cambridge for a year. Then his father died and he had to leave, for money reasons. But he grew acquainted with Mr Munby, a fellow of the college, and found an interest in the education of working men. He met Madge in the cathedral city of Ely not ten miles or so from the college."

Young Gilford hardly sounded like the stuff of which murderers are made. Yet the story took Roland Gwyn some time to tell and he did not find it easy. Emotion sometimes came close to overwhelming him, but he mastered it bravely and kept his course. To me, both as a medical man and a partner of Sherlock Holmes in our detective practice, it was a familiar tale of its type.

The girl's father had been a verger of Ely cathedral, who blessed the love match and the union. Madge Gilford had been a kind and generous girl but a simpleton in the ways of the world. The young married couple had come to London, where William Gilford found his post as an almoner at Marylebone Hospital. They took lodgings in Maida Vale. Madge was already deft with a needle. When the chance came to care for theatrical costumes, neither father nor husband raised any objection.

If the young wife had a vice, it was no more than the credulity of a country girl in the city, rather than a betrayal of marriage vows taken so short a time ago. To Caradoc she was easy prey. By being polite, then helpful and understanding, to a man who seemed so famous and so far above the world she had lived in, she stepped into the quicksands of flattery and insinuation. After she had given way to him and then regretted it, he had only to suggest that any resistance would compel him to reveal to the world what she had already done. I thought at once of Jenks's "blackmail." Did he know something of all this or only of Caradoc's ways with others? At first Madge Gilford, poor fool, was enchanted by this important man who was the age of her own father. At length, love had turned to distaste, tempered by fear of how the spiteful public tongue of Caradoc might curb her disobedience. Perhaps I was over-dramatising the threat, but I wondered if Madge Gilford knew that a public flaying of her quiet character awaited her at the green room supper, after which—as Jenks described Caradoc's threat—she would crawl back to her burrow and dread the light of day.

Because she was honest, she had at first told William Gilford everything and protested that she had fallen in love with the great actor. She could not help herself. The young man was distraught. There had followed a miserable six months of estrangement under one roof, hopeless arguments, threats of self-destruction, wretchedness of every sort. All this was for the delight of a man—once his friend—whom Roland Gwyn described as having lowered himself in recent years to become one of "the scum of the earth."

"Mr Holmes," he said quietly, "I have never forgotten the religion of my childhood. After a few years Caradoc was so changed, without heart or feeling. He seemed like a man without a soul."

I have seen a good deal in my time, but I confess I was shocked by the account that followed. To destroy the lives of two young people in this manner—even as they set out in hope upon their life together. In the course of my practice I had once come across it in the case of a man from the dregs of a European city. He had amused himself by enticing such simple victims into a society where they marvelled at the rich clothes of his companions and the assurances of his passion. Disease happily rid the world of him in his middle years. Forgive me, I rejoiced to hear of it.

We listened to this tale of a kind familiar in the divorce courts and in the small tragedies of everyday life. William Gilford would return from his evening classes. Sometimes Madge Gilford was not at home. Far worse, sometimes he would see her hurrying ahead of him from an assignation with Caradoc, hoping to be in the house first and make it seem that she had been at home all the time. If Roland Gwyn was truthful, which no one who heard him would doubt, William remained loyal. He lived with his embittered thoughts but hoped for better times.

During this account, Gwyn had become increasingly distressed. He was almost in tears before the end. It was clear to me that he had grown fond of these two young people, almost as a father might. Holmes held the gaze of those brown eyes steadily and said again,

"You need have no fear, Mr Gwyn. They are both safe with me."

What did he mean? What else had he kept to himself?

"Mr Gwyn," he said, "You will have heard by now of the letters from Carnaby Jenks to Caradoc?"

"Something of them, sir."

"The story of his sister?"

He shook his head.

"He had no sister, Mr Holmes."

"I thought not."

"She was his friend, sir. I daresay he would not write her name in the letters for the world to see."

"She became, perhaps, one of the ladies of the night who visited Caradoc in the Dome?"

"Perhaps she was, Mr Holmes. I know nothing of that."

"How was it done?"

Mr Gwyn took a deep breath.

"I was occupied with the performance. I never saw them, that I know of. The story was that they came through the private entrance, the street-door, not directly into the theatre. The Dome was his domain, as he said. Now and again I believe they were in his dressing-room with him. He might easily lend them a key to the private door on Maiden Lane, if he chose. More likely, he would leave the Yale on the latch for them. I do not know. Only he could have told you."

Holmes swung round and strode out through the wings. I could hear his voice in the passageway.

"Mr Hopkins! Mr Bradstreet! If you please!"

There was a pause, and then he returned with the trim, upright figure of young Hopkins in attendance.

"Now then," said Holmes to Gwyn, "be so kind as to repeat to Inspector Hopkins what you have just said to me. I promise that neither you nor anyone else has anything to fear."

Gwyn hesitated, looking at the young inspector as though at a man who might be trusted.

"Sir Caradoc was visited by ladies of a bad reputation, sir, in the sitting-room of the Dome. At night, usually after the play. Even in his dressing-room, sometimes."

"Indeed, Mr Gwyn?" Hopkins managed to sound concerned and dismayed at the revelation. "I am sorry to hear that."

"The Dome was his domain, as he called it, sir. My understanding is that he would sometimes give them a key to the street-door, if he knew them well, or leave that door on the latch. I never saw them down here, that I know of. But I could not be sure."

Holmes turned to his Scotland Yard protégé.

"Tell me, Hopkins, has that street-door been examined this evening? Mr Bradstreet has not mentioned it to me."

"So far as I know, Mr Holmes, it is locked. The matter has not been raised, but that is what we have assumed."

"Then had we better not see whether our assumptions are secure?" Holmes inquired innocently.

With Hopkins and Gwyn we climbed the stairs hung with theatrical portraits, went past the sitting-room of the Dome and down the far side. That area seemed little used and the walls were bare. At the foot stood the green-painted street-door. As I looked, it appeared undoubtedly closed and fastened. Only when Hopkins turned the handle and the door swung open was it apparent that the latch and not the lock had been holding it.

"It seems he was expecting a visitor after all," Holmes said for everybody's benefit.

Caradoc's enemies were legion. However, the unlocked door now opened a Pandora's box of the seven deadly sins, any of whose practitioners in London's underworld might have chosen New Year's Eve as the time to level scores with him. It was not impossible that one of them had been in his dressing-room at any time from the pouring of wine into the goblet to the smoking of the last cigar. A prosecutor of Carnaby Jenks would have a steep hill to climb when this was revealed.

The silence that accompanied our return up the stairs was of a depth that follows the dying reverberations of a trench mortar. We retraced our steps as far as the door of the sitting-room. Superintendent Bradstreet and Carnaby Jenks were staring at each other in silence across the table.

"Mr Bradstreet," said Holmes pleasantly, "I think the time has come for you and me to share a little information."

8

Twenty minutes later we took a courteous farewell of Stanley Hopkins and Isaiah Bradstreet. The latter was now full of the theory that some creature of the streets with a grudge had known of the unlocked door on Maiden Lane. With a little knowledge of the play's performance, she—or he—had only to enter before the last act—even in a costume of some kind. There would be no one in the Dome at such a time. From there, it would be the easiest thing to sidle down the stairway with its signed portraits. While the play was in progress, the chances were that the dressing-room passage, even the dressing-room itself, would be empty. The goblet of wine was out of sight while still in Caradoc's dressing-room. On Mr Gwyn's little table, it was the only one containing wine. In the myth that was now being created, it was vulnerable to a malevolent passing shadow, while all attention was on the efficient performance of *Hamlet*.

Even if challenged, an intruder had only to mention a visit to Sir Caradoc in the Dome and postpone vengeance to a future occasion. How easy to believe that such a phantom had brushed past and emptied a powder, from sleeve or pocket, into the wine before withdrawing by the same route. As the cast crowded towards the stage for the curtain calls, there would have been no one to hear the last dreadful sounds of the great actor's career. No one to see a shadow pass along the wall and up the narrow wooden stairs again.

Such was this fable of the poisoned wine which was woven into the history of the great theatre. It was so much more intriguing than the likely truth. The beauty of it was, as Holmes later remarked, that while such a chain of events could not be proved, it certainly could not be disproved for the benefit of a court. Indeed, so long as the world believed Caradoc had been poisoned on the stage, it must be true. Without conclusive proof against any other defendant, this phantom of the underworld would always haunt the minds of an Old Bailey jury. Caradoc's romances of the street must be the first evidence produced by the defence. Who would send a man to the gallows while the wraiths of such women and their bullies lingered among the backstage stairs and passages?

No one welcomed such an unknown visitant of this kind more readily than Superintendent Isaiah Bradstreet. In the space of two or three hours, before Scotland Yard "got its hands" on the case, this amateur of the uniformed branch solved the mystery, even if he created another in the process. Each time the case became a topic of journalism, he was consulted, quoted, and acquired a fame he can never have expected. His rivals, Lestrade and Gregson—even Sherlock Holmes—were nowhere compared with him.

We did not see Carnaby Jenks again. His own alibi seemed proof against all suspicion, as indeed it was, for he was on the public stage while Caradoc was supposed to be dying. As Holmes and I parted company with Roland Gwyn, my friend said softly once again, "They shall he safe with me."

9

Not without reason, the waving placards of the newsboys next day proclaimed the Royal Herculaneum "Mystery." The death of Caradoc Price did not spawn as many theories as the Whitechapel murders of the so-called Jack the Ripper. Yet once or twice a year some penny-a-liner would pen a new solution to the identity of the unknown intruder—and Bradstreet would say a few more words about the unlocked street-door.

Sherlock Holmes was philosophical as our cab took us back to Baker Street in the early hours of the New Year.

"If interest in the case survives, my dear fellow, it will be because people like you persist in quoting curious cases from *The Lancet* and the *British Medical Journal* of men and women who have lived for fifteen or twenty minutes after taking prussic acid. As a result, the members of tonight's audience believe they actually saw him drink it. That will be something to tell their grandchildren. Poor Caradoc is doomed to be one of your rare medical specimens, whether he likes it or not."

"Then what we saw in the dressing-room is not to be given to the world?"

"Apart from my modest powers of deduction, there was nothing that could not be explained by your medical theories and the poison in the goblet. The tobacco ash was a curious mixture, but it might have come from innocent sources."

"And what of the riddle in his dressing-gown pocket? What became of the scrap of paper?"

He patted his coat.

"I know I had it then. I do not seem to have it now. In any case, it was hardly conclusive."

This was too much!

"If you were right, Holmes, as you say you invariably are, young William Gilford has no alibi. True, he did not reach the theatre in time to poison the wine before it was carried on stage. He was certainly there in time to enter the unlocked dressing-room before Caradoc came off during the final scene and exchange the first Real Feytoria for a cigar contaminated by rat poison. The play was in progress. The dressing-room passage would be quiet and empty. Gilford had five minutes for less than one minute's work. He had ample time to spy through the window and go back to the dead man's room soon afterwards. Time to change the cigar and the tobacco ash. He could lock himself in while making these arrangements and lock the room after him when he left, tossing the key through the window, to fall as if from Caradoc's dying hand."

"He might have poisoned Caradoc," Holmes said thoughtfully, "but as it happens, I think he did not."

"Why?"

Holmes pulled a face at the passing scene, almost as if with a pang of indigestion.

"Because of the meeting."

"The meeting?"

"Several reputable witnesses swear that after his evening

lecture he attended a meeting of teachers at Toynbee Hall. It ended about five minutes before nine o'clock."

"He could still have reached the theatre before Caradoc left the stage."

"You miss the point, Watson."

"How?"

"This murder was planned, and he could not have planned it as it happened. He could not have known that he would reach the Herculaneum in time, could he? Among the other statistics a criminal investigator must carry in his head is the speed of traffic in London."

"Which is?"

"Something over five miles an hour but less at difficult times. Gilford could not be sure that he would be there before Caradoc left the stage. A man who must be two miles away by twenty past nine, in order to plant a poisoned cigar, does not attend a meeting of indefinite length at half-past eight. If he does do so, at least he warns his colleagues that he may have to leave them before the end. That did not happen. Under these circumstances, William Gilford could not plan the murder as it was committed. Nor would he poison a cigar on the spur of the moment. When he joined his colleagues at Toynbee Hall, he had not the remotest idea that Caradoc Price would be dead in an hour or so."

"So we are left with the phantom of a street woman or her bully who glided in and left a trail of poison?"

He shrugged and looked aside, studying his reflection in the window of the cab as we crossed Oxford Circus into Portland Place. Small groups of revellers and dancers were walking home, Harlequin and Columbine, Pierrot and Pierette. There was one thing I could not let pass. Almost without considering what I was saying, I broke in upon his thoughts.

"Holmes! Will you give me your word that when you went from the Dome to call Sergeant Witlow and his constable from the green room, you did not first go down the other stairs and put the Yale lock of the street-door on the latch? So that it should later be found unlocked and this story of an unknown intruder put about?"

He had not seemed to be out of the room for long, but I had seen Holmes ascending stairs two or three at a time. Inspector Tobias Gregson was the only man I had ever known to outdistance him.

He smiled at the costumed revellers without turning his head. "I would willingly have unlocked it, old fellow. Unfortunately for your theory, someone else had already done so."

There was a moment's silence before I tried him again.

"William Gilford had ample opportunity to replace the half-smoked cigar and the ash in the dead man's dressing-room, even if he had not planned the murder."

He turned to me with a smile.

"A palpable hit, if we could prove it! I should bet that Gilford never smokes and would not know one leaf of tobacco ash from another!"

"There is very little you could not prove if you chose. Gilford is your man."

"More to the point," he said, gazing at the dancers again, "who is my woman? This is not Gilford's revenge."

"Madge Gilford?" It fitted so neatly—and yet how I wished it did not. Poison is proverbially a woman's weapon against the physical strength of a man. If Caradoc had sworn to her that he would punish her resistance, where more likely than before the elite of the theatre and the gossips of the sporting press during the green room supper? How was she to silence him?

Sherlock Holmes yawned.

"If I am correct, Gilford intervened to shield a murderer. So, I believe, did Carnaby Jenks. I do not much care for him but tonight that broken old player gave the performance of his life."

"Madge Gilford?" I repeated.

"Who else would Gilford intervene to save—in the certainty of the gallows if he was caught in that room? As gallant a gentleman as Henry Hawley Crippen—but more fortunate."

He counted on his fingers.

"That young woman was mocked, threatened, abused by her seducer when she knew her error and turned away from him. Her life, her marriage, all hope of happiness, were at his mercy. You doubt it? Recall his treatment of the lost and unfortunate Oscar Wilde. That serpent tongue had the power to ridicule Madge Gilford so publicly that her husband, her father, the friends of her youth must weep for her but could not save her. She had good reason to dread his harangue at the green room supper. By tomorrow, his pleasantries would be all over London."

He pulled on his gloves.

"Therefore, if I am correct, Watson, Madge Gilford prepared a weapon to silence that man for ever."

"She? And if it was she, you will keep silent?"

"Even you, old fellow, came with me to exterminate Charles Augustus Milverton and silence his threats of blackmail to young women a year or two ago. Had you forgotten? Happily, a young woman whose reputation he destroyed did the job a few minutes before us! We witnessed it but did not betray her, did we? Nor did you ever suggest that we should."*

The porticoes of Langham Place stretched away to the Euston Road.

"I cannot believe Madge Gilford was a Lady Macbeth."

"Precisely my point, Watson. If I am correct, William, on his return, found her stricken by what she had done—the simple

* "Charles Augustus Milverton" in Sir Arthur Conan Doyle, *The Return of Sherlock Holmes.*

substitution of one cigar for another. What followed was quite beyond her, as we saw for ourselves when we passed her in her distress. As the terrible minutes ticked by, if my conclusion is correct, William laid a false trail before Caradoc was found. His one touch of criminal genius was to add what remained of the poison to one of the goblets on the stage, just as Caradoc was discovered and the dressing-room door was opened."

The cab rumbled over hardened snow.

"And that is where the case must rest?"

"Watson, I should despise myself if I did not do as much to save the woman I loved and who had suffered so bitterly. On the evidence, I cannot convict William Gilford rather than an intruder who may have entered by the street door. I would not even if I could. Will that do?"

We turned the corner at Baker Street Metropolitan station. He wrapped his plaid coat round himself and prepared to descend from the cab.

"You set yourself above the law."

"But not above justice. In any case, I have been my own judge and jury so often that it comes a little late in life to alter the practice now. I believe that they are young enough to salvage their marriage from the wreck of their romance."

That last prediction proved correct. We later heard that the couple clung together and ultimately took ship for Queensland. Holmes seemed prepared to bury deep in his mind the evidence of the dressing-room. As for Carnaby Jenks and Roland Gwyn, neither would name a suspect, even to us.

The cab slowed down in the snowy length of Baker Street.

"In the circumstances," I said, "I think this must be one of our adventures that does not see the light of day."

We had pulled up outside our rooms. Sherlock Holmes looked up at them through the window of the cab with something like affection but also as if he were seeing them for the first time in the frosty lamplight. Then he turned and favoured me with the same resigned and rather weary smile.

"Let us say, Watson, that I should not dream of preventing you putting pen to paper in one of your little mysteries. However, I should be obliged if you would withhold this one from the world—as you have withheld certain others—until the day when it can no longer matter to me."

In that, at least, I have respected the wishes of my wayward but greatest friend.